# Don't Be Scared

## AJ Merlin

Thank you Covers by Combs

Paperback ISBN: 978-1-955540-32-2

*NYCTOPHILIA -*
*LOVE OF DARKNESS OR NIGHT. FINDING*
*RELAXATION OR COMFORT IN THE*
*DARKNESS.*

# CHAPTER 1

The pumpkin is excruciatingly heavy.

My fingernails dig into its orange skin as I walk, and I'm barely able to see over the curved, bark-like stem. "Fuck," I breathe softly, knowing I won't be able to curse when I enter the cone of my parents' hearing.

Twenty years old, and my mother still looks offended when I use words like *fuck* or *hell* or *necrophilia*.

Though, I suppose the last one might be reasonable.

I stop on the flat grass, glancing back at the woods that border both the parking lot and one side of the county fairgrounds. A breeze picks up as I do, ruffling my black hair and the leaves in the many trees that form the forest on the north side of town.

It's a famous forest, for all the wrong reasons. Horror stories and folktales about Hollow Bridge and things that have supposedly happened in the forest are more than just whispers in our town. Though, to be honest, the stories that had lived rent-free in my head as a child and teenager seem far-fetched to me now.

I switch my grip again, arms straining, and start walking toward my parents' booth again. They've been doing this for many years and had the same spot enough times that it's muscle memory by now to get to where they are, so seeing isn't as important as it would be in other situations.

When I hear their voices, I switch my grip again, steps picking up so I can get rid of my heavy armful. I pass other tents and booths, but I barely have to glance up to know what they're selling.

Not only have I been helping my parents with their booth at the Hollow Bridge Halloween Festival, but I've also been attending it since before I could walk.

The fairgrounds aren't huge. And overall, there might be thirty-five or so vendor booths on the fairgrounds. The rides and bigger attractions haven't been brought in yet, though from the corner of my eye I can see a stage being put together on the other side of the fairgrounds, furthest from the parking lot. I have no idea who the town has gotten to play this year, though I suspect it'll be someone at least twelve percent of the town has heard of.

My dad spots me before my mom and jogs over to wrestle the pumpkin out of my grip and onto the table. My mom is there already, unloading supplies for the caramel apples that she somehow has perfected until they taste better than any other caramel apple in creation. She makes them fresh, during the festivals, and lets people choose their toppings. What started as a way for the high school choir to make more money has turned into a rather profitable business for my parents. Though, they still make sure most of the money goes right back into the school's clubs, once my mom has covered what she spent on supplies.

"You should, uh, test to make sure all of your stuff works," I tell my mom, helping Dad situate the pumpkin on the ground next to the plastic table that will soon be covered with a cheap tablecloth. Last year's theme was evil fairy tales. This year, from what I can tell, it's a jack-o'-lantern explosion. There's a plastic knife sticking out of one pumpkin, and the one I've just helped Dad move is painted on the front to look like a graveyard. "I'll taste it to be sure it's good, of course," I add, as my mother eyes me with a grin.

"I don't even have the apples here," Mom points out. "If you're that desperate, though, I'll make a batch at home for us."

"I would die for that," I tell her soberly, without an outward hint of the teasing sarcasm that runs through my words. I don't look at her as I talk. The pumpkin is much easier to look at, for one, and I enjoy finding small details in Dad's painting that I can rest my eyes on while I speak. Mom, of course, doesn't take that personally. She'd stopped being phased by the whole 'avoid eye contact' protocol by the time I turned nine.

"Are there any more pumpkins in the SUV?" Dad grunts, moving one of the other orange decorations that he'd spent the last few nights decorating and carving.

I glance around the booth, cataloging the pumpkins Dad and I had brought over from the car. "The cat one," I say at last, realizing it isn't here. "I'll go get it." Dad doesn't need to be carrying it with his back, even though it's far from the heaviest one we've dragged out here today.

Before he can protest, I'm off again. I stay closer to the other vendor booths, even though it takes a few extra minutes to meander back to the parking lot.

Next to Mom and Dad is a knitting booth, their cute crafty setups already lining the tables of the booth. Their actual pieces that are for sale aren't here yet, but with rain due tonight, that doesn't shock me. The only people really setting up for the weekend are those who either have water proof configurations, or can throw a tarp over everything and not have to worry about that failing.

Still, Mom's friend straightens from behind the table, beaming at me as I slide by. "Good morning, Bailey," she greets, and I hold up a hand in greeting. "It's been awhile. I don't see you around the shop as much as I used to."

That's because my phase of scrapbooking had come and gone faster than a hurricane, but I don't tell her that. I smile in her direction, hoping the look is sincere. "Sorry, Mrs. Johnson," I reply, still walking. "I've just been really busy with school late-ly." It's a lie, obviously. I'd graduated with my Associate's degree in Human Anatomy in the spring, and since I haven't figured out what I'm doing with my life or if I'm going to go for my bachelor's, I'm not in school. But thankfully, she doesn't seem to know that. She says something else that's more polite than conversational, and I give her one last smile before moving on, wanting to see what other vendors have ended up at the festival this year.

Sure, most of them are the same as always. Hollow Bridge isn't that big of a town, and it's always the same people who do the same things year after year. Not that it makes things bad. It feels...classic. Like a tradition, to know what I'll be running across at the festival. Comfortable predictability.

But there are always a few vendors, from out of town or even out of state who want to come check out the Hollow Bridge Halloween festivities. From festival to parade to concert, we do more than most towns, or even most cities. But then again, most towns and bigger cities don't have a history *built* on Halloween traditions, witches, and curses.

My eyes fall on one vendor booth I know I've never seen. A large, plastic Michael Myers stands to one side of it, plastic knife upraised in a stiff hand. They're going to regret having him out, unless they have some magical way to weatherproof his blue jumpsuit. I don't think a tarp will do it, though I've definitely been wrong before.

Once or twice.

Two men stand behind the wide table, the bald one's hands flying along with his lips as he talks, as if he needs the movements to make his point known. When I pass by, they both glance at me, one of them narrowing his eyes as I just keep walking.

Whatever they're selling or showing, I don't care enough to stop and let them take whatever their issue is out on *me*.

They don't say anything to me as I go by, and minutes later I'm at Dad's SUV, digging in the back as the last pumpkin eludes my grasp. My fingers wiggle as I lean forward for it, putting myself off balance as I stretch on the tiptoes of one foot, my other leg pointed out behind me as if it'll give me some kind of advantage or extra length to reach.

Just when my fingers curl around the stem, another car pulls into a spot beside me, the engine cutting as soon as it's parked. I'm still dragging the pumpkin toward me as the two people, men it sounds like, share a murmured conversation, the hatch opening as one of them leans in for something.

When I finally straighten, they're done getting whatever it is they were reaching for, and curiously I glance in their direction, seeing them walk to another line of vendor booths. I don't know them, but that doesn't exactly matter, nor is it really a surprise.

Halloween pulls everyone out of their houses around here.

It's not until the SUV is closed and locked that I glance one more time at the two of them, and I see it.

The man on the left, tall with tousled black hair, turns to nudge the other with his elbow, a wolfish grin on his face as he carries a tray of something. The other laughs, not turning to him, but he's not the important one now.

*Phoenix.*

Memories of going over to my best friend's house and trying so damn hard not to let her older brother know I had a crush on him flit through my brain. He'd been forced to babysit his sister, Daisy, and I, more times than I can count, but even though it was clear he wasn't into it, I'd been a lovestruck thirteen-year-old unable to act normally around the handsome, older boy.

God, it's no wonder he acted like I didn't exist at school for the most part. Especially after, when everyone was too afraid to talk to him, since—

I close my eyes hard, my heart twisting in my chest. I have no idea why he's back or what he's doing at the fairgrounds, and I definitely won't be the one asking him. Instead, I make a mental note to mention his reappearance to Nic, knowing she'll at least pretend to be interested.

I also wonder if the guy with him, who looks like he might be around the same age as Phoenix Hawthorne, is his boyfriend. If he is, they make a hot couple, even though I've only seen the other guy's profile, and only for a few seconds.

They don't turn as they walk, so I'm free to stare until I take the pumpkin under one arm and head back to my parent's booth. I deposit it there and leave again, though I make sure to note where Phoenix's parents' booth is. Worst-case scenario, I run into him and he gives me that look. The sad but frustrated one he's so good at, from eyes that are the darkest shade of sapphire possible.

Best-case scenario, he's forgotten I exist or what I look like. He hasn't seen me with my black hair in *years*, since I was thirteen and decided I wanted to be a red-head for the rest of my life. That had lasted until about the time he'd left for college in my junior year.

I don't realize I'm at the strangers' vendor booth until I'm staring up at Michael Myers again, the gray, darkening sky an ominous backdrop above his dirty white mask and shock of light brown hair. The plastic knife is stained with fake blood that wouldn't fool a child, and the two men behind the table have disappeared, likely to get more stuff out of their car.

Sure enough, their voices bring me back to myself, and I

stride behind the vendor tents before they can see me, heading toward the woods that act as a backdrop to the fairgrounds.

My heart twists at the love I used to have for these woods that's dulled over time. I still enjoy them, as a concept. But they'd lost their magic for me years ago, except for around this time of year when the leaves are in the middle of turning and dark branches reach toward the sky like twisting, gnarled fingers seeking help.

I've always liked the contrast they make against the cold autumn or winter sky, though not enough to go exploring in them like I used to.

But maybe the sight of Phoenix makes me bolder than usual. I don't stop at the edge of the woods, though I keep to the lit areas of the forest as I head between the trees that line the parking lot. I don't need to get lost here in October, with the temperatures getting colder every night and me just dressed in an old, ratty hoodie and leggings.

*I won't get lost.* The certainty of the thought is...surprising, if I'm honest with myself. It tingles through my brain like a promise, though the voice that whispers the words isn't quite mine. If it is me, then it's a younger, braver Bailey who had never been lost in the woods in the first place.

My steps slow, then stop. at the last minute; the toe of my sneaker is bright white against the dark ground and the thing that lies in front of me.

It's so close I could touch it.

So close I can smell the sweetness in the air that's been drawing me in this direction for the last ten steps or so, though I hadn't registered that until this moment.

If Phoenix's reappearance in Hollow Bridge has been a surprise, then the only thing I can think as I stare down at the dead crow at my feet is that this is a bad omen.

# CHAPTER 2

My toes curl in my shoes, though I don't make a move away from the bird at my feet. All I can smell is the sweetness of rot, but it's not bad enough or pervasive enough to make me step away. And it's nothing for me to kneel, my knees cracking from a combination of years of falling out of trees as a child and dance classes that had done little more than make me miserable.

Well, I guess not too miserable, since I'd taken three classes a week through high school without much complaint. My hands rest on my knees, thumbs and forefingers squeezing on either side of the joint there in a well-practiced movement that barely requires any thought to hopefully soothe the cracking there. The pain isn't bad.

Certainly not bad enough to distract me from the dead bird.

One of my hands lifts, and I grope on the ground beside me until I can find a suitably long enough stick. It's a little thinner than I'd like, but still good enough that I can poke the stiff bird until it flops onto its back.

The fact that the bird looks like it died from a broken neck is just more proof to this being some supernatural bad omen, if such things exist. The bird's eyes are wide as if it had been afraid before it had died, and its beak is parted just enough that I could wedge the stick in between if I really need to.

I don't.

I resist the urge, the curiosity, and poke the stick up under the bird's wings, looking for some other reason for this bird to have spontaneously broken its neck. I could understand it, if there was something else. Even a sign of some predator having snagged the bird out of a tree, or a hawk having grabbed it out of the air.

But there's nothing.

Just a terrified crow with a broken neck that's lying a few feet from the edge of the trees. With how stiff it is, I can't imagine it's been dead for very long. And not long enough for the predators that roam the upstate New York wilderness to have found it. At the very least, someone's dog will be at it soon, dragging it into a backyard and scaring their owner with a big mess of black feathers.

But I don't have anywhere to take it, or anything to carry it in. So the chances of a dog scaring the shit out of someone with it are high.

"What happened to you?" I murmur, turning it once more. I've looked at enough diagrams and seen enough bird skeletons to know what it would look like if I were to strip the feathers and skin away. Thanks to Aunt Kathryn, I also know what it would take to taxidermy a crow, as weird of a skill as that might be.

But for all the things I've studied and looked at, I cannot figure out how the bird *died.*

Well, apart from the obvious.

But birds don't have a habit of just dropping dead in the woods with a broken neck. At least, not from what I've seen in my life.

I push the crow around one more time with the stick, my

fingers coming close enough to almost brush the bird's feathers. Maybe it was old, or sick, or just...fated to die today.

"Sorry buddy," I mutter, straightening with my hands on my knees that yet again pop under my fingers. One day I'm going to pay the price for the years of dance, more than I already do. If I don't have a knee replacement by thirty, I'll consider myself incredibly lucky.

My eyes catch on something moving as I stand, tracking it in the near-darkness of the woods. At first, I think it's a coyote that smelled the bird and came to get its dinner. Or some neighbor's dog intent on showing its master the cool thing it's found.

But the movement is too tall. Too graceful for that, and the footsteps that reach my ears are definitely of the human variety.

Words catch in my throat. Hooking the inside of my esophagus as my lips part like I'm going to say something, or warn the person walking through the woods about the bird they'll most likely never see. Nothing comes from my lips, and the person keeps walking as I drop the stick and stay where I'm standing.

If they turn, they'll see me. I realize that when their silhouette is highlighted in a break of the branches above. Auburn hair sparkles in the dying, orange sun like a flame; though it's extinguished seconds later when he moves into the darkness of the trees again.

I don't know him.

*Well, I don't know his name.*

It takes me only a second to realize it's the boy Phoenix had come here with. Yet now he's here, skulking through the woods, instead of with my dead best friend's brother.

The thought of Daisy is unexpected, and my brain takes my moment of weakness to pile on all the things that I try never to see.

*Daisy is pale, her lips are blue. She doesn't move when I shake her—*

*My leg hurts, and when I press my knee against the searing snow under me, I can see red blooming around my skin like a poinsettia. Just in time for Christmas, and—*

"What do you mean she's dead?!" He shakes me, holding my arms too tight, but I don't have an answer for Daisy's brother. *I don't have an answer, when I don't—*

I close my eyes hard and consider picking the stick up again to whack myself in the face with it. The pain would help, and to that end I dig my nails into my palms until I can feel the tender skin beginning to give under the sharpness of my nails.

I can't do this today.

I can't have her face in my mind this close to going home.

While I don't know when I closed my eyes, the moment I open them again, I look for the stranger who'd been in the woods. My gaze finds the place he'd been before, and the sunlight that had lit his hair like a pyre. It's fading now, the sun dipping further in its descent as the coolness in the woods picks up to swirl around my arms.

He's gone.

Sometime in the last minute, when I'd been battling bad memories and thoughts I try to keep out of my brain, he'd disappeared into the trees. I can't even say if he'd gone deeper into the woods, or back toward the fairgrounds.

But I do know that I can't keep standing here with a dead bird for company. I hesitate, glancing down once more at the creature, and nudge its wing ever so slightly with my shoe until it's on its back, wings spread, like some artist's rendition of a crow against an earthy background.

There's something gorgeous about it, in death. Something almost surreal that threatens to pull me back to my knees in the dirt to play with dead things.

*But I have to go home.*

Girls shouldn't play with dead things, as my mother so often reminds me whenever I make the trip to my aunt's house by the river. So I force myself to move, to take the steps on crackling knees, protesting the day's lifting and bending from setting up at the fairgrounds.

The trees lessen as I go, thinning so that I don't have to look for paths between them. Soon enough I'm out of the forest entirely, though my eyes rove over the grounds to look for my parents...or Phoenix.

For my own presence of mind, I refuse to think that I'm looking for my dead best friend's brother in the Halloween-themed rows of booths and vendors getting ready to go home now that there's not enough natural light to see by.

When the festival starts, there will be lights, of course. Orange, white, and purple lights are already strung between tents, and, once things are in full swing, I know there will be bonfires that cast both warmth and light on anyone that walks by.

But that's not for another couple days. Right now, the fairgrounds are just coming back to life. Just starting to show the black and orange bones in half-finished parts and debris still littering the ground. While the official fair won't start for over a week, the craft fair that's tradition for Hollow Bridge is tomorrow and the day after, with my parents long-time vendors of the snack and pumpkin painting variety, though it's mostly for fun and not for extra income.

A familiar feeling curls and stirs in my stomach as I make my way back to my parents' booth to help them with anything they're taking back home. It's excitement, despite everything, for my town's favorite time of year. It's genetic for us to love Halloween, I've decided. And even though I'd told myself the bird was a bad omen, I find it almost easy to leave my trepidation behind with every step, and to convince myself that even if Phoenix is back, it doesn't change anything.

Lost in my thoughts, it's a surprise when a man slams into my shoulder, knocking me off balance. I can't help the sound of protest that slips from between my lips, and the gray-haired, wild-eyed man glares at me, like I've done something wrong.

Like I'm the one who slammed into him.

"*Excuse* me," I mutter when he's far enough away that he can't hear me. My steps slow, and I watch as he makes his way towards the parking lot, steps staggering and uneven. But even this rude, strange man isn't enough to drag my thoughts away from Phoenix for long, and in seconds I'm back to trying to convince myself nothing has changed.

By the time I get back to them and accept a pumpkin in my arms that throws me off balance, I almost, *almost*, believe it.

# CHAPTER 3

I f I'd ever needed any evidence that my parents' marriage is the stuff of dreams, their constant date nights would be enough.

From night fishing, to all night cruises, to weekends in the Adirondacks, I'm pretty sure that by this point, my parents have done it all and been in love for every bit of it. While I'm not particularly interested in marriage; if I was, I'd want something like this.

Tonight, my dad has surprised my mom with tickets to a late-night opera, because *those* exist apparently, and a bed-and-breakfast stay afterward. The place they're going, the Adirondack Inn, has been one of their favorites since before I was born.

When I leave them to go to my room on the second floor, my mom is still picking out her outfit, and judging by the drifting of Dad's voice coming up the stairs, he's trying to book roses for Mom.

They're the sweetest, most in love couple I've ever seen in my life, bar none.

Yawning, I close the door of my room behind me, eyes

flicking over the large space. We'd knocked out the wall between two bedrooms when I was younger, and now my room is the size of huge, meaning there's ample room for my sitting area, desk, and bed that's tucked into the far wall. My floor is bare, since we'd ripped up the carpet to redo the hardwood under it, and the soft purples, grays, and dark charcoal color scheme does *everything* for any kind of bad mood I'm ever in, and helps my brain that hates things that are out of place.

A large, taxidermy golden eagle spreads its wings on top of my dresser; the mount it's on makes it look like it's about to attack anyone coming in my door. My gaze lingers on it, and I stride over to stroke my fingers along the silky, feathery texture. It's the first thing my aunt let me help her do, and parts of the mount, like the wood the eagle's claws are clasped on, were my idea.

Though, it's thanks to my Aunt Kathryn that it looks good at all.

My fingers move over the feathers almost without my say-so as I think about the bird in the woods. Would its feathers have felt like this? Or would they have been stiff with dirt and grime? If I had pressed my fingers against its skin, feathers ruffled over my nails like those of the golden eagle, would I have been able to feel the wriggle of beetles whose arrival accompanies the presence of dead things?

For a moment, I imagine I can feel them on the eagle as I let my fingers sink into its feathers. I imagine the squirming, hard carapaces of small creatures against my fingers, scurrying around me like an unfortunate nuisance as they do what they were made to do.

But finally I blink and pull away, dropping my hand to my side to survey the eagle's angry, yellow gaze. It's beautiful, though I always think that when I come in here. The eagle had been killed by natural causes, and sold to my aunt by a company that works with the Department of Natural Resources for conservation. Half of the money she'd spent had gone to a bird rescue, and I'd quickly been able to overcome my trepidation of working with such a beautiful, dead animal that looked like it should still be flying the skies.

I collapse on the sofa with a groan, half-wishing I'd gone for my bed instead. I could still watch television from there, and it's not like I expect to be doing much, anyway. So what if I want to turn in early?

But out of habit, I pull the black and purple comforter off of the back of the couch, draping it over me as the excess hangs to the hardwood floor. It's a king size comforter for a couch, so there's always enough to wrap me up like a burrito if the situation calls for it. My next order of business is finding the remote on the side table without looking, and my fingernails click harshly against the fake-marble top a few times before finally I close around the matte black object and turn on my smart TV.

I know they'll be gone soon. According to Dad, the opera starts at eight, and the clock on the home screen of the television shows me that it's just before seven. If I'm right, they'll be gone within the next twenty minutes or so, leaving me here alone.

Not that I mind.

Really, I don't.

When I start flicking through the live stations, though, I know I've made a mistake. While I love to sleep with the white noise of a movie or show playing, I rarely, if ever, just leave it up to Jesus by putting the television on a live channel. The jolting differences between commercials, and most shows, are good at throwing me into nightmares or worse. If I want to sleep, my best bet is the food network, or some bridal show with gentle, pretty music and mostly polite voices until the mom or grandmother breaks out into their insults.

I'm about to pull back to the menu when the news anchor

catches my attention, my finger freezing on the button before I can do more than consider what I'm going to watch.

*Did I really just hear what I think I did?* The words the woman said ping around my empty head, smacking off the bones in my skull to echo louder in my ears.

*"The body of Emily Forrest, a college student at SUNY Oswego, was found in the lake near the town of Hollow Bridge. The small town, known for elaborate Halloween celebrations, has been the scene of such a tragedy before. When—"*

I close my eyes hard, until my eyelids hurt with the pressure, but her voice continues to flow through my brain unfiltered. She talks about Emily's parents, her academics, and all the things they never got to say about *Daisy* six years ago.

For a moment, I consider jumping to my feet and going to tell my mom. I can imagine her face when she hears, and the worry that will line her eyes as I look anywhere but into them. I know she'll cancel date night with my dad, and that's what makes me mentally put my foot down on the idea.

The last thing I want to do is ruin tonight for them. I don't want them to lose the night they definitely deserve to have. I can survive being here on my own, with my eyes and ears riveted on the news anchor who's still discussing Emily's death while I sit on my couch, numb to everything as my fingers curl and uncurl around the remote.

Where was this attention when it was Daisy getting pulled out of the snow after drowning in the river? Where was this attention when I'd told everyone what had happened to us, and the doctors had said I was lucky I hadn't lost my fingers to frostbite?

My phone rings, vibrating against my arm from its spot under me so hard that I nearly levitate. I'm surprised my heart doesn't slam out of my chest at the sound or the shock of it, and I barely check the name on the screen before I put it to my ear, a deep breath sinking into my lungs as I do.

"Nic," I sigh, greeting my best friend without a bit of surprise. "You saw, huh?"

"Yeah, *I was sort of hoping you hadn't,*" she admits, her voice hesitant. I believe her. I can imagine the speech she had planned out for me, and wonder if she would've demanded to use Facetime, though she knows how much I despise it.

Meeting her eyes is hard at the best of times. I don't need a weird, bad phone connection making it worse.

"Yeah." I lick my bottom lip, eyes still on the television and the crowd they're showing around Keuka Lake. It's the closest of the finger lakes to Hollow Bridge, though most people go to Canandaigua if they want to have a day on the water. At least, people from here who are tired of Keuka, anyway. But I'd know the shoreline anywhere, having grown up here. Even without the label on the bottom of the screen.

"So. No more Emily, huh?" I murmur, sinking down onto the sofa. "They're saying it's an accident, then? She fell in the lake and drowned? That's ironic, poetic justice, don't you think? After what happened to—"

"*She didn't fall in.*" Nic's voice is tight, her tone clipped. I can imagine the dancing worry in her eyes, and the way she can't help but pick at her nail polish when she's upset. Is she doing it now? Or is Nolan holding her hands, not letting her, as the two of them watch the same news broadcast as me?

"What do you mean?" Her words finally make it through the fog of my brain, and I realize that I'm working at less than one hundred percent processing capacity. Well, I can't exactly be surprised.

Not when seeing Emily's pretty face brings bubbles of nausea to my stomach, even if she's dead.

This time, I don't try to push away the memories that she brings to the surface. It's no use. I know for a fact they'll be living in my head more than normal for the next few days, and I hope to *God* I don't dream of her dying now, too.

I can't take that.

"*I overheard my mom...*" she trails off, and I wonder if she's regretting saying that much. With her mom as the chief of police of Hollow Bridge, she's good at knowing things before the rest of the town knows them. Whether she eavesdropped or heard the rumors naturally. I have a feeling that tonight, it's a case of the former. I can't imagine her mother would talk about something like this in front of her.

"Come on. You've started, you have to finish," I cajole, trying to sound like none of this is of any consequence to me.

It's a lie, of course. My heart beats in my throat, making my discomfort known. I'm sure if I look at my hand that's clenched around my phone, it's shaking. But if I don't look at it, then it's not happening.

*None of this is happening.*

But it is, unfortunately. And when Nic starts talking once more, she cements that fact loud and clear.

"*Mom says...well there's evidence that she was pushed. She said it happened early this afternoon, at that part of the shore you can only get to through the park. You know, no one goes there anymore since it's behind all those briars and huge ass trees.*" I know exactly where she means. Daisy and I had spent hours and hours there as kids and then Phoenix started going with us or staying near so we wouldn't get lost. According to him, it was so he wouldn't get in trouble when we'd escaped the house from under his nose.

Even though we'd tried to rope him into our games, he'd always insisted he wasn't interested, of course. Even when he *would* surrender and play with us, he promised it was just so we would stop screaming at him.

My heart twists at the memory of a time that seems too long ago. It's surreal to remember it now, when Emily had met her death in the same place we'd played.

"Ironic," I murmured, knowing I should care more. It's hard

to push my emotions up that high, especially for someone I don't really like. "Do they know who did it?" My mind flashes to the man at the fairgrounds, the one who'd looked at me with panic and violence in his eyes as he'd just kept walking. Is it coincidence that my brain conjures up the weirdest man I've seen in, well, *ever*? We don't get a lot of strangers in Hollow Bridge. Especially ones that look crazy.

Thankfully, Nic is more than used to my weirdness, and knows that just because I don't seem to care doesn't mean I'm falling apart or hiding something.

This just isn't something worth crying over. If anything... though, it's mean to even think, it's the opposite.

Emily had been awful.

"*Not a clue.*"

"Then why does she think Emily was pushed?"

Nic hesitates, and that alone tells me it must be bad. "*Her fingers,*" she whispers finally. "*Her fingers were broken, and it looks like someone stepped on them hard. Mom thinks she was trying to hold on and someone, uh, helped her off her handhold.*"

That's brutal. I don't say the words out loud, but I do sit up, still cocooned in my comforter. There's nothing in me capable of being sad for Emily. I don't even feel mildly inconvenienced. Actually, I'm irritated that she's brought up all the shitty memories inside me that I've worked to beat back with a stick.

*Thanks a lot for dying, Emily,* I mutter internally, conveniently forgetting that Phoenix's arrival in town had done the same to my brain.

But I can't help thinking how weird the timing is. Just as I wonder what Phoenix thinks about this development in Hollow Bridge. He has to care, right? After all, he knows as well as I do that she's one quarter of the reason that his sister is dead, instead of being in college with me.

"Would you let me know if you hear anything else?" The coldness of my voice is worse than I'd hoped it would be. My detachment has to be evident. "I'm going to see if I can find any other stories about it. I'd like to know if they find out who pushed her."

*To thank them.*

Well, no. That would be wrong of me. But *still.*

"*Sure, Bailey,*" Nic says after a moment. "*We're going to a party later tonight at Tasha's, though. It's a costume party.*" Of course it is. Those are Hollow Bridge's favorite kind, and the ones Nic and Nolan love the most. She salivates all year long until this time of year pops up, and hunts down any costume party she can in order to show off her sewing and design skills. "*Do you want to come?*" The invitation is an afterthought, though I'm not offended. She just knows I don't share her love of parties, costumed or otherwise.

"No, no no," I assure her. "Not in the least. Seriously." As if to prove a point to myself, I flop back down and wish my thoughts weren't racing like thoroughbreds. "Like I said. I just want to watch the news. At least for a little while. Just to see if..."

To see if there's a reason for Emily's death, or if Nic's mom's theory makes it on the eleven o'clock news. "Have a good time, Nic. Send me a picture of your costume."

She hangs up a second later, after a quick farewell and plea for me to do something of the self care variety, like drinking hot chocolate in the hot tub. It's not the best idea I've ever heard from her.

But it's certainly not the worst, either.

# CHAPTER 4

I can hear the ice crack moments before my foot falls. Thin, almost crystalline sounds that trickle into my ears, and when I look down, I know what I'll see.

And yet, I'm still too surprised to move.

Spiderweb cracks spin out from the ice under my sneaker, getting bigger and branching off in a myriad of directions against the mostly opaque ice. It's beautiful, in the most terrifying way, and when I look up a little, I see that I'm not the only one with cracks under them.

Daisy, who stands closer to the flag planted in the ice of the lake, stares at me with abject horror on her face, having picked up on our danger mere microseconds before me. Or maybe it's that I don't want to believe it.

That I want to spend my last few seconds in wonderful, ignorant bliss.

"Bailey..." My name is a whisper on her full, chapped lips, and she lifts a shaking hand toward me, her mitten bright against the gray and white of the snow and ice around us. In that moment I see the regret, the guilt, and I know she wishes she'd stopped when I'd begged her to. Or not have done this at all.

*They were never worth this, and I think she knows it in the last few seconds we'll ever look at each other.*

But whatever else she's going to say is lost when she falls. With a dreadful sound like a gunshot, the ice beneath her breaks a second before the ice under me does as well. It's a strange sensation, like the earth getting yanked out from under me, and I hit the freezing water with a scream as my lungs seize up in my chest, protesting everything about the situation.

For precious, terrifying moments, I struggle. My eyes are wide in the water, and freezing. It feels like frozen fingers are trying to claw them out every moment they're open, but if I close them, I won't know where to go.

Fear and ice close in around my chest, and mercifully, my mind plays the memory like a bad projection. One moment I'm sinking, the next my freezing, burning fingers are clawing at the ice to pull myself up. In the dream, I don't feel the pain in my knee where it's sliced open on the ice. Nor do I feel anything past dull discomfort in my hands, though I know that in reality, they'd burned worse than anything I'd ever felt.

In the next moment, I'm crawling towards the shallow edge of the lake, where Daisy lays half in, half out of the water. My heart soars, and I tremble with relief that she's made it out of the lake as well, since she would've had to swim to get this far and not sink straight to the bottom.

At least, until I turn her over, my hands on her shoulders as I try with freezing, bruised lips to say her name.

Daisy.

Daisy.

Dai...sy.

......Daisy.

I shake her once. Then again. A third time, as the syllables of her name become a strange, slurred cry on my lips. Daisydaisydaisydai...sy...

Remembering the others my head jerks up, but when my gaze

*scans the far shore where Emily, Ava, and Jayden had been standing, all I see is the snowy, frozen shore and the trees beyond.*

*The flag from the middle of the lake, having fallen along with us, bumps against her shoe with the movement of the water, but Daisy doesn't move.*

*She'll never move or open her eyes again.*

My eyes open and I stare at the ceiling above me, at the still fan and the dark-painted expanse that matches my walls. My fingers unclench one at a time, letting go of their death grip on the blanket that covers me.

Beside me, a few feet away, the television is on. I can hear the soft murmurs of conversation, and I can see its light playing upon the ceiling, though I haven't yet turned to look at it.

I knew I'd dream of Daisy tonight. Ever since finding the bird in the woods, I've known that tonight will be bad. Emily's death and Phoenix's arrival had simply solidified that fact.

But as dreams about that day go, this isn't the worst I've had. Sometimes my mind contorts the events, replaying them in ways where I die with Daisy or I fall in a different, deeper lake with no way to get out, causing me to be stuck in the frigid darkness forever without the ability to draw air into my lungs.

Compared to that, this one was tame. As far as nightmarish memories go, anyway.

This time, I don't push the dreams away. Normally, I work as hard as I can to get them to fade, to push them out of my brain completely. But this time, with Emily's death so fresh in my ears, I let myself remember what happened next.

Phoenix had been the one to find us. We were too old by that point to need a babysitter, but later he'd told me one of his ex-friends, the brother of one of my 'friends' whose actions led to Daisy's death, had expressed to him that he'd overheard his sister talking about their plan.

Unfortunately, Phoenix had been too late to save his sister, who had so desperately, so *innocently*, wanted to be invited back into the friend group that had ousted us.

So, so desperate that she'd done something she knew was stupid, irresponsible, and dangerous. But it wasn't her fault. It had *never* been Daisy's fault that she'd needed acceptance. They never should've said what they did, or promised her what they had.

*And I should've been faster getting out of the water.*

That thought, and the guilt that sweeps through me, causes me to squeeze my eyes shut as the feeling threatens to overwhelm me. It chills me to the bone, even under my blankets, and I curl my hands tight, nails biting into my scarred palms that have felt the cold more acutely than the rest of me since that night.

God, I hate that Emily's death has done this to me. My normal ability to stay calm and detached has shattered and I find myself gulping deep breaths of air as I try to get myself under control. I open my mouth, prepared to call for my mom to tell her what I'd been dreaming of and talk things out with her. But then I remember that she's gone, and my teeth click together, mouth shutting once more. I'm on my own tonight, to deal with the painful memories and the bad feelings in my chest.

*I can't do this tonight.*

The thought sweeps through me, and there's no arguing with the absolute certainty of it. I'm not wavering on some edge of panic. I'm there, in the middle of it, splashing around in an icy pool with chunks of ice that never melt inside my mind.

*I really, really can't do this tonight.*

In seconds I'm on my feet, my muscles tense and twitching as they come to a too-swift wakefulness along with the rest of me. Before I know what I'm doing, my hand is groping for my phone, and within seconds I have it to my ear while it rings.

God, I hope she answers. If she's at her party already, there's no way Nic will hear her phone going off. Knowing her, she'd skipped to the closest bar or found a beer can in the fridge and is well on her way to being tipsy.

Not that I'll be the first one to tell her that maybe, possibly, she has a bit of a problem and gets blackout drunk too easily and often with how fast she drinks at parties.

Thankfully, Nic picks up, and I don't hear any loud music or yelling in the background as she answers, *"Hey Bailey. What's going on? Did you change your mind about coming to this party with us?"*

"Yes," I reply, barely letting her finish. "I did, actually. Could I come with you, please?" *Pretty please*, I add, because *I can't do this tonight.*

She's quiet for a few seconds, and I wonder if she's changed her plans or doesn't want me there. The second option seems far-fetched, but in my current panic, anything is possible as my heart pounds against my ribs, searching for a way out of the claustrophobic cage my body provides.

*"You're not okay."* Her words aren't a question, and I kick myself for being transparent enough that she knows I'm not okay. Damn it.

"Is that a question?" I ask with a harsh laugh that doesn't do anything to prove my okay-ness. "A statement, or are you about to sing me a song?"

She sighs into the phone as I twist my fingers nervously, still standing in the middle of my large, open room with the television on in the background. *"You know what I mean. It's Emily, isn't it?"*

I hate being so readable. I despise the fact that I'm an open book for her at times like this, and it drives me to grind my teeth together as my jaws ache with protest at the force of the gesture. "Can I come or not?" I ask finally, my voice quiet. "It's okay if not. I'll just—"

*"Of course you can come, Bailey,"* Nic interrupts. *"I'm not*

*trying to interrogate you over the phone. I haven't left yet, but we're about to so you have great timing. Want us to come pick you up?"* If I say yes, then I'll be at her mercy for when we come home, and that's never a solid bet to take if I need to be somewhere at a certain time.

But my parents are gone, and there's nothing going on tomorrow that I care about. If I say *yes*, then I can hunt down alcohol as well, while Nolan, Nic's boyfriend, judges us with raised brows and an almost-frown on his lips.

The same way he always does.

"Yeah, okay," I agree, turning to look at the television that still plays the same cooking show as an hour ago. "I'll ride with you if it's not any trouble." Thankfully I have cash on me I can give her for gas, or more likely, stuff into her car's console for her to find later when she steadfastly refuses to take money from me. "I'll see you in a bit? I need to get ready."

*"Want me to bring you a costume?"* Nic asks, her tone cheeky. *"I have an extra."*

"Of course you do," I mutter, rubbing my eyes. "Can I just go as 'bored college girl from a small town'? I hear that costume is all the rage this year."

*"No."*

"Can I go as *tired* college student from small town?"

*"Is that a different costume than bored college girl from a small town?"*

I consider the question, eyes narrowed, and say finally, "No."

*"Then no."*

"Fine. What's your other costume?" I sigh, wishing I had something lying around that would help me out. "Please tell me it's not a murdering cheerleader. Or a murdering dancer. Or uh, a murdering anything?"

*"A cat,"* Nic replies smugly. *"It's not even a full costume. It's just a tail and a mask."* I can absolutely picture what she's bringing,

and cringe internally at the image of a felt half-mask with ears, and a long, fluffy tail strapped to my ass.

But sacrifices must be made.

"Okay, okay. I'll take it," I agree, once again wishing there were *any* other option available to me. "And uh, I'll dress appropriately." In black, since I'm sure the cat outfit is a black cat for Halloween.

"*Perfect. See you in fifteen? You're on the way, so please don't slip money into some crack of my car. I've told Nolan to look for it, too.*" I doubt Nolan is going to do that, but then again, what do I know?

He'd do anything for Nic, and she's only partially aware of how much he's in love with her. I, for one, can't wait until he finds the courage to propose to my best friend so I can be her maid of honor.

As long as it's not a costume wedding, anyway. Which, unfortunately, is a real possibility with Nic.

"Sure. I would *never*," I lie, trying to sound believable. "Cross my heart and hope to—"

"*I get it,*" Nic snorts before I can choke out the word *die*. "*See you in a few. We'll honk.*"

"I'll already be outside," I assure her, knowing my neighbors will give me the stink eye if she does sit outside of our house in her beat up old Ford honking like a maniac. Already I've had to talk to the security guard for the neighborhood about Nic, Nic's car, and the fact that she *isn't* a robber or serial killer like the neighbors believe.

"No honking, please."

## CHAPTER 5

I f there's one thing I should know by now, it's not to underestimate Nic. My best friend—who'd moved to Hollow Bridge in high school and decided the depressed, quiet girl in the back would be her best friend with no say in the matter—has always aimed to impress. Ever since that first day, she's blown expectations out of the water however she can.

And of course, the cat costume is no exception.

In the minutes before she'd showed up, I'd changed into a short dress, knee-high boots, and a choker, all in matching shades of velvety black. I'd done my makeup as well, though I had no doubt she'd judge me for my lack of great precision in creating wings.

But now, as I sit and stare at the cat mask I've pulled out of the bag, surprise is the only thing I can muster. And a soft, "Huh," under my breath as Nolan puts his foot on the gas pedal to propel us away from the sidewalk in front of my house.

On one hand, it's definitely a mask. And it's definitely cat-shaped. On the other hand, I hadn't expected to be wearing a black cat *skull*. The resin is shiny with polish, and a large, reddish stone is embedded in the forehead of the fake, fanged skull. Instead of just obscuring my eyes, the entire thing goes over my forehead, eyes, and nose. The 'snout' comes to a blunt stop inches from the end of my own nose, and on either side, two delicate fangs protrude toward my upper lip.

It's definitely better than what I'd been imagining.

"So I have ears. But I don't think you need them. And I don't think they look that good with it," my dark-haired best friend says, pulling one of the clip-in furry pieces from the bag. She's right. It's unnecessary, especially with the delicate, bony ears that the mask ends in, up past my forehead. Obviously that makes the mask less anatomically correct, but I for one prefer the 'bone' look instead of adding clips into my tumbling, unkempt hair that I'd barely managed to run a brush through, let alone tame with willpower and hot tools.

"I like the ears it has," I reply, running my fingers over the smooth material again. It feels great against my fingers, and I do the action once more before I curb my enthusiasm for the sensation. I'm nothing if not big on textures, and I wonder if Nic knows she's given me a toy for the night that I won't be able to keep the pads of my fingers away from when I'm bored. "No fur needed." This way, I look *scary* rather than cliche. Though if I'd known this was what she was bringing me, I would've worn something other than the black, lace up dress with straps and off the shoulder, puffy sleeves. Still, the look works. Especially since everything is black.

"But you have to wear the tail," Nic points out, her thin lips in a sly grin for my benefit. "Please? It clips onto whatever you're wearing."

"As opposed to the kind you want *me* to get," Nolan sighs from the driver's seat, sounding dramatic and lamenting.

It takes me a moment, but when it clicks, I snort and look away from both of them. "Still? You're *still* trying to get him to wear a tail like that, Nic?" It's been her goal for at least a year, though I have no idea why. I've started to think that while

Nolan complains, he has to be into it for Nic to keep teasing him about it. And for him to bring it up so casually.

But if he *is* wearing a tail in the bedroom that isn't the clip-on kind, I don't really want to know. Hell, I don't want to know if it *is* just a clip on. That would be way too much information about their relationship for me to be privy to.

Plus, I already know too much about their sex life as it is.

Again I run my fingers along the mask, and pull the tail with its small, black metal pin out of the bag before letting the plastic fall to the floor of the back seat with a soft rustle. It's black, mostly, but with little bits of dark-red, sparkling tinsel mixed in with the fur to give it the same kind of shine as the mask. That alone is the reason I don't refuse, though I keep it in my lap along with the mask as we drive.

"So, where are we going?" I think to ask finally, as I settle against the window. Halloween decorations are on full display as we drive closer to the middle of town, and I can't help the small smile on my lips that twitches into place when we pass the houses well known for their Halloween decorations. One has an elaborate cemetery in the front, with all the headstones hand painted by the guy that's somehow related to the mayor, from what I've heard. Skeletons tumble and dance in the billowing fog and lights placed behind fake stones; one of them is even playing an orange, blow-up saxophone for the 'party' of dead people.

Other houses near the center of town are lit up with lights and inflatables, though only a few are full on, blazing bonfires of light and sound and activity. It'll be like this until after Halloween, and while I rationally know that most other places aren't as obsessed with the holiday as we are, I still can't accept any other way of doing things.

Before I can mention the cemetery, my eyes fall on a papier mâché tree that winds upward through a sloping yard, some of the 'branches' resting on top of the house. It's...crafty, to say the least. Though, there's not much to be scared of with the tree and the fog at its roots.

Except for the dead woman that swings in the breeze that sweeps through Hollow Bridge.

Nolan slows and comes to a stop at a red light, in fierce conversation with Nic about their plans for tomorrow. I've kept an ear on the conversation, knowing they're always nice enough to remember I like being with them, but not usually in the middle of conversation.

Sometimes it's just nice to be included at a distance. Especially when I'm not at my social best, which is considerably *worse* than other people's social best.

Neither of them has stopped to really look at the tree, or the dead woman who's supposed to be Agnes Brown swinging from the branch by a noose around her throat.

It's been a while since anyone included her in their decorations. It's just so...easy here to make her part of the scene. Though, I've never seen such a huge, life-size replica of *the* tree that Agnes was hanged in.

Supposedly, anyway. But that's the entire basis of our town's folklore. *Supposedly,* Hollow Bridge was plagued by the witch, Agnes Brown, after her son had been killed in an accident. *Supposedly,* the townspeople had formed a mob and hunted Agnes down after Emily Riley, the daughter of the town's mayor, got lured into the woods and eaten by Agnes and her familiars.

She'd been hunted down and killed by the people she'd tormented, and lain a curse on them to last all the days of Hollow Bridge's existence. When they'd hanged her, however, Agnes had decided not to stay dead. She'd come back for one final stand and was slain again by the mayor's son on the bridge that gave our town its name.

The bridge that, I'm sure, is dripping orange and purple lights right about now. The sign, labeling it *the* Hollow Bridge, is likely covered in cobwebs as well. Maybe this year, the family that owns the woods on the closest side of the bridge will go back to putting lights in the woods to look like eyes, just to scare and confuse anyone driving into town at night.

The car we're in jolts forward as Nolan fumbles with the gearshift, and I nearly faceplant into the back of Nic's seat as we rattle into motion once more.

It occurs to me I never found out where we were going, though if it was due to my inattention or by my friends' lack of answer, I have no idea. If I have to guess, I'm sure it's the former. I'd gotten interested in something right after I'd asked, and that's enough to make my ears forget their job half of the time.

Luckily, my question is answered before much longer. Nolan slows on a side street packed with cars, and my gaze falls on the house that's more lit up than its neighbors, though the decorations are anything but thoughtfully put together. The residents of this house have just thrown everything and the kitchen sink into the yard, from blow-up witches to lights and fake pumpkins, instead of sticking with some kind of theme.

I can't help but judge, since our yard is lit up quite nicely with orange lights, purple lights, and a light show that spins against the sloping roof of the house that faces the neighborhood for a few hours each night.

It takes Nolan a few minutes, but he finds a parking place that doesn't require a hike and also isn't in front of a hydrant. Nic is out first, predictably. She doesn't love cars and is always the quickest to escape. Though she's gotten better at looking like she's moving deliberately, instead of flailing with all due haste to fall over herself onto the grass.

I stretch when I get out of the back, going up on my toes and then back down with a long sigh that comes from somewhere in my chest that's had enough for today. I'm still drowsy, though the Halloween decorations and chilly air that pervades the sleeves of my dress are doing a damn good job of bringing me back to full wakefulness. If anything, I just need a few minutes out here, staring at the lights and trees, to get myself back on track.

*Emily is dead, you know,* my brain reminds me in a voice that sounds too much like Daisy's to be coincidental. There's no stab of guilt or shock, and certainly no sadness for the girl I hadn't called a friend in years.

She'd never deserved my friendship, or Daisy's. In fact, I wish we'd never met Emily and her brother in daycare so many, many years ago.

"Hey." The word forcefully drags me out of my skull and I look up at Nic's nose, my eyes halting there like there's a barrier preventing them from going any higher. The nose and mouth are my visual comfort zones, especially when I'm feeling less than sure of things. Like tonight. "You okay?" Nic asks, worry in every inch of the curve of her mouth and every note of her voice. "If you're not, we can go do something else. We can go back to your place and watch movies, or go feed some feral cat colony no one knows about except you."

"That would ruin it then, don't you think?" I ask in a slow voice, a small grin curving my lips upward. "If I take you to the feral cat colonies that only I know about, then I'm not special anymore and *anyone* can go hang out there." I'm joking, mostly because I'm not the only one who feeds the cats that live in some of the less-than-nice areas around town and are consistently too-thin.

My parents have banned me from bringing animals home with me after I'd brought home the third cat that does more lurking and hiding than socializing. So, feeding them has become more of a hobby than it used to be, since I worry about their health when I'm not there spooning wet cat food into their bowls.

Nic smiles at my joke, though I know it wasn't a very good

one. "Want me to clip that tail to your ass?" she asks, just as Nolan locks the car.

He looks up, his thick brows disappearing under the tumble of bangs that obscure his forehead. "Don't do it. Last time she used that on me, I ended up naked."

"You end up naked a lot," I remind him, turning and handing her the tail. "Don't act like you don't love her spontaneous sexxing ways."

He looks around, as if he's contemplating my accusation, then nods once. "Okay, yeah, I can't exactly argue, but *still*."

"Plus, I'm not the one she wants to peg," I add, just as sweetly. "So I think my ass is safe, don't you?"

"Shh," Nic teasingly smacks my arm when she's done. "Don't tell him that. You'll spook him."

"He already knows," I remind her, delicately tying the ribbon of the mask over my face as I look both of them over.

From the small wings they're tying to each other's shoulders, I realize they're angels. Or, well, fallen angels, judging by the black attire both of them wear. Nic looks gorgeous in a corset and shorts that barely cover her ass, the paleness of her skin is a good contrast to the black, satiny material of the corset. Nolan, on the other hand, wears tight black jeans and a black tank top, though I can see the goosebumps dusting his arms as he rubs them. Both of them wear dark, smoky makeup, and I'm sure she'd done it for the both of them at least three times before they'd left.

And Nolan, of course, had let her. He lets her do anything, and supports her in every hobby she's ever had, with more devotion on his face than any human should be able to have.

Or at least, more than I've ever felt. Looking at them for too long makes my eyes sting with jealousy, even though my lack of a partner is from a noted lack of trying to find one.

The feral cats are enough for me. At least until I can find

someone who can handle the allergy to eye contact, the sometimes-allergy to touch, and the texture thing.

Seriously, we could never *ever* have fuzzy socks in the house. With the worst texture and feel known to man, they're banned from my room and whatever future house I end up buying will have a strict, no fuzzy socks rule posted right at the door for everyone to see.

Or maybe something less dramatic.

"Okay," I sigh, rocking back on my heels. "It's cold out here. We're going in, right?" Another glance at the house shows me a building I don't really recognize. But that's not exactly shocking or worrisome. Nic has more friends from college than I do, and has met more of them that live here than I thought possible. Of course, there's a college kid throwing a party in Hollow Bridge. I'd be surprised if there wasn't.

"Right. And hey, if you need to leave, we'll leave," Nic informs me, with no hint of frustration or trepidation in her voice. "No matter what."

"Even if you're busy pegging your boyfriend, we'll leave?" I ask, over Nolan's choked indignation that comes a second too late to be real.

Nic stops to ponder that theatrically, one long, coffin-shaped nail tapping against her lips. "I'll get back to you on that one," she tells me finally. "No promises. He has a *really* nice ass and I'd hate to miss out."

"And far be it from me to deprive you," I agree enthusiastically, stepping back off of the sidewalk and onto the road behind the car. "If you're in the middle of, uh, appreciating such a fine ass, I will, of course, look for other travel arrangements. This is Hollow Bridge, so there's gotta be some Halloween-themed transportation I can take home, right? A headless horseman strolling by? A cab driven by a skeleton who doesn't want to help us save Halloweentown?"

Though Nic doesn't share my aggressive love of everything

Halloween and tries to stay on the un-obsessed side of town, even she's seen the classics.

"I'd take the skeleton over a man with no head," she replies nonchalantly, falling into step with me as we cross the street toward the steps of the small, one-story house. It's the kind of house I expect to smell like old beer and socks, and I hope to god I'm proven wrong when we go in.

"But seriously." Nic turns to me, blocking my path across the red solo cup strewn yard. "If you need to leave—"

"Then I'll ring the stranger danger bell. Or would you like me to pull out the monkey backpack-leash so you can strap me to your arm and keep track of me all night?" I shake my head at her, still smiling. "I'm fine, Nic. And I'm just as much of an adult as you."

"Debatable..." Nolan mumbles from Nic's other side. When he sees my look, his smile is all sweetness, like he isn't hurling saccharine insults.

"*Anyway*, Mr. Fine ass, I can handle whatever happens, okay? And I can manage my own emotions. Or so my therapist told me last week. She's really proud of me, actually." Nic snorts, but I just sniff and try to look inspiring or proud of such a feat. "I'm not going to do anything or leave with anyone. I won't take candy or beer from a stranger. And I'm not going to make out with someone in a sexy slasher costume." Probably because I've never *seen* a guy in a sexy slasher costume.

"Just trust me, Nic. I'm happy to be here, and I'm not made of glass. You don't have to worry so much about me." I make the words sound believable, but deep down, just a little, I can't help but wonder just how true they are this time.

# CHAPTER 6

M y first thought when I walk into the house with its open layout and not-so-cheesy Halloween decorations is that this isn't nearly as bad as I'd thought it would be.

My next thought, as I lift my foot off the tile and feel the way the sticky surface clings to the sole of my boot and makes a loud, unpleasant sound as I pull away from it, is that my first thought was very wrong. This is much *worse* than I'd expected.

"Gross," I mutter flatly, not particularly phased but also not impressed. A drunk guy, who's either on steroids or the son of a gorilla, stumbles through the open space, his arms pinwheeling as people dodge out of his way. He disappears into the kitchen, though his crowing laughter remains even as Nolan closes the door gently behind him, his nose wrinkled into a delicate, yet still very disgusted, sneer.

My teeth set together in a grimace, and I lock my jaw against them grinding to pieces as both Nolan and I follow the much more confidant Nic further into the house.

"How do you know whoever lives here again?" I ask Nolan over the spooky-ish party music that pulses from the speakers set up in the corners of the room on small platforms installed just for that purpose. "College?"

Nolan gestures at Nic. "It's someone from one of her theater classes. A brother and sister live here and she's been getting invited to these parties of theirs for *months*. Not that she's ever come." He glances around the house, his brows raised. "You know, without the sticky floor and the smell of stale beer, this place could be pretty. Not as nice as your house, though," he adds casually in my direction. "But your house is pretty spectacular."

"My parents' house," I remind him automatically, without looking at him. I don't love it being referred to as *mine* as if it's some kind of accomplishment that I, personally, have achieved. I didn't do anything to get it, after all. My parents bought the house when I was five, and I barely remember any of our old house, though it was close to being on par with our current one, without the cool Halloween-eccentric neighbors.

But still, as much as I may like it, I still can't say it's *mine* in a way that doesn't make my skin tingle and prickle with discomfort.

"Your parents' awesome house," Nolan amends with a half-grin that borders on apologetic, though it doesn't need to be. I'm certainly not upset with him, and he's only a small part of the reason that I feel so uneasy tonight.

I turn away again before he can notice, since I know for a fact that Nolan is a lot more intuitive than people think when they see his sweet, goofy grin and gorgeous eyes. Nic is the loud one, the more abrasive one, and I've always felt that Nolan is the perfect counterbalance for her personality and the way she goes about things.

They're *perfect* for each other, and I'd be lying if I said I wasn't a little envious of their relationship. No matter the fact that I've never been in love or really *that* attracted to a boy— well, except for Phoenix when my raging hormones pointed me at the most attractive thing in the vicinity—it's still a goal to have a relationship where someone is the perfect other half.

Or at least willing to pick up after themselves and make their own dinner. The bar may be low, but I've learned that it's still a tripping hazard for most of the guys in Hollow Bridge.

*Oh well.*

Absently, I adjust the cat mask on my face, loving the feel of the smooth, cool material against my skin. Occasionally, my tail brushes the backs of my legs, but I'm too busy admiring the other costumes people are wearing to care that much.

Within minutes, Nic has found her friend. The two of them seem to magically clear off a sofa of people that wander away at that moment, and when they sink into deep conversation with grins and enthusiasm, I waver.

Socializing is exhausting at the best of times, and their level of commitment to it right now is overwhelming my brain tonight. Even Nolan looks a little intimidated, though he perches on the edge of the sofa to be the supportive boyfriend of legends.

But I'm not in love with Nic, nor do I feel particularly attached to her at the moment. The longer I stand here not doing anything, the more itchy my fingers get, and the more my muscles twitch with restless, nervous energy.

I need to be doing something other than this.

I back up one step. Then another. Nic glances up and I offer her a smile from under the borrowed mask, my gestures and flicking fingers indicating that I'm going to find the kitchen and, maybe, some kind of alcohol. Being the lightest of light-weights, all I really need to do is sniff an empty beer can to get buzzed.

Well, maybe I'm not *that* bad. But if I try to chug any of the mixed drinks that Nic does, or any of the ones that are on the kitchen island that looms into view the moment I cross into the kitchen, I'll be out before I can realize what I've even picked up a drink.

My fingers come to rest on the cool surface of the island, just as my upper lip sinks lightly into the lower. I have no idea what to ask for, when three kinds of Halloween punch and bottles of tequila, rum, and vodka litter the counter.

I don't want to get that drunk tonight; I don't think.

"The punch isn't that bad." The voice makes me tense, and my shoulders rise, as a guy in a toga that should've been left behind in the nineties swaggers up to stand beside me, elbow brushing mine with obvious intent.

My eyes fall on his bare chest, his questionable tattoos, and move up to his throat, where his Adam's apple bobs precariously. It trembles as he swallows... up and down. Up and down. Finally, my eyes go further upward, resting on thin lips and a thin nose that looks as if it would snap under just two of my fingers.

He opens his mouth and says something again, though my attention is fixed once again on that bobbing piece of him.

"What?" I ask finally, not looking at his eyes. He doesn't speak at first, but does offer me a small, wide-lipped cup made of plastic. In the orange liquid, three ice cubes swim, their edges shiny and going transparent as they lose some of their coldness.

"The punch. It's uh..." he trails off and I see little blobs of ice cream in the drink he's offering. It's that view of melting ice cream, and the nostalgia of park-held birthday parties and homemade punch, that gets me to slide the cup into my fingers, the coolness of it sinking into my skin. "Really, it's not bad," he shrugs, and as I take a drink, I finally look up at his nondescript eyes, the dusting of freckles, and red hair that's a mess of untamed curls.

He's right. It's not bad, and it doesn't taste like alcohol, which is either very good for me or very bad. There's a chance there's still something in it. More than a chance, given the bottles. But the sherbet, juice, and whatever fizzy drink was dumped into it are doing a solid job of masking it, if that is the case.

"You're right," I admit, not oblivious to the grin that flashes across his lips. "I was expecting worse. It's not bad."

Which, apparently, is the wrong thing to say. It launches him into a flurry of words in explanation. His hands up and moving in front of him and distracting me from his words while I absently drink the glass until it's completely gone.

He's still talking when I dip myself another half-glass of it, and for a few minutes, I'm sure of my decision. I haven't tasted alcohol so far, and I have no reason to think that my assessment of the drink is wrong.

Until life shows me that it is.

The feeling is smooth as it hits me, traveling through my veins and snaking fuzzy, warm tendrils through my brain. It's easier, at least, to look up at the ginger-headed boy as he talks when I can feel fuzzy cotton in my skull. He pauses when I finally do make eye contact, his lips still parted to address whatever he'd been talking about.

The fact that I can't remember is my next warning sign.

My third and final one is the way I stumble back when he leans in, his intention to kiss me so clear that he couldn't be more obvious if he announced it to the room. *But I don't want to kiss him.*

My steps teeter, two turning into four as I *subtly* try to express my disinterest, but when my shoulders bump into something solid and an arm slides over my shoulders to steady me, I realize I'm being anything *but.*

"She's not into you, Fritz," a stranger's voice chuckles as someone walks by, a glass of punch in his hand. He salutes both of us and leaves, though after a momentary look of disappointment at me, and trepidation at the owner of the arm on my shoulders, Fritz flees with him.

Leaving me...not so alone.

My head tips back, tilting until I'm resting the back of it against my new friend's shoulder. The mask he wears swims in my vision, the whiteness and smoothness causing my focus to slip and slide on the surface unnervingly. For a moment there's four of him, then three. And with a jolt, I realize that I'm not *completely* hallucinating.

There are two of them, dressed almost completely alike. Their masks, for sure, are identical in every way, and with their black hoods drawn up, it's impossible to even tell their hair color.

"Oh," I murmur, finding it easier to talk with everything so loose and easy. "There's two of you." I say it like they might not know, and the two of them trade a look, with the one not holding me tilting his head to the side in a way I'd say is *coy*.

"Do you need help finding your way home, little cat?" one of them asks, his voice a low, soft purr. I *think* it's the one with his arm over my shoulders, and when he speaks, he pulls me a little more snugly against him, shifting his weight as he does. Another hand comes up to touch my mask, gloved fingers running over the curves of the skull and making me shiver like he's just touched my skin.

The man pulls away, head tilting once more, and glances at his partner with the other white mask. It occurs to me then that there's mesh over the eyeholes that prevents me from seeing their eyes, and gives them more of an anonymous, dangerous look.

"My friends are here," I breathe, not sure why my body is completely content to be right *here*. "I don't need to go home."

"Where are your friends?" the one not holding me asks. "Do you want us to find them for you?"

I shake my head without thinking about it, my thoughts

coming slowly. Even when the thoughts from earlier tonight rear their head, it's easier to chase them off when I'm here, with an arm around my shoulders and these two behind me.

Slowly, uncertainly, I reach up, my knuckles touching the mask of the man with his arm over me. "Do I know you?" I ask, swearing there's something familiar in the way he holds himself.

"No," he chuckles, his arm sliding free of me. Before he can say anything else, however, his partner is there, one arm going to my waist as he inserts himself between his partner and me.

"Would you like to know me?" he purrs in a lighter voice than that of his partner. "What's your name, pretty kitty?"

"Don't," the other says. "Don't ask her that when we're not going to give her ours."

There's something suspicious about them, and it tickles the back of my brain when they trade looks again, as if they're having a silent conversation.

It's a shame I can't read minds. Not that I'm particularly good at reading faces, either, but that's not an issue since I can't even *see* theirs.

"That's not creepy at all," I murmur, leaning forward onto the island and cramming my eyes shut. I'm not *drunk*. Not quite. I'm more buzzed than I'd like to be, but it's not like I'm alone or driving home.

A hand on my lower back turns my thoughts to dust, and I feel fingers carding through the fur of my tail, tugging on it lightly. There's something like a growl, then a chuckle, and when I turn, I see that it's the slightly shorter one with his gloves on my tail, tugging hard enough to make it taut.

"This is adorable," he informs me in a purr. "Really just the cutest thing, right?" he tips his face toward his partner, who neither answers nor moves.

"My mask is better than yours," I assert, and I get a soft scoff in reply.

"Your mask lets everyone know who you are if they look at you for longer than a half second." It's still the shorter one speaking, and he steps closer, until he's leaning on the island as well. "Why did you run away from the cute redhead? He was really into you, little cat."

"Because..." The answer swims away on the tide of his cologne. It's not overpowering, and it invades my nose sweetly, making me forget everything I'd planned on saying. "I don't know," I say finally. "I didn't come here for that."

But if I didn't, then why am I not moving?

"Stop." His partner puts a hand on his arm, drawing him back. "You saw her drinking just like I did. She's *drunk*."

"Not that drunk," I assert. "I'm *barely* tipsy."

"She's *barely* tipsy," his partner teases. "And besides, you have me confused with someone else, surely. Someone *much* nicer."

When he rounds on me again, his fingers are under my chin, tilting my head up. "Do you want us to leave you alone, little cat? We can find you someone not so cute as us to tumble into, if you'd rather. We could even tug that cute little tail of yours and take you back to your friends. It won't hurt our feelings much, I swear."

"I don't need you to take me back to anyone," I reply, trying to keep myself from sounding worse off than I am. I wasn't lying when I'd said I was tipsy...but I'm definitely closer to drunk than sober. As it is, these two are not only intriguing, but fun. Their conversation, their attention, are drowning out the background noise of a treasonous brain that wants my night to suck.

"If you don't want us to take you back...want us to lead you away?" he goes on, teasingly. "Can I wrap a leash around that pretty throat of yours and take you home with us? We'll even get you an upgrade for your tail—"

His partner *growls,* drawing both of our attention.

"Or maybe I'm only allowed to tease you here," the one in

front of me goes on with a sigh. "While he watches to make sure I don't do something *terrible* to you."

"Is that what he normally does?" I ask without thinking, head cocked to the side as I look at the guy standing a bit further away. "*Watch*?" I know how I say it, but I don't expect the slight tension in his shoulders that dissipates when he snorts out a laugh.

"Be careful, little cat," he warns, looming closer without any other warning. "Because I'm only a *little* more polite than him. What did you say, lover?" The words are obviously directed to his partner, but the gloved hand that comes up, fingers encircling my throat, is a love letter addressed to me alone. "We'll put a collar and leash on her and take her home?"

His voice makes my breath catch, and my fingers tighten on the wood of the kitchen island as two girls come in, their eyes on us and the precursor to gossip on their faces.

When I move almost uncomfortably, hating their eyes on me and the way it burns and sizzles at my skin, the taller boy turns to glance at them over his shoulder, unmoving as they walk out the back door instead of staying.

"Go back to Nic and Nolan, little cat," he sighs, releasing his grip on my throat. In my drunken state, I don't think to question how they know my friends' names. The alcohol tells me that's normal, that they're probably Nic's classmates, since they're at a party hosted by her friend.

They're right, of course. I have no business acting like this with two men I don't know; especially with my head swimming just enough to be dangerous. The taller one slides a bottle of water into my hand, closing my fingers around it before he and the other boy step back.

"Scat," his friend chuckles. "But don't talk to anyone on the way back."

"Why?" I ask, cracking the seal on the miniature bottle and

downing half of it. "Will the spell break, fairy godmother? Will everyone at the ball know who I am?"

"Because I said so," he teases. "Isn't that good enough?"

I can't help rolling my eyes as the coolness of water hits my throat and trickles down to my stomach. I definitely should've eaten more today, but at least the cold water is helping chase some of the fuzziness out of my brain.

I hope.

Without another word, I push away from the kitchen island, disappointment sinking into my bones as I walk. I'd liked their company, their mystery, and even the prickle of unease that they'd instilled. It had been more interesting than most of this party, anyway.

But if they don't want my company, then I'm not going to force it on them. Especially if they think I'm too drunk to say yes or no with any kind of confidence.

A hand snatches at mine, pulling me to a stop. It's the redhead from before, Fritz, with the friend that had bodied him out of the kitchen so nicely.

"Are you okay?" he asks, sweetness on his face. His grip is kind and soft on my hand, fingers stroking along my skin. "I'm sorry if I came on too strongly. Is that what happened?"

For a moment, I consider just walking away. I'm really *not* interested in him the way he is me, and nothing he's said or done has really held my attention.

But I smile, turning on my heel and stepping closer to him. "It's not that," I promise. "You were really nice. I just—"

The hand that curls around my shoulder is much tighter than his on my arm, and I can't help but tense.

"My my, aren't we terrible at following rules, little cat," the voice in my ear whispers sweetly. "Seriously, Fritz. She's not into you. She's into me."

The redhead glances between us, but lets his hand fall.

"Sorry," he says finally, in a way that makes my teeth grind with guilt and the urge to apologize. "I didn't realize."

"It's okay," I said quickly, wanting to assuage his hurt feelings. "Really, it's not like that. It's kind of complicated." Complicated, because I don't know them and I'm about to skip back to my friends and probably never see any of them.

But maybe that's for the best.

"So, so complicated," the boy behind me purrs. "Say your goodbyes now, little cat."

I can't help but roll my eyes again, and I tell Fritz to have a good night before I turn, once more facing the direction where I think Nic and Nolan might still be.

Except, the hand on my shoulder won't let me, and the person sidles in closer, until his smooth mask is pressed against my ear.

"What are you doing?" I ask, not turning to look at him. "My friends are over there."

"But you broke the *rules*," he purrs, hands sliding down to my waist to rest there lightly. "So now you can come play with us instead."

# CHAPTER 7

There's no good way to stumble after the boy that pulls me along with a hand on my wrist. No graceful way, at least, and my stomach turns nervously as he leads me through the house, and finally upstairs to a bathroom that I'm pushed into.

The door's lock *clicks*, and the noise makes my stomach drop ten stories straight to hell.

*Did I make a mistake?*

Did I fuck up and let these two take me somewhere they could *hurt* me?

As if sensing my thoughts, the taller of the two approaches me, hands up to cup my cheeks before I really know what's happening. "No, it's okay, little cat," he purrs, his words the sweetest kind of promise. "You don't need to hold your breath like that."

I let out the air I'd been holding, my hands coming up to rest on his wrists. "Why did you lock me in a bathroom?" I ask, some of the panic seeping out from my fingers and toes as his friend comes close, reaching out to stroke my cheek.

"Because it seemed like you wanted to play," he remarks,

head tilting just a touch to the side. "Were we wrong? Do you want to go back to your friends, truthfully?"

*No.* The answer echoes around my head, and unfortunately my mouth is on the same page. I say the word quickly, in a clipped tone, accompanied by a shake of my head that earns a soft stroke from the fingers of the man who holds my face.

"But I don't know who you are," I point out in a whisper, my head still swimming just slightly. "Aren't you going to take off your masks?"

"No," the one in front of me chuckles. "Sorry, little cat. We're not taking them off. Not even for you."

I'm pretty sure he doesn't know me. There's no way he can since his voice doesn't sound familiar in my ears. Surely if I'd met either of these guys more than once, I'd be able to recognize them by the sound of their voices.

Still, flickers of faces swirl in my brain. Jack and Evan, plus a few other boys who'd made it clear I was the easy target in high school. The idea that this could be one of them playing some terrifying prank, no matter how dumb of an idea that is, makes it even harder to relax when their touches draw me to do more than stand here, gaping like a fish.

But it's the man to my left, the one who hoists himself up to sit on the long counter that holds two sinks for the primary suite, who does the best at drawing my attention. From under his hood, I can see a small peek of auburn, but he's too close a second later, cutting off my view as he reaches out to slide a hand up my arm. The leather of his glove is a new, interesting feeling on my skin, and I shiver.

Just as his friend pulls me in to brush the lips of his mask over mine, like he can really feel the kiss. "So gorgeous," he purrs, hooking a finger in my mask. "I won't take this off because it wouldn't be fair, would it sweetheart?" I love the way he talks. I love the way *both* of them talk, truth be told. Though right now, he's more vocal than his partner.

"We just want to play a little. And we're not going to hurt you," his friend says from my left, his voice thrumming with excitement. "Don't you want to play with us?"

My heart hammers even as I dip a nod. Already heat is pooling between my thighs, and as if he can sense it, the man in front of me shoves them apart with his knee, moving so he can stand with one leg pressed against my center.

"Good girl," he murmurs, and presses me back, until my shoulders and the back of my head are flush with the mirror behind me. "Such a gorgeous little thing." He moves his hands, one of them going to my throat where he can wrap his long fingers around my neck, and the other moves to my knee, pressing it further outward so he can stand more comfortably between my legs. "This really is the perfect costume for you."

"Because I'm *purrfectly* cat-like?" I joke, not sure where I'm even going with the stupid pun.

"Nah," his friend murmurs against my ear, one hand wrapping around my thigh and the other tangling in my hair as he leaned close. "Because you're the cat that curiosity killed...and we're the satisfaction that can bring you back."

A thrill shoots up my spine at his words, and irrationally, I want to beg both of them to take off their masks so I can see them. Or, more preferably, so I can kiss them and taste every bit of their mouths.

"You should've worn half masks," I tell the one at my side, as his fingers stroke closer to his partner's thigh and my center. "Then I could've kissed you."

"We should've worn half masks," he agrees, tone sharp. "So my boyfriend could eat you out while I fuck your mouth. I bet you'd look so good sitting on his face." When my mouth opens —either in a gasp or to reply, I have no idea—his friend is there, thumb pressing down on my tongue and his hand gripping my jaw, keeping it open.

"I'd rather hear you moan, even if hearing you two argue is

more than a little enjoyable," he tells me, keeping his grip firm and the leather-covered digit pressed down firmly so I can't say a word. "Lean back against the mirror for us a little more, sweetheart. Let us play with you before we let you go."

My breath hitches at that, and it takes a moment for me to do what he says, my gaze fixed on the narrow eyes of his mask. His other hand leaves my thigh, and it's his partner who surprises me, moving so he's sitting fully on the counter between the sinks and can curl one leg under him, the length of his calf against my hip. He leans forward, the hand on my thigh moving too, until I feel his gloved fingers stroking lightly against my panties, teasing me.

The sound I make is embarrassing at best, and I squirm against the mirror, their touches driving me crazy with how much more I want. One of them chuckles, though I don't know which, and the man in front of me reaches to grip the bow holding up the corset top of my dress. "Can I undo this? I promise I'll help you put it back," he asks, already plucking at the ribbon.

I jerk a nod, most of my attention fixed on the auburn-haired man's questing fingers. The teasing stays at the edges of the cloth covering my damp slit, never once going where I want them to. In some detached, rational part of my brain, I tell myself this isn't what I came here for, and that I'm probably going to question this in the morning.

*But I don't care.* Not right now. Not when I need something, anything, to take my mind off of the memories that plague me in my sleep. My brain is still a little fuzzy with alcohol, and I blame it on that when I let out a soft moan that sounds too much like a mewl, and arch my hips against the man's fingers.

He chuckles, and when my fingers wrap around his wrist, trying to guide him to where I want him, he doesn't seem to mind. But he also doesn't exactly comply. He takes his time as

DON'T BE SCARED    53

his friend unties the ribbon at my chest, unthreading it from the bronze loops that hold my dress together.

*Fuck.* I'm really about to let them, two strangers in masks, do this. But instead of scaring me, the thought fuels me onward, and I try to make a noise of impatience to get both of them to *hurry up.*

But I don't think they get the message. Not when it still takes another thirty seconds for the man to push my panties to the side, and when the man unlacing my dress is still just playing with the ribbon, teasing my skin with the edges of it.

"Patience," his friend purrs in my ear. "You've got to have patience, little cat. Why don't you show me how much you want us, hmm? Close your lips around his thumb and suck on it for me."

When I hesitate, they don't push me. They don't say anything until I lock eyes with both of their masks' eyes, and I hope they can see me do it before my lips and teeth come down around his friend's thumb, just sharply enough for him to feel it. The leather is a bitter tang against my tongue, but I still close my eyes and lean my head back, dragging his hand with me as I trace the seam with my tongue and suckle at it, teeth grazing over the fabric.

*"Fuck,"* I hear him breathe. "You're so hot, sweetheart. Look at you." His hand at my corset ribbon fumbles for a few seconds, but a moment later it rips open, the ribbon pooling on the sink on my other side. He pulls his thumb from my mouth so he can use both hands, fingers gentle as he shoves my dress open as far as it can go, slipping it down my arms until it sits at my waist.

"Come here, darling," his friend murmurs, snagging my knee with one hand and pulling it over his leg. He hooks it there and squeezes my thigh, an obvious message for me to keep it in place, before his hand goes to his boyfriend's jeans. Surprisingly quickly and with only one hand, he unbuttons the taller man's fly, the zipper loud in the small room as he peels it downward to be met with a groan.

"Wait—" He stops himself from what he was going to say, shuddering. "If you do that, I'm going to end up fucking her in this damn bathroom."

"No, you're not," the man beside me purrs. "You're just going to play with her like I am." There's a note of teasing in his voice, but this time, it's not for me. I watch with rapt attention, chest rising and falling with my breaths as he runs his palm over the bulge in his partner's underwear. Teasingly at first, before he grinds his hand against it, eliciting a gasp in reply.

"You don't mind, right little cat?" the auburn-haired man teases. "He's not going to fuck you. Promise we wouldn't do anything like that without you being fully sober and knowing who we are. But he wants to touch you so badly...let me tease him a little with your body, won't you?"

I doubt he's waiting for an answer. Especially when he dips his gloved fingers into his partner's black underwear and frees his cock that's already straining against the soft fabric. As if in response, the man in front of me moves, hands coming up to cup my breasts.

"Can I take this off?" he asks breathlessly, attention back on me. "I'll be nice—"

"I don't think she wants us to be nice." His partner drags my skirt up, hiking it up over my thighs so both of them can see the matching underwear I have on. "Gorgeous," he says again, and shoves them to the side easily. "Do you want us to treat you nice and delicate, little cat?" I can hear the goading in his words, even before I shake my head. "Or would you rather us play a little rough? We'll put you back together and make it all better after, I promise." His fingers spread my slit, index finger free to stroke between my folds which pulls a whimper from my throat.

"He wants to fuck this cunt so bad, pretty cat," the auburn-haired boy tells me frankly. "I bet if we could see his face, he'd be biting his lip and looking *so* stressed out."

"Why don't you fuck me?" I whisper, eyeing up the man in front of me in his all black outfit. It's the alcohol that makes me this bold. I know I'm tipsy, verging on buzzed; but that only makes me speak my mind. "If you want to so badly."

"Because, sweetheart, you're not sober enough for me to do that," he replies with no hesitation. "Didn't I tell you that?" But as if to satisfy us both, he unhooks my bra and slides it off of my arms, hands coming back so he can palm my breasts with a breath of satisfaction. "You really are perfect," he murmurs, leather gloves warming to my skin temperature. "I bet you're perfect *everywhere*. You'd feel so good around my cock."

"Not that you'll find out if you don't fuck me," I point out, still holding out hope for that.

"She has a point," his partner teases. "But he has a better one. We don't fuck tipsy girls. No matter how much they beg for it. Which...I would totally not be opposed to. You begging, I mean." His finger slides into me, pumping in and out while his partner moves to flick his thumbs over my nipples, teasing them until I squirm under him.

"You move around so much," he laughs lightly. "When I fuck you, should I pin you under me with my hand in your hair? He can hold you if that'll make it better, while I breed that sweet little pussy."

"*Fuck.*" I don't mean to say it, but how can I not? He takes it as encouragement, his movements becoming rougher, until he's pinching my nipples hard enough that I yelp at the sharp pain that's definitely not quite unpleasant. My hands come up to grab at his wrists, scratching at the skin between his gloves and the cuffs of his hoodie.

"That's it," he encourages. "Scratch me up all you want, little cat. Here." He pulls away just for a moment, just long enough to jerk his sleeves up to his elbows. "Leave all the marks you want." One hand comes back to play with my breasts again, still just as rough, but the other is once more around my throat, fingers slipping into place under my jaw and pressing until I swear I start to see stars.

Only then does he release me, and as blood rushes back to my brain, I realize I've gripped that arm instead. Sure enough, I can see the red marks from my nails across his wrist and up his forearm. His partner takes advantage of my distraction to slip another finger into me, then pumping them in and out of me while he *still* holds me open.

"Y'know..." His free hand moves, but instead of touching me, he jams his fingers into his partner's back pocket and shoves. The action catches his partner off guard, so he stumbles forward until he's pressed against me; and even with the fingers in my pussy, I *feel* the line of his cock against my folds. "You look much better like that, my love," he laughs darkly, sliding his fingers free.

"*Shit,*" his partner curses, face turning up to mine even though I can't see his expression. "I don't want to hurt you—"

"You're not," I tell him, my eyes wide. Tentatively, I wrap a leg around his hips, and a small grin flicks against my lips. "Fuck, you're really not."

"Are you sure?" he's already moving as he says it, sliding his length along my slit, getting my wetness all over his cock. "I can stop." The hand still teasing my nipple falls, though I find it a second later when he presses his thumb against my clit. "If you want me to, sweetheart."

"She doesn't want you to." His partner is on his knees at my side, fingers wrapped in my hair to jerk my head back so I'm looking up at him. "I want your hand," he tells me, and I realize his jeans are undone as well, and I can see that the man between my thighs isn't the only one worked up. "I want your hand on my cock, darling. Can you do that for me?"

It definitely feels only fair. And I do what he says without him needing to ask again, letting him guide my hand into his underwear, fingers around mine as he forces both of us to grip his length.

"There you go. Just like that," he encourages, still holding my hair tight with his other hand. "You're so good for us. I bet we'd have so much fun with you if we could take you home. Do you want to take her home?" he asks his partner, still guiding my hand up his cock. "She doesn't have a collar, and possession is nine-tenths of the law, right? We *need* a pet. Especially a pet with a mouth that was made to be fucked." His hand leaves mine, coming instead to grip my jaw and force me to stay like I am, his mask filling my vision.

"We're not good pet owners," his partner moans, still grinding against my slit. His thumb rubs against me, sending a burning need throughout my entire body. "And you're so fucking wet, sweetheart. You're just begging me to fuck this pussy."

"Have you ever had your mouth fucked? And I don't mean 'have you ever given a guy head,'" the man gripping my chin and hair asks. "No, I mean, have you ever been put on your knees and had someone's hand in your hair"—his tightens in mine, as if to make a point—"while they fuck your mouth and throat like it belongs to them?"

"No."

"Good. Because I'd love to be your first." My fingers tighten just a little, and his breath hitches as I adjust my movements. "*Fuck,* just like that. How wet is she?"

"She's soaked," his boyfriend replies. "I think she's going to come soon." He's not wrong, I realize with a jolt. I can feel my thighs trembling, my muscles tight from the effort of keeping one of my knees hooked around his thigh.

"Be a shame if you just accidentally slipped in and fucked her pussy," the auburn-haired man remarks offhandedly, like it wouldn't be a shame at all. "I bet you'd look better with his cum dripping out of you. I know I'd rather come inside you than on your fingers, but..." I feel a shudder go up his spine. "Beggars can't be choosers. Tighten your grip, darling, I'm not going to break."

I do what he says, following his instructions whenever he asks me to move or adjust my grip. It's hard to focus on either of them, and when their hands move and touch me all over, I find myself flinching at every new sensation as the heat builds in my core.

"Damn, sweetheart," the man between my thighs breathes. "You're practically begging me to fuck you. Do you know how soaked you are? Do you want to come for me?" he asks, as his thumb speeds up on my clit. "I want you to come for me. In this shitty bathroom while we play with you however we want. That sound good?"

"I..." It's so hard to think or give him a straight answer, with all the different stimuli. "I want to come."

"I know you do, baby."

"Please make me come." It's as good as I can give, especially when the man beside me leans down to scrape his mask against my face like he, too, can feel my lips on his.

"Only if I can come right here," he fires back. "Just like this. Can I do that?"

"Yes."

"Yes, *what?*" the one beside me demands, dragging my attention to him.

"Yes, *please.*"

It's definitely the magic word. The man between my thighs grinds against me in earnest, holding onto my thigh that's around his waist and using his other hand to tease my clit so harshly I definitely see stars. My toes curl in my boots and seconds later I'm coming, body uncoiling like a spring as I cry out a sharp, clear, *"fuck!"* right against his ear as he buries his face against my throat. Black hair peeks out from under his hood, but before I can see more than that and a bit of pale skin, his partner sharply yanks his hood down over his hair, pulling him back up before the mask can do more than move an inch.

"God," he growls, letting his partner tow him back up so he's not in danger of losing his mask. "You're too perfect, little cat." When he pulls away, I look down to see my thighs are a wet, sticky mess of his cum and mine. "But my boyfriend hasn't come yet. Could you help him, please?"

It's the *please* that gets me. I let the auburn-haired man pull me gently off of the counter, and I'm not really all that surprised when he guides me to my knees.

"Open your mouth for me, gorgeous girl," he orders so sweetly I could melt. "And stick out your tongue." I do what he says, though non-tipsy me would be having an internal crisis right now at how I've never done this with anyone, let alone a stranger. But it's so easy to do it, so easy to tilt my head back just enough that I can watch him stroke his cock, gloved fingers gripping it tightly. His partner moves to stand behind him, mask nudging the side of his hood, and pushes his hand away so he can do it instead. He murmurs something in his ear and the auburn-haired man leans back against him, a soft groan leaving him that's just so remarkably vulnerable that I wonder if I heard right.

"Good girl," one of them says, just before he comes. I hear a few soft curses, more murmurs that definitely aren't meant for me, and instinctively close my eyes as thin strings of cum splash against the mask and my skin. My tongue gets it too, and the sharp, bitter taste is such a stark contrast to everything else that I swear it helps sober me up.

But I don't move. Not until his boyfriend is tucking him back into his jeans and he reaches forward to stroke his fingers over my hair, then runs them through the mess on my face, making it worse.

"You sure we can't keep her?" he asks, as they disentangle to help me to my feet. The black-haired one shakes his head, running water over a rag that he hands to me. "Because I swear I could learn how to be responsible for a pet *real quick* if this is the one you let me keep."

His partner chuckles. "You can't keep her," he informs him, though he's looking at me as he gently runs the rag over my face. "Not until you know her better."

I'm in a daze while they talk. It feels like part of my brain is disconnected, and it's made more so by the fact that no one has *ever* treated me like this post-sex. Or, well, post almost sex, since neither of them fucked me. They take their time putting me back together, rinsing off my face, and helping me with my clothes, before the black-haired one leans in, his mask so close to mine I could reach up and take it off to see what he looks like.

God, I would die to know what he looks like right now.

"Go find your friends, little cat," he tells me, as his partner runs his fingers down my shoulder. "Before I let him have his way and you end up with a collar and a bell in our house before you've even sobered up." Then he releases me and, not having any idea what to say, I offer them both a smile that doesn't fit my face and slip out of the door, leaving them in the bathroom by themselves.

# CHAPTER 8

As soon as I swim into consciousness, memories from last night pummel my brain unforgivingly.

How dare I have a few minutes—a few seconds, even—to wake up peacefully, pretending ignorant bliss before remembering last night?

*All of last night.*

*Emily is dead.*

*And I nearly fucked two strangers at a house party across town.*

"Fuck," I sigh, flopping back on my sofa. I'm so used to falling asleep here that I have a second comforter dedicated to this space instead of my bed. The television is still on, proving that I really did pass out the moment I fell onto the sofa instead of setting an alarm.

But instead of *The Golden Girls* that I'm pretty sure I'd been watching, a detective show that I don't recognize is playing at a volume that's too soft to have woken me up.

It's hard to pull myself out of my drowsiness as I stare at the television without really seeing it. So difficult, because my brain wants me to relive every touch, every caress, and every sweet, filthy fucking word that had come out of their mouths.

Though of course, the memories certainly aren't bad ones. Not by any means.

My fingers come up to stroke the side of my neck lazily, running over skin that had been held so tightly by fingers longer than mine.

God, I still can't believe what I did. But I'm also not averse to remembering, so I let myself slip back into drowsiness. My brain takes off reliving the sensations and feelings that had me *scorching* for so much of last night.

My hand moves, fingers stretching around my own throat as much as they're able, though I can barely simulate the feeling of the night before. But it's enough. Enough to remember the growling words of the more aggressive of the masked men.

And definitely more than enough to help me remember everything else. My fingers slide downward, under the comforter, to drag down my chest and splay against my stomach. It's easy to make it real enough that flickers of revived embers seethe to life inside of me, heat pooling between my thighs as they tense and press together.

*I have to get over this.*

No matter how great they had been. I miss sex, I realize now. But more importantly, I miss *good* sex. It's been *months* since my last hookup, and so much longer than that since I can say I've had really good sex, if ever.

But God, there's no way they'd be bad at everything they held back from me last night. Especially if they took their time. *Especially* if I could have both of them at once.

Still, somehow, I chase away the lust and the pleasurable burn that's making itself known in my body. My parents are going to be home soon enough, and there's no way in hell that I want them to knock on my door anytime within the next ten minutes or so.

At least not until I'm awake and not imagining their hands on me.

"Okay, okay," I sigh to myself, reaching a hand up to the back of the sofa. Instead of finding the slightly rough weave of the couch, however, my fingers land on warm, soft fur covering a cat too fat for any cheap cat tree.

Stranger purrs, his body vibrating under my head. I'm careful as I pet him, minding the scars I know rake along one side and the leg that is still sensitive, even after being repaired and six months of living in the house instead of the feral colony.

"Where's Kale?" I ask, as if my fat tabby will know where the orange cat is. Most likely in the cat tree by the window, or on the bed under my desk. Out of the two, Kale is more temperamental and less likely to be cuddling with me when I wake up.

I turn to look up at him, eyes falling on the chubby pouches on either side of the cat as he rests on the back of the sofa. His light green eyes stare at me, heavy with sleep, and I can't help but smile at his adorable nose.

He really is my favorite mistake, since everyone had advised me not to bring home a half-dead feral that would never grow to be comfortable in the house. *Everyone* had been wrong, and my chubby Stranger had moved in like he'd owned the place and had just been waiting for us to realize it.

"You're adorable," I sigh, sitting up and scratching his forehead just over his eyes. His purrs deepen; rattling his entire frame, though he doesn't move, as if he's much too sleepy to get off of his impromptu bed.

From downstairs, I hear the front door open and close, and a moment later my mom's voice travels up the stairs.

"We're home!" She sounds breathless, as if my dad has had her laughing the whole way home at his dumb puns. Though knowing them, he has. They're anyone's standard for marriage, in my opinion. At least, for anyone who wants the perfect American dream. A doting husband, a loving wife.

They've never wavered, though I have no idea how they manage to barely even argue at the worst of times.

"Hi Mom!" I call back, wiggling out of the shorts I'd thrown on to sleep in and chucking my tee onto the bed with them. I don't really care what I wear around the house today, but I rummage around until I find a pair of loose black sweatpants and an orange jack-o'-lantern t-shirt. Over that I slip on a hoodie, then pause.

It's not right.

The hoodie itself isn't *right*, and I immediately know by the way it smells of too much detergent that I'll need to wash it again. It lands in the laundry basket and I frown, glaring at it like it's personally offended me by soaking up more than it should in the machine.

It isn't anyone's fault that I struggle with strong scents or weird textures against my skin, and I try to never make it anyone else's problem, either. If I have to wash the hoodie eight times to get the smell out, so be it.

"Hey Dad," I add belatedly, when I have another hoodie on. This one isn't a zip up, but I've cut the neck hole into a slightly deeper V to prevent it from being as choking as I normally find them to be. Stranger moves when he hears my parents, striding to jump onto my bed and curl up once more on the blankets thrown on top of it.

When a door slams, Kale scuttles out from under my desk, his ears flat and his one eye wide. My parents won't take it personally, and I don't either when he doesn't even stop to look at me before disappearing *under* the bed, as if Stranger's close-ness provides him with the emotional support he needs.

While I wish he'd come further from being feral and settle into the life of a house cat as effortlessly as Stranger, I sigh and remind myself that he deserves as much patience as he needs to get there. And even if he doesn't, even if he stays a little skittish and nervous around anyone other than me, that's more than okay, too.

My door opens a second later, and I raise my eyebrows to look at my mom, who leans against the doorframe with a frown curving her lips downward, accentuating the lines around her mouth.

"Did something happen?" My eyes linger on the different parts of her face, noting how harsh the frown lines make her look and watching as the crows' feet around her eyes rush to answer their challenge. My mother isn't *old*, in my opinion. At only forty-three, her prematurely silver hair and the lines make her look older than she has any right to.

Though if there's one gene I hope I didn't inherit from her, it's how quick her hair went gray and the lines became apparent.

"Do you not know?" Her pale eyes pin mine, and I stare back at her, thoughts from the party crossing into my thoughts. *Does she know I almost fucked two strangers?* I panic, thinking for a wild moment that someone there knew her or told her somehow...but a second later reality sets in and I look away, studying the closet doors.

"Emily," I say, the word nowhere near a question. "You heard about Emily."

"If you knew last night, I wish you would've called us." She strides into the room to hug me around the shoulders loosely, her hands linked behind me.

I lean into her, pressing my nose against her shoulder as I close my eyes and murmur, "I wasn't going to ruin your night, Mom. Nic called and invited me over." She'd also told me more about Emily, and her fucking *fingers*.

But I still can't find it in myself to be, well, upset. Emily was directly responsible for Daisy's death. The fact that she never, not once, made a real apology or had to pay for what she did has always felt unfair. And well, maybe this is karma evening the score.

Mom doesn't need to hug me, but she doesn't realize that. I'm not *upset* like she thinks, though it had dragged up some unfortunate memories of Daisy last night.

But now I can only wonder how Daisy feels, and if it's her turn to feel justified, wherever she is.

If any part of her, like a soul, still exists.

*That's* the thought that makes my stomach twist, along with the memory of Daisy's grin and the way she'd looked at me so shrewdly, once in a while, from bright green eyes under her dark fringe. My fingers tighten against my palms, and I have to almost physically shove the thoughts away before they drown me in a feeling that I know will be difficult as hell to get away from.

"It's okay. *I'm* okay," I force myself to say without a shake or a waver in my voice. I won't let her think for a moment that this will break me, because Emily's death will never have that kind of power over me.

Mom still takes her time pulling away from me, her attention grabbed by Stranger as he gets to his paws on the bed and stretches first forward, then bows his body toward the sheets while arching his voluminous butt high into the air. His tail flicks, and moments later Mom is scratching that upturned rump, her nails providing a better feeling than my bitten-down ones.

I stare at both of them. At my cat begging unashamedly for attention and my mom, who'd sworn she'd never be a cat person as long as she drew breath, but now buys him toys and catnip every few weeks.

What a liar my cats have made out of her. Well, Stranger anyway.

"I'm wondering if we should make an appointment with Dr. Lawson," she says without looking at me, still making the same movements along Stranger's spine. "Just to make sure we keep on top of things."

My chest clenches, stomach following suit, and I shake my head as I walk over and sit on my bed, close enough now that I can catch her eye. "Mom, I'm fine," I tell her, my voice quiet but firm. Emily's death won't break me, and I refuse to let it put me back in therapy, either.

My coping skills are great, and neither anxiety nor overwhelming depression are the things I'm dealing with right now. Not yet, at least.

But I can tell mom isn't going to let it go, so when she opens her mouth to repeat the argument, I find myself shaking my head once more. "Mom, I'm *fine*," I inform her, bunching my fingers in the blanket under me and twisting lightly. "And if you need me to sit here for an hour and explain to you all the ways I will make sure I'm fine and stay that way, then I am more than willing to roll out the PowerPoint."

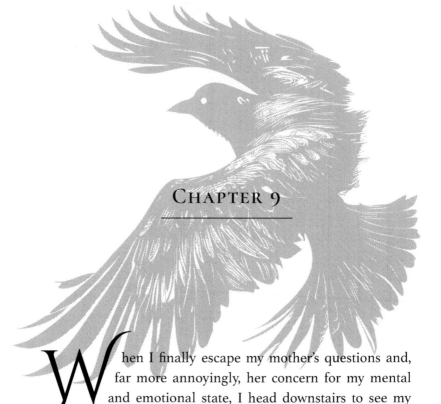

# Chapter 9

When I finally escape my mother's questions and, far more annoyingly, her concern for my mental and emotional state, I head downstairs to see my dad hovering near the kitchen, pretending to be busy.

He's going to give me the same talk, but with more facial expression and oomph. And frankly, I can't deal with that today. Not to the extent that he's going to take it, anyway. I love my dad and he really is the best parent anyone could ask for, but the concern, right now, is going to kill me.

Or maybe something a little less dramatic.

But when I see him standing there, loitering near the kitchen with the remote held in one hand and, for some reason, a potholder, I make a quick, rash choice and spin toward the front door instead.

The Halloween wreath looms as I get close, black and spiderweb patterned ribbons curled and reaching out with ends wired to hold their shape. My hand goes out to touch the knob under it, and it's at that moment Dad realizes what I'm doing.

"Hey, Bailey," he comes toward me across the foyer, the smile hitched on his face bleeding parental concern. "Do you want to talk? I was thinking of making grilled cheese."

"At nine am?" I laugh, throwing him a smile as I stare at the sharpness of his nose instead of his eyes. "Come on, Dad. Mom already did *the talk*. Everything is fine."

He waits, looking me over as he weighs my words. "Okay," he sighs finally, his voice heavy. Though I know for a fact that he didn't want to have the concerned parent talk anymore than I did. He's not as good at making it sink in as Mom is. "But I'm still making grilled cheese for lunch. Do you want pickles?"

"Is that even a question, Dad?" I joke, yanking the door open so that it doesn't stick in the frame. No matter how many times they've had someone come out to fix it, it always goes back to sticking within a few months.

At this point, I'm pretty sure they're talking about replacing the door completely, since nothing seems to work long-term. But I'll miss this door, with its scratches and the purple residue that still stains an area two feet off the floor. Even though Dad has been scrubbing at it for years, the purple cat I drew on the white surface in permanent marker can't be erased completely.

It brings a small twitch of a smile to my lip as I step outside, waving at Dad before closing the door behind me. The bigger wreath, similar to the one on the inside, shakes when I pull the door all the way shut, and I glance back just to make sure today is not the day that it escapes the little golden hook that attaches it to the door itself.

The best thing about living close to the middle of Hollow Bridge is that no matter what, it's easy to get where I want to go. Especially without a car. Barely stopping to consider my route, I cut across the street and down an alley between two houses, one of them currently up for sale, that takes me off of my street of Pine and onto the one next to it instead.

I would be lying if I said it's not because Oak Leaf Street has better Halloween decorations. The people here have taken decorating as a personal challenge, and the scenes littering the yards and even roofs are way better than anything our closest neighbors have.

My feet find the sidewalk again and I glance up at the sky, steps slowing. It looks like it's going to rain. Eventually, anyway. And the sky in upstate New York usually looks like it's threatening rain, at least a little, and especially this time of year. We're not close enough to Lake Ontario for real lake effect weather. But that doesn't mean we're completely safe from it.

If the clouds are anything to go by, tonight I'll be curled up in my room in a blanket burrito, both cats on the sofa, and barreling my way through every Halloween movie I can find while thunder booms outside. Not that I mind, as long as I don't have to go out in it.

My gaze falls, attention no longer kept by the sky itself as I look at the Davidsons' yard. I've always thought our town should do Halloween decoration bus tours, and Oak Leaf Street could be the one and only stop, if the budget is tight. Hell, even if it's not, it's not like Hollow Bridge is big enough to need more than an hour or so of travel to see everything of importance.

This year, the Davidsons have created an outdoor garden cafe that takes up their entire yard. Tables made of ribs and bones have been built or bought, though I'm pretty sure it's not possible to just waltz into Walmart and pick up decorations like this.

No, if I had to guess, the Davidsons have been working on these for months. Skeletons sit at the tables, a few more balanced precariously in bent over positions meant to resemble the wait staff. There's a chef skeleton near their living room window, and though the power to the display is off, I know for a fact that when he's plugged in, the skeleton continuously stirs the barrel labeled *human waste* that he's leaning over, hands clutched around a long stick that serves as the spoon.

I could stare at their display forever, and when I was a kid, my parents had to physically pull me away from some of their more lifelike decorations. The carnival they'd set up, for instance, had made every kid in the neighborhood shrivel in jealousy of the actual, working Ferris wheel that took ghosts, goblins, and skeletons six feet into the air, then back down.

Mom had told me that if I got my butt into one of them, I'd break it, and that I was not allowed to bother their decorations. Even Daisy—

The lump in my throat is immediate, as is the hand that closes hard around my heart. *Daisy* had loved the Davidsons' displays. She'd adored coming over and had begged my mom to take us walking around the neighborhood to see the decorations in the daytime, when things weren't so scary.

It's hard, and becomes almost impossible very quickly, to sweep the memories out of my head as they play out on my face.

*Daisy,* who had found the path between the houses that I use now whenever I don't feel like going all the way to the end of the street.

*Daisy,* who had ranked the houses on the streets around mine and demanded her brother drive us around when he was old enough, and when he wasn't, he'd had to pedal after us on his bike, reminding us not to go too far.

And it's *Daisy* who I can't get out of my head this year, no matter how hard I try.

It's obvious why. But that doesn't make things any better when my dreams consist of things I'd like to forget.

A loud sigh escapes me, breath drawing my chest tight for a few seconds before I release it in a visible puff, thanks to the morning's downright chill. It's not going to get warmer until April, with us being in New York, but I love the cold; so it's fine.

Leaving the Davidsons' house behind is always such a disappointment. No one in Hollow Bridge can live up to the senior couple's decorations, though a lot of other residents of Oak Leaf give it their best shot. Another cemetery full of ghosts and animal skeletons looms, but it's nowhere near as meticulous or impressive. There are too many store-bought decorations for it not to look a bit campy in my eyes. Hell, I can almost smell the plastic of the Halloween store from the opposite sidewalk.

A house at the end, closest to where houses start morphing into small businesses, does the best job without really trying to be similar. Instead of plastic skeletons, blow up ghosts, or loud and large decorations, the people that live here have gone for a huge display of lights.

Even in the daytime, without any of the patterns illuminated, I see the outlines of tombstones and dramatic, monstrous eyes across the yard. Lights wrap around the trunks of trees, and across windows on the two-story colonial that looks a lot like every other house in our neighborhood.

While we may be considered the 'rich end' of town, we certainly aren't the creative side of it, when it comes to house shape and individuality.

Though I see a spider web stretching from the top of the garage down to the grass, and I make a mental note of where I am as I shove my hands into the pocket of my loose hoodie. I want to see this place when it's dark, to see if it lives up to what my mind builds as an image of what it may look like.

I don't have anywhere I'm *going*, exactly. Except that I want to stay out of the house for another hour or so if I can. Mom and Dad are no doubt talking about me, about what they can do to help me, and I don't need to be in any part of that.

Especially because *I don't need any help.*

I don't realize I'm glaring at a small shop next to a taller, older house until a familiar mask catches my attention. Edging closer, my feet nearly silent on the pavement, I can feel my cheeks flushing, and heat rising up the sides of my neck like reaching fingers.

The feeling reminds me too much of last night for me to chase it away, but hell. So does the mask hanging at the top right of the display. It's white and nearly featureless, just like the ones from my, uh, friends I'd met the night before. Right down to the slightly pearlescent color, and material that looks like it would slide smoothly under my fingers, or my mouth—

Someone walks behind me, visible in the reflection of the shop, and I blink, straightening at the familiarity of the hair and the posture. I know that slouch, just like I know that permanently tousled hair.

My mouth opens as I turn, and I almost say his name, catching myself *just in time*, so that instead, I only let it whisper through my mind.

*Phoenix.*

Daisy's brother hasn't even noticed that it's me, but that's not exactly surprising. Half of me wonders if it's because he doesn't *want* to recognize me, and doesn't want me to recognize him. Hell, ever since what had happened to Daisy and me, he's barely said two damn words to me.

And one of those was probably an accident, all things considered.

He doesn't look back as I stare, my hands flexing around my forever scarred palms as I look at him. It's so easy to think of the frigid, sharp pain of the water and the ice. Of the anguish when I'd found Daisy, when I look at her brother who shares so many of her features.

But it's also...more than that. I had been so head over heels with Phoenix as a little girl that I'd written him damn love notes that, thankfully, Daisy had mostly intercepted. The rest

I'm still working on forgiving my thirteen-year-old self for, instead of cringing over the memory every time it surfaces.

But the fact that Phoenix is really here makes my brain whirr.

I can't help it, and it's not a physical decision when my feet start to move, steps mirroring his as I do what I shouldn't do.

*I follow him.*

"This is certainly a choice, Bailey," I murmur, the fall air brushing across my already red cheeks. Belatedly, I check behind me, just in case his friend from the carnival is here, and I hadn't waited long enough to start walking. There's still time to make this look unintentional. Still time to break off onto my own path and pretend I was never following Phoenix at all, it's just some coincidence.

But it isn't, and when I don't see anyone of note behind me, and no one looking at us whatsoever, I keep walking.

Where could he be going? To the mask shop we'd just passed? It's not *just* masks of course. Mrs. Williams makes a ton of crafts and small, handmade favors that are popular with a ton of people my parents' age. But Halloween is where she shines, and she makes or buys some of the coolest masks I've seen. In fact, I wouldn't be surprised if Nic had gotten the cat skull mask there, now that I think about it.

But Phoenix doesn't double back. He doesn't go into the pop-up costume store either, and doesn't stop at the farmer's market currently being set up for tomorrow morning, as it is almost every week.That had been my next guess, since his parents regularly have a stall there to sell some of the produce they grow in their small gardens. It's never a lot, but Phoenix's mom has always made the absolute *best* strawberry jam. Hell, it's an institution in Hollow Bridge. One a lot of people are willing to fight over.

He pauses and so do I, just before the parking lot where vendors are unloading or setting up. A man I don't know smiles and gives me a small nod, while a woman brushes past me, staggering to keep a hold of the box of apples in her arms.

Absently, I lift my hands to rub my arms, trying to look like I belong here, like I'm actually doing something instead of being a creep.

But yet again, Phoenix doesn't notice me. He only waits to cross the street, twenty feet from the nearest crosswalk, and his long legs eat up the distance effortlessly until he can step up on the opposite sidewalk. His hands are jammed into his pockets once more, then he stops, head swiveling back and forth as he looks around.

Is he waiting for something? That's definitely the look of someone waiting for something to happen, I think.

He doesn't make me wait long, at least. There's a whistle that I can hear from my side of the street, and the door of a small diner opens, showing the face of the guy who had been at the fairgrounds with him. The one that I'm certain has never lived in Hollow Bridge before.

The brunet walks to Phoenix quickly, though not as quickly as the latter had crossed the street, and as I watch, hooks one arm over Phoenix's shoulders, dragging him down, mouth open, to—

"Good morning, Miss Bailey." The voice is familiar and creaky with age. I turn to see a friend of my mom's, someone in her book club whose name I'm blanking on, walking toward me from a booth, her smile wide. "How's your mom doing these days? She's been hit or miss coming to book club this month."

"She and Dad have been busy," I tell her, an awkward but automatic smile on my lips. "I know she's been pretty put out about that." That's a bit of a lie. Mom would rather do Halloween-related things than her book club, though it is a close second. "She'll be back full time after this month." Because that's how it always worked, and I have a hard time believing this woman doesn't know that. More likely, she's trying to create polite conversation.

Which is wasted on me, when I barely ever appreciate it, but I'll be nice and not tell her this time.

"Well, tell her I say hi. We've missed her," the lady informs me, coming close enough to reach out and touch my shoulder in a friendly, neighborly way.

But all I can think of is how much I want to slither away from her touch. I hate when people act this familiar, and my hackles rise even as I grin back at her, feet itching to move. "I'll tell her," I promise, counting to three before stepping away and toward the curb, as if insinuating I have somewhere to go. "Have a good Saturday."

Or whatever.

She doesn't look put out. Or that she's even realized the lengths I'll go to in order to avoid the awkward touch of her hand on my shoulder. I don't shudder, which is a big win for me, as I continue my leisurely stroll down the sidewalk and turn my head back to where Phoenix and his *friend* were a minute ago.

Except...they're not there anymore. Naturally. There's no sign of them, even as my eyes travel up and down the road, and for twenty more steps I look for them, thinking that they can't have gone far on foot.

At last, though, when the sun crests the top of the buildings and the farmer's market is more set up than not, I sigh and stop walking, hands gripping the edges of my sleeves as I grind the toe of my sneaker into the cement of the sidewalk under me.

It's useless. Phoenix is gone, and I have to admit defeat, even though it was never my right to be following him in the first place.

Hell, I didn't even have a good reason for it, though now I figure I should take responsibility for that. I can't just follow him, or anyone, around town like a creep. There are names for those kinds of people, and I don't want to be one. And, as I remind myself, I don't have a reason to be doing it.

Just a weird, creeped out feeling in the pit of my stomach and a years-old, unrequited crush that drives me to say something, *anything,* to the brother of my dead best friend.

So really, no reason at all.

# CHAPTER 10

It gets easier to avoid my parents' concern when they start to believe that maybe, just maybe, I'm telling the truth. Emily's death *isn't* tearing me up inside. At least, not how they think. The only thing it's done is make me curious and dragged up thoughts of Daisy that I thought I had under better control.

But what can I do about it in the long run?

When I step out the front door, the evening October breeze smacks me in the face. It pushes my dark hair back over my shoulder as I fumble to pull the door completely closed, pulling it past the place it likes to stick.

It's not as cold as it could be, but I still shiver in my hoodie, dragging the sleeves down over my fingers so I can clutch the soft fleece against my skin. I'll get over it when I get moving, so I force myself to take a few steps off of the porch and onto the sidewalk, not making for the alley between two houses this time, but instead following Pine Street to the stop sign.

Surreptitiously I look around, knowing it's unlikely and unreasonable for me to see Phoenix when he has no reason to be here. His family lives a few miles from us, on the other side of town, and it's more than likely that he's here visiting and staying with them.

Do they wonder, as I do, if he killed Emily? They have to know how he's felt about our former 'friends' just as much as I do.

I even seem to remember him saying a few unkind things that could've been construed as threats after everything happened.

My fingers clench and unclench, but today I'm more successful at sweeping away the bad thoughts. It helps that I'm tired after helping my parents with the last of their fairground setup. It helps even more that I've been working through things like my therapist had taught me.

Slow breaths. Grounding thoughts. Think through the problems and the anxiety rationally, instead of letting them control me.

The three-three-three rule has always been my friend. Especially today, and I find myself almost unconsciously looking around for ways to keep it going.

*Three things I can see.*

*Three things I can hear.*

*Three parts of my body.*

But the effort dies out as I walk. I'm not as bad as I was this morning, and I'm more looking forward to meeting up with Nic and Nolan at the park, where we used to hang out as high schoolers.

The walk takes me a grand total of fourteen minutes and seven seconds, and I applaud myself on being faster than last time, when I'd had a time of fourteen minutes and eighteen seconds instead. Clearly I'm improving, though I'm not sure what the prize is for walking my ass to a park and home. The sun is setting in earnest now, not that it matters, and I glance up at the looming, iron gates that look like they belong in front of a cemetery, instead of our local park.

They, too, have fallen victim to Hollow Bridge's Halloween traditions. Fake spiderwebs hang and sway from the black iron, and lights are wrapped around the solid columns holding the gates together.

The gates are always open; in fact, I'm not even sure they *do* close. As I stride through them, along the walking path that leads toward the trees and the river's edge, my hands go into the pockets of my hoodie instead of curling in the sleeves.

It's breezier than it has been. Part of me wishes I'd put my hair up before coming out, because soon I'm going to look like a witch out of a kid's movie with her hair sticking up and wind-blown. It's also getting colder, though that's not uncommon. The weatherman expects snow by next weekend, and even that is something most of us just shrug off.

After all, the perks of living in Upstate New York in the winter include superior road crews that make it very hard for inclement weather to do more than slightly inconvenience the people that live here, no matter how much snow or ice we have.

For a few minutes I don't see any sign of my friends, but that isn't surprising. I scuff my feet along the sidewalk that winds around two playsets, benches dotted at the sides of it, and squint in the light cast by the decorated light posts that stand every few yards along the path.

Near the trees, two figures on a bench catch my eye, though I can't see more of them than their silhouettes outlined by the light nearest them. Still, judging by their figures, I have a pretty good idea it's Nic and Nolan.

My steps pick up and I give a soft whistle, drawing their attention to me as I raise a hand to wave at them. "Sorry I took so long!" I call, breaking into almost a jog. I enter the light from one glowing lamp above me, then step into darkness once more. "I had to..."

It isn't until I'm under the streetlight nearest them that I realize I'm *not* looking at my two best friends.

Phoenix sits on the back of the bench, his hands in the pockets of his black hoodie that's unzipped over a dark red tee. He stares at me, his eyes so dark in the artificial light that they could be pitch black.

On the seat in front of him, leaning against one of Phoenix's legs, is the auburn-haired guy from the fairgrounds and the carnival. Unlike Phoenix, he doesn't study me with no trace of humor on his face. He *grins*, one hand coming up in a small half wave.

"Don't worry," he chuckles. "We weren't waiting long. I hope the trip wasn't too bad…" He glances up at Phoenix, who barely slides his gaze to meet the other man's.

"Bailey," my dead best friend's brother says helpfully. "Her name is Bailey. She grew up with my kid sister."

*Ouch.*

His words are cold. Frigid even, in the darkness, and I'm surprised I can't see frost emanating from his mouth when he speaks.

"I'm sorry," I say, glancing down at my shoes, though I don't know what I'm sorry for, other than still breathing. "I'm meeting Nic and Nolan here." While his friend won't know who that is, Phoenix sure as hell will. "I thought…I thought you guys were them. It's *dark*."

"*Bailey*." The auburn-haired man repeats my name, rolling it around his mouth like he needs to taste it. He goes to move, only for Phoenix's leg to slide forward, blocking him from going anywhere. Not that it's a problem for him, or so it seems. He just leans on Phoenix's outstretched leg, gaze on me. "I'm Rory," he introduces, when the silence becomes thick enough to be uncomfortable. "Since he's apparently not going to introduce us."

"You have a mouth and a heartbeat," Phoenix murmurs in his clipped, usual tone. He's always been like this. Always been to the point and easy to annoy.

But to thirteen-year-old me, that had been hot.

The smile that catches my lips dies immediately under Phoenix's glare, and when he opens his mouth, I'm sure that he's going to say something scathing or, at the very least, condescending.

"They're further up the trail," he states instead, and I swear his voice softens as he does. "Looking at the lights by the meetinghouse."

I glance up toward the small hill that crests a good forty feet away. Sure enough, I see two figures by the lit up meetinghouse, though the purple and orange lights do nothing except create the semblance of strangely colored stars beside them, instead of actually illuminating the pair.

"Thank you," I say, not looking at Phoenix's face. "I'm sorry for bothering you guys."

"You're not *bothering* anyone, Bailey." Rory says my name again in a way that makes it feel like more than just a word. "You could stay here instead, if you wanted. We'll be your friends for the night."

Now I *do* look at him. My eyes find his, and I search his face for the mocking, taunting look I expect to find there.

But I only find amusement. Easy amusement, without the cruel edge that I'd expected. He waves his fingers at me, still leaning on Phoenix's leg as I look at him. "I bet you have pretty eyes," he adds. "Not that I can see them that well in the dark."

"He's harmless, by the way," Phoenix states lazily, nearly cutting off his friend. "He's just trying to rile you up."

"Maybe," Rory shrugs. "Maybe I'm just tired." He glances up, then back at me. "I just got here too. And I'm pretty sure I had to ask your friends where my tall, dark, and scowling boyfriend was before he took pity on me and loomed out of the shadows."

I can't help but snort, though I see Phoenix's quick look of irritation from the corner of my eye. "He's always been like that, you know," I find myself saying, tilting my head toward Phoenix. "Literally ever since I was *six*."

"Yeah, he had a stick jammed up his ass early," Rory agrees sagely. "I've been working on—"

Phoenix sighs and gently, almost affectionately, curls his fingers in Rory's hair. "They're missing you," he says to me, eyes locked on mine and not letting me look away. Hell, I don't even *want* to, for all his eyes look like yawning pits of black in his face. "If you don't go now, they're probably going to call the cops to send out a search party."

I expect malice in his words. I expect pain or frustration, based on past events. But he's just...talking to me. Like a normal human being who might be either cracking a joke or just trying to get rid of me.

Either way, I get the message. I nod once, taking a step back with no intention of using the path to get to my friends. "It was nice meeting you," I tell Rory, who gives me one more lazy wave as his face skims closer to the apex of Phoenix's thighs.

"You too, *Bailey*," he informs me sweetly, eyes glittering. "Don't be a stranger to our bench." Phoenix shakes him a little for that, almost like a misbehaving puppy, but I don't stick around for longer than it takes for me to realize my skin is prickling, goosebumps rising along my arms demanding me to rub my hands against them to dissipate the uncomfortable sensation.

Without giving things a chance to get worse or better, I ignore the shivers and cut into the short, mostly dead grass. My steps crunch as I walk up the hill the quicker, steeper way instead of following the path that leads past their bench.

Within minutes I reach the meetinghouse, its roof covered in lights and both bathroom signs replaced with Halloween-themed ones instead. There are no sides of the building, save the ones that house the small bathrooms, and only wooden pillars hold the arching roof up above a myriad of picnic tables sitting on a concrete pad that's cracked with age.

The moment my feet scuff in the gravel surrounding the pad, Nic looks up from where she sits on a table, eyes expectant in the dim light. "Bailey," she greets, not getting to her feet. "It took you a while. Everything okay?"

"We thought you might have fallen asleep. Or found another cat to take home," Nolan admits with a small, half-smile of his own. He crosses from one picnic table to another, hopping between them like he isn't afraid of misjudging and smacking the concrete below hard enough to break a bone.

I know I would have been.

"Yeah," I say, slumping onto the picnic table across from Nic. "I'm okay it's just..." From here, it's easy to see Phoenix and Rory, and they haven't moved from their bench. "I thought they were you." I point to where I mean, both of my friends glancing down curiously.

"And I bet that was incredibly awkward," Nolan comments, coming to sit down next to me. "That's Phoenix's boyfriend, right? The brown-haired guy?"

*Brown hair* isn't enough of a descriptor for Rory's thick auburn hair that brushes his ears and threatens to curl if it gets much longer. But I'm also not going to sit here and wax poetic about Phoenix's boyfriend, so I just shrug.

"I think so. I saw them kissing the other day. On the sidewalk." My jaws click shut, because I'm definitely not about to tell them I was stalking Phoenix through town, with suspicions of him being a murderer. After all, there's paranoid, then there's *that* level of paranoid that will get me a nice new pair of grippy socks.

And I hate socks.

My fingers curl and I tap them against the wood, the breeze picking up around me once more to stir my hair around my shoulders. "Things feel weird this year," I say, not knowing who

I'm really saying it to. "I mean, it feels like there's more to things than Emily's death."

"About that." Nic looks up, biting her lip. "They've officially ruled it an accident."

My brows jerk upward, and I look at Nic incredulously, wondering if I've heard her right. "An accident? But you said—"

"And Mom still thinks it's a load of crap that they're doing that," Nic goes on. "Mom says they're making a mistake. But she can't overrule what the coroner said." She shrugs one shoulder at me and fishes a box of gum from her pocket to pull out a silver-wrapped strip before offering the package to me.

I take one absently, still processing her words. "An accident? Even though her fingers were broken like that?" Slowly I unwrap it, looking down at the silver paper before popping the gum into my mouth and shoving the trash into my pocket. "Is your mom sure?"

"No," Nic admits. "No one is. And I think... Well, I'm pretty sure no one in this town wants there to be a murder, you know? I think they're using any excuse they can to label it an accident."

What she says makes more than a little sense. I rub my arms over my hoodie, leaning back on the picnic table. "Maybe I'm just going crazy," I sigh, unable to keep my gaze from drifting to the two men on their bench down the hill from us.

They've moved in closer, and I swear they're kissing again. "Do they not care we're sitting here?" I mumble out loud, feeling the beginnings of the warmth of embarrassment in my cheeks. I certainly wouldn't be sitting there making out in front of people I know from school.

Though, the party from the other night crosses my brain and I cringe internally, feeling like the pot calling the kettle black, or whatever the saying is.

Nic starts to answer at the exact moment her phone rings, making both of us jump. Nolan leans forward to glance at the screen, his brows pressed together. "It's your mom," he tells her, sliding it across the table to her. "She sensed you talking about her."

Snorting in disagreement, Nic shakes her head and picks up her phone, just as mine starts to buzz in my pocket. Confusion shoots through me as I fish it out, surprised that my dad is calling when it's not like I have any kind of curfew and even if I did, it's not that late.

"Dad?" I greet, turning away from the table as if to give Nic some semblance of privacy. "Is everything—"

"*I need you to come home,*" he says, his voice firm. "*Are you still at the park with Nic and Nolan?*"

"Yeah?" Now I'm more confused than anything, my brows knit together. "Dad, what's wrong—"

"*Just come home. Now.*"

I don't reply for a moment. I don't know what to say, so I sigh out a breath and nod, even though he can't see the motion. "Okay, Dad. Sure. Sorry." Is he mad at me? His voice is tight with tension or anxiety or both, but I can't figure out what it is I might've done to warrant an angry 'get your ass home' phone call.

"*Do you need a ride? Maybe I should come pick you up.*"

"I'm not alone. I don't need a ride," I tell him firmly. "We'll all walk home together. As much as we can, anyway. I'll be home in a few minutes, okay? Just don't freak out." I hold my breath, listening to him think it over, before he lets out a long, hard sigh.

"*Fine. Just come home, Bailey. You aren't in trouble, and we'll explain everything when you get here.*" My heart is pounding when he hangs up, and when I glance up at Nic to explain, to apologize, whatever, I see that she looks just as concerned.

"What did your mom want?" I ask, nodding towards her phone as I stand up.

"Probably the same thing your dad did," she replies, both of them getting up as well. "For me to come home. They...they've found another body, Bailey. Outside of town."

"Another accident?" I ask, and she hesitates.

"I don't know. Mom told me not to say anything. She said you'd find out eventually and I'm not the right person to tell you."

"Tell me *what*?" Tension rises in my throat, my heart pounding there as my chest constricts. "Nic—"

"That they found Jack Fairfield dead a few minutes ago, down by the pond where Daisy died."

The words ring through my ears, and for a moment, for one sweet and peaceful moment, I swear I've heard her wrong. I *have* to have heard her wrong, even as memories of the pond where I'd—*Daisy stay with me, Dai...sy*—where *it* had happened.

My hands are so cold that they feel as if I've plunged them into the icy water that took my friend. I take a step back, head still spinning, and half wish that I'd taken Dad up on his offer of a ride.

"I have to tell him," I say, though I swear I meant to say *I need to go home*. My head swings to the side, to where Rory and Phoenix still sit on the bench below us. "I need to. He should know."

"What? No. No, you need to go *home*," Nic says. "All of us do. They're enacting a curfew for tonight and maybe the week. Or until they have more answers. You need to—"

"Go on and go," I tell them both. "You know I'll be fine." I don't wait for an answer. I don't tell them that I need to do this because I need to see Phoenix's reaction.

I need to see his face when I tell him.

It can't have been him, right? Not with him being here for a while. I'll have to ask Nic and Nolan when exactly they got there, or when he did. But surely, if Jack died not that long ago, then Phoenix can't have done it.

*Surely my suspicions are wrong.*

My feet take me to the bench, to where the two of them are whispering, and it's only seconds before Rory looks up at me, his eyes somehow colder than they had been, as if to mimic the falling temperatures around us.

"You want to join in, Bailey?" he asks, voice caressing my name. "Do you want to snuggle? Phoenix is warm as hell, and—"

"Do you know?" I ask, eyes jerking upward until I catch Phoenix's dark gaze. "*Do you?*"

He stares back at me, his mouth pressed flat and his hands unmoving on his lap and Rory's shoulder. "Know what?"

"Do you know that Jack Fairfield is *dead*?"

I don't know what I'm expecting.

Maybe for him to jump up with shock so fake, I can see right through it. Or maybe for him to laugh maniacally and launch into a villain monologue while Rory fills in with song and dance to make this into the family movie no one asked for.

But I don't expect for him to stare at me, eyebrows raised just enough to show that undeniable moment of surprise. He doesn't look sorry.

Though, I doubt I do either. How could either of us be sorry, when Jack was one of five kids at school who had taken my best friend and his sister away from us?

"Who's Jack?" Rory asks, voice barely above a stage whisper. "Do we know him? *Should* we know him?"

Almost as if he doesn't realize he's doing it, Phoenix lets his hand drift down to rest in Rory's auburn hair, fingers curling through the strands as if he needs the comfort.

The movement draws my gaze and I watch him grip loosely before Rory reaches up as well, pulling Phoenix's other hand into his.

"Jack was one of my sister's...." Phoenix trails off, and I wonder if he was going to say something like *friends*. "He knew my sister," he finishes finally, but I narrow my eyes in surprise at his choice of words.

Is this Phoenix trying to spare my feelings? Or to downplay the situation to his boyfriend? My theories about him being the killer are starting to fade, though not completely, since I have no idea when Jack died, or if it was an accident.

Like Emily's death supposedly was.

"Are you going to Emily's funeral?" I blurt out the words like an idiot, and more than anything wish I could grab them and stuff them back into my mouth when Phoenix's gaze finds mine once more, the shrewdness in them as terrifyingly perceptive as always.

Sometimes, it feels like he knows what I'm thinking.

The wind picks up around us, making me shiver and jam my hands into my pockets. October is *cold* here, and somehow one of my super powers is not knowing how to dress for the damn weather. It feels like the wind is swirling around us, trying to drag me closer to the two boys, and for one wild, stupid moment, I think about the crow from the fairgrounds.

"No," Phoenix says, breaking me out of my trance of crow caws and black, beating wings. "I don't have the interest, or the time. And I don't think they'd want me there. Are *you*?"

I open my mouth to tell him no, but there's no sound to be heard. He tilts his head to the side, watching me, eyes narrowing just enough I can see the intrigue there.

"You don't feel sorry for her dying. Don't lie to me," he challenges, causing Rory to shift closer to me from his spot on the bench.

"I...I don't feel bad for either of them," I say, the words soft enough to get dragged into the swirling breeze. "In fact—" But I clamp down on that thought, on those words, just as Phoenix's eyes blaze and his hands tighten on Rory's hair, knuckles going white before he relaxes at a sound of concern from his boyfriend.

"In fact *what?*" The question has all the audacity of a demand, and the confidence of someone who isn't usually denied his wants. But that's how Phoenix has always been, and it only phases me a little.

"No, it doesn't matter." He's not my friend, and he doesn't intimidate me anymore...in theory. I take a step back to put physical distance between us, my gaze slipping to Rory's instead of his, and surprise ripples through me at the intensity I find there.

As soon as he sees me looking, however, Rory smiles and holds his hands up in surrender. "Don't worry, Bailey." He still says my name like it's a treat on his tongue. "I won't growl at you like Phoenix does. He's growl-y enough for the both of us, don't you think?"

I give a one-shouldered, noncommittal shrug. "I just wanted you to know," I mumble, glancing back at Daisy's older brother. "Felt like you should." I don't give him a chance to snap at me, or a chance to decide he's irritated. I pivot on my heel and turn, heading back to the path and the gated entrance to the park.

"Bailey." Phoenix's voice is sharp and impossible to ignore. I turn just a little, just enough to see him lean forward. "Don't stay out so late," he warns, his voice soft. "You know the stories about what happens in Hollow Bridge around Halloween just as well as I do."

This time I don't give him an answer. He doesn't need one, and I don't need to prolong this conversation. I walk away, my shoes crunching on the dry leaves, and try not to think of dead crows and bad omens.

Even though that's *exactly* what this feels like tonight.

# CHAPTER 11

Staring at the kitchen timer has never been the highlight of my day, though there are definitely worse things I could be doing than this. With my shirt covered in cake mix, frosting on the side of my face, and a glob of something in my hair that may or may not be butter or more frosting, I look like the cupcakes have gotten the better of me, instead of the other way around.

I'm good at baking. I just...also have a tendency to wear about five percent of it. My hands aren't as bad as usual, though red stains mar my fingers, looking like I've dipped them in blood. I have no doubt when I make the blood in about an hour, I'll really look like the murderer of Hollow Bridge, or the next best thing.

The timer ticks down to two minutes just as Mom comes in, glancing my way as she opens the utility drawer under the television. "Cupcakes going okay? How many dozen are you making again?" she asks off-handedly, more from interest than a desire to cook anything herself. While she is the baker of the family, and can make a mean burrito, she has very little interest in my ideas about taking box cake mix and doctoring it into something twenty percent better.

Well, maybe twenty percent is pushing it. But at least I make the frosting myself, so that has to count for something.

"Four dozen." I sigh, pressing my cheek on the wood of the bar in the middle of the kitchen. "Two dozen for Dad's work. Two for the fundraiser. But I think I'm out of the sugar I need for the, uh, shattered glass?" I look over the bags I'd brought home from the store, looking for the familiar shape and color of the bag I apparently didn't get with my pickup order.

If I have to go get it from the convenience store now, I'll have to actually go *inside* like a real adult. And I'm not sure I'm willing to change out of these clothes just for a ten-minute trip down to the end of the street and back.

Fuck it, I'm really not. No one I know shops there, and I doubt anyone is going to care that I look like I've been baking in hell with the bodies of my enemies. Hell, maybe it's a good look for me.

The timer goes off and I slide to my feet, go to the oven and hit the button with one finger before pulling the door open with my other hand. My mother looks at me in disapproval, hating the way I let the oven door bounce on its hinges. According to her, I'm flirting with disaster by giving the door the opportunity to come back up and close around my wrist.

I disagree. The urge to be lazy and use as little effort as possible is much more important than the possibility of being burned. Quickly, I pull my last two trays of red velvet cupcakes out of the oven, setting them on top of it with the others before I turn the heat off completely. I know this isn't the *best* way to cool cupcakes, but I'm not Julia Childs, nor am I trying to get my own baking show. I let them sit as I prowl to the bags one more time, looking through them as Mom opens the refrigerator door.

"I have to run down to the store," I announce, standing up

with a grimace. My lower back isn't thrilled about today's baking feats, but she'll just have to suck it up. "I need sugar for my broken glass."

Mom glances at the bags, her own eyes hunting for the missing ingredient. "Could you grab us some orange juice?" she requests thoughtfully, looking at the door to make sure she isn't missing a sneaky carton.

"Sure. Anything else?" When she shakes her head, I check the oven once more, my finger brushing over the button just to ensure the heat is off. The light is off as well, and I remind myself the oven can't lie to me.

It's *fine*.

Tearing myself away from the kitchen, I grab my hoodie from the night before and shrug it over my shoulders, not caring I'm dressed in just a tee and leggings under it. My sneakers are by the door and I toe them on, making sure everything I need is in my pocket before opening the door and yanking when it wants to stick.

One day, I'll ask Santa for a working front door, just to see if I get my first ever Christmas miracle. But until then, I push and pull with extra oomph, moving the door past the spot that it always catches, no matter what direction it's moving.

It's warmer than it was yesterday, if only by a few degrees. The sun's rays sink into my black hoodie the moment I step outside, and I stay on the porch to soak it in for a few moments, reveling in the feeling. The sun won't be out for long, I'm sure. Not with the weather forecast that calls for more clouds than sun for a while.

While it's difficult to force my legs to move, I manage. The sun makes it easier, still beating against my hair and clothes as I walk down the sidewalk toward our little local convenience store that's stood the test of time for fifty years or better. Thankfully, my parents have no issue with me going here, even with a curfew in place while Jack's death is investigated by the police. It's close enough that they could probably see me with government grade binoculars, and well-lit enough that, even at night, I could read every marker-written message on the back of the small, house-turned shop if I wanted to.

Even the ones with half scratched out phone numbers.

My eyes linger on them as I walk, hands jammed in my pockets. When I was younger, I'd tried to read some of them, to the exasperation of my parents every single time. But now my eyes barely skim the faded words that are marked over, some of them in handwriting I couldn't read if I had a magnifying glass. They usually repaint over the words every few years. But I guess the owners are running late.

The business itself is old, but not ugly. The brick is always as clean as possible, and shines with the work put into it a year ago, save the writing on the back. Even the door, which looks like a very proper front door of a house like mine, is brand new and hung with a welcome sign and a Halloween wreath attached to it. I pull the door open easily, rocking back on my heels before stepping inside and turning to look for the aisle that might have sugar suitable for what I need. While the shop looks like a house on the outside, Lauren had completely redone the inside so it's much more suited to a small convenience store layout, with her bakery counter near the front along with the cash register. In my experience, the shop and bakery combo is good about keeping things in stock that aren't expired or two days from it. But I know that doesn't negate the need for me to check, and I glare at the bags of sugar with my nose scrunched in scrutiny.

I could just pick one. I *should* just pick one, since the brand I normally buy isn't here and anything else probably tastes just as good as the one beside it. The bell clanging against the door only makes me stand on my tiptoes, while still focusing on the blue and red bags of one brand, and the light purple of another.

Have we bought either of these before? Surely we've come to Lauren's for sugar—

A long arm moves into my vision, smoothly reaching out beside my face toward the options. Fingers pluck a small cylinder of sugar from the shelf, and then slide down just enough to reveal a few inches of pale, flawless skin.

Somehow, I know it's Phoenix even before I turn around.

But I don't expect him to be so close. Phoenix stands there, just out of reach, his arm still over my shoulder as he drops his gaze down to mine. And unfortunately, I'm not quick enough to avoid his eyes before they can catch mine. Their coldness is just as palpable as it had been the night before.

At least...I think it's the cold that seethes in the depths of his gaze. If it isn't, then it's an emotion I can't name.

"Why are you staring at the sugar?" he asks, bringing his hand and his own cylinder of sugar back over my shoulder. "Especially like *that*."

"Like what?" I ask, hating that I can't pull my damn gaze off of his. This close, I'm reminded that his eyes aren't black, but the darkest blue I've ever seen. Wisps of sapphire show themselves in the light from the sun that peeks through the windows before retreating when he tilts back into the shade.

It should be a crime for him to be this gorgeous, quite frankly.

"Like it's disappointed you and you're trying to glare it into submission," he murmurs, quieter than the situation calls for.

"They're not the brands I know. The brand we use," I explain, trying to play it off like the most normal thing in the world, like I'm not obsessed or something about brands. Even if I sort of kind of am.

"Oh." He says it so simply, like I've said the most reasonable thing in the world. My brow arches at the casualness of his tone, and the way he looks up over my shoulder and scans the shelf. When he reaches out again, his arm brushes my cheek so lightly I could have imagined it, if not for the way his eyes flick to mine to look for a reaction.

But I don't give him one.

He plucks a bag of sugar off of the wall behind me and pulls it back to his chest; cradling the five-pound bag between us. "This is what we've always used. It's as fine as sugar *can* be." Then Phoenix holds it out to me, as if he's a consumer expert on the type of sugar I should be buying.

But considering the way I take it and holster it more firmly in my grip, maybe he is.

"I'm surprised you didn't tell me that sugar is sugar," I say, trying to go for my own version of casual while following him to the register. On the way I snag a bottle of orange juice for my mom, belatedly remembering she'd asked.

He shrugs one shoulder and slides the cylinder toward the young cashier, then lets his gaze fall on me once more. "Different things matter to different people. Who am I to judge? After all, I'm buying my boyfriend sugar from a convenience store because he doesn't like the sweetener at the hotel." He turns with the plastic bag the cashier had put his sugar in looped over his fingers, and I'm sure he's going to leave.

Instead, to my absolute surprise, he doesn't. Phoenix waits, watching me pay and take my bag with all the judgment of God himself, causing the back of my neck to prickle as I try not to look like it bothers me.

Then, when I turn, I see he's walking away, as if all he'd wanted was to make me squirm under his scrutiny. But I'm not letting him get away that easily. Not with my curiosity burning at the back of my throat so sharply that I can taste it.

Not when there are so many things I want to ask them, and only about half of them are concerning *murder*. My steps are quicker than his to match his long strides, and I catch the door that he doesn't bother to hold open for me, as if giving me a very clear, silent warning about following him.

But I don't care. I follow Phoenix anyway, needing about twenty seconds to catch up to him on the deserted street where houses and businesses meet and mesh, where the neighborhoods of Hollow Bridge end and downtown begins.

"Are you mad at me?" It's not the question I'd thought I'd ask. It's not even the first one that had come to mind. But it is the one that still keeps me up, especially now that I can see Phoenix's dark gaze that pins mine, and the shrewd coolness he has every time we interact.

I don't realize that I'm holding onto his arm until he looks pointedly down at it, and I feel his biceps flex under my fingers, another reminder of what I'm doing and what he wants me to do. Not that I let go. He can't frighten me into letting go, and now that the question is out of my lips...I don't even want to take it back.

Because I need to *know*.

I've needed to know for years.

"Mad at you?" Phoenix tilts his head to the side in a motion that strikes me as cute, his eyes narrowing. "Because of the sugar thing?"

"No," I tell him flatly, unimpressed. There's no way he doesn't know what I'm talking about, but I don't expect the sudden ache behind my eyes that has me pressing them closed tight.

God, this has been such a bad Halloween season, and it's barely started.

"For Daisy," I force myself to say, the words grating up my throat like blades. "Are you mad at me for letting Daisy—"

I definitely don't expect him to cover my mouth with one of his long-fingered, tattoo-covered hands. I don't expect his fingers to curl around my face, his palm warm against my lips. "Stop," Phoenix murmurs, in a voice that's both so dreadfully cold and yet laced with a heat that I don't understand.

Is it anger? Annoyance or severe frustration? His hand

gentles against my mouth, and I have a wild urge to lick him that I thankfully don't act on.

"I have never been mad at you for that," he tells me in a calm, cool tone that doesn't match the look in his eyes. "Not *ever*, Bailey. Do you hear me?"

I nod, and he slides his hand from my lips, dropping it to his side again as he just watches me. I don't get it, nor do I understand why it's so easy to stare at him, to meet his dark gaze, to ignore the nipping breeze that catches at my fingers and throat.

And yet again, I can't help but think that it's him. That *Phoenix* is the one killing people, and that the accidents aren't, well, accidents. After all, I've never seen him the moment a murder was committed, have I?

Unless Jack was killed last night, instead of earlier in the day yesterday. But even that seems unlikely, given that his body wasn't dumped in the middle of town or on the sheriff's doorstep. Surely it took them hours and hours to find him.

"Are you sorry about their deaths?" I turn as he walks away from me, though I don't expect him to stop mid-step before relaxing onto his heels with a sigh. "Jack's and Emily's—"

"I know who you mean," he breaks in smoothly, still not turning to look at me. The silence stretches between us, until the birds in the orange and red trees overhead are the only things I can hear. I'm about to either ask again or walk away when Phoenix says, in a voice as clear as can be, "There is nothing in this world that could make me sorry about them. But whether I'm sorry or not doesn't give you a reason to ask the next question that I'm *sure* you're just dying to ask. Aren't you, Bailey?"

My hands clench and unclench at my sides, the handle of the bag around my wrist, and I feel like the wind is picking up, creating a small pocket of air that drags me forward. Closer to my dead best friend's older brother that has always, *always* known me better than he should.

"I don't—"

"Yeah." He turns and glances at me with eyes as forgiving as black ice. "Let's maybe keep it that way, don't you think?" Phoenix doesn't give me the opportunity to answer, though I'm not sure what's left to even say. He starts walking again, as nonchalantly as if none of this had ever happened, and I wasn't about to accuse him of being a murderer.

*But what if I had?* The thought is a whisper as I turn and walk away, back around the store to step foot back on my street and toward my house with my bag of orange juice and sugar clenched between my fingers. My eyes stray to the side, back to the wall with the bits of writing, and fall on a splotch of black that looks suspiciously, ominously, like a sideways crow.

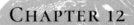

# CHAPTER 12

**M**y fingers flex under me against the hardness of the bench, curling around the metal slat closest to the edge. Around me, wind whips my hair into a mess around my face, though I try not to give it more thought than I have to.

I don't know why I'm here again. It's not like I'm going to magically find some bit of evidence that shows me who the killer is, or at least, who the killer *isn't*. Especially in the daylight. Nothing happens when the sun is up, and nothing ever happens in the Hollow Bridge community park.

With a groan I get to my feet, fingers coming up to zip and unzip the jacket I wear over my tee. It's not nearly heavy enough—a trend I've come to accept as one of my flaws in dressing for the weather—but it's better than nothing.

"You're so dumb, Bailey," I can't help but sigh, looking at the bench where Phoenix and Rory had sat a few nights ago. "No inspiration is going to strike, and you're not about to magically learn to see the past or future." Though, that would be pretty cool in a lot of situations.

I hesitate still, stuffing my hands in my pocket before

mentally relenting. I should just go home, if my entire plan is to stare at a bench and hope for the best.

Though in my defense, I didn't come here just to mope or speculate. I'd needed to get out of the house for a little while, and walking the trails of the park is an easy way to do that, along with being relatively safe.

*Unless I'm next on the to-be-murdered list.*

My eyes flick upward, following the trail up the hill to the little covered meeting house that sits near the top of it. When I was younger, my school had taken day trips here, always renting out the meeting house on the hill where all the teachers could sit and make sure none of us were throwing one another off of trees or burying someone in the dirt.

Elementary school kids are feral creatures, after all.

Today it's empty, like it is most of the time when it's too cold for kids to be here from one of the surrounding daycares or schools.

Except...it's not so empty. Not when I look again, head tilting to the side at the movement I swear I'd seen near the back of the small, open-sided building.

"You really don't need to go up there," I inform myself, speaking aloud in the cold, autumn air. "You really *shouldn't* go up there." It would be stupid if I did. If I go up there and die, I'd deserve people saying how stupid I was at my funeral.

*It's probably that creep from the fairgrounds,* my brain supplies unhelpfully. That makes it even clearer that I should stay away.

Yet I find myself walking up the hill, once again forsaking the trails as my thigh muscles burn with exertion. I don't know why I'm doing this, except to prove my eyes wrong and to make sure there's nothing actually here. It's the most reasonable option, and the most probable one.

I even start to believe my reasoning, when I make a circuit around most of the open sided, concrete-floored building with picnic tables jammed together end-to-end inside.

I'm being jumpy, for one. I can't do shit like this while there really is a killer around, or I'm going to drive myself crazy.

And I need to go home, before I start seeing Godzilla instead of just—

The moment I round the back of the building, my eyes catch the flurry of movement from between the two doors leading to the bathrooms. It's a recessed alcove, the doors blocked off by large fences to give people going in and out of the bathrooms some privacy, so the person standing there could have gone completely unseen, if he hadn't moved.

But I'm not fast enough to do anything other than jerk away from them, even as hands close around my wrists and yank me around, shoving me back against the concrete wall of the building.

A small yelp leaves my throat as the person leans closer, face obscured by a black face mask that pools at his neck and is thrust up over his nose. His hood is pulled down as well, leaving only his unfamiliar, pale gray eyes staring me down from inches away.

"Who the hell are you?" I murmur, hyper aware of his hands on my arms. "What do you want?"

He doesn't answer. He leans forward instead, his eyes impossibly close to mine, and one hand comes up to gently, *oh so gently*, press against the base of my throat.

"What are you doing here?" the man murmurs, in a voice I don't think I've heard before. "Shouldn't you be at home, darling? There's a murderer on the loose."

My fingers itch, trembling to reach up and rip his mask down so I can see who he is.

"Are...are you the murderer?" I find myself asking, and kick myself when I realize what I've said. *Shit.*

"Don't you hope I'm not?" I hear the hint of a laugh in his voice, and when he releases my other hand so he can swipe my hair back from my face, I flinch back into the wall. "You can't run away from me," he points out, the hand against the base of my throat unfurling so his long fingers can wrap gently around my throat. When my hands come up around us, fluttering, looking for a purpose, his gaze flicks to the one, then back to my eyes. "Don't do anything you'll regret, gorgeous."

"Who are you?" I mean it as a demand, but it comes out a softer, less sure request.

"No one who you want to be around."

"It's really awkward that you're going to give vague answers like that," I sneer nervously. "Or is this you trying to be cool?"

His head cocks to the side, like he's bemused by my words, and I feel the heaviness of his attention fully on my face. "Are you trying to make me feel bad? Or are you trying to make me think you aren't absolutely terrified right now?"

"I'm not afraid of you," I'm quick to snap, though it's a lie.

"If you're not, then walk away from me. Pull my mask down and see who I am." His gaze is goading, and his voice holds a challenge I'm not looking to accept. So I just stare at him, hating how easy it is for him to call my bluffs. "Oh, no? You're not going to do that." His fingers tighten just slightly, and my breath catches in my throat. "What a shame." With the words, he relaxes against me, though I'm still as tense as a board as he presses a knee between my thighs, the scent of his sharp cologne tickling my nose when I suck in a breath.

"Stay away from shit like this. Do you hear me?" He's so careful when he says it, making sure to enunciate every word. "Stop looking for shadows or suspects. Because eventually, you're going to pay for it. Curiosity killed the cat, you know." The words whisper through my brain, reminding me of the party and the two masked boys I'd met there that night.

But there's no way this is one of them. He can't be.

"Fine," I reply in a whisper, my heart pounding against my chest. "Let me go." He doesn't have to. In fact, he has the upper hand here, and when he moves, I see the hilt of a knife under his jacket that makes me choke on the air I'm breathing.

The man reaches a hand down to where I'm looking, and I swear he's frowning behind the mask. "I'm not going to hurt you. Not as long as you *stop* looking for trouble. Now, before this goes any further." He presses against me, eating up the empty space between us and forcing his thigh against my center, which I'm hyper aware of. Especially when he moves, his jeans rubbing against my leggings, and it's suddenly *really* hard to breathe in the cold, enclosed space.

"Promise me you won't go looking for a killer, Bailey," the man orders, and it's hard enough to come to terms with the fact he knows my name, when he's so close I can feel the heat from his skin radiating to me.

God, he's like a *furnace*.

"I promise," I agree without hesitation, breathless with fear

"Mean it."

"I literally mean it. And I don't know how to convince you that I do," I promise, my voice wavering. "Let me go." *So I can run home and hide under the blankets.*

He hesitates, searching my face like he wants something else. Something *more*. But I don't know what else I have to give, especially when his fingers brush over the skin of my throat, still holding me against the wall.

"It's such a shame I don't get to play with you," the man sighs at last, pulling away so he's no longer touching me. "But he'd be upset...so. *Run away, Bailey*." His voice turns sharp, prompting me to jerk away from him as my heart pounds in my chest, no part of me believing I'm going to get out of this unscathed.

"W-what?" I ask stupidly, eyes wide as I pull away from the building.

"I said run," he repeats, stepping toward me. "*Now*."

I don't wait for him to change his mind, and I'm quick to

escape, my feet flying over the ground as I run away from the meetinghouse and the stranger who has every part of me on high alert.

"Hate to break it to you, Bailey, but there's no physical way that Phoenix could've killed anyone two nights ago." Nic's voice is apologetic, as if she's under the impression this is somehow important to me. That I need Phoenix to be the killer, or some bullshit.

In reality, I'd rather him not be. But the hunch has been there, and only now do I feel my grasp on that certainty slipping away, as does the fear from this afternoon.

I haven't told Nic about what happened. Not yet. And maybe I just...won't. Not until I know how to say it or what I'm going to do with the memory of what had happened.

"How?" I ask, dragging my knee up to my chest as I swivel on my gaming chair. My headset cord pulls slightly beside my knee, the pink microphone too close to my mouth. I brush it away lightly, being careful not to snap the light pink and silver headset appendage. "Yesterday he..." I trail off, definitely not wanting to talk about yesterday at the store. She doesn't need to know, and something like embarrassment keeps me from telling her. "How do you know that for sure? Are you telling me it was accidental again?"

"No," Nic informs me with a sigh. "I'm telling you that he was killed about twenty minutes before you showed up at the park, and Phoenix was already there, waiting for that other guy who showed up later. Sorry to burst your detective bubble, Bailey."

Some private investigator I'd make, I guess.

"But it was definitely a murder, right?" I ask, probably with too much enthusiasm, by the way Nic pauses. Again the man from the fairground swims into my thoughts, and I look at my fingers trying to remember his face more clearly.

"*Yeah. It was definitely a murder. They're not releasing it on the news, and Mom would kill me if she knew I was telling you, but...*" I can hear the indecision in her voice, even as she goes on. "*He was stabbed about twelve times. Insides all ripped out. It was bad, she said. One of the worst things she's seen ever, even back in Portland.*" Hearing that this murder was one of the worst things the former Portland, Oregon police officer had ever seen is certainly something to think about.

"Had to have been someone who really hated him, huh?" I ask, trying to think through a list of Jack's enemies. I can't think of many offhand, except one.

But she's, well, dead.

Then again, if I'm being honest with myself, I don't know much about what their circle does anymore. Not since Daisy died. Emily, Jack, Jayden, Evan, and Ava were still as close as ever, from what I know, but that's not much. But maybe they pissed off a serial killer or held a seance and there's a ghost that's now taking them out one by one, horror movie style.

"I wonder if the others are afraid," I find myself murmuring, before I can stop the words from leaving my mouth.

"*What?*" Nic not hearing me is probably a blessing and I tilt my head back to stare up at my ceiling.

"I was just muttering. Sorry." *Just muttering,* because that's probably not a very normal thing to say, given the situation. My fingers drum against my thighs, nails catching my leggings every once in a while as I try to work through the thoughts taking up too much space in my brain.

The way he'd looked at me. The way he'd spoken and the tone of his voice...I'd thought for sure he was the killer, and taunting me with it. But maybe he was just taunting me with his innocence instead. The idea isn't incredibly far-fetched. Especially if he had been trying to scare me off.

"*Bailey?*" Nic's voice is hesitant, concerned, and makes me wince, though I'm thankful she can't see it. "*You okay?*"

"I'm fine." It's great that she's trying so hard not to talk about the things that she thinks will trigger me, since it gives me so much extra time to dwell on them in my own head instead. "Thanks for telling me. I hate asking you about super secret police stuff." I do, because she doesn't always like going behind her mom's back, even when it's something she knows Nolan and I will die to hear.

"*It's okay. It's a special occasion,*" Nic snorts. "*But are you sure you're okay? Do you want to come over tonight?*"

"Nah, I don't think so. I'm helping my parents with caramel apples tonight." With only two more days until the fair starts, Mom and Dad are in hustle mode. Meaning, they'll take all the help they can get. "But—"

I levitate at the knock on my door, and don't get the chance to say anything before Mom opens it, peeking her head in. "I need you, Bailey," she says, her face strangely distant and serious. I glance over her features for more clues, find none, and frown.

"O...kay," I agree, figuring that if she were going to give me a reason, she would've already. It's probable that it's a *family* thing, and she doesn't want Nic to hear it too, though I don't know what could be so serious that she wants to talk to me alone.

Unless there's been another murder.

Except...Nic would tell me if there had been, I think.

*So why is Mom looking at me like that?*

"I gotta go," I say, sitting up and dropping my legs to the floor. "Talk to you later?" I'd give her a better explanation if I had one, but my palms are already clammy from the way mom is still looking at me with something I can't place.

"*Okay.*" Nic sounds as confused as I am. "*See you later.*" I'm the one to hang up first, and I get to my feet, fingers digging into my thighs as I turn to face my mom.

"What's going on?" I ask, straightening as she opens the

door wider. "Did I do something wrong?" I hate that it's my go to, but anxiety nearly chokes me when she looks at me like I've definitely done something wrong, or I'm about to.

"No," Mom assures me, her voice firm. "You did *nothing* wrong. It's just." She looks hesitant, dismissive, and then sucks in a breath. "There's a cop here, and she'd like to talk to you about Emily and Jack's deaths."

I don't know this detective by name, even though I'm sure she's lived here all her life, just as I have. Her uniform is pressed, creating solid lines around her frame that give the severe look on her face even more meaning.

I hesitate at the entrance to our formal living room, hand on the edge of the archway that leads up into the room and the step I've tripped over at least thirty times. She sits straight in an armchair. My mom's favorite armchair that she doesn't like people sitting in.

After all, she's told me in a grumble, long after guests have gone and she's finished most of the straightening up. "Formal living rooms aren't made to be comfortable in." I've never argued with her, never voiced the thought that if they're not made to exist in, why have them?

But of course, that kind of argument would be lost on my mother, who came from very little and built a life and a home that so many people can't.

Trying not to look like a deer in headlights preparing to meet its doom, I carefully step into the room, knowing that if I fall in, I'll probably look even more suspicious. Slowly I cross to stand in front of the detective, who rises to her feet smoothly, her blonde hair pressed back in the smoothest, tightest pony-tail I've probably ever seen. I wonder how much hairspray she uses, and how much of a flame hazard her hair now is.

"Bailey Scott?" She reaches out a hand and I take it, hating the feel of her fingers against mine. It makes me nervous, like she can read some truth through palm-to-palm contact that even I don't know about. "Hi. I'm Detective Angleson."

I went to school with an Angleson, though I don't remember liking her very much.

"Hi," I reply, knowing I look just as nervous as I feel. "Umm. My mom said you wanted to ask me something?" Well, it isn't exactly what she'd said, but I'm sure paraphrasing probably won't get me thrown in jail.

"I'd like to talk to you, yes." If I had to peg the detective's age, I'd put her somewhere in her early forties. It's hard to tell, with the hair and the uniform that fits her a bit poorly, but she lets go of my hand and sits, some of the severity leaving her face as if it takes a real, concentrated effort for her to look human.

"You knew Jack Fairfield and Emily Donahue, didn't you?" she asks, getting right to the damn point. Apparently, she's not going to waste words on the little things like *hello, how are you,* or at least, *how are things after we failed to do anything about the incident on the ice six years ago?*

My fingers drum on my knees, and from the corner of my eye, I see my mom sit down in one of the other chairs, her eyes firmly on Detective Angleson's face.

It's an easy question, at least. I don't have to think about it before saying, "Yeah, I went to school with them. High school and middle school. They didn't go to the same community college I had."

Emily and Jack were much too good for community college, or in Jack's case, maybe not good enough academically.

"And you used to be friends?"

I blink, head tilting just enough that I know she's seen it. That's definitely not the question I'd expected, and even though I know the answer, I struggle as the words stick to my tongue like soft caramel, though much less pleasant.

"Years ago, we were friends. Yes." I've seen enough cop shows to assume I should've offered the word *lawyer*. Even though I haven't done anything wrong and I have nothing to admit to. There's no lie she could find and point her finger at me, crying, *I knew it*. And there's definitely no reason in hell that her handcuffs will inch anywhere near my wrists.

*I didn't kill them, after all.*

"But you aren't anymore." I hate the way she says it, shrewdly, leading me on as if *this* is the hidden truth.

But it isn't, and I'm not afraid of the words she wants to hear. Still, an irritated, humorless grin pulls at the side of my mouth like a puppet's string, though I'm sure my eyes are anything but amused. "No, we're not friends anymore," I agree, hoping I sound at least a little polite. "Because Jack, Emily, and three others killed my best friend and almost me as well. I'd say we're *definitely* not friends anymore."

When she shifts uncomfortably on her seat and looks away, it dawns on me what camp she belongs to. Back when the investigation had happened and everyone had been worked up, upset, and grieving, there had been two sides to what had happened. Some of the police, and the other parents, had been firmly on our side. On Daisy's side. That it wasn't an accident, or just a stupid childish prank that wasn't really anyone's fault. Those people called for a harsher punishment than, well, nothing, but in the end, things hadn't gone our way.

But then there were the others. Some cops and parents, especially the parents of my former 'friends,' who swore I was making parts of it up. That it was hearsay; my word alone couldn't be trusted about whose fault such a sad, devastating, 'accident' had been. They'd sworn that kids just didn't think, and that's all it was.

A sad, unfortunate, episode of kids not thinking.

And by the look on her face, the dismissal in her gaze, and the way she's clearly uninterested in what I've just said, Detective Angleson is definitely one of the people who thought it was just *kids not thinking.*

Something *strange* slots into place in my chest. Like a gear that's been jammed and is misfiring over and over and *over*, causing a pain I didn't know existed. But before I can examine the feeling, the relief, further, she's speaking again.

"I'm not here to talk about what happened years ago." She brushes me off with the practice of someone who's been doing just that to people for long enough that it's become natural. "I'm here to talk about Emily and Jack. I think it's fair to say that you, among some others, have reason not to be sorry about their deaths. Is that right?" She snaps her gaze up to mine lightning quick as she asks, like she's trying to catch the smallest of micro-expressions before I can hide it.

But really, truly, there's nothing to fucking hide.

"Not liking someone isn't a crime," I point out. "Not crying over their deaths isn't either. Or they might have been in more trouble back then, huh?" She doesn't rise to the bait. I hadn't expected her to. It'll take more than my polite and less-than-subtle needling about a topic she doesn't care about to push her beyond her carefully coiffed calm.

But that's okay. My schedule is wide open, and I have nothing but time.

"It goes without saying that you're the person in this town who would have the *least* reason to cry over their deaths. Doesn't it?" she pushes, and I know right then she's made a mistake, because my mother stiffens, her eyes narrowing.

"Detective, if you're going to accuse my daughter of *murder*, then I'm going to have to ask to speak to someone higher up than you," she says coolly, her gaze on the blonde woman. "Someone with more knowledge of how things work, maybe?"

Mom has her own angle of attack, and it's less subtle than mine. I almost grin as Detective Angleson's gaze cuts to her, but my mother works in finance and is not easily scared. If old fat men in the boardroom can't do it, I know for sure this woman can't make her back down.

"I'm only asking questions, Mrs. Scott," she tells my mother finally, her voice still just as stiff as it had been when she'd spoken to me. "I'm not making accusations."

"You're kind of trying to lead me into one though, aren't you?" I add so helpfully. "You want me to admit to not being friends with a group of people anymore. Which, last I checked, isn't a crime. So you also want me to admit that I'm an awful person who is *not* planning to go to their funerals. Actually, I'm hoping the line at the coffee shop on Third, you know, the place that does the donuts on Saturdays?" I ask her the mostly rhetorical question blithely, but she doesn't answer.

"Maybe you don't," I continue, "I'm hoping that they're less busy during the funeral, so I can go get a donut, hunt down coffee, come home, and not give a damn that they're dead." I know it's reckless. The look on Mom's face says so, though she isn't glaring at me or giving me any kind of warning to stop. She doesn't feel anything for those kids, either. I know that for a fact.

"Sounds to me like you more than just don't like them," Detective Angleson says, her attention solely on me as she turns away from my mom.

"Does it sound like I...hate them?" I ask, rather dramatically, if I do say so myself. I'd almost wiggled my eyebrows during the words, but I really don't *need* to end up in jail that badly.

"It does. Did you kill them?" The words are so natural, the question just so *there* that I can't help the surprised scoff of laughter that nearly chokes me.

"Did *I* kill them?" I shove my finger into my chest, trying to make sure she means me. "Did *I* kill Emily? Track star Emily? Or wrestling... Well he wasn't a star by any means, was he? Uh. Wrestling...*enthusiast* Jack of the six-foot-five clan?" I shake my head at her stupidity, and her audacity. "I'm five-six in tennis shoes and one-fifty soaking wet. I've never played a real sport in my life. How would I have killed them, exactly?"

"And she has alibis for both deaths. Which, as far as I know, have still been ruled as *accidents*," my mother points out icily. "Or is this you coming to our house to tell us that maybe that's not the case?" Thanks to Nic, I know she's wrong. But the fact that they haven't released the truth about Jack's death is interesting.

Detective Angleson doesn't look at my mother, but she holds my gaze with her pale blue eyes. "People get creative, Miss Scott," she tells me, hand resting on her knee.

"Creative enough to be in two places at once?" I mirror her for only a moment longer before flopping back in my seat. "Mom's right. I can give you the names of multiple people who saw me when Emily died, and four people who saw me when Jack died."

"Are you one of those people?" she asks my mother, clearly harboring some kind of death wish.

"I am," Mom replies icily. "Or is that against the law now, too?"

"I asked because I wanted to see your reaction to me asking. But I wasn't expecting you to be so casual about it." She looks me over again, scrutinizing every part of me, as if trying to find the piece that's broken. Joke's on her, though. It's my brain. Well, and my achy palm from the night she doesn't care about.

"I'm just so sorry to disappoint you like this."

"Because now I wonder if you'll tell me the truth when I ask you if you know who could've done it." She pins me with those eyes, her face looking younger for a moment. Almost vulnerable. Is this something more important to her than just her job? It's starting to look like I should pull out a yearbook just to look up what Angleson I knew from school, just in case there's a connection I'm not seeing.

I don't answer her right away, but mostly because the first four answers my brain conjures up include a fancy four letter word beginning with F, in a sentence that starts with *go* and ends with *yourself*.

But also because I *do* have an idea of who might have killed them. It's impossible, obviously. Like me, Phoenix can't be in two places at once, as far as I know. And I'm *sure* Rory is his always-alibi, true or not.

Still, his presence in the park when Jack had died, the fact that he'd been there waiting on Rory for longer than Jack had been dead, proves my suspicions incorrect more firmly than anything else could.

Blinking, I realize it's been too long since I've answered and I drag my gaze back to the rounded tip of her too-wide nose. "I don't know anyone who hates them more than me," I lie to her, my voice as trustworthy and level as I can ever hope to make it.

*Especially since I'm lying.*

"I don't know of anyone who can blame them more than me and Daisy's parents. But I'm *pretty sure* Daisy's mom and dad were at the fairgrounds that night, too." It rules them out, and I'm hoping it helps rule Phoenix out as well.

The cop stares at me and finally, *finally,* gets to her feet with a sigh. "We're just chasing leads and checking all of our bases," Detective Angleson informs me, glancing around the room like she's never seen it before or hadn't really looked when she came in. "You have a lovely home, Mrs. Scott."

My mom's lips thin as she stands as well, but she doesn't respond. Normally she'd give a kind thank you, and direct the person's attention to some piece of art or sculpture or lamp that she'd picked up somewhere unique.

I follow Detective Angleson to the door with Mom looming behind me like the literal iteration of a *momma bear*, but neither of us offer any help as the detective struggles with our bratty door that is suddenly my favorite feature of our glorious house.

When she does get it open, her own weight causes her to stagger back a step, but she collects herself as if the two of us aren't looking and judging her.

"Thank you for answering my questions," she tells me, walking out to stand on the front porch. I follow enough to lean in the doorway, my head against the side of it. *Good door,* I think to it, fighting not to pet it like a horse's rump.

"Thanks for being so thorough with your work." Not a hint of truth finds my words that drip with the sarcasm of a thousand preteens. "Wouldn't want a crime in this town to go unpunished."

She smiles but again doesn't answer, clearly being the benevolent bigger person as she slides her sunglasses onto her face. They're just as severe and unassuming as the rest of her, with black aviator frames outlined in more black.

"I'll call next time if I have more questions," she offers, like that's the problem here. "I know it must be jarring to have a cop just show up here. Especially after everything." If she's trying to play my game against me, I hope she's better than that.

"You call," I agree. "I'll keep my phone on twenty-four seven. Want to text me, so I can save your number and give you a special ringtone?"

Her grin widens. "I notice you aren't telling me what ringtone."

"Yeah," I agree, nodding back at her. "You caught me. Probably nothing you'd listen to on the job." Though I very much doubt she listens to anything other than the police handbook while working.

"Just try to stay out of trouble this season, Miss Scott. Things are weird this time of year, anyway. This year is just..." I expect her to look away cinematically, out onto the street from behind her glasses. But she stares at me instead, like I'm the spooky landscape hiding secrets.

Boy, is she going to be disappointed if that's what she sees me as.

"Extra weird." She tilts her head at my looming mother and turns, trudging down our front porch stairs and, unfortunately, not falling. "Oh, by the way. I totally forgot to mention..." She looks back at us, her smile falling. "Did you know that Phoenix Hawthorne is back in town? He's your best friend's older brother, right? I drove by their house earlier, only he's not staying there. Weird, right?" She offers me one last smile that couldn't fool a blind donkey and starts walking again.

"Detective?" I hate that it's taken me this long to remember, but now that I have, I can't push the memory of the man in the fairgrounds away. If he's the killer, and I don't say something, I really *will* feel guilty.

She stops, looking at me with arched brows, but doesn't speak.

"There was a guy at the fairgrounds a few days ago. He didn't do anything..." Now I just sound like I'm making shit up, and I shake my head. "It's definitely nothing. But it was weird. *He* was weird. Middle age, gray hair. Weird eyes. He slammed into me and just—"

"I'll look into it." The way she cuts me off causes me to go silent, and I blink up at her owlishly. "Have a good day, Bailey." She starts to walk again, as if I hadn't said anything of value whatsoever.

"Sure you will," I mutter, watching her approach her unmarked car that looks just as normal, if at a lower price point, as most of the ones on our street. "I definitely believe that."

# CHAPTER 13

Out of all the places I could be, or should be, the park probably isn't one of them. Especially when I'm here alone, close enough to sundown to be suspicious if Detective Angleson has some kind of tag on me, which I doubt.

It's not like she got close enough to spritz me with overwatch spray, or shove a bug into a coffee that I didn't even have at the time of her 'interview.'

I pull my hood up anyway as the wind blows my hair further across my face. Nature seems to have remembered what month we're in at last, and the milder temperatures from last week are officially a thing of the past. My teeth try to chatter before I set them, wishing I'd get used to the weather quicker, or that I'd worn a jacket more suitable for protection against the cold, instead of my favorite *Friday the Thirteenth* hoodie over my fleece-lined leggings.

I don't even know what I'm doing here. The trees aren't about to talk. Not even the one in the middle of the park where, supposedly, the witch Agnes was hanged with a colossal effort on the townspeople's parts.

Though not before she cursed us, if the stories are right. And this year, it's looking like they are.

The trail leading to the tree is only marked a few times, which has always surprised me given the tourist nature of our town. Shouldn't we *want* people perusing the park, going to take pictures by the ancient white oak tree instead of, well, not?

But I'm not the mayor, or any part of her staff. Nor do I have any desire to be. I know the unmarked paths in the park well enough to get to the tree without really trying. Most people who grew up here do. But apparently—when my eyes fall on the water of the river that looks gray under the heavy clouds above us—I don't know it well enough to avoid this place.

I'd played here so often that the riverbank was a second home to me. Even my mom and dad knew where to find us if Daisy and I had gone out without asking or accidentally went too far into the park itself. We'd made this place our fantasy land, our beach, our boardroom.

And now it's her memorial that lives in my head, causing every inch of the river that I can see to burn into my thoughts like boiling water.

Movement makes me blink, and I'm so far down the rabbit-hole of my thoughts that the first shock of dark hair appearing around one of the bigger trees by the bank has my mouth forming the familiar, yet no longer so familiar, name on my lips.

*Daisy.*

I don't say it, and it's a good thing. Instead, my lips press flat as Phoenix stares at me, his gaze distant and cold.

"I didn't know you came here anymore," I say finally, before the silence grows too heavy for either of us to break. He looks as uncomfortable as me, though at least he's dressed in two hoodies instead of just one like my dumbass. I shiver in envy, and that at least makes him look at me.

"I didn't know you did, either." Our standoff continues,

though today I can't meet his eyes, just the tip of his nose. The only sound is the rush of water and the far-off call of birds saying their farewells for the day. At best, we have an hour of daylight left, though I'd lean more towards forty-five minutes.

He's the next to break the silence, though he doesn't speak. He walks over to me, sneakers crunching over dying leaves as he stares me down.

The crack of a small stick under his foot makes me jump, but his hand is on my shoulder a moment later to calm me, the soft *shhh* that leaves his lips the cherry on top.

Fuck. *Fuck.* If anything can bring back my attraction to him, this is it by a landslide.

"I didn't mean to scare you," he murmurs in the quiet, broken only by natural sounds. "Not this time." A small smile hooks at the corner of his mouth and I snort, looking away. "What are you doing here?"

His hand falls from my shoulder, and I turn back to survey the semi-changed riverbank. "They let this shit grow, huh?" I mutter, making the decision to step off of the comfort zone of the path and into the taller, lusher grass. I make my way past the stump that we'd used as a table or a platform. The flatter ground near a jutting, flat rock is familiar, if overgrown. But the areas we'd used for our more fantastical games, the ones Phoenix normally got roped into playing a *dragon* for, are so grown up with briars that it would take a month to fix it up again.

It hurts more than it should, for reasons I refuse to name. Just as I refuse to name the feeling in my chest when I'd admitted just how *not sorry* I am for Emily and Jack.

"Do you remember?" I ask recklessly, pivoting to look at Phoenix. "Back when we were kids, and we'd always make you be the dragon for us to fight?"

He doesn't answer for long enough that I'm sure I've fucked up. My lips part, and I'm ready to apologize, when he says, at last, "That's not quite how I remember it, Bailey. In fact, I remember you *constantly* volunteering to be the princess who the dragon kidnaps, and telling Daisy she had to go through all these tests and puzzles just to find you."

I can feel the heat creeping up my cheeks at his words. Mostly because he's right, and I'm definitely mortified that he remembers. "Yeah, umm. Well, you know," I laugh, trying to sound like I'm not regretting everything I'd said a second ago. "I just really...loved dragons as a kid. Loved all reptiles."

"You were afraid of snakes."

"Well, yeah, but—"

"You made me pick up a frog from the flat rock because it looked at you funny. I had to toss it in the river before you were satisfied."

"You're looking at me funny," I counter, my embarrassment causing me to snap. "Does that mean you'll throw yourself in the river for me?"

He cocks his head just a little, and I hate the cute, coy expression it brings over him. It's unfair for him to still be this damn attractive and for me to still be *this* into him.

*Fuck.*

"I don't think so. Ask me again in the summer when it's warmer," he hums. "I hear it's pretty bad to swim in this week."

"Oh, yeah?" I ask with an incredulous laugh, already looking away and starting to create distance between us. "Who the hell went swimming in it and told you *that*?"

"Emily."

There's no way he's just said that. His face doesn't change. The almost amused look is still there as I try to filter the word through my brain, and the audacity of his casual attitude.

"You can't. You can't make jokes like that," I murmur, and turn without thinking to walk away from him. It isn't that I feel bad for her. Obviously, it's never been about that. But he can't say things like that without my brain going back to the idea of him being the damn killer.

*Even if it's not scientifically possible.*

"Why? Did I hurt your feelings?" His words aren't as gentle as they had been, and he follows me as I march up the hill, no longer staying anywhere near the sidewalk.

"Of course you didn't," I hiss, barely glancing back at him. Sure enough, he's still behind me, and I definitely can't help how jealous I am of how warm he looks. "Why would either of their deaths hurt my feelings?" I don't know why I'm still walking, except to get away from him.

Not that he's going to let me, apparently. He follows me no matter how fast I walk, his longer strides preventing any distance from growing between us.

"You're acting like they bothered you. You're acting like *I* bother you," Phoenix amends quietly. "Last time I checked, Bailey, this wasn't how you treated me."

"How *I* treat you?" I can't help but whirl around, surprise in every line, every movement of my body. "Phoenix..." It's hard to do more than stare at him, his lips parted for breaths that puff out into the air in front of him. "In case you've forgotten, you stopped treating me like *anything* after Daisy—" I don't finish the sentence.

But his frown twitches at his lips and he steps forward to grab my hoodie with his long fingers. "She *died*, Bailey. Daisy *died*. You can't just pretend it didn't happen by not saying it. That's not respecting her memory, and it is *certainly* not going to bring her back."

"I know she died! I know just as well as you!" Embarrassment fuels my anger. So does rage at the memories he's trying so hard to dig up. "*I was there, Phoenix.*"

"I know you were. Bailey, wait!" He doesn't let me turn away. He grabs me and drags me to the side, further from the path. "I didn't mean to say..." he curses, looking away with a grimace. "I didn't mean to upset you," he says at last. "Sorry, I shouldn't have joked about Emily's death."

My anger ebbs, though that's not saying much. All of it was superfluous. Trivial. Nothing he's done could *really* ever upset me for more than a fleeting moment. Subconsciously I step back, and I'm surprised when my back brushes up against a large, solid shape.

"Careful," Phoenix murmurs, stepping forward too, his hand going up to my shoulder. I barely look at him, however, as my head tilts back so I can look up above me.

Somehow, Phoenix has brought me to Agnes' hanging tree without me realizing it. Reaching back, I rest my hand on the white, smooth bark, gazing up at the centuries old tree that's been here for longer than anyone alive in Hollow Bridge.

"I never understand why we don't do more to like, bring tourism to the tree," I admit, echoing my thoughts from earlier. "And no one ever touches it with Halloween decorations, either."

Phoenix sidles closer, staring up at the tree as well. "It would feel disrespectful," he admits, apparently not noticing how close he is to me. I can *feel* his warmth now. How his hoodies and internal heat are like a radiator that I'm so goddamn envious of it hurts. "And I always figured the town was too afraid of tourists ruining it if they had signs and a trail pointed straight here." He stares up at the tree, his eyes thoughtful.

"Why did you come to the park tonight?" he asks without looking down, and when he shifts casually, it takes me way longer than I should to realize he's trapping me against the wide trunk of Agnes' hanging tree.

The realization makes my heart pick up in my chest, fluttering upwards into my throat. My hands, though, press against the bark. My nails clench against it and dig into rain-softened bark. "What?" I ask, even though I know exactly what he'd asked.

"Why did you"—he leans his head down until his eyes find mine—"come to the park tonight? Haven't you heard, Bailey? Even though the curfew isn't being enforced, it's certainly encouraged. I can't imagine your parents are thrilled that you're out here."

"What about your parents?" I counter, not feeling much of a need to look away. "What do they think of you out here at night with no one to watch your back? Or do you think you're invincible because you haven't been here in a few years?"

"I think I'm more capable than you of taking care of myself. And not for any of the reasons you'll accuse me of implying, so save your breath."

"A detective came to my house today," I reply, refusing to rise to his goading words. I see the small surprise on his face. The way his brows jerk up toward his bangs is unmistakable, and so is the spark of sapphire in his normally dark eyes. "She wanted to ask me about why I'm not worked up about Emily or Jack's deaths. And she asked me if I had any idea who would want to hurt them, if this, hypothetically, wasn't an *accident*."

I think we both know it isn't.

I also think that, even though Phoenix isn't the killer, he knows more than he's letting on.

"Did you tell her your suspicions?" he inquires when it's clear I'm waiting for his reaction. "Did you tell her to come knocking on my door? She did, you know. Is that where you told her to go?"

"No." I suck in a breath. "I told her I had no idea. That I can't think of anyone that would want to kill them."

The resurgence of surprise is different this time. It's... warmer. Fondness surges in his gaze before he shoves it back down. "I won't tell you I'm surprised, since I'm sure you'll take it as an insult. But...thank you. For not sending the mob down to my hotel room with pitchforks."

"Well, you couldn't have, right?" I ask, still watching every movement of his face. "I was telling the truth. You couldn't have done anything. You have an alibi. I saw you and Rory at the fairgrounds before Emily died. I saw Rory in the woods," I add. "Then Nic said you were at the park when Jack died. I can do the math." One of my shoulders lifts and falls, but I'm too interested in the look on his face to think about anything else.

He looks surprised. Impressed, I think, but if it's just at my ability to tell time and do basic math, I'm a little offended.

"You saw Rory in the woods?" he asks, not asking what I'd expected him to. His arm muscles tighten, and he presses harder against the bark over my head, still trapping me against Agnes's tree. "But you didn't see me?"

"So what if I didn't see you?" I can't help the way I'm basically snapping at him like a feral dog. His hot-then cold-then hot again attitude isn't doing it for me, and he makes it so difficult to figure out the situation, or my response. "Were you hiding from me?"

"Obviously," he shrugs. "Specifically you. What were you doing in the woods that night? Last I saw, you were getting pumpkins out of your car. I figured your parents were there setting up, like mine were."

A feeling of surprise ripples through me. I blink away the small spark of excitement that he remembers, that he'd seen me and thought enough about it to mention it now, or to have assumed as to what I was doing. But it doesn't take long for me to realize he's asked me a question I should answer.

And, well, is still holding me against a *tree*. Which helps in making all of those cute, fuzzy feelings die in my stomach.

"I was just walking," I tell him with a shrug. "Then I smelled something dead. So I followed it."

He chokes at my words, as if somehow they've grabbed his

throat and surprised the shit out of him. "You smelled something *dead* and followed it?" he repeats, eyes widening a fraction of an inch. "What the hell?"

"It was a crow," I go on flippantly, as if he hasn't said anything at all. I figure this is better than answering the outrage that he has absolutely no right to. "A dead crow without any discernible cause of death. Which is weird, by the way. Crows don't just drop dead mid-flight like that. Do you know what most people around here would call that?" I can't help the way my attention magnetizes to him, even when I don't want it to. I can't help the way I meet his eyes, wanting to be the one to catch anything there that might change.

But he stares at me, expression unfathomable. "A dead bird?" he assumes, though to his credit I can see he had tried to think it over.

"A really, *really* bad omen," I correct him flatly. "Especially the night that Emily died."

"Which, I'll remind you, they ruled an accident," Phoenix slips in almost casually.

"Except that it's starting to feel like no one believes that. Cops don't show up at your door for accidents, Phoenix." My eyes narrow, brow furrowing slightly. "Would you tell me if you knew something about their deaths?"

The question stretches between us, long enough that I regret asking it when his lips finally part and he leans in closer, so he can see me in the waning light of the park. It feels even darker here, against Agnes' tree, with the branches obscuring most of the light that tries its hardest to make it to us. And what the limbs don't block out, Phoenix's body does.

"Of course not," he murmurs, and I swear I can feel his breath against my lips, making my heart leap for the confines of my throat, as if choking me is the safer option. "Why in the world would I do that, when you can barely admit that you agree they deserve it?"

My mouth opens, then closes. My lips feel hot from the hiss of his words, and I wish, *God*, I wish I could back up or at the very least climb the tree from this position. "I never said they didn't," I point out carefully. "I've never *once* cheered for their innocence or picketed for them not to be in trouble for what they did."

"And what did they do? Everyone around here is too afraid to say it. I think they worry that saying it out loud will make it real. Will make them realize how bad it was. Too bad for us that we can't help but know it's real, huh, Bailey?" This time I know it's his hot, burning breath on my lips, hotter still with the heat of his hate-filled words. "So, what did they do?"

"Why are you doing this?" I challenge instead. I can feel my limbs shaking from the effort of not collapsing into a puddle of nervous fear on the ground, and I wonder if Phoenix can see how close I am to breaking as his eyes rake over my form.

"Because I want to know who the Bailey that still lives in this town is," he tells me smoothly, reaching out his other hand to grip my shoulder. "The Bailey that had to be carried out of the courtroom before she could kill Emily herself, or..." He looks at me, disappointment glazing over his eyes. "The Bailey that can't even say what they *did,* thanks to staying in this town for too long."

"What was I supposed to do?" My response is a sharp hiss, as if I'm not avoiding the question. "I'm not like you, Phoenix. I can't just *leave* and expect to have people gravitate to me for my looks and my personality. What was I supposed to *do*, when I don't know how to be *alone?*"

I throw the words between us like a burning, boiling hot potato and leave it there. I've never been any good at being alone, and he knows it. He's known it since the first day of kindergarten when I stuck to Daisy like glue and half-transferred to him the moment she brought me back to her house.

He's always known, but he's never made fun of me for all

the times I needed Daisy's reassurance, or his. He's always known my brain works differently, and yet unlike a lot of people I could name, has never, not once, held it against me.

When he looks away, I think that I've won. Or at the very least, brought this discussion to its natural end. A stalemate that was inevitable all along. He knows why I didn't leave. I know how he feels about everything; me included. But when I take one step away from the tree, expecting him to step back and let me go, he surprises me with a hand at the base of my throat and a sudden closeness that I'm definitely not expecting.

"But you didn't answer my question, Bailey," he murmurs against my skin, his eyes no longer the cool, dark sapphire of a cold gem but instead, are somehow molten night skies that burn with accusation and curiosity. "Which one are you?"

He's not literally asking. I get that much. My hands shake as I bury my fingers in the tree again, but something in his gaze spurs me forward until the fingers of one hand are gripping his outer hoodie, and my other is around his wrist.

"They told Daisy and me that the only way we'd have friends is if we did what they said," I grit out, though it's hard to look at him when I do. "They told Daisy that—Don't make me say it, Phoenix."

"Tell me what they said," he demands, his hand tightening ever so slightly on my throat, and his other gripping my wrist that holds his hoodie.

"They told Daisy that she'd really have to work for it, since her birth mother gave her up because she was unlovable. It was..." The words *dumb kid shit* die on my tongue, because I know that's the comment that did it for Daisy and had us on the too thin ice of the pond in the woods on a day too warm to trust it hadn't melted.

The red of the flag stuck in the middle by Emily the night before is still as vivid in my memory as it had been, and I close my eyes on it as I try to pretend I can't feel how Phoenix flinches against me at the cruelty in my words. I hate having said it. I also hate that he asked.

"Don't make me do this to you," I whisper, suddenly feeling like I'm the one who has him by the throat, instead of the other way around. I hate the feeling enough that it makes my teeth grind harshly, but when he looks down at me, there's clear conviction in his gaze, instead of the sorrow I'd thought to find.

"Nothing you tell me could ever hurt as much as Daisy's death and hearing it the first time around," he promises me. "But you don't have to go on—"

"So they told us, go get the red flag. That's all," I snap, eyes burning into him. He wanted to hear it, and I'm not going to swallow the words now. "Bailey can even go with you, Daisy. It'll be easier with two of you. Except no one mentioned the ice had been cracking. Or that two of us going onto it was a death sentence. And we were *fourteen,* like fuck, Phoenix. We were kind of dumb, sure, but I definitely don't think we were the problem when you didn't get to hear the social threats Emily's friends made. We were so fucking *afraid* of being outcasts that we walked right out on that ice. And when we fell in, you know what they did?"

God, I wish I could stop talking. I wish I could stop, but I can't. Even when Phoenix's hand drops from my throat and I inexplicably surge forward to hold on to him, to turn us and press *him* back into the tree like the spirit of Agnes has possessed me.

"They *left.* I yelled for them. Did you know that? Were you there in the courtroom when I begged Emily to tell me why she, Jayden and Evan ran away?" I barely notice when his hands come up to cup mine, though he doesn't try to push me away. "Is this what you *want?*" Heat sears my cheeks, and with a jolt, I realize I'm fucking crying.

God, I feel so weak.

"No," he tells me, his voice soft. "I never liked seeing you cry, Bailey. I hated it every day in that courtroom when you were all wrapped up in bandages. And I hate it now." He moves forward, like he's going to push me away, but instead just presses his forehead to mine and sighs, the tension leaving his body.

As if it's a signal, my body does the same, the fear and anxiety and anger drain out of my feet and into the ground under the giant tree. "I'm not sorry though," he admits, but I don't open my eyes to see if he's smiling. It sounds like he is. "Because now I know exactly which Bailey I came home to."

*I think he's going to kiss me.* He's so close to me, and I can feel the heat from his body radiate into mine as I open my eyes to stare up at Phoenix, my childhood dragon and teen crush. Clearly, I should've made a move on him sometime between the grief, counseling, and him emancipating himself for an early escape from Hollow Bridge.

"Do they deserve to die, Bailey?" he asks, leaning forward so that when he speaks, his lips brush my forehead. "Do they all deserve to have 'accidents' like Emily and Jack?"

Everything is so quiet. The wind whips around us up on the hill under the giant white oak tree, and all I can see in the scant space between us are our sneakers. "I have to go," I tell his shirt, still not willing to look at him. The wind picks up, as if in protest, and his arms move, sliding around my shoulders until he's actually hugging me.

"Oh Bailey, Bailey, *Bailey*," he sighs, with that same chuckle that has always made my stomach twist. "What are we going to do with you if we can't even get you to admit that bad people deserve to die?" But thankfully, he releases me. His arms falling suddenly to his sides as he looks at me with an expression in his eyes that I refuse to read clearly.

Because he has Rory, for one, and for two...I'm already in enough trouble tonight. I don't answer him or pretend to have any composure left in me. I stumble, taking off towards the path that'll take me home and try to forget how his hands felt on my shoulders, on my face, and most importantly, on my throat, with varying degrees of minimal success.

It isn't until I'm close to the big gates that I look up, and my heart jolts up into my throat when the man from the fairgrounds, eerily light eyes fixed on me, catches my attention from twenty feet away.

He isn't trying to, I don't think. But how can I not let my steps drift to a stop when he just *stares* at me, hair greasy and curled into small ringlets. He looks...off, for one. But he still has that unnaturally uncomfortable look, like he's going to vomit or scream at me. His hands clench, then unclench, and I've never once thought someone was a killer based on their appearance before now.

But if he's not the one killing people, even though I've never seen him in my life and can't imagine why he would, then there's no one else more fit for the role. My own palms feel clammy as I scrub them against the fabric of my hoodie, and I hate that I have to swallow back my racing heart.

I won't let him keep me here, and it isn't like he's blocking the gate. But it's hard to make my legs move forward, harder to try to make my escalation into almost a jog look casual when I'm almost parallel with him on my way out.

"It's cold out here," the man mutters, facing the ground but probably talking to me, since there's no one else around. When he looks up at me, I find myself slowing, curiosity getting the better of my common sense. "And it's only getting colder. Shouldn't you be at home, instead of out here all alone?"

I don't hang around to reply. Thankfully my brain snaps back into action and I take off once more, not caring about looking subtle or caring about what he thinks of me. It's much more important for me to get home, where the most dangerous thing in the world is my sticky front door.

# CHAPTER 14

I f there's a part of me that's disappointed when the rest of the week goes by murder-free, it's a part of me that I refuse to admit exists. The curfew falls away completely on Wednesday, and on Thursday I take my anxiety meds and stare at myself in the mirror, wondering if I look 'family friendly' enough for the first day of the Halloween fair. The events kick off with a kids-only event where children can dress up and safely trick-or-treat a few weeks early.

For our town, two nights of trick-or-treating have always been normal. I don't know how other towns exist *without* two days of kids bouncing off the wall with a sugar rush. Or, hell, how the dentists stay in business outside of Hollow Bridge.

No matter how much I want to borrow Nic's cool cat mask again, I know it'll probably scare some of the little kids. So instead I dress all in black and go as a regular cat, with painted on whiskers and cute ears. My only job is to hand out candy with my parents for a couple of hours, then run a few last checks with them to make sure everything is set for the *real* opening of the annual Halloween Fair on Saturday.

Thankfully, my parents don't remark about my insistence

on all but setting up a surveillance station to stare over at Phoenix's parents' booth. But to my disappointment and relief, I don't see Rory or Phoenix there, handing out candy or otherwise.

But what did I really expect? I'm sure a lot of people in town aren't Phoenix's biggest fans, given his attitude and how vocal he'd been back when Daisy died. Still, my heart sinks just a little when it's obvious he isn't there, and the boredom that sets in at the realization is hard to ignore for the rest of the night.

Twenty-hours later, I find myself sitting on my sofa, staring at Leatherface on my television as he wraps a guy's leg in butcher paper. I eat my red velvet ice cream without really paying attention to the movie itself, or the amount of screaming echoing through my room.

I want to do something before the fair. Sure, going is nice. Helping out is... Well it's not *fun,* but I definitely don't mind. And this isn't my last night of freedom by any means. But this year more than others, I feel almost stifled, like somehow I've wrapped myself in a blanket burrito to protect myself from the outside world but forgot to poke air holes for me to breathe.

Or something like that.

Fumbling for my phone, I sink down in my seat until I can flop over onto my side and stretch out on the sofa comfortably, scrolling to my contacts until I find my best friend's name preceded and followed by star emojis.

*Do you want to go somewhere tonight*? I ask, typing the message fast enough that it autocorrects *tonight* to *tongue* just before I send it. I fix it, then send the message and wait, knowing that Nic is good about keeping her phone on her come hell or high water.

Sure enough, the *delivered* on my screen changes to *read,* and seconds later the gray bubble pops up to show me she's typing.

*Where do you want to go? We'll have to pick up Nolan. He's actually not here.* That's a surprise, and by her words, she knows it too. Normally, they spend most waking moments together.

*Oh no, is he deathly ill? Possessed?* I tease. *Has to be right? To be outside of your bubble?*

*Probably possessed,* she shoots back.

*Haunted house?* I ask, unable to deny how much I'd like to go to one this year.

*Haunted field? You know where I mean. Field of Nightmares.*

*Done.* I love Field of Nightmares, and we haven't been in three years. Not for any real reason...I think. Things just haven't seemed to line up lately. And by lately, clearly I mean the last few years.

*I'll pick you up in thirty minutes?* Nic asks, never one to waste time. I'm on my feet and going for my closet even as I reply in agreement, careful not to step on Stranger's tail as he saunters to the food bowl where Kale is currently standing guard, eyes wide as he watches for imaginary danger.

From my closet I pull out a pair of leggings, shimmying into the fleece-lined clothing and yanking them up over my *Friday the Thirteenth* underwear. It's Hollow Bridge, after all, so I feel a certain call to be at least a little on theme as much as I can for the month. I snatch a red top from my bed, pulling it on over my leggings and tugging it down until the long shirt with thin straps covers me to my thighs, before finally gripping a ouija board-themed hoodie and pulling it on as well. As with most of my sweatshirts, it's technically too big and falls to my thighs, the sleeves needing to be pushed up to my elbows so I can have use of my hands. While it'll bother me and I'll probably sweat aggressively until Nic picks me up, I've looked at the temperatures for tonight and I know that even in this, I'll still end up being chilly at the Field of Nightmares.

*I'm ready when you are,* I text Nic, knowing she'll be a little while. *Just watching Leatherface slaughter home invaders until then.*

*They're not home invaders. They're victims,* Nic shoots back a few seconds later.

*They invaded his home. In the original, anyway. They're sooo home invaders and I'm sure Texas has pretty solid stand your ground laws. I'm making us 'Leatherface did nothing wrong' shirts,* I can't help but tease.

*Make mine green,* she replies, then sends another message before I can reply. *Leaving now. See you in 10.*

The Field of Nightmares has never been this expansive. At least, it hadn't been when I was here a few years ago, when I was a giggling, nervous eighteen-year-old. Now I'm still just as nervous, but I do less giggling to make it not so obvious.

"I see it's more than just a *field* now," I point out, seeing the entrance to the corn field maze near a clearing on the farm where a large projector is set up to play horror movies. Tonight, I see the telltale street that Michael Myers frequents on the screen, and a very young Jamie Lee Curtis dressed in brown, walking down it, talking to someone. The clearing also hosts a huge fire pit and chairs, most of which are filled with other teenagers or college-aged adults drinking cider, hot cocoa, or off-brand bottles of water.

To the left of the field, the old barn that had been empty and closed off the last time I was here, has a sign above one door that says *enter here,* and a line of ten or so people waiting to go in. It looks larger than it did, with an area outside made of boards and fences signifying the attraction isn't *just* in the barn.

Excitement pools in my stomach, taking flight like a thousand little birds as Nic parks and I pop out of the car, closing the back passenger door behind me as I stand on my tiptoes and stretch. "I feel like a teenager again," I admit to Nolan as he comes around the car and zips up his hoodie. "I was so excited every time we came to one of these, remember?"

"I remember you bolting at the first rev of a chainsaw," Nolan chuckles, giving me one of his kind smiles. Even when he's joking or taunting one of us, it's clear he's too nice to actually hurt anyone's feelings.

"The barn expansion's new this year, I think," Nic remarks, sweeping her hair off of her neck and into a ponytail. "Ticket sales are still over there." She points to a stand near the empty field dedicated just to parking, where two people stand inside of a small shed-like building behind a low counter. Nic takes the initiative to trudge across the damp grass and I follow, thrilled that we've gotten to the farm on the edge of the woods at the best possible time, an hour or so before the sun sets.

"Three adults?" the woman at the shed asks, glancing between us. "Do you want just the field, just the barn, or both? You can add the hayride onto either for ten dollars extra."

"Do we want to do just both haunts for now?" Nic looks between the two of us and I nod. Nolan shrugs in agreement, forking over his twenty dollars as I do the same. "Just both the field and barn," Nic says, handing our money to the lady, who nods her head and gives her six tickets that Nic folds up into her pocket.

Again, excitement ruffles my insides, and I clutch my hoodie sleeves in my fingers as a smile grows on my lips. We haven't done this in too long, that's for sure. And I love being scared at haunted houses. While chainsaws definitely used to be the bane of my existence, it's been a few years and a few Texas Chainsaw Massacre movie marathons since then, so I hope I'll be okay. Or at least, at the *very* least, not make a fool of myself.

But we're here and all is right with Hollow Bridge this week, so what could go wrong?

That's the thought in my head as I turn, my lips parted so I can say something about the movie playing on the screen... until all of that flies out of my head at the familiar, curling blond hair and the more familiar laugh coming from the person *under* that hair.

"It's going to be so fucking fake," Evan Davids laughs, sliding his arm more comfortably over his girlfriend's shoulders.

The brunette, Ava York, grins back up at him just as ferociously and says in a voice I'd grown up hearing, "You're such an embarrassment when you drink, Evan. Shut the fuck up for a minute."

But it isn't that sentence that rings through my mind as I stare at them. It's the other one, the last one she'd said to me before the courtroom. Before *everything*, with her eyes locked on mine after I'd said that going out on the ice wasn't going to happen.

*Don't be such a freak, Bailey. Can you at least act normal about this so Daisy has a chance of making friends?*

The flash of memory makes all the guilt that I'd tried to push away—the guilt at that sentence being the thing that tipped me into doing the thing that got Daisy killed—pours back into me like boiling acid.

"Shit," I murmur. Then, taking a step back, I manage to fall to my ass all in the same, unfortunate motion that has more people than I'd like looking over at me.

Including Ava.

# CHAPTER 15

E van turns after her, his gaze on me so I can clearly see
the surprise on his face, then the way he tries to hide a
grin. His mouth opens, and I know he's going to say
something openly scathing, probably as a remark to Ava, and
my stomach twists, hands digging into the soft dirt.

God, I look like an idiot. I brace myself for his words, but
before I can do more than grit my teeth, a shape steps between
Evan, Ava, and me, and Rory bends down until he's in my
personal space.

He's not who I'm expecting. And I certainly couldn't foresee
the kind smile on his lips, or the way he reaches out one hand
for me, fingers curling around mine when I place my now-
scuffed palm in his. "They're not worth it, Bailey," he murmurs
sweetly, helping me to my feet and holding my hand until he's
sure I'm not going to fall over again. "Don't worry about what
some small town loser thinks about you. He's *really* not worth
it. Have you looked at his eyes? They hate his face so much that
they're actively trying to escape from both sides."

The insult is so off the wall, so unexpected and rude, that I
snort out an undignified laugh and let Rory pull me away from

the uneven ground. He reaches out to gently brush my sleeves off, his smile crooked, and when he looks back over his shoulder pointedly, I follow his gaze.

And see Phoenix. He's prowled over to where Evan and Ava still stand, every inch of him seething with menace as he says something soft with a cruel smile etched on his lips. I have no idea what it is, but when he walks away with his hands shoved into his pockets and doesn't give any of us a look from his dark eyes, I admire the effect it's had on the now-silent Evan and unhappy Ava.

She looks at me suddenly, our eyes connecting for half a second before something like indecision crosses her gaze and she shakes her head. It prompts me to drop my gaze to Rory's shoulder as they walk toward the field.

"Are you okay?" Nic is insistent at my side, but before I can answer, Rory turns to look at her, less than impressed judging by his frown.

"You weren't going to say anything?" he asks her, rather impolitely in my opinion. "You saw the way they were looking at her. *Neither* of you were going to stick up for your friend?" He says it quietly enough that people don't stop as they stream around us toward the parking lot or the mazes. But I still busy myself with dusting off my leggings and my ass as much as I can while trying not to look embarrassed.

"You didn't exactly give me a chance," Nic snaps, squaring off against him without hesitation. "You just swooped in like she matters to you and grabbed her off the ground. Should I have wrestled her out of your arms?"

"Maybe," Rory shrugs, looking between them with one hand still on my waist. "That's what best friends do, right?"

"Maybe that's what asshole *boyfriends* do when they're trying to make a point," Nic counters hotly. "Speaking of, your menace is prowling toward the corn. Better stop him before he scares off the kids." She nods in Phoenix's direction, but I'm too busy watching Rory's face for any sign of anger at her words.

But the expression I'm expecting never comes. He just melts into friendliness, his pale gray eyes glittering with amusement. "Oh, come on," he chuckles, suddenly the polar opposite of how he'd just acted toward her. "Give him the credit of being a *sexy* menace. But you're right. I do have to stop him from stealing the souls of the children."

He glances at me one more time, hand rising a few inches and bunching my hoodie up with it, until I can feel his cold fingers against my heated skin and shiver. "You're good?" he asks, and I nod to assure him of it. "Good. Don't let them bother you, okay?"

"Okay," I reply in a tiny voice, feeling suddenly a lot younger than twenty. He grins once more, though the look softens at the edges, then takes off after Phoenix, following him to the field's entrance.

"It's a shame he's that hot," Nolan says with a sigh. I turn to look at him, brows raised for clarification. "It's a shame he's that hot and that much of a dick," Nolan explains. "That's all."

"I don't think he's that much of a dick," I admit. "He seems nicer than Phoenix."

"Which is a rather low bar," Nic points out, looking me over with worried eyes. "Seriously though, you're okay?"

I nod and bite my tongue, not wanting to remind them Phoenix wasn't *always* this quick to anger or so cold. Sure, he was never exactly friendly. Especially when he was saddled with babysitting or dragon duty. But I wonder if there's still a part of him under all of that anger that reminds me of the Phoenix I grew up with.

Unhelpfully, my brain flashes to the night at Agnes' tree. When I'd been the one holding him against it and his *eyes*—

No, it's definitely not a good time to think about that, so I sweep the memory into the ever-growing pile under the mental rug. "What do you want to do first?" I ask, looking between the two attractions. "Field? Before it gets super dark?" Not that it would matter, probably, since I know the trail is lit enough to see by.

"That's what I was thinking," Nic agrees, excitement streaming back into her and, by extension, me as well. We'd come here to have fun, and though it's hard, I shove away the humiliation with one last glance around the area for Ava and Evan.

But wherever they've gone, I can't see them. As I look, I fall into step with Nic, walking with her into the clearing where I can see a girl on the screen in her t-shirt and underwear, doing laundry in a dark room. Yeah, because that's always gone well in movies. Not that I haven't seen this one before, so admittedly, I know the dark room was never her downfall.

The line is short enough, and as soon as we fall into it, I hear screaming from the field that makes me jump, my heart fluttering in excitement as I let a smile creep onto my face. A shiver wracks me seconds later, and I let my sleeves fall as far as they'll go, covering my fingers even when I hold them straight.

God, I love October in Hollow Bridge.

Another group screams, and I hear a chainsaw rev. The sound makes me flinch, and my fingers curl against my palms, but any trembling is from cold and excitement, not fear.

Ahead of us, about seven people up in line, I can see the edge of Phoenix's black and red jacket. But more than that, I can see his back pocket, where Rory has unobtrusively slipped his fingers in for a better handhold as the two of them talk too softly for me to hear.

God, to have a relationship like that. Nic and Nolan are enviable, of course. But I don't have a crush on either of them. Phoenix, though? And now, after his comment and the way he'd helped me to my feet, Rory is definitely a contender for this year's unexpected crush award.

But it's not like either of them is obtainable for a relation-ship. Even if they *would* give dating me a thought, they're so taken with each other that the thought of coming between that is laughable. Not with the way Phoenix's jaw softens just a little when he looks at Rory with his entire focus. And certainly not considering the possessive curl of Rory's fingers in Phoenix's back pocket.

I blink as the line moves, admitting them and the group of three behind them. Rory grins as they enter the maze and, unexpectedly, turns directly to me and sends me a little salute, as if he knew where I was and that I was watching them this whole time.

Which, admittedly, is more than a little embarrassing. I smile painfully back at him just as both of them disappear into the corn maze, and I'm left to listen to Jamie Lee Curtis scream and the crackle of the huge fire.

"I'm glad you thought of this," Nic says, nudging me gently with her elbow to bring me back to the conversation. "I've been craving getting scared lately."

"I haven't," Nolan remarks helpfully, and Nic snorts at his words. "But I'm sure I'll be the loudest one screaming. So if anyone asks who sounds like a toddler, it's definitely me."

"You're not *that* bad" I argue, as the attendant says some-thing into a walkie talkie in her hand. She steps forward and waves the next group of two on, then glances at the three of us and holds up 3 fingers.

We nod and she ushers us in, Nic's hand snaking around mine and Nolan gripping onto her with both arms.

When I see that they've both fallen behind me as we walk in, I can't help but scoff lightly, my stomach tightening. "You want *me* to lead?" I hiss, seeing that the couple is far enough ahead that they'll hit things way before us.

"You're the brave one," Nolan says sagely, nodding like it's a foregone conclusion. "We're just chickens beside you, Bailey."

"Chickens," I repeat, brows raised. "*Chickens,* sure." Normally they're the extroverts. The brave ones. But seeing as I'm sure I've done this to both of them in numerous social situations and made them all but throw me into a fireman's carry when we've gone somewhere I haven't felt comfortable, I decide that I can take one for the team this once.

Sucking in a breath, I start walking. One foot in front of the other, and my heart starts to beat a little more normally *just* as the corn to my left rustles and a short woman comes out, screaming, her head and arms held in a pillory unattached to the ground. Jerking to the side I gasp, her hands rattling the wood as she screams curses and warns us off the sour land.

Because *that* isn't more ominous than it has a right to be or anything. Nolan does scream, but Nic laughs nervously, holding tighter onto me as we navigate around the well-dressed pilgrim still screaming her threats. Another pilgrim sits by the side of the trail in a pillory as well, this one looking a little more foam than wood, and rocks back and forth while she sobs.

"Don't go," she whispers, turning her gaze up to mine. "Don't go. Go *home.*" Somehow it's scarier than the screaming, and I hurry forward, to a narrower section of the trail that leads us to what looks like the remains of a broken village in the cornfield itself.

Finally, after what feels like an hour but was probably closer to fifteen minutes, I stumble out of the maze, my muscles tight with fear, and suck in a deep breath. "Hooooly shit," I murmur, thankful to leave the screaming behind. "Holy *shit.*" Somehow after chainsaws, jump scares, and an actor that had screamed right into my face that I'd regret this, the pilgrim on the ground has stuck with me the most.

"You guys good?" I ask, seeing how pale Nolan is as he holds onto Nic. "Do you want to go get hot chocolate?" I offer, while I could go again. My bones vibrate with adrenaline and I feel like climbing a mountain all of a sudden.

But Nolan gives the line at the hot cocoa stand one look and shakes his head. "Barn first," he mumbles, straightening so he's no longer plastered to Nic's side. "Then hot cocoa. It'll be our reward for not crying like little kids."

"Speak for yourself," Nic laughs, and gestures at me. "Did you see her? She kept cracking a smile. She wasn't about to *cry*."

"Sorry," I admit with a shrug. "This is just my jam, okay? I love everything about Halloween, and I haven't been scared like this in forever." This is the fun kind of fear. The artificial, harmless shit that we all buy into for the season.

"Then by all means." Nic gestures toward the barn and the small line outside of it. "Let's continue with the fun. Afterward, though, we're getting hot chocolate and food on the way home. Mexican food?" She looks between us as we fall into the small line.

"I could go for a quesadilla," I agree, wishing we could go through the maze and the barn again or that we'd signed up for the hayride. Really, I'd forgotten how much I love this place, and the feeling of the cold air on my skin as we go through haunted experiences and past people doing their best to make us scream.

Does it say something about me that this is one of my ultimate ideas of having a good time?

Just before the people in front of us go inside the barn, I realize that Phoenix and Rory aren't in front of us. Though, they could've already been through the barn. Or just not bought tickets. Still, the disappointment in my chest brings a small frown to my lips. But when I see that we'll be very first in line for our group, that disappointment turns to anticipation.

An older man stands up from a stool beside the door, glancing behind us as he listens to someone on his walkie-talkie. "Aren't you guys lucky?" he chuckles, smiling at the three of us. "First in line *and* you get your own turn."

"Own turn?" I repeat, confused until I look behind us and realize he's right. There's no one behind us waiting for the barn. Instead, a large group is slowly coming out of the maze, one of the girls sobbing into her hands while her boyfriend pats her back awkwardly.

"Unless you want to wait for more people," the man continues. "Doesn't bother me either way."

"I want to go in just us," I say quickly, my eyes going to Nic's and then Nolan's. "If you two are okay with that."

"More than okay, as long as you take the back," Nolan supplies, wrapping an arm around Nic's again. "I'll just hold onto her for safety."

"And you can hold my hand if you get scared," Nic adds. "Or just if you want to hold my hand. It's a pretty great hand." She flashes a smile of thanks at the man as he lets us in the door, and this time, I can feel my heart in my throat as we're plunged into an almost absolute darkness.

At least, until my eyes adjust. I stumble, realizing a second later that Nic and Nolan have already started moving down the corridor. Someone slams a door open to their right and screams, scaring both of them into a shout, and I snicker into my hand as I follow them, trying not to get too far behind and miss all of the scares.

Quickly it occurs to me that the barn is *huge*. The maze twists and turns, taking us into different rooms all themed like parts of a slaughterhouse. Blood is spattered on the walls, and the actors are able to get close, nearly pulling us into separate spaces as they scream, threaten, or beg for help.

I don't notice the growing distance between my friends and me until a man walks out of a side room, his heavy boots thundering on the concrete as he looks at me from behind a featureless mask and stares. His breathing is loud enough for me to hear it, and he holds his chainsaw in one hand, a hammer in the other, like neither of them weigh more than balloons.

There's an apron that shines with fake blood on his body, shining in the dim, red-tinted light.

"Oh," I mutter, stopping. "I'm uh, with them. Not the group behind me," I tell him, though I haven't actually heard the group behind me except for a few moments ago, when it sounded like they were incredibly far away.

He doesn't say anything. But he does lay the hammer against one wall and holds the chainsaw in both hands. As I watch, he revs it, coming closer to me as my heart flips, trying to burrow up my esophagus for escape. *Shit.* Seems that up close, I'm just as afraid as ever of a chainsaw coming toward me.

I can't help my step back. Or the one after it as my hand goes out and *sticks* to the wall at my left, which draws a small sound of disgust from my throat. The man keeps coming, getting in my face for long enough that I'm sure my soul has left my body entirely and the rest of me is just waiting to expire from the earth.

"*Go,*" the man growls finally, as the chainsaw motor ebbs.

"Gone," I whisper, trying not to sound terrified as I squeeze around him, my steps turning to a stumbling jog as he revs the chainsaw just as I pass.

I can't see Nolan or Nic, but I try to walk at max speed, doing everything except actually breaking into a run as I head down the slaughterhouse hallway.

At the end, two doors sit open, which is incredibly unhelpful. I have no idea which way to go, and without an actor to menacingly point me in the right direction, it comes down to a guess.

Well, I guess if I get lost, someone will tell me that soon.

I take the right-hand door, following it down another poorly lit hallway until I see a cracked door at the end of it, where dim, red light pours out onto the cement from inside.

"Oh thank god," I breathe, pushing open the door and

trying to slow down. "I really thought I was lost." Sure, I might be talking to the actors like they're going to answer, but still—

The room comes into focus a piece at a time, and it isn't until the last piece clicks into place that I realize why I suddenly don't feel so great.

A masked figure kneels on the floor. Which, given the location, is completely normal. So is the blood-spattered mask he wears, and the knife dark with blood that he holds in his hand.

All normal things for a haunted barn-turned-slaughter-house, even if this just looks like a regular storage room without any decorations other than the red lighting.

The body he leans over is just as normal, with its myriad of stab marks that slowly stain the *SUNY Plattsburgh* hoodie the 'victim' is wearing.

But this isn't a part of the haunted house.

*And the person on the floor isn't an actor.*

Evan-fucking-Davids stares up at the ceiling, choking out gasping breaths as his hands search for something, anything, on his chest to make the bleeding stop. He turns to me, eyes wide, and one hand comes toward me, eyes begging for help as his lips move in the same pattern over and over again, blood trickling from them to stain his red-lit skin.

*Help me. Help me. Help me.*

"Evan?" I breathe, forgetting for a moment that there's someone else in the room. "Holy shit, *Evan*—"

I dive forward, or start to just as the man in all black rises smoothly to his feet, shakes his head, and slides his gloved fingers over the blade to clean it.

For some reason, for some stupid reason, my eyes stay fixed on the blade, on his gloves, and finally on the mask itself. Until the man takes a step toward me and every cell in my body has the same idea.

*Run.*

# CHAPTER 16

*I* *have to find Nic and Nolan.*

Hell, I'll take finding anyone as I scramble down the hallway, too afraid to look over my shoulder. My stomach reels, heart speeding up like a terrified rabbit's in my chest. I scream, wordlessly at first, then manage to turn the sound into something more productive, until I'm begging anyone for help.

Except it all just blends right in. My screams mesh with the others coming from all parts of the barn, and I can't find *anyone* as I run down the red-lit, cement-floored hall with my heart in my throat. Surely there has to be someone here.

A quick glance over my shoulder shows me exactly what I don't want to see. The man in the white mask walks confidently after me, eating up the distance with strides that are worth at least two of mine.

*Fuck.*

The knife glints in the red light, and I can feel goosebumps crawling up my skin. I don't have a lot of time before I end up like Evan; so, I have to find someone.

*Anyone.*

My hands land on a closed door and I grab the handle,

shoving on it so hard I hear the door groan. There's something pressed against it from the other side, but the door isn't locked, so I keep trying.

After all, thanks to me cornering myself at the end of the hall, I don't have anywhere else to go. Another shove gets the door open a few scant inches, but it's not enough for me to crawl through. One more shove, then another, and finally, *finally,* I can cram my body through the opening, shimmying through the doorway into the darkness beyond.

When I'm almost through and prematurely celebrating it by taking a deep breath, however, a gloved hand grabs my wrist, yanking me hard back against the barn. I shriek, stumble, and pull *harder,* trying to make him let go.

The white plastic mask he wears appears in the opening I've made, one that's too narrow for him to fit through, and I swear I hear a soft curse from behind it as he reaches his other hand through, aiming for my hoodie.

"No!" I scream, my free hand coming up to slam his wrist back against the door. This time he definitely says something, though nothing pleasant or informative judging by the garbled sound. I'm finally able to rip my wrist free of his other hand, staggering back as I do while I cradle my wrist to my chest to inspect it for injury.

Nothing. He hasn't cut me, and other than grinding my bones together with his strong grip, I'm fine.

But, *fuck,* I've put myself in a bad situation. This side of the barn backs up against the woods, and even though I look to both sides of the building, all I see are the barn walls or tall sheets of plywood nailed together, to keep people out of the woods I'm currently at the edge of.

Screaming won't help, either. Not with—

The *slam* on the door makes me flinch, and I take a step back when I see that masked man doing exactly what I had just done, using his body weight to open the door faster than I had.

It should take him a few times...but it doesn't. With only two shoves he has it open enough that he can walk through, and I see the hilt of the knife in a sheath at his belt as he stares at me, hood up and mask so fucking creepy in the low light from the barn.

There's a moment where I just stare at him. I take a breath in, and I swear he does the same, like he's staring at me and trying to figure out what to do.

Then my body tenses, and as if we've trained for this, both of us move at *exactly* the same moment. The man lunges for me as I whirl around and take off into the woods, knowing I won't make it to the open side of the barn, or be able to yell loudly enough that someone realizes this isn't part of the show.

I'm not a runner. At least, I wasn't until this moment as my feet eat up the distance between me and the thicker, older trees of the forest that borders most sides of Hollow Bridge. I barely stop to look where I'm going as I run, trying to ignore the way my heart quickly starts to protest me doing any kind of rigorous physical activity.

I should've tried harder in gym class, clearly, but who in the world can predict that they'll be running from a murderer a few years after high school?

"Fuck," I pant, looking behind me to see how close the man is. Not as close as I'd feared, but he's still in sight. Which means there's no way I can stop.

Not unless I can break his line of sight.

I dodge behind a big oak tree, heading for the deeper, darker parts of the woods that can hopefully conceal me better than the open clearings. A root trips me and I nearly go down, instead only getting whipped in the face by branches that make my eyes tear up at the burning sting on my cold skin.

*Ignore it,* I tell myself, swiping away tears as I duck behind another, larger tree. There's a ditch near it that I quietly scramble into, tucking myself into the hollow that's partially covered by the huge roots of the old tree. If I can just stay here and be quiet. If I can just stay out of sight, he should go on by.

It's hard to gulp air silently into my burning lungs, but I do my level fucking best to try. One of my hands clenches, twisting my hoodie tightly in my fingers as I lean back against the side of the ditch and just *breathe*.

Footsteps crashing through the leaves meet my ears and I tense more, if that's possible. I *force* my breathing to calm down until I'm sucking in silent breaths through my nose and letting out air slowly from my mouth. My chest hurts less and less with every breath, and I open my eyes just enough to see out in the darkness ahead of me, though I'm too afraid to move to see where the killer is.

*I can't let him find me.*

For once in my life, my preference for darker clothes is doing me a favor. My shoes, leggings, and hoodie are all black, and thankfully zipped up over my bright red shirt. If I'm still and quiet, I don't think anyone can see me.

The footsteps sound again, slower this time, and finally I see the man come into view, hands at his sides as he searches the area for any sign of me. He even looks *up* into trees, which surprises me. In the movies, killers never look up. Belatedly, I think that it was a good idea not to climb a tree. Not that the possibility had even occurred to me, truth be told.

He searches a few more places, thankfully never once looking toward my sheltered ditch, and then walks further off into the woods, the crunching of his steps in the leaves fading until finally, *finally*, all I can hear are the sounds of the surrounding woods. Wind gusts past my ears, and I swear the night gets colder the longer I sit here. I shiver in my hoodie, wishing not for the first time that I could dress like I know what temperatures and forecasts actually mean.

"Fuck," I whisper after a few more moments, my muscles screaming in protest at the running I'd done. Still trying to ignore it, however, I reach into my pocket and fish out my phone, noting with relief it's not broken or even a little bit cracked.

But I also have no service. The light flares from the screen, nearly blinding me, and I have to squint my eyes against it as I hurriedly turn the brightness down to its lowest setting. "Come on," I whisper, begging it to find even a single bar now that it's not in the pocket of my leggings and smooshed against the dirt. "Please, *please*—"

A sound grabs my attention and I whip around to scan the small clearing, eyes wide as I curse the brightness of my phone that's now made me night blind. There's no way he's come back without me noticing. No way he's seen my phone when he's nowhere near me.

*Right?*

I'm still looking when the first gentle tug comes on my phone. It's not a demand, but a request, and the gentle casualness of it doesn't set off my alarm bells...at first.

Until I remember there should be no one here tugging on *anything* of mine.

When I turn back to my hiding place and my phone, it's so quick that I'm surprised I don't get whiplash from the action.

*It's him.*

Somehow, though, I don't understand how he could be here when he was just walking in the other direction with no sign of being anywhere near me or knowing where I am. But I can't deny the bright white of his mask, or the black hood that obscures his hair.

I shriek. Weakly at first, until he grabs my phone more tightly and yanks it out of my hand, his other coming toward my throat.

But I don't give him the chance to stab me or snap my neck. I give up the losing battle for custody of my phone and throw myself out of the ditch, landing on my hands and knees that scream from the abuse before finally scrambling to my feet.

When I take off running again, however, it's a short-lived journey. The masked man slams into me from behind, both of us skidding in the leaves, until he can roll me over onto my back.

I kick up at him, still shrieking, trying to do anything to not let him capture both of my hands. I can't let him trap me, otherwise I won't get another chance to run.

*He'll kill me.*

It's the fear of my certain death that pumps adrenaline through my veins. Terror at knowing what comes next as my mind oh so helpfully provides me with graphic images of the knife stabbing into me over and over again, like it had with Evan.

*It'll hurt.*

And I'll *die.*

"*Plea*—" I cut the word off hard, nearly biting off the tip of my tongue as well. I'm probably going to die and it's *definitely* going to hurt. But I'm not about to beg him to spare my life. I don't want to go out like that. I want to leave with something, even if it's just the small, very tiny, moral victory of knowing I didn't beg.

Whatever that's worth in the afterlife.

"*No!*" I scream instead, arching up to shriek the word in his face. He hisses a sneer back at me, and finally, unfortunately, manages to straddle my hips, weight pinning me down just as he gets ahold of both of my wrists, transfers them to one hand, and slams them to the ground above my head.

Leaving his other hand free for the knife I can see at his belt.

Tears prickle at my eyes, though I squeeze my lids together hard to lock that down. Crying goes along with begging, and I refuse to do either. My hands ball into fists as I try to push him off of me, but both of us know that it's a futile effort going nowhere.

A touch on my stomach, my skin bared by my shirt and hoodie riding up during our struggle, is enough to unlock my teeth for a soft whimper to pass between them, but it's not a knife.

It's only his gloved fingers. They trail up my skin, dragging my hoodie with them a few inches until moving over it instead. The man repositions, leaning down closer to me until I can feel the smooth coolness of the unblemished white plastic mask slide against my cheek, and his fingers wrap almost lovingly around my throat to tighten ever so slightly.

He's going to strangle me, and in a moment of cold calmness, I can't decide if this is worse or better than getting stabbed.

"Stop fighting me," the man purrs in a cold voice that's slightly muffled by the mask. "I don't want to hurt you."

"Yeah, that's so believable," I spit, wishing I could bite him. "God, I'm so reassured already."

"All I want is to ask you a question."

"If the question is 'stabbing or strangling?' I haven't decided yet, thank you—" But he interrupts me with his fingers squeezing my throat, and shifts until he's looking at me straight on from behind the bright white mask.

*"Who should be the next to die, Bailey?"*

" *hat?*" I breathe, staring up at the blackness of
the sky above me that I can see over his mask. I
know branches obscure parts of it, but in the
darkness and the clouds, I can't tell where the trees end
and the sky begins. The only thing I can see that isn't darkness
is the killer's mask, only inches from my face. "What did you
say to me?"

The hand on my throat moves slowly, and the backs of
gloved fingers trail against my skin, the leather smooth on my
face. It gives me a minute to think, and when I look at his mask
again, something clicks.

I've seen this mask before. Fuck, I've all but *licked* this mask
before, and the thought curls in my stomach. "Do I know you?"
I ask, trying to move my hands and failing. Instead, I settle for
turning away from his fingers, but he only chuffs out a small
laugh and follows my face with his hand. If anything, I'm pretty
sure it's to make the point that I can't get away from him, more
than him wanting to touch me.

"Do I look familiar?" he goads in a soft, low voice. "Does
this *feel* familiar?" He strokes my face again, then moves his

hand to grip my chin to force me to look at him. "Or is it something else you find *familiar*?" He rolls his hips against mine, and I can't help the hitch in my breath when he does.

There's no way he was one of the guys from the party that night. I know for a fact that at least one shop in town sells the masks, so they aren't exactly unique.

"No," I dismiss, wishing he would get off of me. "I don't know you."

He doesn't laugh like I'd expected, or tease me about it. Instead, the man is quiet, though I can't stop looking at the hilt of the knife he still hasn't drawn, or the bright white of the mask that, for some reason, is throwing me off.

I *know* there's something wrong with the picture I'm looking at, but I can't for the life of me figure out what.

"If you're sure," he only replies, and I swear there's a hint of disappointment in his voice. Does he want more fear from me? More *terror* at my impending death. "But you still haven't answered my question."

*What was the question*? God, my brain and heart are working so quickly and at such a terrified level that my thoughts are too scattered for me to do more than just blink at him. "What?" I mumble at last, feeling like an idiot.

"Oh, Bailey," the man sighs, adjusting his grip and leaning back to sit up as much as he can while still holding my arms. "*Bailey*, what am I going to do with you? You have to pay attention. Especially this year. Especially *now*. There are so many mistakes I've made with you tonight, and you haven't even seen any of them, have you?"

Mistakes? I have no idea what he means by *mistakes*. The only mistake he made was not finding me the first time. Or maybe not stabbing me in the barn when he was killing Evan. Still, the word has my brain turning, and it's hard to fully focus on him when it feels like he's given me a puzzle I'm somehow supposed to solve.

My thoughts go out the window when he leans in again, however, face *inches* from mine. I take a deep breath, trying not to cry out or jerk away, and get a nose full of his scent. For a killer, he wears great cologne. It's mellow enough, with hints of vanilla under the sharp spice, and I wonder how much of that is just *him*.

Fuck, I cannot be sniffing a murderer in the middle of the woods while on my back, about to get either stabbed or strangled or both. Inappropriate doesn't even begin to cover it.

"Pay attention, Bailey," he purrs in a voice too-sweet and much too velvety to belong to a murderer. "Because you're going to choose."

"No," I whisper, shaking my head. "I'm not."

"Yes, you are. Who gets to die next? You have to pick, or I'm not letting you leave these woods tonight." *Alive* is implied, I'm sure. Even though he doesn't say it. My heart flutters in my chest, and with the way his body is pressed to mine, I'd be surprised if he doesn't feel it.

"I'm not picking," I say more firmly. "You think I'm just going to name someone in this town for you to *kill*? Are you fucking crazy?"

"I think you're going to give me the name of someone who hurt you and deserves to die," he clarifies. "And I think you're fooling yourself if you're going to pretend you haven't already thought of a name."

*He's right.* The realization is painful with its clarity, and I cut my gaze away, trying to turn my head to stare at the leaves instead of him. But he doesn't let me. The man holds my jaw in his leather-gloved hand and makes me face him, though I stare at the black sky instead of the white mask.

I do have a name.

And that makes this so much worse.

"What's their name?" he purrs so sweetly that I feel it in my bones. "Come on, Bailey. This isn't difficult." He presses the mask against my throat, as if he can actually feel the skin of my neck and shoulder against his own.

"I'm not doing this. You can just kill me." My fingers tighten into fists and I twist my wrists, looking for a way out. *"I'm not doing this."*

"Yes, you are." I hate how certain he sounds. How sure of himself, and how sure of *me* he is.

"No."

"And I'm not going to let this devolve into an argument. I'm not *arguing* with you, Bailey, do you hear me?" Yeah, I hear him and the stupidly hot voice he's using, though it's barely more than a whisper.

"How do you know my name?" I ask instead, moving my legs to see what I'm working with. Not much, as he proves when he readjusts his weight to pin me more thoroughly, just to prove he can.

"Does it matter?"

"It sure as hell does if you're actually trying to get me to name someone in this town for you to *kill*. And why are you doing this?" I jerk away from him just so I can stare at the mask, wishing I could grab it with my teeth and pull it off of his stupid face so I could glare at him, spit on him, or both.

Well, okay, I probably don't have the guts to spit on the man with a knife who just offed Evan in a storage room.

Fucking *Evan*.

I don't feel bad. I can't, and that just makes this worse.

"One day, I'm sure you'll be in my position." He rolls his hips into mine and nearly makes me choke, in case I was unclear about what his *position* was until this moment. "And then you can ask me all the questions in the world, *Bailey*." I hate the way he says my name. Like he's goading me with the knowledge of it. "But unfortunately, the odds aren't in your favor tonight. So tell me who it's going to be."

"I could wait you out," I reply, just because I can and I'm not giving him a name.

*Especially the one that's at the front of my mind, begging to fall from my lips like a stone.*

"You aren't that patient," he chides, cradling my face in one hand easily. "And you're cold."

"You're warm," I quip. "It evens out."

His head tilts at that, and I swear he's studying me like he can't figure out what my problem is. Though honestly, if he could, he would deserve a lot more money than my therapist gets. But whatever his thoughts are, he's quiet as he looks at me, as he studies my face like I've stumped him.

For a few precious seconds, I'm sure that I've won. If he's not going to stab me, then I'm not going to give him a name. He should leave before I do something menacing. Like figure out a way to bend my knee backward and kick him.

Then a scoff grabs my attention, and I realize instantly that it hasn't come from the man above me.

"You should've known she wasn't going to give up that easily." A man strides out from behind the large oak tree, the same mask on his face and dressed in all black, though his hood is down. As I watch, he unsheathes a bloody knife from his belt and flips it up into the air, catching it by its hilt. "I told you to let me do it. You're too *nice* to her." He sneers the word like an insult, and the man above me makes a grating noise of displeasure.

He says something then, too, but I don't hear it in the whirring of my racing thoughts.

Because the man standing up has blood on his mask and he isn't whispering. *And I know that voice.* But if I know his voice, then I know who's on top of me as well.

"Fuck," I whisper, drawing their attention down to me and interrupting whatever conversation they were having. "Are you *fucking* kidding me? Now I really wish I could hit you."

"What?" he asks, though now that I know who he is, the growl in his voice is obvious. I've heard it a thousand times before, and only my adrenaline and fear have kept me from figuring it out so far. And God, now that I know, the pieces of the puzzle won't stop sliding into place.

Of course there's two of them.

*There were always two of them.*

"Were you really going to stab me?" I ask, leaning my head back so I can look at the man leaning against the tree. "In the barn?"

He doesn't answer. He just looks at me, still flipping the knife.

"Are *you*?" I challenge, looking at the one on top of me with much more bravery in my voice than what I feel. My heart still thrums against my ribs, and it's so hard not to struggle to get him off of me once again. I'm still afraid of him. Of *them*. But not quite so heart-poundingly terrified.

"Do you think I am?" he asks. "Do you think I haven't killed people?" He lifts a hand to comb through his hair, pushing his hood back in the process.

"I think if I told your mother you chased me through the woods, took my phone, and pinned me on the cold ground, she'd kill *you*."

"He didn't chase you," the other man corrects from where he leans against the tree above us. "He's just the one who caught you. *I'm* the one that pushed you to that ditch and made sure you stayed there for him."

"Wow, gold star," I tell him, voice dripping with sarcasm. "Let me go home and I'll make you one out of aluminum foil to glue on that stupid mask." He doesn't reply. Instead, he pushes away from the tree, sheathing the knife a second before he falls to his knees just above my pinned arms. My breath catches, and I wonder if I've gone too far with the one of them I don't know well at all as his bloodstained mask looms closer and closer to my face, then dips towards my ear.

"You didn't think my mask was so stupid when you were in that bathroom begging us to *fuck you*," Rory purrs. "Or have you forgotten so soon?"

I swallow hard, looking at my situation through something other than the lens of indignant fear that thrums through my veins. I really am in a bad spot. Especially if Rory decides he doesn't like me enough to put up with me.

*But I'm not about to give them the name of someone to kill.*

"It was you at the park, wasn't it?" I ask, realizing suddenly that Rory is much more likely to have been the one there. I would've recognized Phoenix's voice, I think, and Rory is so much more...

Sadistic.

The auburn-haired killer tilts his head to the side and I'm sure he's grinning behind the mask. It's certainly good enough for me, even if he doesn't answer outright.

"You said you were cold, right?" he goes on, dismissing my question with one of his own, and sits up to push Phoenix's hand off of my wrists. "So, so cold. Right, darling?"

Suddenly, I don't want to be warm anymore. But he doesn't give me a chance to tell him I'm fine, because in seconds he has me sitting up. Phoenix pushes back so he's trapping my legs instead of holding me down. Rory settles me in the v of his thighs, yanking my hands tight in one of his before I can do anything, and rips the mask off with the other.

It feels final, somehow. And the feeling doubles down when Phoenix removes his more carefully and lays it to the side. I can barely see his face in the darkness. Hell, I can barely see *either* of them in the darkness, but I feel it when Rory's mouth grazes the side of my throat.

"Rory..." Phoenix's growl of warning is soft, but his boyfriend doesn't stop what he's doing. His hand does let go of my wrists, though, so he can dig both sets of fingers into my hoodie and grip my ribs hard enough I worry they'll break as he holds me against him.

"What?" Rory asks, voice not nearly as soft or as careful. "She's cold, Phoenix. I'm helping. Aren't you always telling me I should be more helpful? And who better to practice on than precious, sweet Bailey?"

A shiver trails up my spine as he says my name, and I take a deep breath that catches in my throat as his teeth sink into my skin, but he pulls away to whisper his next words in my ear loudly enough for Phoenix to hear as well.

"I guess the question now is how long are you going to keep us here before you tell us who we get to kill for you?"

# CHAPTER 18

"I'm not keeping you here," I murmur into the darkness. "*I'm* not doing anything—" I break off with a hiss when his teeth sink into the juncture of my neck and shoulder, and I can feel him sucking a mark into existence on my skin to prove that he was there.

My hands reach up to do something—whether that's to stop him or motivate him to keep going, I'm better off not knowing —but Phoenix catches them, fumbling in the darkness until he's holding my wrists again, his body still pinning my legs to the ground.

"Rory," he warns, his voice sounding forced and more than a little strange. "What are you doing?"

"What you've wanted to do since you left her in this shitty town," Rory replies hotly. "Besides, she clearly doesn't want me to stop." He kisses up my jaw, nipping at my lip to draw a whimper from me.

"How do you know?" I ask, making the mistake of turning into him, our mouths brushing when I form the words.

But he doesn't pull away. He stays there, so I feel every shape of every word when he says, "Because if you wanted me to stop, you'd tell Phoenix a name. Don't play dumb. You know who you want to see dead in this town just as much as he does. If you don't like this, then give us one. We'll kill them, anyway. You're barely contributing at all."

Yeah, but there's a big difference between not contributing and *barely* contributing. Like, jail time difference. I open my mouth to present my argument, knowing it won't convince him anyway, until Phoenix moves, his shape only barely visible as he shifts to press one knee between my thighs, shoving them wide enough that he can sit between them with my knees on either side of his waist.

I kick at him, surprised at whatever the hell he's doing, but with how he's sitting, I can't even do that much. Hell, I barely feel balanced with the way I'm perched between them, most of my weight on Rory's chest as he holds me against him.

"What are you doing, Phoenix?" I demand, hating the small waver in my voice that belies the fear I feel.

"Making sure Rory doesn't hurt you, obviously," he scoffs. "Making you play your part, if we're being technical." I have no idea what he means for all of two seconds, until he releases my hands to grip my waist, gloves sliding against the skin that's been exposed from how Rory holds the fabric of my hoodie in his grip.

"Why?" I demand, feeling more than seeing him as he leans in. My brain is frantic and scattered—I wonder if I'm dead or dying and this is the fancy fever dream my mind has created to keep me from realizing it.

But if this is a dream, then why are they so *warm*? Why can I feel the pressure of his knee that rubs at the apex of my thighs, and the discomfort of my protesting ribs when Rory pulls me more tightly against him?

"For fun?" It's Rory who answers first, predictably, as he jerks my hoodie and shirt upward with one hand, his other disappearing. Though from Phoenix's soft exhale of surprise, I have a pretty good idea of where it's gone. "For legal reasons? If you're our accomplice, you can't tell. And I'm pretty sure giving us a name would put you *firmly* in the accomplice category."

"I'm not giving you a name," I remind him, in case he's forgotten since the last time I said it ten seconds ago.

"Well then, I don't think I'll stop," he murmurs against the shell of my ear. "And I'm pretty sure if we fuck you out here in the woods, you're still an accomplice. So I get my way no matter what."

"I'm *definitely* not letting you fuck me," I say, not feeling as strongly about that statement as I should.

"You're not? Really? Not even if I ask nicely? Not even if I make you come on my fingers, or hold you while Phoenix fucks you with his tongue? He's so good with his mouth, and he's wanted to taste you so badly since that night in the bathroom." I hate how his words make me feel. I hate the way my stomach coils, and how part of me seeks out his warmth every time he touches me. Then when he pulls away, I shiver and sorely miss the heat of his skin, but he shushes me like I've made a physical sound and leans back in, cheek brushing mine. "Don't worry, Bailey. I'm not going anywhere. I'll share my warmth with you for as long as it takes."

"You're lying," I find myself saying, my voice unsure and shaking.

"About what, sweet girl?"

"About him. About *Phoenix.*" I feel the black-haired man stiffen between my thighs, taken aback by my words.

"What about me?" he asks, cutting Rory off before he can answer.

"You've never been interested in me," I shoot back. "I had a crush on you for *years* when we were kids." There's no use denying it now. And it's better ammunition for me to throw back at him. "And you never said a *word.*"

"That's because I would've hurt you. And I was too *old* for you," he protests. "You were sixteen when I left. What was I supposed to do? Kidnap you?"

"You could've, I don't know, given me some kind of indication you didn't hate me for what happened to *Daisy*," I snap, and immediately, instantly wish I hadn't.

His hands tense on my skin for a few seconds, though I can feel him stroking his thumbs over my hips. He's so quiet I can hear all three of us breathing, and even Rory seems to be waiting for him to say...something.

But it's me who breaks first. "I'm sorry. I shouldn't have said—"

"If we took things any further at that party, I thought we'd break you," he interrupts, his voice completely cool and unaffected. "I thought if you knew it was me, you'd stop me. That you'd taste what we wanted, and you'd *run*. I didn't think you'd beg us for more. We're not people you beg for more, Bailey."

God, I wish I could see him in the dark, but it's just too pitch-black to see more than outlines and some movements. He shifts, and I can feel his warmth crowding closer, until he's almost as close as Rory is, if that's even possible.

"You want to go home?" he purrs in my ear, opposite the one Rory's teeth have found. "You want us to let you go that badly?"

I nod my head, knowing both of them can feel it.

"Then tell me to go back to that farm and slit Ava's throat."

"No," I reply, before I can even think things through. "*No, Phoenix.*"

"Fine." He strangely doesn't sound very put out by it. "Don't." I feel him moving and I start to say something, but when his lips find mine, I forget very quickly what that was.

Phoenix kisses like it's a competitive sport. That's the first thought that crosses my mind as he urges my lips to part like it's the easiest thing in the world. He uses Rory to his advantage, hand cupping my face as he leans over me, pushing more of me against his boyfriend's chest so I'm not holding myself up at all. For his part, Rory's arms encircle me more firmly, and at some point, I've closed my eyes as Phoenix devours my mouth like he's always known exactly what I enjoy.

His hand on my face moves, urging me to follow until my head is tilted *just* enough...and I'm definitely not expecting Rory's mouth on my neck, on the same side he'd marked my skin already, lips and tongue tasting every inch.

*Fuck.* I've got to get them to stop. Guilt, and something else, keep the name in my head sealed behind my lips, locked in silence.

"I wonder how hard I have to kiss you," he purrs, pulling back just slightly.

"W-what?" I gasp, not thinking straight, if at all.

"I know you have a name for me. It doesn't have to be Ava," he continues. "I wonder how hard I have to kiss you to taste the name on your tongue, Bailey."

"When you figure it out, don't ruin the fun," Rory chuckles. "I want to find out, too." He raises my hoodie again, and I shiver when the night air finds my skin.

"Don't," I protest. "It's too fucking cold to take it off."

"You don't trust me to keep you warm?" the brunet behind me teases. "I bet when I make you come, you'll be begging for me to take this off." I don't know if that's a promise or a threat, but it sends a shiver down my spine, straight to the heat pooling between my legs, either way.

"You know he's right," Phoenix states, some of the cool aloofness back in his voice. "The longer you let us play with you, the more you seem to have wanted it all along." He grabs my thighs, fingers digging into my leggings. "*I'll* keep you warm, Bailey."

I don't realize what he means until his hands *jerk* my leggings down. He doesn't even bother with my shoes, only jerks them off over one of my sneakers through sheer willpower alone, leaving the other alone.

"Shit!" I squeak, barely able to do more than twist in Rory's grip. Just as I knew it would be, it's *cold* without my fleece-lined leggings covering my skin. "What are you doing?"

"Exactly what Rory told you I've wanted to do since we came back to this town," he *growls* against my thigh. "I want to taste your fucking cunt, Bailey."

His words do more for me than any porn I've ever watched. It does more than it has a right to, and I can feel my thighs tremble when he pushes them upward, hitching them over Rory's knees so I'm spread wide between them, with only my underwear left as a barrier between us.

"I can't..." I trail off, barely knowing what to do with my hands. Phoenix sits up, pressing against me to kiss me sweetly once more.

"You don't want my mouth on you?" he asks, and there's a serious note in his otherwise playful tone that surprises me. "You'd better tell me now, then. It'll be a lot harder for me to pull myself away from you later."

The silence that follows as both of them wait for an answer is the longest and *shortest* silence of my life. I fidget, knowing they can feel all of it.

The worst part about it? I do want this. And they know it. They know it because every *nerve*, every *cell* in my body, knows with certainty that I want them. Even though I didn't until about five minutes ago. I may be able to make my mouth say the word *stop*, but all three of us will know I don't mean it.

So instead, with my lips close enough to his that I feel them with every brush of every word, I say, "I'm not giving you a name, Phoenix Hawthorne. No matter what either of you do."

Instantly I feel his smile, the way it curves upward. I feel the lack of softness in it, and somehow the greed as well, before he shoves my knees wider and presses his ungloved fingers against my inner thigh, skimming them up toward my center.

"Then we'll just have to make you, won't we?"

"*Fuck,* those are the best words I've heard all night," Rory groans, his hands back on my hips, bunching up my hoodie until he finds skin. "Next time, I'm going to chase you to our hotel. I'll kidnap you," he rambles, his gloves gone as well as his fingers explore my stomach, and finally trace the line of my bra. "I want to rip your clothes and take my time playing with you."

"You sound like a serial killer," I inform him dryly, but Phoenix only chuckles.

"He is," my childhood babysitter informs me, his fingers finally hooking in my underwear teasingly.

"He's killed Evan and..." I think back, mathing out my nights. "Jack, right? I don't think two murders makes you a serial killer."

"Oh, Bailey..." Rory's sigh in my ear is accompanied by the feel of something sharp and metallic on my thigh.

"Who in the world told you that I've only killed *twice?*" In an instant one of them cuts through my underwear, yanking the scraps off of my legs as Phoenix's fingers find me again, this time with nothing between us.

"B-but—" the new information makes me stammer, and I reel. "But Phoenix—"

"*Phoenix* has only killed twice," Rory agrees, one hand leaving my stomach to trail down my body. He finds Phoenix's fingers and his own replace them, spreading me wide as I feel Phoenix's hair brush my thigh, then his lips. "He killed Emily. I was so proud of him. He did so fucking good without me. That's why you saw me walking around in the woods with your dead crow at the fairgrounds. I was worried about him."

He, honest to God, *giggles* against my ear. "I told him that night we could just kidnap you. He wanted you so *badly.*"

"Fuck, Rory, you're going to scare her off," Phoenix

murmurs, and I jump at how close his face is to where Rory holds me open.

"No, I'm not," Rory argues. "I won't scare her off. I know how much you want to keep her."

"You can't...you can't *keep* me," I protest, hyper aware of Phoenix's breath against my slit. I can't stop the whimper that escapes my lips when he licks a line up to my clit, and my thighs tense where they're hooked over Rory's legs. "I'm a person. That's not how it works."

"We can't?" It's Phoenix who answers, and some of that darkness that's laced Rory's tone all night has found its way to him. "Not even if we promise to take such good care of you?"

I swear I have something good to say. Some valid argument waits at the tip of my tongue, but instead I *yelp* when his mouth finds my slit. His tongue licks at me teasingly, both of his hands on my thighs, and seconds later I feel his tongue press into me, licking every part of me he can.

When he moans in appreciation, Rory shifts behind me, letting me feel his hardness that rubs against my lower back. There's no way in hell Phoenix's tongue should feel as good as it does. But somehow he defies reality as he holds my thighs in his iron grip and tongue fucks me lazily, like he really is willing to do this all night.

But it isn't until Rory's middle finger finds my clit that I can't keep still. My hips move, and when I open my mouth for another protest, his other hand leaves my stomach, three fingers pressing insistently between my barely parted lips until I can't do more than moan.

"Suck on my fingers, Bailey," he breathes, biting at my ears. "I want to know what it'll feel like when I fuck your mouth." I shudder at his words, drawing a breathy laugh from him as he thrusts his fingers languidly in and out of my mouth.

"Does she taste good?" he asks, effectively keeping me quiet with his fingers so I have no choice but to hear the soft sounds

Phoenix makes between my thighs. "You're not saying much, so I'm guessing she does."

"You want to find out?" his boyfriend asks, pulling away for just long enough to say that before his tongue dips into me once more.

"Make her come first." Rory talks like this is a regular conversation. Like he isn't holding me open while his boyfriend tongue fucks me and his fingers aren't keeping me from doing more than making embarrassing noises against them.

"You're impatient," Phoenix accuses, one of his hands leaving my thighs. "You're going to make me rush."

"Then rush. I'll kidnap her for you sometime this week and you can eat her out as much as you want. But *I'm* starting to get cold too, and unless one of you is going to let me fuck you, I don't see myself warming up anytime soon." He turns when he says it, nipping at my ear. "Like I said, though," he tells me, knowing I can't do more than try not to choke on his long fingers. "I'll gladly fuck you if he wants to drag this out. It would be so easy. You're already right here. You're already sucking on my fingers, and I bet I could open you up for me without you minding much. Can I fuck your ass while he takes his time with your pussy, Bailey? I promise I'll be gentle this time."

"She's probably never let anyone do that," Phoenix says, his fingers sliding into me to replace his tongue. His thumb slides against Rory's finger, and it's so strange for both of them to rub my clit that I can't help the tiny sound that leaves me.

"You haven't, have you?" Daisy's brother purrs. "Poor little Bailey. Stuck with having to pick from the guys still in Hollow Bridge. I bet none of them have ever fucked you how you really wanted, have they? Have they ever made you come more than once?"

He's not really asking. If he was, I'm pretty sure Rory would have removed his fingers.

"Maybe you should let me be your first. I'll be so nice," he says, then adds a third finger to my pussy, fucking me with them until it feels like my muscles can't get any tighter.

"I let you taste her cunt, Phoenix. I'm even holding her open for you. But you have to give me that at *least*." Rory can't help but laugh. "You have to give me *something*."

"I'll give you the chance to taste her when she comes. I think that's pretty nice of me, since she was mine first."

*His* first? I'm not anyone's, last time I checked.

"Possession is nine-tenths of the law."

"Yeah? Well then, she's still mine, since it's my fingers in her perfect little cunt."

He twists his fingers and I moan, nearly choking on Rory's fingers as my head falls back against his shoulder. From my barely open eyes, I see the clouds move off some, exposing a half-moon that fills the small clearing with just enough light that I can finally see both of their faces.

They're way too pretty to be real. Or to be *real* serial killers, at least. Phoenix ducks his head back down, mouth sealing against my slit once more as Rory continues to rub my clit.

If I could, I'd tell them that I'm close. But instead, I just whine around Rory's fingers, hips arching into Phoenix's face as his tongue sinks into my folds, nearly pressed against his fingers.

"Come for us," Rory breathes, hotly against my ear. "Come on, sweet girl. Precious *Bailey*. I want to find out what it tastes like when he makes you come with his mouth. And I'm so sick of waiting." He rubs my clit harder, his fingers spreading on my tongue to take up more room in my mouth.

Even Phoenix feels impatient between my thighs. His fingers curl, fucking into me hard, and when he and Rory manage to match up their movements, I'm done for. I shriek around Rory's fingers, my head against his shoulder as they throw me off of the proverbial cliff I was barely hanging onto.

My muscles clench around Phoenix's fingers, and I nearly bite Rory's, though I stop myself before I hurt him.

Not that I think he'd care.

But Phoenix doesn't stop moving his fingers for almost a minute. Rory continues to rub my clit lazily, even as I plead wordlessly for them to stop. It's too much, after my orgasm rolls through me, and it's starting to become almost painful.

"We'll let you get away with just one this time," Phoenix murmurs finally, sitting up and with one hand he catches Rory's hair, pulling him over my shoulder for a kiss before shoving his wet, glistening fingers into his boyfriend's mouth.

And it's way hotter than it should be. I'm grateful for the moonlight that lets me watch them, and I'm shocked when Rory hollows his cheeks around Phoenix's fingers, sucking on them like he's savoring every bit of my taste.

It makes my stomach clench, and heat to pool between my thighs again, even though there's no way I can go for another round right now.

When I blink, I realize both of them are looking at my face, and I'm not sure how I feel about the expression I find in the depths of their gazes.

It doesn't exactly bode well for me, I'm pretty sure.

"You want to find out how you taste?" Phoenix purrs, and doesn't give me a chance to answer before Rory's fingers are gripping my jaw, pulling me back against his shoulder so that Phoenix can loom over me. "Open your mouth."

"What—"

"Open your *fucking mouth*, Bailey. And stick out your tongue."

My breath stutters in my throat, heart hammering against my ribs as my fingertips tingle. I don't understand what he wants, or what he's going to do, but I still hesitate before doing what he'd said, mouth opening.

"I said stick out your tongue," he adds, too-sweetly to be genuine. "Or did you not hear me?"

It's terrifying when he's this hot. And the sheer amount of absolute sureness in his voice makes me open my mouth wider so I can stick out my tongue.

"Good girl," he praises softly, so softly, and leans in closer just as Rory's hand on my jaw tightens and Phoenix, honest to God, *spits* in my mouth. I move, or try to, and nearly spit out the mess of my cum and both of their saliva right back out before Rory's hand moves to keep my mouth shut, still not letting me move.

"Swallow it," the serial killer hisses in my ear. "Swallow it, Bailey, right now. Come on, don't you want to be the *good girl* he just called you?"

But I still whimper, my throat locked, unwilling to swallow.

"Swallow it or you'll be on your knees in the cold leaves with my cock down your throat," Rory threatens in a soft, velvety purr. "Your fucking choice."

I swallow with a shudder, eyes never leaving Phoenix's. A second later, Rory moves his hand, though not enough for me to pull away from the two of them.

"Good girl," Phoenix murmurs again, pressing closer. "Even if it was too difficult to make you do it. But that's okay, huh?" He skims a finger up my face, thumb stroking under my eye. "We'll just have to practice until you do it when I tell you for the first time."

"No—"

"*Shhh.*" He barely seems to notice that Rory's fingers have slipped into me, or that he's teasingly, lightly, fucking me with them. "We're not done yet." He cups my jaw, smiling so, so kindly. "They'll all die anyway, Bailey. They all deserve it. So what's the harm? Just tell me a name. I've even *told* you what to say. I just want to hear you say it."

But I shake my head, gasping when Rory's fingers sink deeper into me.

"Give me a name, Bailey," Phoenix all but hums, barely reacting when Rory pulls his fingers free and swipes them across my cheeks.

"I *can't*," I gasp, feeling pliant and willing when Rory pulls me in for a kiss while Phoenix watches.

"Just one," he murmurs, pulling away. "Just say *Ava*. He wants to take care of her next, anyway. You'll barely be doing anything wrong."

"I *can't*," I beg, my eyes falling onto Phoenix's.

"Yes, you can." He sounds way too sure of that. Way too calm as he pulls me in for a kiss of his own, Rory trailing his mouth down my shoulder. Phoenix nips my lower lip, and I want to cry at how their mouths on my skin make me feel. "Just say—"

"*Jayden*," I gasp, locking gazes with him, my own eyes impossibly wide as my mouth betrays me. "I want you to kill Jayden next."

# CHAPTER 19

*We can't walk back with you.* The statement from Phoenix had been pretty obvious, and a conclusion I'd come to before he'd even said it. But he'd helped me put my clothes back on and brushed off the dirt and leaves from them with the weirdest look on his face that I couldn't glance away from.

It almost seemed like...fondness? Like he enjoyed putting me back together after taking me apart. Rory hadn't helped. Only stood behind me, an arm hooked around my waist intermittently, or a hand in my hair when he'd shift to do something else. Like he, too, wanted to touch me for as long as possible.

*I don't get it.* I'd wanted to say that out loud, but I'd barely been able to say anything at all. It's only now, as I trudge through the trees using my phone as a light, that all the questions and statements bubble up to my lips, begging to be spilled and answered. But now that I'm alone, there's no one to ask them to.

I follow the directions they'd given me on how to get back, my legs and my brain buzzing with exhaustion. It takes more out of me than it should to find the barn again, and an extra five minutes to trudge around it, bringing my phone up to my ear with the light off once I don't need it anymore.

Nic's phone rings once, just as my eyes fall on the flashing lights of the ambulance and the stretcher being wheeled toward it.

Only, there's no zipped up plastic bag being transported to the local morgue. Instead, the shape on it is uncovered, an oxygen mask over their nose. Two paramedics rush to the ambulance, a third already in it, and I watch as they load Evan inside, with a sick realization in my stomach.

*Evan isn't dead.*

And he saw me in that storage room.

"*Hello?*" The urgency in Nic's voice makes me think that isn't the first time she's tried to get my attention, and my eyes scan the outdoor area outside of the barn.

"Hey, Nic," I sigh, knowing I sound as tired as I feel. "Where are you?"

"*Where am I? Where the fuck are you?!*" she screeches into my ear. "*You disappeared and then someone found a body—I thought you were dead, Bailey!*"

I have to make a decision. *Now.* Otherwise, I'll be hiding lies or making up stories later, unless I can cement the details here and now of what I plan to tell people.

"I almost was," I tell her, letting my voice wobble. It hurts a little to lie to her. She's been my best friend for years. But on the other hand… Phoenix's face flashes through my brain, and the brush of his lips in my memory is perfection. As is the ghost of Rory's touch that I can conjure up, and his teeth on my ear, and —*Fuck.*

There's a hickey on my throat. I can feel it there, and know that if it's not already incredibly visible, it will be soon. Which means I'll have to lie about it, to both Nic and whoever else I have to talk to. "Somehow, I got lost in the slaughterhouse. The barn," I explain, before she prompts me to. "Also seriously, *where are you?*"

"*Near the police cars.*" I look around, but don't see any police cars. "*On the other side of the ambulance. Come over here. They'll want to talk to you since you were in there, too.*"

Yeah, and thankfully, at least, I have some idea of what I'm going to say piecing itself together inside my skull. "Okay," I agree without a fight. "Okay, I'm coming over there." At least this means I don't have to say it all right now. I can tell her when I tell the police. Hopefully.

I hang up and shove my phone in my pocket, wishing I could do something to cover the mark on my throat. I also wish that Phoenix was in my contacts, or that I had any way to get ahold of him. But as it is, he'll have to find out on his own.

The two cop cars are exactly where Nic told me they would be. As I approach, my fingers flex then clench into loose fists against my hoodie sleeves, and I hear what sounds like cracking, high sobs.

Sure enough, when I look over at two female detectives talking to someone, I see Ava's face screwed up in misery, cheeks dirty and tearstained as she explains her side of the night's events to the police.

I expect a surge of sympathy, or at least something close to it. I expect *something* to happen when I look at her. Empathy isn't my strong suit, but surely, even I'm not so bad as to feel nothing for Ava nearly losing Evan.

And yet here I am, wishing he was dead, so I wouldn't have to go through the trouble of making up stories about what happened after I ran out of the barn. God, what is *wrong* with me? I should be thrilled that he's alive. All life is precious and...whatever.

But I'm not.

And I'm too tired to feel particularly bad about it tonight. Before I can look away, however, Ava's eyes find mine, somehow knowing exactly where I am. She stares at me with that hope-less look, and I just don't know what to say, or how to respond.

So I start walking again until I find Nic and Nolan speaking softly to a male cop that nods and takes notes. That seems like the place to be, and I trudge over to them, my feet dragging in the grass until finally Nic looks up, her eyes wide.

"Bailey!" she gasps, breaking away and slamming into me with her arms going to my shoulders in a hug. I wince, too sore and worn out for this, but hug her back awkwardly, anyway. "Holy *shit*, Bailey. I really thought you were dead."

"Yeah, same," I admit, glancing at the cop who I know is listening. "But maybe hug me a little less? I'm really, really exhausted."

"Sorry, *sorry.*" She pulls away and looks me over, her gaze critical. "You're filthy," she informs me, and I look down to see what she sees, in the light from the cars, the ambulance, and the lampposts that *Field of Nightmares* has littered around the place.

I'm a mess. My palms hurt, aching in the background like a constant, thrumming sensation in my mind. The knees of my leggings are ripped, though thankfully my skin isn't bloody or raw. My hoodie isn't much better. Dirt is streaked across it, and I'm sure my hair and face are just as bad.

Thankfully, she doesn't look too hard at the mark on my neck barely covered by my hoodie. But before I can open my mouth to say something or ask to speak to the officer, a familiar voice from behind me makes my teeth clench.

"Do you have a minute to talk, Miss Scott?" I would know Detective Angleson's cold tone anywhere, and I have to fight to suppress the shudder it urges from my body.

Fuck. This night really is getting as bad as possible.

"Yes," I say tiredly, pivoting to look at the blonde detective. Her hair is up in its scary smooth ponytail again, and I let my shoulders sag in exhaustion. I'm too tired to protest. Too tired to do more than *exist* and I want her to know it. "Whatever you want. Then I just want to go home."

She looks me over and nods, glancing around until she spots an empty picnic table. "Let's go sit. You look like you need to."

I'd be a lot happier going home, but I follow her with another nod, falling onto my side of the picnic table with a long sigh. "This night is awful," I say, letting my voice carry my exhaustion. It's not hard to play the part. My brain supplies me with all the expressions I'm sure I need. Of the mannerisms, attitudes, and even tone of voice I've heard in others. Sure, I may not be able to instinctively and naturally pick up on the moods of my friends or, hell, anyone. But I've been alive long enough with a brain that works weird to pick out little details that I can apply to myself in this situation.

"You were in the barn with your friends, right? I hear they couldn't find you." It's not a very subtle hint to tell her what happened, but I take a deep breath and press my hands to the table, eyes finding hers.

*And* the people behind her. Near the large fire that still roars in its pit, Rory and Phoenix have reappeared, both looking shocked as they talk to an officer who writes down whatever they say.

I know they'll be able to cover for each other. After all, that's the joy of there being two of them in this. And the point of that detail, if I had to guess. Especially since when they do kill, they wear the exact same outfits.

"We went in together. It was only the three of us in our group. Just a weird timing between people being there and at the corn maze, you know?" She nods even though it's not a real question, a pen in her hand that she uses to jot down sloppy notes on a small notepad in front of her. "Some huge guy got between us. Did his little show and tried to scare me for long enough that when he moved, I couldn't see them. I didn't see *anyone.*" This part is easy, for the sheer fact that it's not a lie.

Not yet, anyway.

*I could turn them in.* It would be easy, I think, as I recite being lost and looking down the red lit hallways for Nic and Nolan. It would be so fucking easy to tell her that it's both of them, together. They're murderers, and obviously they're going to kill again.

I should stop them.

I could do it so easily, and they wouldn't have time to know it was me.

But instead of telling her what happened in the woods, I paint a different picture. I tell her about running from the side door, about how hard it was to get open and how quickly the man came after me. I even tell her about what it had felt like to see Evan. How I'd thought he was a prop at first, but when I'd tried to help him, the man with the knife hadn't let me. My voice shakes, but it's not from fear. It's from tiredness so bone-deep that I can only assume my adrenaline is the only thing that's been keeping me going this long.

No, I'm not afraid or traumatized by what happened tonight. But I need Detective Angleson to think I am.

"I hid in this, uh, ditch?" I wave my hand, trying to explain the embankment and the roots of the large tree that I had hid in. "Waited there for him to go away. I was so scared—" I drag in a breath, eyes closing hard. "I thought he'd find me. Or that he'd come back. I hid for too long, I know, but I couldn't come out. I was *so afraid* he was right there waiting for me."

"What did the mask look like again?" Detective Angleson asked, her pen moving fast across the paper. "You said it was white?"

"White with blood on it, yeah. Just the same Halloween mask I see at all the stores. You know, the one some craft stores sell to for you to self decorate? And he was all in black, otherwise. Hood up and everything. I'm sorry." God, I hope I sound like I'm telling the truth. I hope I sound genuine. "I wish I'd gotten a better look." She won't buy any sorrow I have for my former friends.

But she'll buy it if I frame my emotions as fear for my own life.

"But why come after me?" I all-but whisper. "I don't know what I did to him. Why would anyone want to kill me?"

"Not even Phoenix Hawthorne?" God, she's like a dog with a bone with him. Unless she knows something more than she should, I have a feeling it's just well-placed suspicion after seeing how he acted when Daisy died.

"He says he isn't mad at me." I hang my head, staring at my hands. "A few days ago I begged him to talk to me. He said..." This is another lie, and I lick my lips to give myself a moment, like this is somehow hard to get out. "He said he knows it isn't really my fault that Daisy died." My heart twists as I force the words out, this really isn't as easy as I'd expected. "But he said that doesn't mean he wants anything to do with me."

My eyes even burn, like I'm actually going to cry, and I turn the look up on Detective Angleson, who watches me with her pale gaze. "I don't think he'd do this. At least not to me."

"It doesn't help that he has an alibi for at least one of the deaths," Angleson agrees reluctantly. "And tonight's attack as well. He was seen by the fire for a lot of the night, and given the timeline, we don't think he would've had the time necessary to stab Evan."

I'm surprised she's telling me this. But it makes something in me uncurl. She's not suspicious of him, because he's so good at making sure she can't be. This really is a smart game they're playing, and I wonder if it was all Rory's idea.

*He's a serial killer.* It's hard to reconcile the auburn-haired man's easy charm and constant, flirtatious jokes with the idea that he's been killing for longer than this year's Halloween season. But I have no choice, do I? Especially when he makes it obvious he knows how to *not* get caught.

"But I'm going to find who did this." Angleson's declaration drags my attention back to her, and I glance up from where I've been staring at my hands. "You need to go home. I'm sure there will be a curfew in place for a while after this. There's no way the town can brush this one off as an accident." When she gets up, I'm surprised. I'd expected way more questions, and more suspicions.

"Did you ever check out that man?" My lips move faster than my brain, but I pat myself on the back as my tired question makes her stop, obviously having forgotten what I'd said about him at my house. "The guy from the fairgrounds. A few days ago he was watching me in the park. Middle aged, gray hair, weirdly light eyes?" It's hard not to be frustrated that she hadn't taken me seriously.

But after what looks like some internal resignation, she slides a small notebook free from her belt, and jots down something with her pen. "You saw him the night of the first death, right?" she mutters, writing down my answer when I give it. "Then at the park..." she writes more notes, then shoves it back into her belt. "I should've looked into it more," she agrees, and I swear for just a second, she's almost apologetic.

Though, the second is gone when her gaze finds mine, and her hard eyes make the rest of her look just as frigid. "We'll find who did this, okay, Bailey? Before they can hurt you again."

Unfortunately, I'm not on the same page as her, and I brace myself for a lecture when I don't reply with enthusiasm or much more agreement than a tired smile.

But instead her smile is nice. She helps me up as well, squeezing my hand with reassurance in the motion. "Go home for me, all right?" she orders kindly. "I may be in touch if I need more information from you."

"Okay," I agree, still sagging from genuine exhaustion.

"Honestly, I just want to go to sleep." When she doesn't say anything else, I turn on my heel, eyes falling on Nic and Nolan as I head toward them and, by extension, the car.

"Bailey?" The detective's voice is a little less kind this time, and a little harder when she says my name, and I look at her over my shoulder, brows raised. "Are you sure that's all you remember? All that happened, as far as you can tell? If there's something you're leaving out, or something you think isn't relevant, I'd rather you tell me."

I think about it. I think about Rory's easy movements with the knife. Of the look on Evan's face as he'd reached out to beg me for help with so many stab wounds in his chest.

I think of them, and I shake my head slowly, from one side to the other. "I'm sorry, detective," I tell her, eyes wide and earnest. "But that's everything."

# CHAPTER 20

*Oh my god*, doesn't really seem to cover the situation that slams through my skull in broken memories as I crack my eyes open to stare at my dim ceiling. My brain tells me that it has to be at least ten am, if not later. So the only things saving my peace are the blackout curtains that I easily would sell a kidney never to lose.

*Oh fuck*, is the next epithet that flutters through my thoughts. It seems more fitting, at the very least. And better suited to, well, just about everything that happened last night.

I've never really regretted having a *very* good memory. And I don't right now...exactly. But it's hard to do anything other than lie here when my brain oh so helpfully replays each touch, all the smirks, and everything in between. The feelings of humiliation, of squirming in Rory's grip, shouldn't make heat pool between my thighs. I definitely shouldn't be replaying Phoenix telling me to open my mouth.

Or how exactly it felt when he spat my cum and their spit onto my tongue.

"Fuck," I mutter, rolling onto my side and curling into a ball under my blankets. My window is cracked, and will always be

—come hell or high water—so my room on the second floor is too chilly for me to walk around without blankets or a few layers of clothing.

*Did I really do that?* I know it's a rhetorical question. I can remember every touch, every surge of heat, and every hot breath on my skin as they replay in my mind with such clarity that I could be watching a movie. A really hot movie.

Slowly, I drag myself up and out of bed, groaning as I slam my eyes shut against being awake. A sound catches my attention, a rusty meow, and then Stranger is butting up against my hands, looking for attention and demanding my affection in quick succession. I give it, and when I open my eyes, I'm surprised to see Kale on the foot of the bed, glaring down at the two of us with irritation.

"No one did anything to you, Kale," I sigh, reaching one hand down so my fingers are inches from his nose. He considers my hand, considers me, and deigns to lean forward so he can sniff the very tips of my fingernails.

I wait while scratching Stranger's belly that's on proud display. His tail flops against the bed. Once, twice, then a third time, and as if that's a signal, Kale gets up to stretch. Unhurriedly, he pads my way, not stopping until he can rest against my folded legs, a soft purr echoing from his throat. I carefully pet him as well, knowing that if he gets spooked by anything, real or imaginary, he'll be gone like a bullet.

The knock on my door is enough to do it. Kale dives for the safety of the floor, scooting under the bed while I watch with a disappointed breath. "Come in," I call a few moments later, dragging one knee up to my chest.

My mom comes in, her face paler than it should be, and a note of seriousness about her that doesn't bode well for me. "Hey," she murmurs, walking across the room to sit with me. She knows what happened last night, and by the dark circles under her eyes, she's worried about it.

Well, at the very least, she knows the story I'd told Detective Angleson. Past that...I'm certainly not about to tell her I know who the murderers are, or that I was ready to beg them to fuck me last night.

Or, worst of all, that I'd told them who I want to kill next.

*Jayden* hasn't spoken to me in years. Not even when the others tried to smooth things over for the sake of looking sympathetic. Jayden had made it known he'd never cared. He'd never once felt bad for Daisy, or me. And Jayden has starred in the highest number of my nightmares out of all of our former 'friends.'

"Hey Mom," I sigh, leaning back against my wall after scooting myself around to do so. "Everything okay?"

"*Is* everything okay?" she fires back, eyes jerking upward. "Are you okay?"

"I'm okay." She knows I don't like or care about the five of them. But I worry she thinks I'm taking this hard for reasons that don't matter. Or things that aren't true. "I'm not so tired anymore. Things don't feel so bad when the sun is up." I wave my hand stupidly at the window, as if she doesn't know what time it is.

"Have you seen the news on your phone or anything?" she asks, watching my face to see if she can see a reaction before I can hide it. Not that I'm very good at hiding my expression from anyone, and I slant my gaze to the side when her gaze becomes too heavy for my eyes to hold.

"No," I say to my blankets, shifting my leg to tuck it more comfortably against my body. "Why? I like to think I'm caught up on last night's..." *Murder* is a strong word, and not something I should probably say with my mom in the room. It'll make me sound too cold. Too uncaring. Too...over it.

She'll really send me back to therapy if I act like I don't care about Evan's death. But when I open my mouth to try to say something, anything, about my condolences for his family, at least, I can't seem to find the words.

*Because I'm really not sorry. Not for any of them.* And that just makes me think of Rory's voice in my ear, of Phoenix's gaze, and the way they both had taken it upon themselves to get the justice for Daisy she more than deserves.

"He's not dead," my mom replies, and it takes me longer than it should to process that thought. My gaze narrows, then widens, and my brows lift as I turn to look at her in confusion.

"What?" I ask, my voice flat and strange as it leaves my mouth. "What did you say?"

Because she has to be mistaken.

Evan *has* to be dead.

"He made it." From her tone, I can't tell how she feels about it. I can't tell if she's relieved or just repeating the news to me. "I hear it was touch and go for a while, but he's going to be fine."

The flood of disappointment brings a flush of embarrassment to my chest, and I close my eyes against it. It's inappropriate to be disappointed that someone I went to school with isn't dead. It's embarrassing to know that I can't control my feelings, and I clench my fingers hard against my palms, as if I'm keeping her from seeing how I feel about the situation.

"Wow," I murmur, blinking at her owlishly. "I remember...I think...he had a lot of wounds. I can't believe he made it." I don't *want* to believe he made it, is the more truthful statement. But it's definitely not going to leave my lips while my mom is here.

"Are you sure you don't want to go see your therapist?" My mom is asking, sure, because she can't force a twenty-year-old to go if I don't want to on my own. "Seriously. I think it might be a good idea. Just so the two of you can touch base. There's nothing wrong with that, Bailey."

"I know there's nothing wrong with it." It's so damn hard to keep the derision and bitterness out of my voice. Harder not to seem like I'm snapping at her. My mom has my best interests at heart. I *know* that. But I also know that I don't want to go see my therapist, because there's no way in hell I'm going to be honest with her. About anything.

The best case scenario is that my mom is instructed to 'watch me for signs of a dangerous situation' and my emergency meds are refilled. The worst case scenario is that I get hospitalized for what she thinks is something leading to said dangerous situation, just because I don't give two shits about the people who led to my best friend's death.

"I'll think about it," I add, realizing belatedly I've interrupted something that my mom has said. "I'll consider it, okay?" There's an electricity in my veins that makes me restless, and though my plan was to take the day off from worrying about everything, and just exist in my room with my streaming services, my cats, and some oatmeal...I find myself at the dresser, yanking out a pair of loose sweatpants, a tee, and a hoodie. "I'm going to go walk," I add, glancing her way. "Okay?"

"That's fine," My mom takes a moment before she says it, and gets to her feet. "As long as you're okay."

"I'm totally okay."

"And you'd tell me if that had changed?"

It's so hard to meet her eyes, but this time it's more because of the guilt that threatens to swallow me than how uncomfortable I find it. I bite my lip, teeth sinking into it, then say without faltering, "Yeah, Mom. If something has changed or does change, I promise you'll be the first to know." At the very least, it'll placate her. She won't worry so much if she thinks I'm being honest with her. Even though it hurts to lie by omission to my biggest supporter and the woman who got me through the worst times in my life.

*But I just need to think for a while.*

"I won't be gone long," I assure her, knowing from Nic that there's another curfew. "I'll be back before mid-afternoon, probably. I just want to go for a walk so I can clear my head. You know how things are sometimes, right?" I wiggle my fingers at my head. "Things are loud up here."

"And you need to quiet them." My mom nods in understanding. "You're so much like your dad sometimes. He's done that ever since I've met him. I think it's genetic." Her tone is teasing, but her ease is forced. I know she's worried about more than just my mental state, but she's at least nice enough not to push it right now.

For that, I flash her a quick grin, hoping it's good enough to help reassure her. Quickly I grab a pair of sneakers, toeing them on while she turns to scratch Stranger's ears when he meows for her attention.

"If you're home early enough, we'll grab Indian food for dinner," she tells me, wiggling her brows theatrically. "I'll even go pick it up."

"You bless me with your graciousness. With your *kindness*," I bow to her, making large, sweeping movements with my arms as I do. It brings a smile to her face. A *real* one, and something in me lightens. I don't feel so bad anymore, and it's easier to unglue my feet from the floor, hoodie yanked over me as I open my door and wait for her.

"I know," my mom sighs, patting my shoulder. "I'm just so good like that. Be home before dark? I don't want to have to send out the cavalry."

"On my honor," I assure her, heading for the stairs. "Or however the Girl Scout oath goes."

"I don't think that works for you," Mom points out, striding by as I unlock the front door. "You were never a Girl Scout, remember?"

"Oh, right." With the door halfway open, I turn to grin again. "Clearly I missed out."

# Chapter 21

I don't exactly stop to think about where I'm going. I just *walk*, letting the rhythm of my steps help my brain as I think through the night before, and the news that Evan is still alive.

There should be some amount of 'good person' in me, right? Something, somewhere, that's so happy that hope is real, prayers were answered, and Evan didn't die in the barn.

*Where he should have bled to death.*

Is it my fault for showing up and making Rory chase me away from the body? If I hadn't been there, if Rory hadn't left, would Evan be dead right now? By this logic, Evan definitely owes me his life, and I'd more than happily collect.

My exhales of breath are visible in the cool morning air, and I curl my hands tighter in the pockets of my hoodie. I'm sure I look like a mess. Before leaving the house, I hadn't even brushed my hair, and for some stupid reason, I extricate my hands from the warmth of my pockets to correct that as best I can. I don't want someone seeing me and thinking I've lost it. God forbid that's the call my parents get from our neighbors in the middle of the day.

Thankfully, it doesn't take me long to get my hair in some semblance of being acceptable for the public eye. Though I wish I had a hair tie with me to take care of the problem until I want to deal with detangling it. Either way, I'm out of our subdivision before long, my steps taking me along the outskirts of town instead of really going into it. But that's fine. I don't want to go somewhere I'm more likely to actually *see* people.

On that front, I scuff my shoes on the sidewalk and look up, not exactly surprised to see myself outside of the park yet again. Lately, this seems like my happy place. It's too cold for kids to be here for long, especially this week. And as long as I swerve the errant jogger, biker, or dog walker, I'm good to go.

And staying off of the main trails is exactly how I do that. I don't stick to any of them, but I tread through as much grass as possible as I walk deeper into the one hundred and fifty-acre piece of public land. It's easy for people who are just visiting to get lost here. Especially if they don't follow the trails, sidewalks, or roads. But I've never had that issue.

The woods that dot the edges and stream through the middle of the park have always felt like home to me. Even when I didn't know them as well as I do now. As I walk, my steps crunch through leaves coating the ground, and I try to step over the bigger piles so I don't disturb them even more.

It isn't until I see the tree that I realize where my thoughts and my feet have brought me. But I can't muster up any kind of shock as I stare up at the tree where Agnes was hanged so long ago.

"I should know better than to play with dead things," I murmur thoughtfully, gazing up at the long, winding branches bereft of most of their leaves already. This tree is always the first to lose its leaves, and the last to get them back in the spring for some reason. I don't stop until I'm right up against the white oak tree, and the sweet scent of leaf mold tickles my nose when I reach out to spread my fingers along the smooth bark.

For all its pretty colors, isn't that all that autumn is? The season of dead and dying things, showing off their prettiest colors as rot eats them from the bottom up. Even the gorgeous leaves will turn brown and curl on their branches or atop the dead grass. By spring there won't be any trace of them at all, and new leaves will bloom to herald in a new year.

But not yet. In my mind, autumn is the perfect season. It's balanced between living things and dead ones, and I wonder how many people see the irony of their love of autumn colors, when all of those colors are the shades in which things *die*.

My fingers curl against the smoothness of the bark, and I close my eyes seconds before I press my forehead to it. Wondering, not for the first time, how much truth is in the story of the witch Agnes. Every kid in Hollow Bridge hears the story from their parents, from teachers, from anyone who likes the season enough to celebrate it.

But I've never stopped to wonder if any parts of the fable could be based on reality. After all, isn't that where folklore comes from originally? Surely there has to be some kernel, some *atom* of Agnes's story that's real. Even if she wasn't a witch that had successfully cursed the town and nearly brought it to its knees before she was killed once and for all.

My hand comes off of the bark, though I don't move, when a crunch in the leaves behind me proves I'm no longer alone. My eyes open a second later, and there's a moment of regret that I'm going to lose my peaceful solitude, but I push it away as I turn, pivoting in the colorful, dying leaves that are nearly ankle deep on the ground at my feet.

I'm expecting Detective Angleson.

Hell, I'm half-expecting my mom or dad to have followed me out here, wanting to check that I'm okay. But when I see Phoenix's face, his eyes wide and soft and full of concern, standing a few feet away from Rory, who just exists without giving me any indication of how he feels, though his gaze is firmly on mine.

"Oh," I sigh, turning to lean my back on the tree as if it'll give me some kind of support. "It's you." I let my gaze slide between them, from Rory's unreadable existence to Phoenix's expression that's too much for me to take in right now.

At least without an emotional support bottle of wine.

"Are you stalking me?" I ask, when neither of them speak, and go back to my favorite hobby of studying their body language without looking at either of their faces.

"Yes." It shouldn't surprise me that Rory is the one to answer, and that he does so with very little hesitation. "You're easy to stalk."

"I wasn't exactly trying *not* to be," I point out, sinking down to sit against Agnes's tree. I see Phoenix stiffen a little as I do, his hands shoved in his pockets.

"You know it's bad luck to sit under her tree," he points out mildly, like he isn't too sure of his words.

"Sit under it, sleep under, walk under it. I think the *tree* is just bad luck in any circumstance," I reply, dragging my feet through the dead leaves. "But I've been coming here all of my life and I really don't think the tree has made things any worse." Especially this week. I've been under the tree at least twice now, but nothing has killed me in a freak accident, or whatever form the bad luck is supposed to take. "Why are you stalking me?"

I don't get a response. Instead, I get Rory's sigh, and he trudges up the hill to the tree that's obscured by the woods beyond. He flops down beside me in the grass and dirt, shoulder brushing mine as he leans against the smooth white oak as well.

But Phoenix doesn't move. He stands there, fidgeting, and I can feel him looking me over as I shred brown leaves between my fingers.

"You look like you just crawled out of bed," Rory informs

me, turning to grin in my direction. "*Did* you just wake up before you came here? Are your parents looking for you?"

"Yeah," I retort. "Dad's about to appear from those trees behind your boyfriend; you just wait." As if mentioning him has summoned him, Phoenix walks up the hill slowly, until he's standing right in front of me and I have to tilt my head up to see him.

"Why are you stalking me?" I ask *again*, not moving when his hands rests against my hair, fingers scraping against my scalp. "Pretty sure I'm not that interesting, or worth your time while you have more important things to do." I arch a brow, but when I see the hilt of the knife Phoenix carries at his waist, my stomach flips. "Unless you've changed your mind and decided I'm responsible for Daisy's death, too?" I hate the hiccup of fear that trembles through my voice. I *despise* the way my tone goes up a few notes, and worse still is how I'm sure Phoenix hears it too. Otherwise, his hand tightening in my hair is just really good timing.

"Well, we're certainly not about to kill you," Rory scoffs, turning to rest his chin on my shoulder. "He thought you would run away when you saw us, so we've been keeping our distance since you left your house."

"That's not creepy at all," I mutter, turning to look at him while praying Phoenix doesn't pull his hand away. His nails against my scalp are comforting, and I could definitely go to sleep fast if he'd do this for me while we're in bed, or at least somewhere that my ass isn't getting colder by the minute thanks to the almost-frozen ground below us.

"Are you okay?" Phoenix interrupts Rory when he starts speaking again, and sinks down in front of me, hands moving so he can cup my face with them. His eyes are filled with more worry than I expect, and it's hard for me to hold his gaze.

Worse than hard. It's *impossible*. In seconds, I've cut my gaze to the side to focus on a particularly bright orange leaf, though the guilt that I feel at doing so makes everything worse. "It's not you," I tell him, in case he's forgotten after not having heard my stupid explanation for my allergy to eye contact in a few years. "It's—"

"Heavy," he cuts in, using my exact word. "Too heavy for you to hold. You're not hurting my feelings, Bailey. I know you need time to process and not look at my eyes."

If he wasn't a murderer, he'd be the perfect boyfriend. Though if I'm honest with myself, I'm not sure *murderer* is the red flag for me that it should be.

My hands come up and I stroke my fingers over his knuckles, wishing I could stare him down until he understands that I'm not afraid of him after last night. "If you ever chase me through the woods with a knife again, I'm throwing a rock at your head," I inform Rory, turning my head in his direction so he knows the threat is all for him.

But all I get is a snort, and his arm wrapping around my shoulders. "Oh *Bailey*," he sighs after a few seconds. "What am I going to do with you? After Phoenix, I said I'd never date a murder virgin again. But you really are just too tempting, aren't you?"

"Date me?" I blink owlishly at the words, feeling stupid. "But you're dating Phoenix." *Did you break up?* Is on my tongue, but surely not, if they're still here, acting like this. Frankly, they feel like they're in it for the long haul, and I'm surprised there aren't already rings on their fingers.

They're just *that* good together. That natural, and that... perfect, I suppose.

"Oh, sweetheart..." Phoenix's lips twitch into a smile. "You didn't think we just wanted to have fun and leave you behind, did you?"

Of course I did. All of his pretty words were nice. Especially the ones about keeping me. Not that I have any plans to air *that* particular personal point of interest.

"I..." I don't know how to reply without my disbelief coming through loud and clear. One of my hands leaves his, wandering up to Rory's hair, where I gently sink my fingers into the auburn strands I've wanted to touch for days. *Fuck,* his hair is just as soft as I'd imagined, and the low, grating groan he lets out against my throat shows me he has no problem with me exploring it. "Yes?"

"*No,*" Phoenix replies flatly. "He was right when he said I've been interested in—"

"Obsessed with," Rory corrects. "You've been *obsessed* with her since we came back. Since before that, if you're being honest with yourself." He sniffs, then nuzzles my jaw to whisper, "If I were a lesser serial killer, I might be jealous."

"I don't think that's what you're supposed to say in this situation," I point out, turning to look at his lips. God, he has such kissable lips.

"Was I not? How sad." He leans back against the tree and reaches out to tug Phoenix down as well. To my surprise, instead of moving to sit on Rory's side, however, he stretches out in the leaves, his head on Rory's lap and his legs out in front of him.

It occurs to me that before this, before Rory, I'd never seen Phoenix be so...*soft.* Sure, he's still the jerk I knew him as growing up. And he could still kill me with his glares or fits of sarcasm. But lying here, with Rory's fingers threading through his hair and his lashes obscuring his eyes just a bit...he doesn't look like the sad teenager I remember leaving Hollow Bridge.

Blinking, I realize that I've found his eyes, and he stares at me, waiting for me to notice, before his lips curl into a grin. "I'd say I'll stop stalking you, if it bothers you. But that would be a lie," he tells me, reaching one arm out to coax me forward.

"And you know how I hate being lied to," I murmur, letting him drag me down against him.

"And I know how you hate being lied to," he agrees quietly,

his palm cupping my cheek. "What do you say, then? What will you do if we keep stalking you around Hollow Bridge for a while?"

I reply, my voice easy, "Depends on when you plan on stalking me. If it's at night and you're sitting on my windowsill, that's a little weird."

"We'd just come sleep in your bed," Rory snickers. "Clearly."

"And if you're stalking me when my parents leave, or when I'm ordering food, it would be cool if you tell me so I can get you food too. Otherwise I'll just feel so guilty looking at your sad faces outside of the windows in the rain," I say with a dramatic sniff.

"Who said anything about outside in the rain?" It's Rory again, and it seems he has a quip for every bite of sarcasm that leaves my lips.

"But I think there's a bigger issue than you stalking me," I point out, eyes flicking between them. "You know, the one from the news this morning?"

Both of them give me blank, confused looks, and I can't help the roll of my eyes as I sit back against the tree. "Evan's not dead. He *made it*. And with your luck, he remembers everything from last night."

# CHAPTER 22

I t's hard not to think about Rory and Phoenix for the rest of the day. It's worse the day after. Then, when Friday finally rolls around, I realize it's been a bit since I've heard from them. But hadn't they said they might be scarce, especially with Evan still alive?

Since, after all, Phoenix is still somewhat of a suspect, despite him having pretty solid alibis for a few of the deaths.

"Come on, Lover Boy," I murmur, curling my fingers toward the white cat hiding under the bench. This part of town, the part with mostly not-so-great-houses and less-than-savory neighbors, isn't my favorite place in the world to be. Especially in the cold and the wet. Even with my hood up, the wetness seems to seep into my bones, making me feel creaky, old, and *tired*.

But the cats are here. And I refuse to abandon them.

The cat in question, Lover Boy, contemplates my existence. He's been caught before, proven by the tip taken out of his ear and the tattoo I know exists on his belly where he'd been neutered. And he's even let me touch him, once or twice. But today doesn't seem to be my day on that front.

Sighing, I sit back on my ass, food bowls strewn around me as the majority of the feral cats eat their fill. I'll make sure to fill up the other bowls before I leave, knowing there are at least six older cats that won't show their faces until I'm gone.

I'd just hoped things would be different with Lover Boy today. Instead, he bristles from under the bench, shifting his weight from one haunch to the other.

"Okay," I say finally, rolling my head on my shoulders to relieve some of the stiffness from my neck. "Okay, I get it. You're not feeling very social today."

"Does he usually let you touch him?" The voice behind me shatters the peace of the small courtyard outside of the abandoned shoe factory. Cats scatter in every direction, some of them not stopping until they're back in the safety of the broken down, hazardous building. Even though I'm not a cat, my own heart leaps into my throat, pulsing there a few times as I turn to see who's scared the cats so badly.

Though when I see her, disappointment dips into my fingers and I let out the breath I'm holding. I should've guessed it would be her.

"When no one is around to scare them, yeah," I tell Detective Angleson, knowing that irritation colors my voice. "I work with them to get friendlier so we can catch them if they need vet care." Or take them home, in the case of Stranger and Kale. But I'm not about to tell one of my least favorite people on earth that I'm two steps away from becoming a crazy cat lady a few decades early.

Her hair is pulled into the same smooth ponytail as before, and she wears a bulky brown jacket over her uniform that carries the same badges marching down her arms. It looks thicker than what I'm wearing, and I'm sure she's warmer than me today, especially since the sun is starting to set.

"What do you want?" I ask before she can even open her

mouth. "I'm not doing anything other than feeding cats. Can't you leave me alone for once?"

I swear a flash of guilt shows up on her face, though it's wiped away quickly by the careful blankness she's so good at wearing. "I just want to talk," she replies, glancing around us, presumably for a place to sit.

"Please don't scare the cats," is all I can deadpan in response. "If you'll just give me a minute, I can finish feeding them and we can leave so you don't scare them away from eating." I know my voice is harsh, but I hate being interrupted when I'm trying to do something.

Especially for this conversation, because I know how it'll go. I know what she wants, and I'm not exactly thrilled to be on the receiving end of her looks or her investigation.

It's not like I've done anything to be investigated for, anyway. At least...not really.

True to my word, I finish with the cats, dumping the last of the bag into bowls under benches and structures to help keep the food dry. They'll eat when they don't feel threatened, and I know from experience I've given them enough food to share. Worst-case scenario, I'll come back tomorrow and do this again, just in case Angleson has scared some of the more fearful ones away for more than the next couple of hours.

"Do you name them?" the detective asks as I roll up the bag of food and stuff it into a nearby dumpster. My nose wrinkles at the smell, and I shrug at her when I'm done.

"Some of them. But it wouldn't be feasible to name them all." It's hard for me to say it, but I continue with, "A lot of them don't last long. And I don't want to get too attached."

"That's rather sad." As if I didn't know that. But she follows me, keeping up her small talk about the cats, until we're out of the courtyard and in front of the building. We reach my car where it sits with hers pulled up neatly behind it, close enough that it looks almost like she's touching my bumper.

Is that a threat? I wonder. Some way to tell me that there's no escaping from her and her antiquated Ford cruiser that could probably do with a new paint job?

Sinking down to the sidewalk in front of my car, I glance up, brows raised, and wonder if she'll do the same. Unless she's arresting me, I don't care to move to any kind of secondary location, and if I can give her any hints that I don't want her here, then I'll do my best to make sure she gets every single one of them.

Including my sigh of disappointment when she does sit down beside me, hands shoved in her pockets as she stretches her legs out in front of her. "Have you gone to see Evan?" she asks out of the blue, and from the way the words hit me in the stomach, she might as well have just punched me.

"No." There's no point in lying to her. "Why in the world would I?"

"Because he's one of your old friends. Because you were peers." She shrugs. "Because Hollow Bridge is a small town."

My fingers drum on the concrete beside me and I spare a look around. I wish this was the one time Rory and Phoenix *were* stalking me, instead of keeping their distance to look like we aren't involved in the wake of what had happened at the barn.

But they're not here. Or at least, not visibly so. And I'm on my own with Angleson.

"This is weird," I admit finally, turning my insincere smile on her. "You know that, right?"

"No, I don't. What's weird?" I hate the color of her eyes and the way she looks at me, as if trying to suss out some secret that she thinks I'm hiding.

Unluckily for her, there's really nothing for her to find.

"Well, when Daisy *died* and it was their fault, no one was on them for visiting or going to her funeral or whatever. But now Evan, who took any chance he could in high school to distance himself from me and *mock me*, is in the hospital, and you're here telling me I should visit him? Out of peer obligation or something? Shall I get him a bouquet of flowers, too? Maybe linen bandages to wrap around his wounds? Perhaps you'll have me self-flagellate next, to show my repentance?"

"I don't know what that means," Angleson is quick to admit. "Self-what, again?"

"Never mind," I mutter, trying not to let my irritation go further than it is already. "It doesn't matter. The sarcasm is lost on you if I have to explain it." I know my look isn't nice, or friendly, or welcoming toward Hollow Bridge's finest, but nothing in me cares whatsoever. "Want me to visit Emily's grave, too? With a bunch of flowers? Should I send Jack's parents a pie? Or a casserole?"

I can feel her frustration with me even before she looks at me with her tiny, unimpressed frown. "You're not doing yourself any favors, you know," she informs me. "If you were a suspect—"

"If I were a suspect and didn't have all kinds of alibis, I'm sure you'd have me in jail by now," I agree. "I mean, I think we're all pretty clear whose side you're on, detective."

"You're right," she agrees. "It's clear I'm on the side of the kids who've been *murdered* here the past few weeks. What about you? Whose side are you on, if not the side of the people trying to catch a killer?" It's a smart question. It's meant to make me squirm, or to make me reveal something that I don't want to.

It's just a shame that she doesn't scare me, and that all of my unease around her has turned from discomfort, to hesitation, to dislike. After all, I've never been very good at hiding how I feel, as I'm sure she's picked up by now.

"Daisy's side. You know, that side no one was ever on? You included?" I can't help but hint dryly.

"I don't think that is a side." She gets to her feet with a sigh, rubbing one knee. "I know you don't like me, but you should stop to think of something, before you blow me off again," the officer advises me, not really looking in my direction.

When she doesn't continue, I let out the breath I've been holding. "And what is that?"

"That you were involved in Daisy's death too," she reminds me. "And maybe that makes you just as much a target as anyone else."

*She's wrong*, is the first thought that whispers through my mind, the faces of Rory and Phoenix swimming into my mental vision at the same time. *She's wrong, because they wouldn't.*

At least, I hope they wouldn't.

I hope they won't, honestly. But them hating me is probably just as believable as Phoenix *liking* me, or having a crush on me. Especially now, with Rory in the picture.

*Do I really believe they came here to do more than kill people?* Do I really believe, for a moment, that they're telling the truth about me, instead of toying with me before I meet the same end of their knives that the others had?

Whatever Angleson sees on my face, it seems to mollify her somewhat. "I'll see you around," she says casually, already heading back to her car as if she didn't come here wanting answers. Hell, maybe she just came here to upset me.

If she did, then she's succeeded. And I hate the feeling of doubt crawling at my insides, whispering just below my skin.

*What if she's right?*

"I'm sure you will," I agree with a too-sweet grin. "But uh, don't hurry over to talk to me if you see me. I have a life too, you know."

"Oh, I know," she replies, flashing me a smile full of false goodwill. "Don't worry about that, Bailey. I know all about your life." And with that—like it's not two steps away from a veiled threat—she gets in her car, starts the engine, and drives away.

Like she never had any business here in the first place.

. . .

W hen I run my fingers over the mask I wear, a small twitch goes up my spine at the feeling. It isn't exactly the same as the one I'd borrowed from Nic, but it's similar enough. The black smoothness of the cat skull is covered in small, black rhinestones that wink in the dark, and the large scarlet stone on the forehead soaks up the light from everywhere around me and flickers with deep red hues in response.

Though I'm obviously not dressed as I was at the party, since the Hollow Bridge Halloween Fair is family friendly until the last couple of days before Halloween.

Unfortunately, the curfew has kept the fair from opening most nights. But now that it's been almost a week with no murder and Evan hasn't been attacked in the hospital, Hollow Bridge seems to have breathed a sigh of relief and gotten back to celebrating the holiday at hand. For tonight I'm wearing all black; a hoodie for practicality, and leggings decorated with cat faces that go sheer at my knees, up to my thighs, though a good part of them are covered by the black, lacy skirt I wear.

Seriously, it would've looked better without the hoodie. But even with it, I'm out here shivering, my bucket of candy balanced against my hip as I hand out goodie bags to small children who are emitting squeals that hurt my ears. More than anything, Halloween always convinces me I do *not* want any of my own.

"Yes, take one," I mutter, as a little girl dressed as a zombie snatches it out of my hand. "And don't say please or thank you. Just take it all." The group of them runs off, leaving me momentarily alone near my parents' booth.

At least, until the Gothic Vampires show up.

Well, I think Rory and Phoenix are going for vampires. And their outfits look like they were picked up from the 'historically inaccurate Gothic period' section of the costume store, even without the plastic canes I'm sure came along with them. Their faces are painted to look like skulls, giving both of them an inherently menacing vibe that sends another twitch up my spine.

"A cat with candy," Rory teases, picking up one of the small, childish grab bags. "You're adorable."

"You're stealing from underprivileged children," I retort, snagging the bag back and dropping it in my bucket. The tail I wear clipped to my leggings brushes the backs of my knees, and Phoenix's gaze drops to it, eyebrows raising slowly and pointedly.

"You just can't get enough of being a *little cat*, can you Bailey?" he purrs in that terribly distracting voice of his, and it's so hard not to step closer to him with some kind of flirty, witty reply on my lips.

If only I had a witty, flirty reply, then I might do just that. Instead, I sigh, flicking my eyes back to my parents' booth to remind them of where we are.

"And you must've dug for hours at the costume shop for that," I tell both of them belatedly, letting my gaze wander over their costumes, the black jeans they're both wearing, and up to their faces. "Did you wash off the plastic smell, or has it just yet to hit me?"

Rory snorts and steps forward, eliminating most of the space between us as he stares at me, the black paint under his eyes giving him a much more aggressive appearance than usual. "You should introduce me to your parents," he murmurs, gaze never leaving mine. "I feel left out, since I'm the only one who hasn't met them."

"They're not your type."

"Well, I would sure as shit hope not." He rolls his eyes at my words and looks to the side, drawing my attention and a small, strangled sound from my throat.

Phoenix is already walking over to my parents, his hands

shoved in his pockets as he waits politely for a little girl to finish decorating her candy apple.

"Shit," I mutter, moving to stand closer to Rory, the bucket pressed against my other hip. "I can't believe him."

"Why?" He reaches into the bucket again, his arm sliding against my lower back as he does. This time I don't stop him, and he pulls the bag back to examine it before pulling out a Tootsie Roll. "Do they not like him?"

"On the contrary." It's hard not to groan when my mom's face lights up and Dad clasps Phoenix's hand like he's a long-lost son of the Scott family. "They *adore* him. They always have. It's like he has some spell on them, or something."

"Then they'll love me." He doesn't wait for my answer. He just goes to my parents' booth, leaving me to make small, unfortunate noises of protest where I stand.

"Is that free?" The sullen voice brings my attention downward, where the boy with a blue headband, green sweats, and a homemade turtle shell stands. "Mom says candy is free."

"Your mom is right," I tell him, moving the bucket around so I can hold it in front of me. But I don't look at him for long. My attention is immediately drawn back to the guys, and the way my parents look so thrilled at having two of them to talk to.

"Are those your boyfriends?" the kid asks, looking to where my face is turned. "Their costumes suck."

When I peer down at him, eyes narrowed, he only meets my glare with one of his own. "Isn't that word above your age range?"

"I'm ten."

"Do other ten-year-olds say *suck*? And why do you think they're both my boyfriends?"

"Because a girl in my class has four boyfriends," he shrugs, like it's the easiest, most obvious thing in the world. "So I've seen it before."

When he glances at the bucket again, I surreptitiously hand

him two more bags, able to spot the small, surprised smile on his face from the corner of my eye as he takes them and stuffs them into his own trick-or-treat bucket.

"If they are, then I don't know what I'm going to do with them," I sigh at last, surprised they're *still* talking to my parents. "Any advice?"

"Well, Kylie—that's the girl in my class—says they're all going to get married." He looks at the ground, clearly thinking, then says, "You could do that?"

"I don't think the country has caught up to that kind of liberal thinking yet." It's hard not to smile at him, at the way he thinks these things should just be obvious. "But I'll take it under advisement. Want one more?" I pull one more bag from the bucket and he takes it without a word, slipping it into the depths of his own. "Have you been to the booth with all the lights?" I ask, searching my brain for something that might interest him. "You can't miss it. There's a lit up witch flying a broom. And stars."

"I don't think so."

"You should have your mom take you there. They have full size bars, and you can go back for seconds. Plus, they have games you can play to win these little spider rings. Seriously." I show him the spider ring I'd 'won' from being over there an hour ago, and his eyes widen just a tad. "Three rows over, about even with here."

He nods hurriedly, gives me a bright smile, and trots off to his mother, who's talking to someone at the booth across from my parents'. As I watch, his excited face turns up, and he tells her what I'd said, only for her to smile, nod, and say goodbye to whoever it is she's been talking to.

That's adorable. If I *were* ever to become a parent, I'd want to be one like that, who cares about their kid's little joys. Just like my parents had.

*Speaking of...* I turn, unsurprised this time to see Rory and

Phoenix still there and my parents preoccupied with whatever they're saying. Knowing they've gone unmonitored too long for public safety, I march over as well, place the bucket on the edge of our table, and stand directly behind both of them, trying to figure out what they're saying.

But I certainly don't expect Phoenix to reach back and loop an arm around my waist, dragging me between them and forward a step, so I'm directly in line with them and facing my parents as well. Even Mom notices and gives a small, confused, look in my direction. Specifically at Phoenix's arm, still around my waist.

I just look back at her, giving her my best deer in headlights look that has worked on many less worthy foes than her.

"I miss Halloween here," Phoenix is saying, an almost sad smile on his face. "And Rory has never been. I'm happy I was able to drag him out here this year."

"It wasn't as difficult as he's making it out to be," Rory snorts, the sweetest grin on his face and the same glint in his eyes. It's amazing how he goes from serial killer to puppy dog so fast, and my parents have absolutely fallen for it. "I like Halloween, and I really like Phoenix."

*Uh oh.* This is about to go somewhere that I'm not sure I'm comfortable with, and *fast.*

"I see..." Dad is still oblivious, but Mom's words are full of doubt as her gaze falls again to Phoenix's hand around my waist. As if to make it worse, because he can, Rory throws an arm over my shoulders, pulling me to him so I really am trapped between them.

And sure enough, Mom's gaze goes *right* to mine.

Fuck.

"They said they'd walk around with me," I lie, reaching up to gently, gingerly, rest my arms across their shoulders. Like we're some big happy threesome-er-*family.* Family definitely sounds better in my head. "You don't mind, do you? The trick-

or-treaters have died down." I hope to God my winning smile is enough to convince them, though Dad is already nodding his approval.

But he was the easy sell.

It's Mom who watches my face, looking for any hidden sign of distress or anything else that might concern her. Her eyes go to both Rory and Phoenix once more, then she shrugs her shoulders. "If you want to, sure. Just make sure you're back before we leave."

"Or give us a shout that you're with them, if it comes to that," Dad adds, clearly not understanding what he's saying. "There's some crazy out and about in the tri-county area, remember. I don't want you ending up alone with some sicko."

Too bad for him, that's exactly what he's signing off on.

I swear I can feel the laughter radiating from Rory, though his face is as perfectly straight as if he didn't have insider information on the *crazy* running around. "Sure, Dad," I promise, giving him a mock salute with one raised hand. "I'll be careful."

"*We'll* be careful," Phoenix amends. "And we'll take care of Bailey, Mr. Scott. We'd never leave her alone in the woods or anywhere else."

"Especially not with some *murderer* on the loose," Rory puts in slyly, leaving me fighting not to punch him.

It's hard to escape, but I disentangle myself from all but Phoenix's arm, letting him pull me down the row of booths with Rory on my other side. "What are you doing?" I ask them both, bemused and feeling my heart thump in what could be anticipation but is more than likely nerves. "If my parents think—"

"Your parents think we're lovely people," Rory purrs against my ear. "Don't ruin it for them, Bailey. And *God*, it's such a shame we don't get to play with you much tonight." Shivers travel up my body as he gazes at me with none of the sweetness still on his face. It makes it so hard not to remember what

Angleson said about me being in danger as well, for being associated with Daisy's death.

"Why?"

"Because we have to help my parents," Phoenix answers, a small trickle of amusement and fondness in his tone. "That's why we're dressed up." He pulls me between two tents, to the outer edge of the fair, where we at least have some semblance of privacy. "It is just so easy to lure you away from prying eyes," he purrs, eyes dancing as his hands slide up my arms until he's gripping my elbows and not letting me move away.

The moment I'm really trapped, though, is when Rory buries his face in my neck from behind, arms going around my waist. "I don't really care that someone might walk back here," he murmurs against my skin. One of his hands slips around my hips, dragging against my skin over my costume before his fingers curl, nails digging into my thigh.

"Shouldn't, uh..." It's really hard to think when I can feel Rory's teeth on my neck, scraping against my skin in ways that send heat pooling to my center. "Shouldn't you guys be focusing or planning or, umm... Practicing?" When Phoenix just looks at me, I move my hand in what might be a stabbing motion, but looks like something a lot less public appropriate.

"Should we be...?" Obviously, Phoenix doesn't see it for what it's supposed to be either, because the grin on his face is too quick to be wiped away or ignored. "I mean, if you'd rather, we could probably skip this and take you back to the hotel for some *stabbing* practice, Bailey—"

"Fuck you," I hiss, only to end up with a yelp on my lips when Rory bites down on my throat.

"Yeah." The auburn-haired serial killer chuckles against my skin. "That's absolutely the plan."

"We can't do anything until closer to Halloween," Phoenix whispers, leaning in close to say it. "It's just not the right time yet. You'll see, Bailey. Everything will be taken care of by Halloween, I promise."

"Will you leave again, after?" I find myself asking, though I swear I hadn't meant to let the words escape my lips.

Neither of them answers. Instead, Rory runs his fingers up and down my sides, nose soft against the side of my throat. "It's still a little while away," he mollifies, and my heart dips at his words. He doesn't want to answer, because the answer is *yes*.

"You can't finger her behind a tent," Phoenix observes, one brow raised as he pulls back enough to watch Rory's hand dip under my clothes, dragging downward. I whimper in protest, gripping his forearm with nails that bite into his skin.

"Why?" Rory's head tilts, a cheshire grin on his face. "Why the fuck can't I? All I have to do is step here..." He takes a few steps, pulling me with him, until we're better hidden between two storage areas of the vendors behind us. But the sound of the festival is loud in my ear, reminding me of where we are and how close my parents are to us.

Yet I'm not exactly stopping Rory. My eyes close hard as Phoenix steps forward, forming a wall between us and anyone that might walk by.

"Someone is going to see," I hiss, reaching out to grip Phoenix's hand hard. "My *parents* are going to walk by, or something."

"Maybe I should be offended you aren't willing to risk it to come on my fingers." Rory's voice is light, mocking, and not one bit serious. But he does let his hand slide up my body, snagging under my shirt so he can splay his fingers against my stomach.

"Maybe you should be," I agree slyly, leaning my head back with a sigh of relief. "So sorry I'm not willing to get disinherited for sex."

"Good sex," Phoenix points out.

"I'm not arguing that." I lean forward to slide my lips against his, aware of Rory using it as an excuse to palm my ass through my leggings. "I'm sure it's *amazing* sex. But it's going to have to wait."

"The longer we wait, the more I'm going to ruin you," Rory murmurs quietly, seconds before voices alert us to the fact that we're about to have company.

Thankfully, by the time the young couple comes around the tents, we're no longer in any kind of compromising position. We smile at them, trying to make it look like we were just back here to pick up supplies, and the fact that these tents aren't ours doesn't factor into us looking like we weren't doing something inappropriate.

"I'll see you later." I sigh, once the two of them are gone. "Mom and Dad are going to send out search parties soon."

"Yeah, my mom is going to start calling, I'm sure," Phoenix agrees.

Rory just smirks. "My mom is probably working with one of our neighbor's horses to teach it how to drive cattle. She doesn't mind if I'm out late."

"Your mom sounds cool," I say over my shoulder, hand raised in farewell. "We get to meet her next, right? Since you know our parents?"

"Sure," Rory assures me, hooking an arm around Phoenix's shoulders and pulling him close so he can press an open-mouthed kiss to his jaw, as if he's worried Phoenix might have felt left out before. "I hope you both know how to ride, though. Everyone in my home town does, and Mom's going to have horses ready the moment we show up."

I don't say anything else, but I do turn quickly so I can hide my smile as I walk back to my parents' booth. I'm ridiculously pleased and surprised at the fact Rory comes from such an idyllic background, and that he's apparently willing to show both Phoenix and me.

# CHAPTER 23

I don't realize how little I want to be alone until I'm sitting on my own, in my room, feeling like the walls are closing in around me. My fingers clench and unclench around the blanket pooled in my lap, and I have no idea where either of my cats are.

Not that they'd help much with the lonely, empty feeling that's hollowing out my chest and making its way ominously towards my stomach. I run my fingertips along the softness, staring up at the ceiling. I could always call either of the guys, I suppose. They'd probably come back and get me, or at least let me walk across town to the small hotel they're staying at.

But something about the idea makes my stomach twist into knots. I don't want them to think I'm weak, or clingy, or attached.

*I don't want them to have any reason to get rid of me.*

My fingers tighten at that, but my grip relaxes a second later, my shoulders falling from where it feels like they're on the same level as my ears. Mom and Dad won't be home for a while, I'm sure. And since it's still light out, if only somewhat, I just feel like I should be doing something.

Something stupid that would be good for any kind of alibi I might need to cook up.

Something like visiting Evan. The idea makes me feel sick, and a gross, icky sensation climbs my nerves, whispering that it's below me to go see him when I want him dead. It's probably all kinds of taboo, as well. Since I could be the one saving him from any future stabbings.

Too bad I really just don't want to.

Obviously, Phoenix and Rory won't skip to the hospital with me. Why would they? But they're not my only options, and my ribs unclench as I think of Nic and how her scathing, witty humor would absolutely be enough to get me through a visit with Evan.

My phone is in my hand within seconds, and immediately it's at my ear, every ring making me set my teeth against my impatience.

"*Hello?*" Nic picks up on the third ring, sounding concerned already. "*Bailey? Is everything okay? I thought I'd hear from you last night, but you went dark on me.*"

"I'm fine," I assure her, trying *not* to think about last night in their hotel room. "Really, I was just kind of under the weather." It's not that unbelievable. I'm always the first person I know to get hit with a fall cold, and since it hasn't happened yet this year, I figure I'm due for one soon. "Could I ask you a favor, though?"

"*Of course you can. What's up?*"

"I want..." I take a deep breath as my heart pounds, all of my senses telling me *this is a bad idea*. Not that I have any intention of listening, apparently, because my lips keep moving. "I want to visit Evan. It was terrifying, seeing him almost die in the barn." Not really that terrifying, given the only fear at the time was of *me* dying, not him. Now that's out of the picture, the whole ordeal just seems like a thrill I can relive in my head whenever I want to. "And I feel like maybe I should visit him for some closure or something."

Thoughts race through my head. Does she believe me? I could've thrown in that my therapist agrees, because that definitely sounds believable. If she doesn't believe me, or asks me more questions than I'm prepared for, then I'm not sure what I'll do.

Seconds go by, my thoughts and worries looping on repeat, but it's nearly half a minute before I realize Nic hasn't said a word.

Confused, I check my phone, making sure we're still connected. We are. But she's still not saying anything. "Nic?" I press, bemused and unsure what's going on. "Are you still there?"

"*Yeah, I'm here.*" She lets out a breath and from somewhere on her side of the phone, I hear Nolan say something, though he's not close enough to the phone for me to make out the words. "*Don't get mad. But you know Nolan's brother is friends with Evan's brother. He wanted to go, and Nolan volunteered to take him. So I said I'd go.*"

My stomach hollows out, but I just stare at my fingers as I tear at one of my nails without really noticing the pain.

"*We've been at the hospital for a few hours now. Evan's...well he's okay. And Ava asked about you.*" Worse than making me feel hollow, the mention of Ava slams into my stomach harder than it should, and I worry I won't be able to catch my breath properly ever again. "*Bailey?*"

I don't answer when she says my name. I'm quiet, my only movements still using one hand to rip at my opposite thumbnail. It burns, the skin stinging as blood wells up to drip lazily down my thumb. It disappears on the black blanket below, and I blink away my stupor. Or try to, anyway.

It's hard to think of anything positive when it feels like Nic has slapped me in the face with her words alone.

"I need to go," I say finally, the words barely more than a mumble.

"*Wait. Do you want to come? I can pick you up—*"

"No." I *sneer* the word, unable to keep myself from sounding as upset as I feel. "No, I wouldn't want to drag you away from Ava and Evan. Do me a favor and don't say anything to them about me."

"*Bailey, wait. Please don't be upset—*" But I *am* upset. I'm hurt, and the anger bubbling in my stomach quickly turns to disappointment and something cold I haven't felt in six years.

Like I don't know Nic and Nolan as well as I'd thought. *How could you do this to me?* I want to howl in her ear. *Why would you go visit them? Especially without telling me?*

*Don't you know what they did to Daisy?*

But I clamp my teeth in front of the words piling up in my mouth, knowing if I open my lips to say anything, even goodbye, that they'll come out. Instead I hang up, tossing my phone down onto my blanket with bloody fingers and get to my feet so quickly I nearly overbalance.

"You're fine," I tell my reflection as I walk past her on my way to the bathroom. "You're *fine*, and everything is fine."

I just need to walk. Or run.

Or not be so alone anymore.

I *hate my costume.*

But then again, I hate everything about tonight. Not to mention if I dress up as a cat one more time this year, I'll scratch my own eyes out with the nails I have left.

My thumb throbs at the thought, and my fingers brush over the bandages that cover my finger to keep me from bumping it but also from worrying it until it starts bleeding again, which is way more likely than the bumping.

My costume is hasty, and I barely care how I look. The mask

I'd bought is in place, along with my tail, and I have a skirt on over my tights that are way too light for the weather. So is my tight, zip-up shirt with a cut out across my sternum and collarbones, but I just shiver and do my best to hurry in my platform wedges toward the house where the party is.

I really, really don't want to be here.

But anything is better than being alone right now. All of me would rather be at the boys' door, banging on it and waiting until one of them lets me in. I'd rather have Rory's hands in my hair and Phoenix's mouth on mine, neither of them being shy about how much they want me.

But I'm here instead, to prove a point to myself that I don't *need them* just because my day has been derailed and I don't know what to do with myself or my feelings.

"Fuck," I mutter, rubbing my arms as I walk into the house. I never go to things like this alone, and thankfully my shoes don't stick to the floor, even as the smell of cheap beer invades my nose unpleasantly.

A girl grins and makes her way over to me, slinging her arm over my shoulders and making my teeth grit even as I try to give her my friendliest smile.

I hate being touched by people I'm not comfortable with. Especially when my emotions are running high and I just need a moment to think. But she doesn't care. Not when she tells me how glad she is I've come, or steers me into the kitchen, where all the alcohol is lined up on the gross kitchen table half-covered by a stained white cloth.

"You never come to my parties," Frankie giggles in my ear, pressing her face to my shoulder. "What made you change your mind this time?"

*Desperation.* The word tastes bitter on my tongue, and I swallow it down painfully, the sharp edges of it slicing along my chest as it goes down. "I just really wanted to," I lie, flashing her a smile that I don't feel. "Come on. Invite me enough and I'll show up, *eventually*." That's not true. Invite me out enough and I'll make sure you lose my phone number is much more like it. But she, in her tipsy state, accepts the stupid explanation and pours me a cup of something that might be charitably called punch, if the barely orange color of it is anything to go by.

"Just have a good time, okay?" Frankie giggles in my ear. "You always look like you need it." It's clear what she means by the way her eyebrows wiggle up and down, but a second later she's gone, attaching like an octopus to someone else who has the audacity to walk by.

My phone rings, but I don't move my hand toward the pocket in my shirt, knowing that it's just Nic trying to call me for the eightieth time. Instead, I busy myself with staring at the punch, wondering if it'll poison me if I drink it.

"Well, things can't get worse," I mutter, and down the contents of the red solo cup within a few swallows, shuddering as it finally goes down.

Yeah, punch would've been a compliment the drink doesn't deserve. Sure, there's something in there that tastes like it was once orange juice. And maybe some kind of other fruit juice, too. But the overwhelming taste of straight vodka overpowers everything, to the point where I can't help the full body shudder that goes through me.

But with nothing else to do, I frown at the bowl of punch and consider getting another. It's not like anyone's here to stop me, or drag me away, or make this night somehow not as bad as it's been.

"Bailey?"

My eyes close at the soft voice, and I groan behind my mask. Apparently, there *is* a way to make this night worse, and I have a feeling that either this punch is laced or Ava is standing right behind me.

Fingers tightening to dimple the plastic of my cup, I swivel on my platforms to look at her, eyebrows arched behind the mask that apparently isn't doing enough to hide my face.

Sure enough, Ava is there. Alone, and not dressed in a costume, she stands leaning against the kitchen counter, her blue eyes on mine before I look away. Her dark hair looks less perfect than usual, with some of her curls not quite ironed out to their normal curtain-straight perfection. She also looks like she's been crying.

"What do you want?" I mutter, now really wishing I had more to drink. But thankfully it doesn't take much to fix that, so by the time I lean against the wall, my shoulder blades pressed uncomfortably to the white plaster like she's somehow trapping me here, I have more of the god-awful punch to focus on. "Last I checked, we weren't friends."

"Nic said you were thinking about coming to the hospital today." Her voice almost wavers, but she crosses her arms like she can hide the unsteadiness I hear there. "She said maybe that you were upset at her and Nolan for visiting him."

All I can do is blink at the contents of my cup, wondering why in the world my best friend was spilling my words to one of the people I hate most on the planet.

"Things like this..." She takes a breath, then lets it out, and continues slowly, "I know you don't like me. I know you're not a fan of Evan anymore, either. But this isn't some stupid shit, Bailey. He almost *died*. He was almost murdered, like Jack and Emily. And we were your friends."

"This is an interesting argument coming from you," I point out blandly. "Since I definitely don't remember you or Evan crying at the side of *my* hospital bed."

"That was different." She's quick to defend herself, voice placating. "That was a long time ago. We were *kids,* Bailey. It was an accident. Can't you see that?"

All I can see is the bottom of my plastic cup and, occasionally, the inside of my eyelids when I close my eyes and count to three, so I don't say something too unkind.

"We're not friends," I tell her at last, intent on ending this conversation. "Not anywhere close. So I don't know why you'd even want me to show up. I don't know either of you anymore."

"Because we didn't do anything wrong." She says the words quickly, then frowns, like she hadn't meant to. "I'm sorry, that's not what I meant to say. I just wish we could move past everything that happened. Back then, I mean. I thought we were friends."

"Me too," My words of agreement are too harsh, and too loud. My voice echoes off the plaster, making me wince at the severity of the sound. "Me too, Ava. I was *sure* we were friends. But I guess I was wrong." I mock-toast her with the cup, then toss it into the trash can. "I'm going to go vomit or something before I leave. If you're here, I don't want to be."

I walk by her, only for Ava to reach out and grab my shoulder with fingers too-tight to be anything other than painful. She whirls me around, eyes wide, and steps in so she can say, "I know you know who's doing this."

My stomach plummets.

"I *know* you do. The way you've been acting? The shit you say, and how you haven't come to any of their funerals? Tell them to stop, Bailey. Tell them it's *enough*."

I don't reply. I don't know how to, without screaming at her or, worse, hitting her. But I don't look away from her frantic, wide eyes, as I wonder how in the world she's come to the conclusion I know who the killer is.

I do, obviously, but still. *She* shouldn't know that.

"Why do you think I know who the killer is?" I ask patiently, reaching up to shove her hand off of my shoulder. "And don't touch me. If we were *friends*, you'd know how much I dislike being touched by someone I don't like."

Instead, she steps as close as she can, her eyes only inches from mine. "Because look who's died," she whispers, still not breaking eye contact with me. "And look at how you're acting. I know you didn't do it. You couldn't. But you *know*, don't you?"

My heart thumps in my chest, and time seems to slow for a moment as I take in every bit of her expression.

She's afraid. That much is clear. But she's also impatient and irritated. And not one bit of her looks like she's happy to be in my space, or believes any of what she's said about being my friend.

"Would we be having this conversation if you didn't think that?" I whisper finally, keeping my words calm and neutral. "Or would you still be at the hospital, instead of tracking me down on a long shot?"

"I'm not the only one who thinks you know," she replies. "And it's not like you're doing a very good job of denying it."

"Yeah?" I tilt my head to the side. "Why? Because you weren't dead first?"

She takes a step back, momentarily stunned, but I see her resolve come back to play, and in seconds she's back in my space, breathing my air, and looking a lot less friendly than she had a few minutes ago. "Whatever you think I did—"

"We both know that without you, Daisy would still be alive," I counter. "We both know you could've stopped her from going out on that ice."

"You could have, too." The words are out of her mouth seemingly before she can stop them, and her eyes widen. "Wait. That's not what I—" I step back from her and she reaches out to grab my wrist in her fingers, her grip like a vice that grinds my bones together painfully. "Bailey, *wait*. That's not what I meant."

But it is. It *is* what she meant, and it makes it worse because I've had that same thought over and over again. I wrestle my arm free from her, not saying a thing, and this time I make it to the door and slip past a group of college students with no idea where I'm going.

My phone buzzing fuels me on, though, and somehow my platforms aren't painful in the least as I walk down the street, strides eating up the distance between me and wherever the hell I'm going.

It isn't until the first drop of rain, however, that I realize where I've ended up. My steps slow, and I gaze upward at Agnes's tree in surprise, my brows furrowed.

Had I really walked this far in the cold without realizing it? Had my brain really been so out of it that I hadn't known at all? I shiver, my arms lifting so I can hug myself while I look up through the limbs at the dark sky beyond them.

I need to go home, or I'm going to get caught out in this storm.

Before I can turn, however, there's the sound of rustling leaves behind me, along with the snap of a branch. I whirl, fully expecting Nic or Ava there, but instead, my eyes fall on two familiar, masked figures that stand a few feet away from me, further down the hill in front of Agnes's tree.

It's easy now to tell them apart, since I know what and who I'm looking at. Phoenix stands on my left, his stance tense, his hair not quite hidden by the hood pulled up over it. To my right, Rory's stance is more relaxed, and his hand rests easily on the hilt of the knife on his belt. Both of their masks are clean this time, and they look like monsters my brain has conjured out of all that hurt inside of me.

"She thinks I know." I have to talk loudly over the wind that whips my hair around my face. "Ava thinks I know who you both are. And that I can talk you out of what you're doing."

Phoenix's head tilts to the side, and for a few moments, both of them are deadly silent. He breaks the quiet, however, by taking the three steps up the hill that close all the distance between us, and leans in until his mask is barely inches from mine. Even though I can't see his eyes, I can *feel* his gaze, and tip my head up as if I can meet it.

"She thinks I could've stopped Daisy from going out on the ice," I tell him without meaning to admit it. "She said—"

"Who do you want me to kill next, Bailey?" Phoenix's voice is soft. A whisper on the wind that somehow makes it to my ears just as his hand comes up to hover centimeters from my cheek. The question makes something in me relax, and I tilt my head to let him cradle my face sweetly. "Who do you want us to go find tonight?"

"Ava," I whisper, the hesitation and mental resistance leaving me as the word exits my mouth. I don't owe them, or her, anything. They'd kill her with or without me, right?

But *with* my encouragement suddenly feels a lot better than the alternative.

"I want you to kill Ava."

# CHAPTER 24

For a few long, precious seconds, I don't know why I've woken up.

Thunder cracks outside of my window, and I feel my muscles tense ever-so-slightly in response. But it isn't that. Storms rarely wake me up, and this one has been raging all night. Turning my head, I see that it's only three thirty in the morning, and the realization makes me groan.

"Stranger?" I murmur, my hand going to my pillow where he normally sleeps. "Did you bounce on me—" My words fall off with a gasp when my fingers slide against something wet and smooth, instantly causing me to jerk backward.

Lightning strikes as I move, illuminating the figure in my bed who's lying beside me, and who undoubtedly woke me up. For several tense moments I'm absolutely terrified...until my eyes trace the shape of the familiar mask, and I reach forward to push Phoenix's hood back, exposing his hair that's just as dark as everything else in my room.

"Hi," I whisper lamely, fingers trembling when I touch the mask again. "What are you doing here? Not that I'm upset," I amend, still jumpy and nervous from earlier and how upset I'd been. "I'm sorry. I'm kind of off, I just—"

"Can I touch you?" It's his voice that melts something in me and dispels the shakes from my fingers. "I know how your brain gets when you're upset. Is it okay if I touch you?"

*Fuck.* He's the first person to say something like that to me in longer than I care to think about, and I sit up to tuck my legs under me, glancing around the darkness of my room. "Where's Rory?" I ask, just in case the answer is unpleasant, even though it means I'm ignoring his question.

My desk light flares to life, the color changing LED lamp less harsh than most of the other lights in my room. But I blink the spots away all the same, noting the outline of the other masked killer in my room tonight.

"How did you get in?" I can't help but ask, even as Phoenix sits up and braces himself on his knees in front of me. "Don't tell me you broke in."

"Is that a no to me touching you?" He's so careful to keep himself a hair's breadth from me, so fucking careful to hold himself back that I consider marrying him on the spot. "If you tell me no, then neither of us will break that boundary, Bailey."

Scratch that. I'm prepared to marry both of them on the spot for that alone.

"I'm sorry," I apologize, not meaning to let my thoughts run away with me. "I'm okay now. You can touch me." He doesn't waste any time, his knees pressing against my legs as he leans in to run his fingers through my hair, the mask still obscuring his face.

Slowly, I reach up to pull it off, thrilled when he lets me. When Rory sinks down onto the bed to my left, I do the same with his mask, marveling at the still-wet blood that's spattered over both of the white, plastic faces. "Is she dead?" I ask dumbly, leaning into Rory's touch on my arm. "Like, actually dead, and not like Evan 'dead?'"

"Evan will be dead soon enough," Rory informs me dryly. "And Ava is *very* dead. I thought about bringing you a souvenir." I swear his eyes glow in the darkness when he says it, but I don't react.

"I told him not to," Phoenix assures me, hands stilling when I reach out to touch the blood sprayed up one side of his face.

"Did you take your masks off?"

"I wanted her to see me before she died," Phoenix confirms. "Rory thinks it's stupid, and no, before you ask, he didn't take his mask off for Evan. But Ava was different." His hand tightens around my wrist. "Ava deserved it more than anyone for what she said to you tonight."

It's hard to swallow the words he's thrown at me. Ava *died* tonight because of my feelings. Because of the guilt she stirred to life in my chest. Ava could still be alive if I'd just been able to walk away from her instead of getting so upset.

And God, that should really bother me.

But instead of being angry, I lean in, my eyes on Phoenix's as I swipe my fingers through the blood on his face, dragging it over his skin. "Tell me how she died?" I ask, looking between them. "Please?"

I shouldn't know. I shouldn't *want* to know. But something inside me demands it, starves for it, and needs it so I can go on breathing.

"How much detail do you want, darling?" Rory purrs; and when I transfer my gaze to him, he opens his arms wide for me in an almost theatrical gesture. "How much do you want to know about all the screams and promises she sang for us?"

The shudder that goes up my spine when his arms close around me like a cage is only partly from fear, and I don't fight the arousal, the heat his words stir to life in my body. *Fuck*, I shouldn't be turned on by this. I shouldn't want to hear about how she'd died, or be so thrilled that they're here to share it with me.

"Did it hurt?" I find I'm not too keen on him repeating the whole murder to me, maybe, but there are a few things I wouldn't mind knowing.

Such as where my sense of morality went, for one.

"It hurt," Rory promises, his fingers creeping up my hips, dragging my t-shirt up with them. I'm only wearing it and a pair of thin shorts that cover very little, and I'm sure by now both of them have noticed.

Especially when Phoenix's hand curves over my thigh, pushing upward over the curve of my ass and bringing the shorts up with them. "No underwear?" I hear him chuckle.

"I'm sleeping," I reply dryly. "I wasn't expecting you two."

"I stabbed her first." Rory is definitely more into the murder side of this than I am, but I don't mind that much. Not when he reaches up to cup my face, as Phoenix moves so he's more behind me than he was and shifts me onto my knees between the two of them. "We chased her for a while. We made it *fun*." Lightning flickers outside of my window, lighting up the upper half of his face and touching on the wide, manic grin he wears. "I like the chase. Phoenix just wants the kill."

"*Phoenix* didn't want her telling anyone," the murderer behind me murmurs, his fingers stroking over my hips. "She could've found someone if you let her run much longer."

Rory eyes me, brows raised. "We both know I wouldn't do that. Don't we, Bailey?" His fingers skim my lower lip and, knowing what he's after, I part my lips obediently so he can press his fingers into my mouth for me to suck on them. At the same time, Phoenix pulls my shorts down my thighs, his hands moving to spread me wider so he can see all of me, as if it isn't still pretty dark in my room. "We both know I'm always so careful. I don't want to spend the rest of my life in jail, you know?" He's slow as he fucks my mouth. His fingers are so careful and teasing against my tongue.

"He stabbed her first," Phoenix agrees in a soft purr, leaning over me. "But *fuck*, I'm the one that got to kill her. He stabbed her in the thigh. Just to make her scream." His teeth close on the nape of my neck lightly, grazing against my skin, as one of his hands brushes my upper thigh. "Then I cut her arms." Both hands come up, nails scraping the skin just below my shoulders. "She tried to get away, so I stabbed her in the back." One hand moves to grip my lower back, nails sinking into me lightly.

"And then do you know what he did, Bailey?" Rory murmurs, looking over my shoulder. "Wonderful, sweet Phoenix slit her throat. That's where all the blood is from. People just bleed so much when you cut their necks."

I'm not surprised when Phoenix's fingers curl around my throat. He grinds his hips against my ass, and I groan around Rory's fingers, when I feel his hard length through his jeans. "Sit back for me, sweetheart," he murmurs, drawing me back as Rory pulls his fingers free from my mouth. Bemused, I let him rearrange me, until I'm leaning against his chest and staring at Rory in almost the exact opposite way of that night in the woods. By the time I'm settled, my shorts are nowhere in sight.

"You stabbed her first," Phoenix states, rubbing his cheek against mine as he stares at Rory. I can hear the amusement, the pleasure in his voice when he pushes my thighs apart, two fingers spreading me open for him. "You can fuck Bailey first this time."

I hear the hitch of Rory's breath, and watch his gaze flit from my face to Phoenix's. "Are you sure?" he asks, fingers already inching the zipper of his hoodie down. "You've wanted her—"

"And I've tasted her," Phoenix agrees enthusiastically. "Unless you don't want to play with her first. If not..." He starts to move, but Rory's hand flies out to grip his wrist.

"No. If you're offering, you know I'll accept." He lifts a hand from Phoenix's wrist, shucking off his hoodie and his shirt, moments later. "*Fuck*, Bailey," he moans, looking between my thighs as Phoenix lazily strokes his fingers over my slit. "You don't know how good you look right now."

"Better or worse than a dying Ava?" I ask, half snark and half real curiosity.

Rory's grin is wolfish, and Phoenix's chuckle against my ear is predatory. "Better," Rory promises without hesitation. He leans forward on one arm, his lips slanting against Phoenix's while I crane my neck back to watch. "Don't think you're getting off easy, lover," he purrs. "I'm going to fuck you while she watches. While you *beg* me to make you come." I feel Phoenix shudder against my back, and suddenly I realize that's a show I'd rather die than miss.

They practically attack each other, Phoenix's hand coming up to bury itself in Rory's hair. The auburn-haired man, in turn, leans into him, fingers grazing Phoenix's face before resting on my knee. They're so gorgeous that I would be satisfied just watching them.

But as if they could hear that thought, Rory pulls away, and immediately crushes his lips against mine like he wants to consume me. "You both taste so good on my tongue," he tells me, hand sliding between us. Within seconds he's sliding a finger into me, then another, and I share my approval of the way he touches me when I moan into his mouth, only for him to devour the sound.

"You both drive me insane. Especially when you're touching her," Phoenix admits, hands pulling gently at my shirt. Before I realize exactly what it is he's doing, Rory moves just enough for Phoenix to yank the shirt over my head, leaving me completely bare between the two clothed killers.

It's terrifying, in a vulnerable and nerve-wracking kind of way. A full body shudder travels down my limbs, making my toes curl against the bed.

"Shhh." Phoenix's soft whisper in my ear is pure warmth,

and when he cups my breasts in both hands, thumbs toying with my nipples, I give Rory another moan to swallow.

"Hold her while I fuck her," Rory growls, pulling back suddenly. "Do you want me to open you up more, Bailey? I don't want to hurt you, but I need to be in your cunt *soon.*"

"Then fuck me," I tell him, leaning back into Phoenix's hand that grips my throat. "I don't need you to be gentle with me."

"You want us to play rough with you?" Phoenix's teasing is a hiss against my ear. "Did you like it the night in the woods?"

"We've corrupted her," Rory replies with a chuckle, stroking his thumbs over my inner thighs. "Relax for me, darling girl." While Phoenix had my attention, he unzipped his jeans and shoved his underwear down enough that his cock is free, curving against his stomach as he waits for me. "If she's loud, Phoenix, you'll have to help her be quiet. But I know you can find some use for her mouth." His grin is wolfish, and without waiting for an answer he strokes his length along my slit, a shudder of his own causing his shoulders to tremble slightly. He takes a breath, and with his eyes on mine, he slides into me slowly, not stopping at my whimper or Phoenix's murmur of encouragement.

He doesn't stop moving until his hips are flush with mine, and I clench my knees around his hips, holding him there while I try to adjust. "I need a moment," I tell them both, holding in my surprise at how deep Rory is inside of me. Taking him without much prep is certainly proving to be a fun, just-this-side-of-painful challenge. "*Fuck.*"

"You're fine," Phoenix murmurs, thumb stroking my jaw. His hand moves, fingers teasing one of my nipples to stiffness before he moves to the other. That only makes things worse, and I find myself clenching my knees more tightly around Rory's thighs, a soft sound leaving my throat as I can feel my muscles clamping around his cock.

"Oh, *fuck*," Rory growls. "Fuck, Phoenix. You have to stop if you want me to not wreck her. You too." He looks down at me, one hand coming down to rest against my lower stomach in warning, keeping me still. "I can't give you a moment if you're clenching around me like that, Bailey."

"Is he right?" Phoenix's voice is barely more than a whisper, and he puts more effort into what he's doing. "When I touch you like this, do you clench around him?" His fingers pinch my nipple, dragging a gasp from my throat that makes his other hand close a little more firmly around my throat. "Did she do it again, Rory?"

"*Yes.*" Rory's voice is strangled. "Phoenix—"

"What if I touch her here?" He moves his hand further down, nails brushing over my skin as he moves to stroke my inner thighs. My muscles tremble, and he runs his finger inward, toward where Rory's cock is pressed so deep. "What if I do this?"

I don't expect it when he spreads my folds and uses one finger to stroke over my clit. My hips arch off of the bed, my thoughts spinning when I clench around Rory without meaning to, though the quiet yelp of surprise from him hits my ears just as his hand clenches over my hip.

"*Phoenix—*"

"What if I keep doing it? Hmm?" He makes good on his threat, putting more effort into rubbing my clit.

"Phoenix," I whimper, reaching down to grip his wrist. "Phoenix, I can't—"

"If you say red, he'll stop," Phoenix promises me. "But you won't, will you, sweetheart? You want him to ruin your pussy, don't you, baby? She wouldn't be clenching around you like this if she didn't. Haven't you told me the last few days how much you want to ruin her for anyone else? That still stands, right?"

God, listening to him tease his boyfriend is hotter than it

should be. Rory realizes what he's doing as I do, a low sound grating in his throat.

"You want me to ruin pretty Bailey for anyone other than us?" he asks, his voice a low rumble. "Is that what we're doing, Phoenix?" His thrust is harsh and deep, and I can't help the soft gasp that leaves me. "Go on. Keep playing with her clit like that. The harder she grips me, the harder I'm going to fuck her."

I swear, both of them take it as a challenge. It's impossible to stop my muscles from clamping down when Phoenix strokes my clit, his movements become more and more insistent as Rory's thrusts pick up until he's slamming me back into Phoenix, who has to adjust his grip on me in return.

"You're unfair," the auburn-haired killer says breathlessly, one hand comes forward to cup my breast in his fingers before teasing my nipple as well. His other grips my thigh, nails scraping at my skin. "You'll hold her just like that for me when I come in her pussy, won't you Phoenix? Keep her leaning back just like that so it all ends up where it belongs?"

"*Fuck,* you can't say things like that and not expect me to come," I reply with a half-hearted sob. One of my hands wanders up to Phoenix's hair, gripping it, while my other finds Rory's wrist. He doesn't pull away. He doesn't really seem to mind as my nails dig into his skin, if he even notices it.

"Oh, darling," he laughs. "I want you to come on my cock. But..." He slows down, obviously hating doing so. "Where do you want me to come? I can pull out and—"

"You can come inside me," I tell him breathlessly, craving his much more brutal rhythm. "Don't stop, Rory, please. I want—"

He doesn't wait for me to finish. He lunges forward until he's leaning over me, one hand going to grip Phoenix's hair and pull him forward over my shoulder. "Watch," he orders, his voice low. "Watch me fuck your pretty obsession, lover. Did you hear what she said? That I can come in her pussy?"

"Then come in her. She'll be even more perfect with your cum dripping out of her," Phoenix purrs in reply, slamming his lips to Rory's just as his boyfriend's thrusts falter.

He falls apart moments later, his movements erratic until he finally rips away from Phoenix's mouth to attack mine instead. One last thrust of his hips is all the warning I get before he's coming. To my slight disappointment, Phoenix pulls his hand free, but I don't say a word as Rory devours my mouth, nipping at my lips until finally he can pull away, spent.

"It's your turn now," Phoenix murmurs against my ear. "Or did you think we forgot?"

Glancing up at him, I blink, a little shocked at his words. "Well, no. But it's fine if—"

"I'm going to lick his cum out of your cunt while you finish on my tongue, pretty girl," he interrupts as Rory grabs my thighs to pull me around none-too-gently. In a movement way more graceful and thought out than what I could accomplish, he has me against the bed seconds later, my thighs open wide around Phoenix as he leans in to press a hand against my stomach, staring down at me.

"I was right," he adds, eyes glittering while Rory pulls my head onto his thigh. "You look so perfect with his cum dripping out of you."

I can't help the flush of heat in my chest and neck, nor can I help the way I look away from his words, a little embarrassed by them. But Rory grips my chin, jerking me back to look at Phoenix. "Don't run away from us, gorgeous," he tells me, as his thumb strokes my lower lip. "Because we'll always chase you down. Whether it's your reaction here or something out there. Let him see it. All of it. You want him to make you come, don't you?"

"Yes," I admit, clenching my fist in the sheets. "I'm really close, Phoenix. Please—"

"You can come on my tongue and fingers," Phoenix interrupts. "Whenever you want, sweetheart." He doesn't waste another second before he leans down, tongue licking up my slit and then over my folds, causing my breath to hitch in my throat.

It takes me longer than it should to realize he really is licking up as much of Rory's cum as he can. And when I try to move, he loops his arms around my thighs, keeping me in place as securely as Rory's hand around my throat does. He's...*thorough* for lack of a better word, and by the time his tongue finally slides into my entrance, I nearly scream with relief.

"God, it took you long enough," I moan, tilting my head back on Rory's thigh. "Fuck, Phoenix. Your *mouth*—" My shriek is cut off by Rory's hand clamping over my lips, and I can feel him laughing as Phoenix yanks my hips to him, pressing his mouth more tightly to my body as he tongue-fucks me harder than I'd expected.

"Not so loud," Rory snickers. "Unless you want your parents to come in and see this. Doubt they'd be thrilled." Phoenix's glare matches my own that I level up at Rory, but he looks unbothered. Instead, he switches his grip to his other hand, keeping his fingers around my throat to hold me here, half on his lap. But now his other hand is free to wander, and though I can't see it, I can certainly feel it when he busies himself with teasing my nipples to stiffness once more.

Within minutes, I want to cry. Phoenix's tongue has me on the edge, and with my knees clamped around his shoulders, there's nothing I can do but take it. "Phoenix," I beg, eyes burning with frustrated tears. "Please, *please* Phoenix—"

"So greedy, aren't you sweetheart? You want me to fuck you?" I nod fervently, as much as I can while Rory grips my throat. "Then *beg me* for it. Tell me how much you've dreamed of me pinning you down to fuck you like you deserve."

"Please fuck me." It's not a difficult choice, and the words

fall from my lips without stopping. "Please, Phoenix. *Please*. I've
wanted you to fuck me for years. *Please*."

"One more time?" I feel his arm leave my thigh, and his
fingers brush my slit teasingly. "For me?"

"*Please*." I force every bit of longing I can into the word.
"*Please* fuck me, Phoenix."

"Good fucking girl." He slides his fingers free, shoves my
thighs wider around himself, and slides into me all in the span
of a few seconds. He's longer than Rory, though not quite as
large. Though it's hard to tell when I'm sure I'm about to go
cross-eyed from pleasure the first time he pulls back just to
*slam* into me. It's overwhelming, and I cram my eyes shut as
Rory's fingers close on my throat, tightening until I'm gasping
and seeing stars.

Somehow, that just makes it better.

I reach the peak with his hand on my throat and Phoenix
fucking me as hard as he can without sending the bed into the
wall. Both of them are speaking, their words addressed to me
with varying levels of filth and encouragement. But I barely
notice. I'm too busy trying to hold out, just enough, just to feel
this for a *little while longer*—

My orgasm rips through me like a bolt of electricity, and it's
only Rory's fingers in my mouth that stop me from screaming.
He forces me to close my lips around them, and I sob as he
finger-fucks my mouth, eyes crammed shut.

"It's unfair how hot she is when she comes," he remarks to
Phoenix, barely minding that my teeth are pressing against his
skin and I'm biting down harder than what's probably comfortable. "I wonder if we could make her really scream for us. If we
teased her for a while."

"It's unfair how perfect she is," Phoenix agrees, his voice
losing some of its carefully controlled edge as he grips my hips
hard enough to bruise and slams into me again. "I never knew
how much I'd love fucking Bailey while you hold her for me.

She looks better between us than I ever could've thought possible." Those words make me groan in protest, and I hear Phoenix chuckle. "Did we wreck you?" he asks, not sounding at all apologetic. "Poor little thing. Poor Bailey." He pulls away when I whimper from over-stimulation, though his fingers curl around his cock, moving along his length that's slick from fucking me.

"That's okay, Bailey," Rory assures me, sliding his fingers from my lips. He moves, helping me sit up so I can lean against the wall with my head spinning. "You can watch me play with Phoenix for a while. Until you feel like getting ruined all over again."

I don't expect him to just go for it. But he does, grabbing Phoenix's shirt to rip it off over his head. There's a brief moment of shock on Phoenix's face, like he hadn't expected him to move so quickly either. But he doesn't protest as Rory manhandles him, throwing him down onto the bed with his jeans undone and his cock free to curve against his body, pre-cum leaking from his tip.

"You're just as perfect as Bailey," Rory informs him, on his hands and knees over Phoenix. He moves just enough that he can yank his jeans off to shove them to the floor, and I'm left to stare at the perfection of Rory's flawless skin, the curve of his spine, and the muscles that slide smoothly under the expanse of his back as I watch.

"You're both more perfect than *Bailey* could ever be," I remark, thumping my head back against the wall again.

"Don't make me fuck that insecurity out of you," Rory warns, tilting his head back at me. "Because I will."

"You should," Phoenix murmurs, eyes on Rory as his boyfriend comes back to straddle his hips again. "Fuck, you're not going to—" Now it's his turn to be pinned. Rory grips his throat in one hand, using his other to line up Phoenix's cock with his entrance.

"Good thing I let you fuck me before we left, huh?" he asks, voice strangled as he sinks downward in one movement, eyes on Phoenix's face. "There you go. Just relax, baby. You can be just as good as her when you want."

I can see Phoenix tremble under him, and when he reaches out a hand, I take it, only for him to tug me down on the bed beside him, my chest pressed to his side.

"He's so sensitive when I ride him," Rory remarks, rolling his hips slowly, then a bit faster, as he grinds down hard enough to make Phoenix choke. "And he's so good at this. At being him."

I move just enough that I can lean over Phoenix, and I run my teeth teasingly up his collarbone, while looking down at where Rory is fucking himself on Phoenix's cock. Warmth surges in my belly, but there's no way I can do more than appreciate them both as I watch.

Rory is just as good at this as he is at everything else. Phoenix seems to agree, judging by the sounds he makes and the way he reaches up to curl his fingers in my hair desperately. "Rory..." he whines, his voice soft as he leans his head back to give us more access to his throat.

His boyfriend takes the invitation without any hesitation, leaning down to fasten his teeth in the skin of Phoenix's throat. His movements become more thorough, more forceful, as he sucks a bruise into view on Phoenix's skin. Somehow though, he maintains his composure so well it's a little unreal.

"Kiss it and make it better, Bailey," he orders, voice raw. I move to do as he says, and find great pleasure in licking over the bruise. My attention has Phoenix honest-to-god whimpering, his muscles twitching under us as he writhes. "Just like that. Make one of your own if you want. He loves to wear the marks of his lovers, don't you, baby?"

"*Yes*," Phoenix hisses, turning half-lidded eyes to me. "Bailey..."

But I definitely don't need more of an invitation. Grinning wolfishly at him, I lean down to nip at this throat a few times, teasing him as Rory continues to ride him. Finally, when his breath falters, I bite down, my hand gripping his hair to hold him in place as I make my own mark a few inches from Rory's. I take longer than he had, feeling Phoenix writhe under me and enjoying the way his hand at the nape of my neck tightens in his desperation.

"Bailey..." he warns, panting. "Bailey, I'm—"

"You have no idea how much I want to see you come like this," I tell him, pulling away just for my hair to fall between us like a curtain. "Because you're gorgeous like this, Phoenix. Desperation is a good look on you."

My teasing doesn't fall on deaf ears, and a grin crosses his face. "You'll pay for that," he tells me, though in the next moment he's throwing his head back again, nails scraping against my scalp. His other hand is in Rory's hair, and he curses once, then again, calling both of us a few choice names, before his hips slam upward just as Rory grinds down again.

"Fucking *perfect*," Rory murmurs, riding him as he comes. "But you're both always perfect, aren't you?"

"If by 'both' you mean you and him, absolutely," I agree, my voice hoarse from exhaustion. The adrenaline is wearing off, and the lightning outside reminds me it's not even four am. But I'm much more interested in watching Phoenix come back to himself than going to sleep. I kiss up his throat a few more times, and when Rory sits back on my bed, using his own shirt to clean himself up, I move to shove him down against my bed, staring down at him with a sudden unsureness.

"Is this okay—" I start to ask, but I get his reply in the way he jerks me downward to kiss me.

"It's more than okay," he tells me, before going back to devouring my mouth with his. At least, until Phoenix starts moving. At that point Rory moves, helping me get up as well, and when I find myself pressed between them on my bed, my blanket across our shoulders, it's...

Well, *perfect* can't be the word of the night for much longer. But I can't think of any other way to describe their heat on either side of me, and the way they make me feel with both of their arms draped across me.

"We should go on a date tomorrow," Phoenix remarks, his voice heavy with sleep. "Breakfast?"

"I'm not waking up for breakfast," Rory complains. "But I'll do something tomorrow night."

"I have no life," I remark, my voice small as I bury my face in Rory's chest. "We can do whatever you want." Already I feel the allure of sleep calling to me, and I'm pretty sure if I fall asleep here, between the two of them, it'll be the best rest I've ever had in my life.

"We'll figure it out," Phoenix promises, lips brushing my hair. "But Bailey? Are you awake?"

"Mhmm." *Barely.*

"We'll have to leave before you wake up so we can clean up and change. Don't freak out, okay?"

"We're not abandoning you," Rory agrees, fingers skimming over my arm. "And once Halloween is over, we can all sleep in and you won't have to wake up without us."

I want to question his words, and the way he sounds so sure of us. That we'll last for longer than whatever this is, and past Halloween, when things will feel more real. But I don't. I wait, trying to find the right words to use.

By the time I have the right words, however, Phoenix is moving behind me, fingers soft whispers against my skin as he pulls my hips backward enough that he can snag my leg up over his hip. A soft gasp leaves me when he enters me again, his soft growl against my skin causing me to shiver.

"Shh, Bailey," he purrs, while Rory reaches down between

us to play with my clit. "Don't you want to come on my cock just one more time? I'll be so gentle, I promise."

I'm so exhausted, so spaced out, that all I can do is whine and whimper and writhe between them, until at last I can't hold back anymore.

My second orgasm is easier, not as intense as the first. But still so, so good and I reach back to grip his hair, turning him against my face for a quick and sloppy kiss that Rory steals me from as Phoenix's thrusts turn erratic.

His low gasp is the last warning I get, and Phoenix buries himself in my body once more, arm hooking around my waist to drag my body back against his as tightly as he can, though Rory is quick to erase any space created between him and me as well.

"It's unfair how perfect you are," one of them murmurs, though by the time I've ridden out my orgasm, sleep has come back to claim me with a vengeance and I can't tell who's speaking.

"So perfect that we're never letting you go," the other replies.

*Good,* I wish I could say, loving the fullness of Phoenix's cock still buried inside of me as I drift off. *I don't want you to.*

## CHAPTER 25

*Are you ready, sweetheart?* The text is just sitting there on my phone, unanswered, even though I am absolutely ready to go and expecting him. But things are different in the daylight. It's harder to reconcile that I'm maybe a little bit in love with two murderers, and everything that goes along with it.

Not to mention I've been checking my sheets for blood all morning and even running my fingers through my hair to make sure nothing was left behind after my shower. God, I wish they'd stuck around for that. My tub is definitely big enough for three people. Especially if I'm sitting on someone's lap.

*Yeah,* I text back finally, ignoring the three texts from Nic that come through at the same time. While my anger towards her has cooled and I'm not so actively upset as I was yesterday, I don't want to talk to her. I can't, not right now, when I'm fighting the guilt-by-association feelings over Ava's death.

God, I wish things weren't so different in the daylight.

*Are you here?* I fire off, sliding on my ankle boots that make me a few inches taller. Paired with my black jeans and an over-sized hoodie with cracked, faded graphics showcasing one of the old *Texas Chainsaw Massacre* movies so that I'm living up to the Halloween spirit, I trudge downstairs, eye on my phone as he writes his reply.

*Of course I am. I'm outside.* Sure enough, as my feet land on the last step of the staircase, I hear our doorbell ring; the sound reverberates throughout the house and summons Dad. He smiles at me, obviously a little surprised to see me up and dressed at only nine am, but opens the door anyway without a word.

Even from where I am, I can feel the shock emanate from him in waves as he stares at Phoenix standing on our welcome mat. He's dressed similarly to me, in a pair of fitted black jeans, black and white sneakers, and a jacket over his gray hoodie that's just as faded as mine.

"Good morning, Mr. Scott," he greets pleasantly, hands in his pockets as he peers up at my dad without a trace of malice on his face. "I'm here to pick up Bailey."

Dad looks back at me, brows raised in curiosity. I give him the same look, and he grins. "You should come in, Phoenix," my dad invites, and I have to fight a roll of my eyes at his reaction. I step off the last stair, just in time for Dad to close the door behind my maybe-boyfriend. "Where's your friend? The one from the fair the other night?"

"He's sleeping," Phoenix replies, offering my dad an apologetic smile. "He doesn't do well in the mornings. Definitely more of a night owl."

"What was his name again? He's not from around here, right?"

Phoenix nods, walking with my dad to the living room as I follow. "He's from Montana, actually. Just as far north as us, but a hell of a lot further west." He holds up his fingers to show a small amount of distance, and dad chuckles. "And his name is Rory. We're dating, actually."

That makes my dad stop, and he turns to give me a pointed look, as if I hadn't heard.

I had, but I'm still surprised Phoenix is admitting that to my parents. If I could hand signal him to silence, or ask him why without looking suspicious, I would. But already Dad is urging him to sit, and when Phoenix takes a seat on the sofa, Dad plants himself on the other end of it, zoned in on the younger man's face.

"Dating?" he repeats as I sit down on my favorite recliner, thrilled to see how Phoenix is going to work this out. "Sorry, I'm not trying to seem shocked. I just... Well I kind of thought..." He glances at me, and Phoenix gives an apologetic chuckle.

*Right* as my mom walks in, just in time for Phoenix to answer.

"Well, yeah. That too. Bailey likes Rory, and he likes her. They really hit it off when we first came back. He and I aren't exactly traditional, you know? And Bailey knows exactly what she's getting into with us." When he throws me that fond smile that's only partially a show for my parents, my heart melts.

"And you're okay with that?" Mom insinuates herself smoothly into the conversation, eyes on me. "You're fine knowing they're together and were first?"

"*Technically*, I'm the one who was in love with him first," I point out. "Remember in third grade, Mom? I announced to you I'd marry Phoenix one day. Daisy even helped me make wedding invitations." The shock on Phoenix's face is short-lived, and he hides a snort. "So, yeah. And it's not like we're fighting over Phoenix." God, I never thought I'd be explaining to my parents I'm in a *throuple,* and it's worse than I could've ever imagined.

My dad doesn't look put out by his words, especially with my input. "You know if you hurt my daughter I'll have to make all kinds of dad-threats, right?" he says lightly and shares a grin with Phoenix, who nods enthusiastically.

"Oh, I'm sure. But I also think Bailey would kill me first." His gaze falls on mine and I fight to remain where I am, instead of throwing myself onto his lap in front of my parents. God, I hate it when he looks at me like that and I'm not in a position to just jump him. "Isn't that right, Bailey?"

"Let's...tone down the talk of killing," my mother interrupts. "After last night, are you sure the two of you should be going anywhere?"

I get to my feet with a sigh and Phoenix follows suit. "It's fine, Mom," I tell her, grabbing his hand and lacing my fingers with Phoenix's in case I need to tow him out the door for a grand escape. "It's not a big deal. Well, Ava's death is." The words prickle down my spine, and I swear Phoenix moves closer, as if he can feel it too. "But we're not doing anything dangerous. We're going to get breakfast, maybe hang out until Rory wakes up, and *not* go out wandering the town after dark. I promise."

"I guess I can't convince you to come home early? You can bring them and we'll even leave you alone?" My mom half-protests.

"No, you cannot." I'm already mostly to the door by the time I stop and Phoenix offers them a small wave. "Now we're leaving. Together. On a date. And I promise, I will call you if I need help."

"Bye, Mr. and Mrs. Scott," Phoenix calls in his best good-son voice while I tug him out the door. "It was nice seeing you again." He remembers the door sticking, and I watch, impressed, as he closes it behind him without much issue.

"It's weird to see you act like that," I admit, dropping his hand as we walk down my porch stairs. "All nice and innocent."

"But I am nice and innocent," Phoenix purrs, hooking an arm around my shoulders and leaning in to kiss my cheek. "That's what you like about me."

"Is it?" My brows jerk up. "Because you weren't nice and

innocent to *me*. You just made me admit to my parents I'm in a throuple. Or at least, fucking a couple, I don't know—"

"You're not just fucking a couple." Phoenix's voice is flat, leaving no room for argument. "I wouldn't do that to you. And since he's not here, I have no problem telling you that Rory likes you more than he thought he would. I think he's falling for you, sweetheart." He nuzzles against my face, leaning me back against his SUV that sits in our driveway to say, "Though how could either of us say no when you take us like you were made just for us, hmm?"

"*Fuck*." I have to pull away, and I feel redness on my cheeks as I shake my head. "You can't say stuff like that in my driveway while the sun is up."

"Oh, yeah?" he chases my lips to give me a quick kiss, then opens the door for me. "I'll say it later, then. Is that better? In your bed, after I've climbed through your window again so I can hold you down and fuck you like you deserve to be fucked."

By the time he's in the car and my door is closed, I've almost managed to calm my body down, reminding her that this is neither the time nor the place to get so worked up.

But then Phoenix smiles at me, his hand brushing my fingers, and all of that work goes straight out the window as I stifle a groan and buckle my seatbelt like a responsible passenger.

"Have you ever been here?" The small restaurant he stops in front of looks new, judging by the paint and the shiny, unblemished sign stating we've arrived at The Young Cricket Grill. We're not in Hollow Bridge anymore, but I've been to Ivesborough, the town we're in now, more than once or twice.

"To this restaurant? No, not in my life. But yeah, I mean. Didn't you play a lot of soccer here?" Being the closest high school to Hollow Bridge, I'd been dragged along to Phoenix's soccer games back when he'd played.

He visibly winces at the memory. "Don't bring that up. I meant the restaurant."

"Are you embarrassed because you were a great soccer player, or because Daisy and I made signs and stood in the stands screaming your name?"

"More the second," Phoenix replies, and I realize it's gotten easier to talk to him about Daisy, like the more I say her name, the less it hurts. If he feels differently, he's not making it easy for me to see. In fact, whenever I've brought her up, he's been just as into the conversation as me. As if he doesn't mind talking about her, either.

*Maybe it helps him too, like it helps me now.*

"But also because I explicitly remember a game where you were standing on the bleachers yelling at some girl, telling her you loved me. Do you remember that?" He peeks at me as we walk into the small building together, and I fight to hide my scoff of indignation.

"I would never. Probably."

"Oh, you did." Phoenix snorts. "Daisy had to calm you down. You know you're not subtle, right? That I've known you've been into me since you were in second grade?"

"I didn't have a crush on anyone in second grade," I demure, shaking my head as we seat ourselves at the hostess's instruction. Phoenix takes the lead, finding a booth in the corner of the restaurant and sinking down onto the bench. I follow suit automatically, sitting across from him and leaning back so I can look at him as I say, "It was the summer after second that I had decided I was in love with you. I turned down a *lot* of eligible third graders for you. Did you know that?"

"I didn't," he drawls, and his legs inch forward until they're pressed to mine, one calf trapping mine playfully as his ankle hooks with my own. "And what did you tell all the boys in third grade who wanted to buy you a milk carton, hmm? That you were taken by a fifth grader who you forced to play knights and dragons with you on the weekends?"

"Something like that, for sure," I agree. It's hard to remember why I'd been so afraid of him for so long, but easier for me to fall back into the familiarity of being in love with him. "Phoenix?" I scratch at the plastic laminated menu that serves as a placemat, and I feel his eyes on me as he looks up at me from his own. "You'd tell me, right? If you... If this..." God, it's hard to get my feelings out when they're embarrassing and complicated.

The waitress saves me momentarily, taking our drink orders and promising to be back in a minute while we finish looking over the menu. Though I know for a fact the delay is on me, and I scan the options while she gets our drinks, hoping to find something that catches my eye.

"You two know what you want?" she asks, setting the drinks down on the small napkins in front of us. "Or do you need another few minutes?"

I can feel Phoenix watching me, waiting for me to say something, but I don't look at him as my thumb slides over the plastic. "Can I get an omelette with, uh, cheddar cheese, ham, and onions?" I ask, sitting back up as the toe of Phoenix's shoe rubs lightly against my ankle.

"Sure can, hon," she agrees, her gaze going to Phoenix. "You want your usual? And for me to bag up your boyfriend's usual too?" The dark-haired murderer nods, his smile friendly, if not particularly welcoming.

"Thanks," he tells her, but the woman is already walking away, going behind the counter presumably to take our orders to the chef. I'm pretty sure we won't be waiting long, since there are only four other tables with people sitting at them, out of the sixteen or so in the restaurant.

"Would I tell you what?" Phoenix prompts, voice carefully empty.

"If you..." God, it would be so easy to just derail my thoughts and make a joke out of this. But one look at Phoenix's face, at the shrewdness of his gaze and the serious set of his lips, makes me realize he wouldn't let me get away with it.

"Sometimes I'm afraid Angleson is right," I explain in a rush. "Or my mom, or whoever. That you're going to kill me, too. That you don't actually like me, or I'm just here until you're bored. You have *Rory*," I remind him, watching him reach across the table to gently, ever so gently, wrap his fingers around one of my wrists and pull my hand toward him across the table.

"Rory is definitely hard to say no to," Phoenix agrees, humming lightly as he runs his nails up my fingers, making them twitch. "And Angleson can be convincing, I guess. But she wouldn't be half as intimidating if she clearly didn't spend four hours a day spraying her hair to look like that."

The corners of my mouth twitch upward, but I fight the smile that threatens to appear.

"The easy one first, I think. Have I ever given you any indication I blame you for my sister's death?" he asks, eyes pinning mine and keeping me frozen. Not that I could move anywhere, since he has custody of my legs and one of my hands. It's so distracting that he's still touching me, and I try to remember my well thought out arguments.

"It's just that Ava said—"

"Ava said a lot of things last night," Phoenix whispers, leaning closer to me. "And only a few of them were true. It was not your job to talk Daisy off of the ice after what they'd done to get her on to it. Do you understand me?" His grip tightens and my fingers curl, just for him to flick my index finger pointedly, making me straighten them again so he can run his nails over my skin just the way I like.

"I guess." Relenting at last, I look away. "But it's hard sometimes. You don't know how I've felt all this time."

"I think I have a pretty good idea," he remarks in a mutter. "You think I don't blame myself? When I knew something was going on with the two of you that Daisy wasn't telling me. Look at me, Bailey." As much as I don't want to, it's impossible not to, and his eyes, his gorgeous, dark blue eyes that glitter like sapphires, are more open and honest than I've ever seen. "It is *not* your fault. It has *never* been your fault. And I have never, not once, lumped you in with the others in any capacity. Do you understand me?"

When I nod, he looks at least a little satisfied, and his grip loosens, though he doesn't let go of my wrist. "And for your second concern. I *love* Rory." The words twist in my stomach in a way I hadn't expected, but he still doesn't let me pull away or retreat from him. "But you know what I've learned in the past few weeks since this all started and I saw you again?" As I watch, he draws my palm to his face, lips brushing over my pulse point before he says, "I am more than capable of loving more than one person in this life, Bailey. And I promise neither of you will suffer for it."

If he hadn't already melted just about every line of resistance, that would've done it. It's so hard not to launch myself across the table and kiss him or cry with relief. I don't doubt him for one moment, though I do find myself saying, "And Rory knows that? He's okay with it?"

"He's a little obsessed, I think. In a positive way." He's quick to add the second part, though I can tell he's worried about how I'll take it, by the way he searches my face for answers.

"There's a positive way when a serial killer is obsessed with you?" I ask softly, teasingly, after making sure there's no one around to hear.

"Uh, yeah. He was obsessed with me and look at me. I'm fine," Phoenix laughs, finally letting go of me.

"Debatable," I reply, not shocked by the small pinch to my knee I feel under the table that nearly makes me yelp.

"Mouthy," he teases, settling back in his seat.

"Hey, umm…" A thought strikes me like painless lightning, and I tap my knuckles against the table under me. "Can I tell you something?"

"I'd be insulted if you weren't spilling your weirdest secrets to me by lunch," Phoenix replies lazily, leaning back in his booth. "What's up?"

"I thought I knew who the killer was." My words are soft, and I lean towards him when I say them. "Well, before I knew it was you and Rory. There was this guy at the fairgrounds on the first night you saw me there? When Rory was stalking me in the woods?" He nods, waiting for me to go on.

"He ran into me that night, and it creeped me out. Then after we talked in the park for the first time. He was there too, but—"

"Ernie McMann," Phoenix sighs, resting his hands on the table. "Yeah, he's a creepy guy."

Shock ripples through me, and it takes a few moments for me to say, "Wait, you know who he is?"

"That is who we're thinking about dumping suspicion onto," he explains. "Ernie isn't that nice of a guy. Rory called his brother in Montana—it's a long story. His brother is an investigator or something and looked into him. Ernie has problems keeping his hands to himself. Especially around women." His head tilts to the side as he waits for my reaction, expression neutral.

"Oh…" I mutter, shocked. "That's not what I was expecting."

"He's just a drifter. A violent, handsy drifter with a bad record. Please don't end up alone with him, okay, Bailey? But by now the cops are interested in him, from what I can tell. So I can't really wish he wasn't in Hollow Bridge this year." Phoenix rolls his shoulders in a shrug, some of the tension ebbing out of the conversation.

"That's fair," I agree at last, tapping my knuckles on the fake wood of the table one more time before relaxing back into my seat. "Creepy, though. Since when do violent drifters show up in Hollow Bridge?"

"Since we needed one for an alibi?" Phoenix chuckles. He picks up his straw paper, folding it between dexterous fingers before saying, "So catch me up. What's it been like in Hollow Bridge since I've been gone, and how haven't you perished from boredom by now, hmm? Clearly, there has to be a secret."

After our meal and taking up more time in the diner than is probably polite, Phoenix holds the door open for me when we leave. I brush by him, purposefully letting my hand graze his hip, only to hear the catch in his breath that's oh so satisfying. His hand tightens on the bag of Rory's breakfast, plastic crinkling under his fingers, and he's quick to lean down, just in time to whisper in my ear, "We are leaving the public eye, you know. I could pull over and repay you for all the times you've done that today."

"Do it," I dare, already on my way to his SUV. "Then you get to explain to Rory why his breakfast is cold."

"Lunch, by the time we make it back," Phoenix mutters, unlocking the car so we can both get in. I take the food when he starts to put it behind me, the warmth of it sinking into my thighs. "Thanks. Do you need to go home, or anything? I thought we'd spend all day together, but if you don't want to—"

"We should parade ourselves in front of Detective Angleson's house," I reply enthusiastically at his hesitation. "Just to make it known that we're not upset that Ava is dead and, you know, we're together. Since she hates you so much."

Phoenix stares at me, and for a few seconds I wonder if I've gone too far with my teasing. Before I can say anything, however, his lips split into a smirk and he shakes his head with a snort. "You really are a vicious little thing these days, aren't you?"

"Oh, like that isn't the pot calling the kettle black," I shoot back, as he turns the key in the ignition and sets to programming his navigation system to take us back to the hotel.

# CHAPTER 26

For a serial killer, Rory is absolutely adorable when he sleeps. It's hard to reconcile the sadistic, blood-loving murderer I've come to adore with this man, curled up on his side on the hotel bed with his face relaxed in sleep.

"He looks so...harmless," I admit in a whisper, edging closer to Phoenix.

"It's why I don't always wake him up," Phoenix agrees, shoulder pressed to my own. "He's adorable when he sleeps."

"He's not asleep." Rory's voice is rough and heavy with tiredness. His words drag, and as I watch, his eyelashes flutter ever so slightly, signaling that he really is awake. "Are you guys back already? What time is it?" He opens his eyes to slits, just to roll over and bury his head in the pillow next to him, inhaling what I assume is Phoenix's scent.

"It's almost noon," Phoenix tells him, striding past me to kneel on the bed so he can dangle the bag of food near his boyfriend. "And I brought you sustenance."

"You also brought me Bailey." Rory rolls over onto his stomach, face now more firmly in the pillow. "If I can only have one, I want Bailey."

"Because I'm great at wake-up calls?"

"Because waking up to you riding me would be way better than food."

Phoenix snorts and moves, straddling Rory as he drops the food onto the bedside table. "You're so lazy," he murmurs, rubbing circles on his boyfriend's shoulders. I join them on the bed, legs crossed under me as I sit in the warm spot Rory has left empty.

"*Me*?" Rory's protest is strangled. "*I'm* the lazy one? I'm the one who did most of the clean-up last night. And yes, I mean that for both situations. Plus I ran more than you to catch Ava." Still, he lets out a soft, pleased groan as Phoenix's fingers dig into his muscles. "Fuck, you can keep doing that." His other hand reaches towards me blindly and I tap his palm, flicking it when he twists his wrist to grab my hand.

"Sleep in, then?" I offer, lacing my fingers with his. "Take a day off?"

"This is my day off."

It takes a while to wake him up, but mostly because I think Phoenix enjoys seeing his boyfriend sleepy and relaxed. I can almost feel how much he loves being the one completely in control, especially when he presses his open mouth to Rory's throat and his boyfriend can only moan.

But finally, when he does sit up, he immediately grabs the bag of food beside him, inhales, and opens the box to find the massive stack of pancakes waiting for him. "Thank fuck for you two," he groans appreciatively. "Just give me, like, twenty minutes to eat and, I don't know, a few to get ready. Where are we going? Should I dress up or look for a new clutch to match my eyes?"

. . .

"Sometimes it's creepy that you don't live around here anymore, but you still know way more places than I do," I point out as we stand in the short line for the hayride that he'd somehow known about from two towns away, even though he technically lives two hours from Hollow Bridge and shouldn't have known anything about it. Hell, even I hadn't known this place existed before now, and I'm much closer than him. I can already hear the tractor slowly chugging its way up the lane, and I shiver despite the two jackets and beanie I'm wearing. "Do you just like, look up shit to do for fun? I'd think Rochester is a lot better than here, even at Halloween."

"Rochester doesn't have you," Phoenix reminds me sweetly, shaking his head.

"Yet," Rory mutters, half to himself and half to his shoes.

"I used to go to all kinds of places when I was in high school. Every haunted house or corn maze I could find, you know? Even if they weren't in Hollow Bridge. I just remember places and check to see if they're still open—" He breaks off when my phone rings, but by the ringtone, I know I don't need to answer it.

It goes off again as I scuff my foot against the grass, aware that both of them are looking at me, expecting some kind of answer. "Cold tonight, huh?" I ask, gazing up at the cloudless sky. "At least it's not raining again." According to the news, the rain from the night before is still making it difficult for detectives to make much of the grisly scene of Ava's murder.

What a shame.

"Your phone is ringing." Rory says it almost like a question, like he isn't sure if he's hearing it correctly. "You know that, right?"

"Uh, yeah. I forgot to put it on silent." God, I'm awful at lying. Even by omission.

"Whose ringtone is that?" Phoenix's question is more suspicious, less confused, and I just shrug.

"Does it matter?" When my gaze snaps down to his, it's a mistake. I can't look at him *and* lie, so I give up the eye contact, letting my gaze slant to the ground instead. "It would be rude to answer it while we're on a date."

"Well, I'm giving you permission to answer it, and we won't consider it rude." The challenge is clear in his voice, and his brows arch when my phone starts ringing again, obviously daring me to refuse.

"I can't." I step closer to Rory, who looks a lot less curious about the phone thing than Phoenix. But when he wraps an arm over my shoulders and pins me to his side, I realize that was probably a bit of a ruse.

Phoenix steps toward me sweetly, cupping my face in one hand while the other reaches into my hoodie pocket to fish out my phone. If he takes too much time, or touches me more than he probably needs to, I don't say anything about it. But I do cringe away from him when he squints to read the caller ID.

"Why aren't you answering Nic?" His sharp tone needles me, the suspicion coming in waves. "Are you fighting?"

"Is she jealous?" Rory suggests, tucking my hair back from my face. "I'd be jealous."

"She's not jealous," I insist, rolling my eyes in Rory's general direction. "We're fighting right now. Well, I don't know if it's *fighting* technically. I just don't want to talk to her right now. Or Nolan. So if you see him calling, don't pick it up either."

"Why?" Phoenix scrolls through the notifications, then drops my phone back into my pocket where he'd found it. "What happened?"

"She bought me tomatoes. You know how much I hate tomatoes, and I consider forgetting it a capital offense." At least it's easier to lie when everyone knows I'm not even trying to make myself sound believable. "It's a three day ban on communication, but she's trying to reduce her sentence."

I make the mistake again of looking at him, though it's supposed to be just a quick check to make sure he doesn't actually appear angry. Instead, his gaze catches mine, holding it with his own dark blue, disdainful look.

"I gave you a tomato out of Dad's garden when you were a kid and you didn't three-day-ban me."

"I think we've established you're a special case."

"I think you're lying to me." The tractor pulls up to a stop in front of us, the wagon it's pulling is covered with a myriad of hay bales that create different levels of seating inside the wooden boards that make up a flimsy barrier between the wagon and the ground beyond.

"I think we're about to go on a really cool haunted hayride and I don't want to ruin it by discussing how my supposed best friends went to see Evan at the hospital then sat around talking to Ava about my *feelings*," I hiss, a little more loudly than I intended to. My heart thrums in my chest, making my palms tingle as I finally move to glare up at Phoenix, who is definitely standing closer than I'd expected.

But his expression is unreadable. He watches me, clearly thinking about something, before leaning forward to brush his lips so slightly, so sweetly, against mine. I could sigh like a fairytale princess, but somehow I hold it within myself.

"Sorry," he murmurs, his forehead pressed to mine as the people in front of us start moving.

"Don't be." I point to the small line, glad that we're some of the few people here tonight, which probably has something to do with Hollow Bridge setting an advised curfew and telling people not to go out for their own safety.

But that doesn't really apply to the three of us, when Phoenix and Rory *are* the danger, and I'm here to cheer them on, apparently.

*I'm a bad person.* The thought has been swimming around my skull all day, and hits me again as I step up onto the wagon. I follow Phoenix as he winds his way past and over hay bales, until we reach the back. He perches on one, Rory next to him, and without hesitation I sink onto the floor of the wagon, my back pressed to Phoenix's knees. Immediately he opens them, drawing my back against his thighs and leaning forward so he can hook an arm around my shoulders, pressing a kiss to the top of my head as he does.

"Well, I didn't know the floor was an option," Rory mutters, sliding down to sit beside me instead of perching on the hay bale. He leans against my side, and I tentatively reach out for his hand, noting that Phoenix moves so both of us can sit against his legs and he can throw an arm over Rory as well.

Rory, in response, pulls my entire arm to him, wrapping his fingers around my wrist and keeping it in his lap.

"Just don't *do* anything to them. Please," I request softly, hating that I can't trust that they just won't.

Rory chuckles as he turns, face close to my ear, when he says, "I'm not a fan of killing someone for hurting your feelings, darling. Even if it's for one of you two. That's how one of us ends up in jail, and I like myself way too much for prison."

"You really do," I agree whole-heartedly. "I just..."

"Don't trust me?"

"It's not just you." I glance up at Phoenix, who raises a brow in my direction as the tractor hitching into motion throws me back more firmly against the v of his thighs.

Including us, there are only eight people on a wagon made to seat at least twenty. The others are up near the front, three of them in one group and a couple as the other. They pay no attention to the three of us, nor can they hear what we say, I'd bet, unless we make an effort to be heard.

"I feel like a bad person today," I admit, wishing this

wouldn't keep coming back to make my day suck. "I mean, more than just today. But *especially* today."

"Why?" Rory's own tone is callously casual. "You knew we'd kill her anyway, with or without you last night."

"Well, yeah... But it's not just that."

"Then what is it?" he presses, his attention almost too much for me. I look away, to the edge of the woods as a woman with a cleaver runs out, begging us not to go into the woods beyond. A smile hitches at my face as she runs after us, her voice hoarse from all the screaming I'm sure she's done over the past week alone. Phoenix, for his part, seems content to listen, his fingers ghosting through my hair as he does the same for Rory.

"I don't *feel* bad," I whisper, unsure if either of them can hear me. "For Ava or Evan or Emily or Jack. I don't *feel bad* for them." When I glance at them, it looks as if they're taking that information in stride.

"Why would you feel bad, sweetheart?" Phoenix murmurs in my ear. "They got what they deserved."

"Yeah but, if I were an okay person, I'd feel bad."

"You also wouldn't be fucking us, going on hayrides with us, or having starred in about half of my dreams this morning," Rory agrees. "I fail to see the issue." From the corner of my eye, I see Phoenix smack the back of his head lightly, but I don't react.

"I'm not like you two," I say at last, hating that I'm feeling so conflicted on our hayride date. "You're so good at being...well, it's going to sound like an insult, but I don't think it is. You're good at being *killers*."

"He wasn't, when we first met," Rory is quick to point out. "Or do you think he already wanted to stab someone? Have you stopped to think that maybe, instead of being *not like us*, or so far on the other end of the good-person spectrum, that you've been waiting to cross that line, too?" My face falls lax with shock when I look at him, but his smile just grows. "Oh, I see we *haven't* thought of that, have we? That maybe you're just a budding serial killer in disguise, Bailey—"

"Stop," I tell him, voice quiet. "I'm *not.*"

"You—"

"Knock it off." Phoenix interrupts him dryly. "Don't say shit like that when she doesn't want to hear it."

*When she doesn't want to hear it,* he said, instead of *when it's not at all true.* Does Phoenix agree with him? That I'm way more like them than I think I am?

Well, it would definitely explain why I can't seem to feel a damn thing for any of my dead peers, but that could also be the lack of natural empathy or the childhood trauma coming out to play.

"Fine. I can be nice," Rory agrees, scooting closer to my side so he can lean against my shoulder. Someone near the front of the wagon screams when a man runs beside us, yelling and making vague threats while fake blood streams down his face like he'd just poured it on himself.

"Does stuff like this scare you?" Rory asks, more curious than anything. I feel him reach up, and from the corner of my eye, I can see their entwined fingers on Phoenix's thigh. "At all?"

"No," I assure both of them, tilting my head back on Phoenix's other thigh so I can stare at the stars. "This stuff hasn't scared me in a really long time." I feel Rory's teeth lightly against my throat, but he doesn't do more than tease for a few moments before turning to do the same to Phoenix's thigh. "But it's still fun."

"My family was never much into Halloween," Rory tells me, pressing his leg to mine for warmth. He really does run hot like a radiator, and I fight not to stretch out on him like a lizard to steal some of that heat. "So I never got to do most of this as a kid."

"That's why you have Phoenix," I tell him without hesitation. "Since he hails from the most Halloween-heavy town in the US, he'll fill the void your lack of celebration has clearly caused in your soul."

I expect a quick quip, or a witty, snarky retort like he's good at. I don't expect him to stare at me, watching my face like he's waiting for something. "What about you?" he asks, with a seriousness that surprises me.

"Me? I grew up here too. I've been celebrating Halloween—"

"That's not what I mean. I mean *you*. I get you too, right? You and Phoenix, like the sexiest matched pair alive? To—what was it?—fill the void in my soul left behind by years of not celebrating Halloween?" His grin is wolfish as he waits for an answer, but unfortunately, my brain is stuck buffering long enough that it falls slightly. "What?" he questions.

"You want me around that long?" The words slip out before I can stop them, but the moment they're out, Phoenix drags me tighter to him, arm tight around my shoulders as Rory all but climbs into my lap, forcing me to meet his gaze so I can tell how serious he is.

"To clear this up, yeah," Rory informs me, eyes bright. "*We* want you around that long. Longer, actually. We want you around when we're all old and gross and *gray*."

"He'll go gray first," Phoenix murmurs against my ear. "He's the oldest by a year." I can't help the laugh that sneaks past my lips, though I manage to lock it down at Rory's withering look.

"I just worry you won't, after Halloween," I admit soberly, leaning back to press my cheek against Phoenix's. "I worry that I'm doing the same thing I always do. Where I fuck up and try too hard, too soon, and spill my feelings all over the floor. It never ends well, obviously. And I just worry that you'll get tired of it, too."

"Nah," Rory denies. "I like mess. I like feelings. Spill your feelings so I can clean them up for you and watch you do it all again. So long as it's for me and Phoenix, and no one else.

Because you know..." He tilts his head to the side, cheer in every inch of his expression. "If you ever decide you're falling for anyone else, I'll have to kill them."

"And I'd have to help," Phoenix agrees quietly. "Half because I don't want him to go to jail and half because, I mean..." He shrugs, a soft laugh huffing against my ear. "The moment I made you come in the woods was the moment you were ours. And it'll take a lot more than whatever you have to throw at us emotionally to undo that."

"If you say stuff like that, I'll get attached," I warn, one hand coming up to grab Phoenix's wrist, the other gripping Rory's hoodie so I can pull him closer to me. "And then you'll never get rid of me."

"Good." Rory's purr is instant, his grin curving wide and cruel over his lips. "Because no one else deserves to even *touch* you, darling."

It's not until after the hayride when we're halfway to Phoenix's SUV that Rory suddenly stops me, one finger grabbing my hoodie so he can drag me to him, his gaze serious. "I worry," he informs me, shooing off Phoenix with a quick flick of his fingers. The latter hesitates, then goes, unlocking his car as his low, melodic whistle drifts back to us.

"That we won't get home before midnight and you'll turn into a pumpkin?" I shift uncomfortably in front of him, not sure what he wants.

"That you think you're a consolation prize. Or an accessory to Phoenix that I have to put up with. Just because we didn't grow up together and I'm not the one who's been obsessed with you for years." He goes quiet, watching me as I struggle to deny what he's said, even though it's totally true.

"It's not...I mean, I get that I'm not Phoenix or the boy you—"

"No," he agrees, cutting me off and dragging me that last step closer. "You're *Bailey.* Not Phoenix's Bailey, or that girl we fucked in Hollow Bridge during our murder spree. You're *Bailey*. *Our* Bailey. Not just his. I may have not known you very long..." He drifts closer, mouth inches from mine, causing my breath to hitch in my chest. "But one of the perks of being like me is that I know what I want from the first moment I see it. And I've wanted you since I watched you walk alone into the woods." Before I can say anything, he brushes his lips to mine, then lunges forward to sink his teeth into my lower lip, drawing a surprised, pained yelp from my throat.

"I think this is the part I tell you that if you hurt Phoenix, we won't be friends anymore," he informs me, still with that too-serious tone of voice that reminds me of the man who wears a mask and carves up my peers in moral support of his boyfriend. "But I don't need to, because you won't. Because you're drowning in us, and I'd rather pull you down to the depths of the ocean with us then send you back up for air." With one hand splayed against my lower back, he worries his teeth across the small wound he's made in my lower lip.

"And as nice as Phoenix is? He'd take your arm and pull you down with us just as quickly as I would." Then he licks the blood from my lip, and the seriousness evaporates, his normal boyish charm and smile coming back to his face. "And also, we should do something soon. I'm not getting up early, but I deserve some Bailey alone time, too."

"Maybe Bailey's boring alone," I point out after a few seconds, finding I'm not willing to remark on the other parts of what he'd said that have my feelings in chaos and my stomach feeling like it's full of birds in flight.

"That's okay," he chuckles. "Because Rory isn't. Now please smile at him so he knows I didn't hurt your feelings, or it's going to be super awkward later when I fuck you and make him watch."

"He's going to just watch?" I can't help but ask, surprised.

"You really think so?" Phoenix doesn't seem much like a *just watch* person to me.

But Rory flutters his lashes at me, twining his fingers with mine as we near the SUV. "I have so much confidence that he will. Especially after we've handcuffed him to the desk. Now smile, Bailey, or he'll start to think we have a nefarious plan in store for him."

"But we do."

"Maybe, but he doesn't need to know that."

# CHAPTER 27

I gnoring Nic's calls lasts three days. Though I have a feeling it would've lasted longer if Rory and Phoenix weren't around to distract me from how upset and hurt I'd been. But by the time a few days have gone by and Nic calls again, I realize I'm not nearly as upset as I had been. Not by a long shot. In fact, I'm on the verge of asking if she wants to hang out when the doorbell rings, drawing my attention from the kitchen island and toward the foyer.

"Weird," I mutter to myself, remembering that Mom and Dad are out. It's not like we get a lot of visitors anyway, and unless this is a surprise visit from the boys, or Nic and Nolan, I have no idea why anyone would be dropping by at four in the afternoon for a social call.

"I'm coming," I say to the empty air, brushing by the living room furniture on my way to the door, just as the bell rings again. Whoever it is seems impatient, and they had better be dying if they're going to ring the bell more than twice.

The door catches, because of course it does, but I've already yanked it open by the time I see Angleson standing there, a frown on her face. Unfortunately, it's too late to pretend I'm spontaneously having a heart attack.

"We need to talk," the detective tells me, without waiting for me to say anything. "About your friend, Phoenix. Do you know where he was about four nights ago, when Ava died?"

More than anything, I wish I could slam the door in her face, but instead I smile, tilting my head to the side thoughtfully as I say, "Maybe with me?"

"Maybe not," she replies, her grin unfriendly. "Can I come in?"


M y knuckles are beginning to sting from slamming on the hotel door by the time it opens, but since I'm barely looking at the door, Phoenix has to grab my wrist so I don't hit him in the face.

"Sorry," I breathe, unclenching my fingers. "I'm sorry. I know it's a weird time, and you weren't expecting me, and I definitely didn't tell you I was coming—"

"You're fine." Phoenix's tone is patient, but the look in his eyes shows me he's suspicious and, above that, worried. "What's wrong?" He tugs on my arm, gently pulling me inside, even though I'm still glued in place, looking around the parking lot to make sure no one knows I'm here.

But even if Angleson did follow me, she has to know I'd come here, since I'd admitted to her that I'm in a relationship with the two of them.

*I hadn't known what else to do.*

"I'm sorry," I say again, letting him pull me into the large room with its huge, king size bed planted firmly against one wall. "Where's Rory?"

"Trying to shower," the auburn-haired killer comments, pushing the bathroom door open with his shoulder, dressed in only a pair of sweatpants. Seeing that much skin on display distracts me temporarily, and a grin hooks his lips upward. "Good to know looking at me can soothe even the most troubled soul."

"Angleson came over," I say, looking between them instead of letting Rory's teasing do anything to calm my nerves. "I thought it was going to be just her stupid threatening nothings. You know, it's not like she's had *any* evidence against you guys. So I thought—" I take a deep breath, realizing I'm rambling, and will my heart to stop pounding so hard. "I thought this would be the same."

"Why don't you sit?" The worry on his face isn't strong enough for the situation, but Phoenix still hasn't looked away from me. "Come on, Bailey. It's okay, whatever it is."

"It's not okay," I assure him, letting him drag me to the bed. I sit down, toeing my shoes off as I do, and curl my legs under me, trying to rub some warmth back into my bare calves. Given that I'd been in a hurry to get to them once I was sure Angleson had left, I hadn't even thought about changing out of my lounge shorts and light-weight, long-sleeve t-shirt. I'm paying for it now though, and shiver from the lingering chill from outside.

"None of us are dead or in jail, so it definitely is," Rory argues, wrapping his arms around me from behind and pulling me against his radiator of a body. As per usual, it feels like someone has cranked up the heat to eleven when I'm pressed against him, and I let out a sigh, trying to force myself to relax.

"She knows, or thinks, anyway, it's you," I tell Phoenix slowly, my gaze finding his as I say it. "There's some evidence that she swears points to you, and she thinks I know more than I'm letting on. Which I do, obviously. But..." I trail off. "She says your alibi isn't strong enough to keep you out of jail. Says she *knows* you're the one doing it, since you have the most reason. I kind of argued with her and said that I'm pretty sure *I* have the most reason." A strangled laugh leaves my throat, and Rory hugs me harder. "I'm sorry. I tried, I said you were with me when Ava was killed, but she wouldn't believe me. We're screwed, I'm so sorry."

Phoenix doesn't react like I'm expecting. Hell, he barely reacts at all, and only looks at Rory, who rests his head on my shoulder.

"Kind of expected it." Rory shrugs behind me. "She's been gunning for you since you came back. What's her deal with you, anyway?"

Phoenix grimaces. "Her little brother was in my grade. He had a huge crush on Daisy, but he was a jerk. Remember him?" he looks at me, and I nod. "He tried hitting on her when she was thirteen, and I politely asked him not to," Phoenix shrugs, like that's the end of it.

"He broke his nose," I supply, sensing Rory's disbelief. "For sexting Daisy. It was a big thing. Pretty sure she's holding a grudge, based on how she's acting." Rory makes a face at my words, but his deadpan gaze lands back on Phoenix, all of that sweet human charm draining out of him.

"You had that coming," he informs his boyfriend coolly. "Stop shaking, Bailey. It's okay. We knew they'd try to blame him and look for ways to prove he did it. We knew the moment we came here he'd be suspect number one. I'm actually surprised it's taken her this long to grow the balls to actually accuse him."

They...*knew?*

My fingers stroke over the skin of his arm as I talk, and I bite down on my lower lip. "Are you going to leave?" I ask, not sure what's going on or what their plan is. "Or...stop?"

I'm expecting Phoenix to answer, but it's Rory who chuckles and kisses my cheek sweetly. "No, darling Bailey," he purrs in my ear. "No, we're not going to do any of that. We don't need to. This is why I'm here. And, even better, why you're here."

"No." Phoenix's voice is sharp. "No, I told you, Bailey isn't getting roped into this—"

"Bailey roped herself into this," Rory snaps. "And it's not like I can force her. Either she wants to help, or she doesn't. Either way is fine, by the way," he informs me, eyes flicking back to mine. "But it would be really great if you could help us out."

"Help you out?" I reply, my words slow and soft. "How? I've tried telling her—"

"No, there's no *telling her* anything," Rory laments, shaking his head. "We have to show her that Phoenix can't have done it. We give him a concrete alibi, one that she can't poke holes in."

"How?"

"By killing Jayden while Phoenix is in plain sight." His answer is instant, like it was obvious all along, but Phoenix shifts uncomfortably, his attention all on me.

"Then what do you want me to do? I can take Phoenix to the fair, or something? It might be a little obvious if we parade him into the police department, but I'm open to ideas." Caught up in thinking of potential solutions, it takes me longer than it should to realize neither of them are saying anything. My heart seems to freeze, the beats of it taking longer than usual to pump blood through my body, and I feel slow, groggy, lethargic even for a few seconds. "But you already know what you want me to do, don't you?"

"Don't ask her," Phoenix warns, shaking his head again. "I'm serious, Rory. This is *Bailey*. She's not me. She's never wanted to—"

"How badly do you want to help Phoenix, Bailey?" Rory interrupts, his mouth pressed to my ear. "Bad enough to, I don't know, put on his clothes and mask, carry his knife, and come with me tonight?" His teeth graze the shell of my ear, and I can't help the full body shiver that goes through me.

"Do you like us enough to help me kill him, if it comes down to it, so the town knows that it can't be Phoenix after all?"

His voice is soft, almost inaudible in the small space between him, Phoenix, and me.

But I can feel every twitch of my nerves as the room stands still. I can feel my lungs filling up with air acutely when I take in a breath, and the scrape of Rory's skin under my nails as I drag my gaze up and up, until I'm staring into the sapphire depths of Phoenix's gaze. "Help you kill Jayden?" I repeat, my lips numb with the words. "You trust me to do that?"

"Yes," Rory replies. "One thousand percent."

"But he's asking too much," Phoenix argues, shaking his head. "Tell him no, Bailey. We'll find another way, I promise. Just—"

"Yes." The one, singular word that falls from my lips causes Phoenix to go quiet, and he's so impossibly still I wonder if I've turned him to stone from shock. "Yes," I say again, with the conviction I can actually feel replacing the cold surprise in my chest. I turn just enough to look at Rory, seeing the approving look in his eyes as I add, a moment later, "What do you need me to do?"

"Oh, Bailey," he sighs, kissing my cheek. "You really are too perfect for us, you know that? Don't argue, Phoenix," he adds, looking up at his boyfriend again. "You need this, and she's offered. Respect her choice, or leave."

"*Is* it your choice?" Phoenix asks, kneeling in front of me, one hand on my knee. His nails scratch at my skin, and his eyes won't let mine look away. "If you're afraid, or you're just doing this because you think there's no other option—"

"*No.*" I interrupt him, shaking my head in case he somehow hadn't heard my too-loud reply. "No, Phoenix. I don't need you to try to give me a way out, or talk me out of this." Surprising myself by realizing that it's true. I *don't* need a way out. Though, I'm definitely more scared by the idea than I want to let on.

"Let me do this. For you. For Daisy, and maybe just a little bit for me, too."

# CHAPTER 28

Phoenix looks amazing in his murder clothes when he wears them.

    ...I do not.

Standing in the mirror of the hotel bathroom, I pull at the sleeves of his black hoodie, staring at my reflection in the mirror. I look like him, at least. Our heights aren't too far apart, and I'm not well endowed enough that a sports bra can't take care of the issue of my breasts being an obvious giveaway that I'm not a guy. But I just don't look like him. I don't look as menacing, or as, well, hot if I'm being honest as either of them do.

"I can't believe I'm doing this," I mutter, tugging on the sleeves one more time. My hair is braided into a crown that loops around my head, making it appear shorter than it actually is so that when I pull the hood up, I'm a black-haired guy just like Phoenix. My face looks pale in the mirror, and I wince when banging on the door sets my heart racing.

"Come *on*, Bailey," Rory calls, sounding impatient. "We need to go. Phoenix needs to be at the fair in an hour, max."

"Yeah—" The word comes out as a soft, unsteady croak, and

I clear my throat. "Yeah, okay. Sorry, guys." I've been in here way too long, I know, but it's still hard to grip the doorknob and pull it open, revealing what I look like to the two guys.

Immediately Phoenix's brows shoot upward as he looks me over, and after a moment he comments, "I don't know if it's the murder look, or the fact that you're wearing my clothes, but I really want to fuck you right now."

"Both," Rory replies conversationally, making a motion for me to spin around for him as he continues, "Because I want to fuck her too, and I think she makes a pretty hot murderer. We can fuck her another time."

"Right, because murder is much more important." I laugh uncertainly. "It's really okay?"

"More than okay," Phoenix promises, and reaches out both hands holding the rest of what I'll need.

His mask rests in his left hand and I take it, marveling at the smoothness and the cleanness of the plastic mask. A ribbon is attached to the sides, and I wonder if this is really what they've been relying on to conceal their identity every single time. If it were me, I'd be duct taping the damn thing to my face.

The other thing he holds out to me is his knife. It's cold in my fingers, and heavy, but when I start lifting it out of his grip, Phoenix closes his fingers around it and steps close to me.

"Let me do it," he murmurs, reaching out to my belt and sliding the sheath onto it. When it's done, his fingers linger, pushing up the bottom of his shirt so he can stroke along my skin.

"Stop." Rory slaps at his hand with a roll of his eyes. "Touch her after. And remember to give her your gloves."

Phoenix snorts and fishes in his pocket for them, then hands them over to me. "They're hot," he warns, when I slip them on and flex my fingers in the fleece-lined leather. "You'll thank me for it later, but you'll be miserable for a bit."

"I'm never miserable when I get to be where your fingers

were," I reply lamely, eyebrows wiggling like I've made some kind of genius innuendo.

Rory groans. "I'm going out to the car," he announces, sticking his tongue out in disgust, "before I puke. Maybe when you're done making bad jokes, you'll even join me."

We do join him, and the ride to the edge of town, near the fairgrounds, is just as tense as I'd hoped it wouldn't be. Finally he pulls over, but before I can climb out of the passenger seat, where Rory had so *graciously* told me to sit, Phoenix snags my arm in his fingers, concern dominating his face.

"Please be careful," he murmurs, when Rory's door is shut. "I just got you. I can't lose you."

The door whips open as he speaks, and Rory looks at him, unimpressed. "What about losing me?" he demands, hands on his hips like he's actually offended.

"You're good at this. You won't get hurt, or lost, or caught," Phoenix growls. "She's new. She's...*Bailey*."

"Bailey is about to get offended if you say her name like an insult again." My words are sharp, but my eyes are soft when I grin to show him I'm joking. "I'll be careful, okay? But you have to let go of my arm so I can, you know, go do the thing with Rory."

"Seriously," Rory agrees. "Kiss her and go enjoy the fair."

Phoenix makes a face at that, but leans over to brush his lips to mine. "Come back safe," he whispers, and releases my arm before blowing a kiss at Rory as I slide to the sidewalk beside the SUV. "You too, lover," he calls, and Rory just waves at him in response.

"Don't get eaten by hordes of children, or whatever," the auburn-haired killer replies. Phoenix blows him another kiss and I close the door, prompting him to pull away from the sidewalk and back onto the road.

"He's such a worrier," Rory comments, pulling his hood up over his head. He doesn't add anything else, but reaches over to tug mine up as well, hand lingering on my shoulder when he does.

"Right, and you aren't?" I ask him dryly, falling into step with him when he starts to walk into the woods, away from the street.

Somehow, he'd already known where to go, and had told me earlier that seventy percent of being a serial killer that doesn't get caught is research. He'd then informed me that he'd been tracking Jayden's schedule for a week, and knew for a fact he'd be at the gym until late tonight, probably playing basketball either with his friends or practicing alone.

From where we are, the gym is a mile or so walk.

"It *was* me in the park, by the way," he says suddenly, falling back so he's in step with me, his strides equal to mine when he makes an effort to make it happen. "I thought I could scare you out of looking at us too closely, or trying to figure out who we were."

"I figured it was you," I admit, hand clenched around Phoenix's mask. "When we were in the woods and I asked, I wasn't really asking. I can tell by your cologne. And your voice." Not to mention his eyes, which are so different from Phoenix's.

"And it was sexy as hell, right? With my knee between your thighs and us out there, where anyone could see?"

"Not the word I would've used at the time, unfortunately."

We walk in silence for a bit, the trees as tall and silent as judgmental, immortal sentinels. It makes me shiver, even in Phoenix's warm clothes, and I'm definitely glad that he's better at dressing for the weather than I'll ever be.

"How did you meet Phoenix?" I ask at last, breaking the silence. Rory looks down at me, surprise on his face, and I watch as he thinks it over, considering.

"College is the easy answer," he admits, not missing a step. "We had a math class together our freshman year, first semester. He was...different," Rory explains. "He was in rough shape. Lashed out at everyone, especially me anytime I riled him up. I thought it was funny for a while. Until he flipped out on me and pinned me against the wall in the bathroom." His smile curves, widening over his lips. "It was hot as hell. I kissed him."

"Right then? Before you were even friends?" I can't help the shock that makes my brows twitch upward, and Rory chuckles in spite of himself.

"Right then. I just grabbed him and tried to devour all of that anger that was eating him up inside. He punched me, by the way. But then kissed me back the next day, so it was okay. I wasn't lying when I said I've always known what I want, Bailey."

"Yeah, I guess you weren't."

"I'm really glad you never punched me. I would've let it happen. And I guess if you still want to, that's on the table." He flashes me another quick grin, and I shake my head in response.

I'm not going to punch him.

"Who was the first person you killed?"

That causes him to stop, and Rory turns to look at me. He's not as tall as Phoenix, so I can meet his gaze without tipping my chin back. His hand comes up, and he touches two fingers under my chin, as if he needs to hold me there to keep sight of my eyes.

But I'm getting better at eye contact. With him and Phoenix, at least.

"You ask the strangest questions. Even Phoenix didn't ask me that for *months*. He was too afraid to know before the idea became appealing to him. But that's not why you're asking, are you? It's not so you can figure out if you want to be like me."

"You're right." If I'm going to be a murderer—as weird as that sounds even in my own head—I'm not going to use Rory as a business and ethics model. It'll be for myself. For my own feelings, or to do something that can't be done another way. "I just want to know, I guess. I'm incredibly curious, okay?"

"Yeah, you really are." He lets go of my chin and starts walking again, taking a few moments before he speaks. "I was seventeen, she was sixteen. We were dating, and she cheated on me. I got upset, and she thought it would be cute to have her boyfriend come threaten me. Only, he didn't stop at threatening." His voice is clipped, words almost cut off when he says them, like he wants to get this over with as quickly as he can. "When he tried to slam my face into a mirror for the second time, I grabbed one of the broken pieces in the sink and stabbed him with it. He was nineteen, and huge. Obviously, everyone knew. I mean, my bloody hands and that same blood all over him were a dead giveaway." He rolls his shoulders in a shrug.

"But I was never charged for anything. It really was self defense, after all." But his voice darkens as he speaks, and I'd give anything to see his face. "If they'd seen how I taunted him, how I made sure it hurt as much as it could, then I doubt I would've gotten away with it so easily. Does that scare you?" His eyes are suddenly back on mine, like he's looking to catch a reaction before I can hide it.

"No." My reply is honest, through and through. "He deserved it. Why would self-defense bother me?"

"Because I stuck my finger in the cut and wanted to see if I could rip it open like moth-eaten curtains?"

"Okay, well, I'm still not upset. Could you like..." I lift my fingers, wiggling them back and forth. "Feel his jugular under there? Was it slippery from all the blood? That would've been pretty epic of you to like, grab his jugular with your finger and rip it." Hypothetically, of course, I add mentally, for my own personal benefit.

"...You are a violent little thing. Vicious, too. Has anyone ever told you that?" From the other side of the trees, the lights from the gym loom in the darkness, illuminating the parking lot.

"A few times," I admit. "Mom says it's because I play with dead things, and girls shouldn't play with dead things."

"Interesting." He doesn't leave the trees completely, but does glance at the cars as he walks. Finally he stops, and I recognize the old Jaguar as the present Jayden's dad gave him for graduating high school. Even now it looks messy, with dirt and mud sprayed up the sides and dried in clumps.

If that were mine, I sure as hell would be taking better care of it. Rory kneels, settling back on his heels as he stays within the darkness of the trees. Stillness creeps over him as I sink down beside him, and it strikes me that he has to be good at the waiting game, especially by now.

I don't tell him that *waiting* is one of my weak points. My weakest, if we're being honest. But I settle down on the ground beside him, leaning against the tree to my left, and tell myself that I'm going to do the best I can, given what I have to work with.

We don't have to wait long, and I'm definitely grateful for it. The last of the big lights from the public gym are flicked off, and when the doors open, Jayden comes out, talking to someone who veers off from him almost immediately to go in their own direction.

Immediately fear seizes me, and for a moment I'm sure I'm going to vomit.

"Thank *God,*" Rory mutters, getting to his feet in the darkness of the trees. "If we're going to do this more often, we've got to teach you how to wait."

"I waited just fine!" I argue, scrambling up and gripping onto his forearm without thinking.

"That is undeniably false," Rory murmurs, his hand coming up to splay against my chest, as if he can feel my racing heart even through the jacket and the shirt underneath. "Put your mask on, Bailey. And stop panicking. You don't have to do anything except be here, okay?"

He'd told me earlier that I didn't *really* need to come at all, but that one of his rules with Phoenix was that they worked in pairs, at least for the kills that really mattered and they weren't creating separate alibis for.

But I'd told him, forcefully, that I'd rather come to make sure nothing goes wrong.

Now, some part of me regrets that. Especially when Rory helps me, taking the mask in my trembling fingers and guiding it to my face so I can tie it around my head and flip my hood back up where it's covering my hair. He puts his on next, with practiced ease, and reaches out to grip my shoulder.

"Don't freak out. Don't talk. Just in case someone else sees," he tells me kindly, and pulls me back into the deeper shadows with him as Jayden slowly walks towards his car, paying attention to his phone instead of his surroundings.

Most of the other cars are gone by now, and the few that aren't are parked in the employee section. Before Jayden gets into his car, the man he'd been talking to pulls out of the parking lot; so by the time Jayden is close enough that I can see the details of his face...he's alone.

And not paying attention.

Both those things make things easier for Rory. My companion looms out of the darkness, steps silent, and just walks up to Jayden, unsheathing the knife at his waist.

It isn't until the very last moment that Jayden turns, eyes wide, and his phone falls to the ground. He gets his hands up, and for a second, I'm sure the ex-high school basketball player is going to put up a real fight. I'm so sure, in fact, that I take a step forward, ready to help.

But he doesn't get a chance. There's a word on his lips I don't get to hear as Rory jams the blade into his stomach and rips the blade upward like he's trying to open him up from belly to sternum.

And in the darkness, the blood just looks like tar as it stains Jayden's clothes and drips to the asphalt below.

Now my feet take me out of the woods, and I edge closer to his car, shoulders hunched, as Rory stabs him again, this time in the chest. My steps draw his attention, and he looks at me from behind his mask as he grips Jayden's coat, the jock's hands scrabbling at Rory's hands, silently begging him to *stop*.

It's only then I see that Jayden's lips are moving, his eyes wide as he stares at Rory with silent pleas dripping nonstop from his lips. I tilt my head to the side, not saying a word, and find that the fear has been replaced with something else.

Something all-consuming that forces me to *watch* as Rory digs the blade into Jayden's throat and pulls.

I don't expect the blood spatter to reach me. Even when it sprays on the hood of his silver Jaguar, I don't think to move until hot, wet blood has sprayed across the mask and the sliver of exposed skin at my throat.

*It's so warm.* Hot, really, as I smear the fingertips of Phoenix's gloves in the blood at my throat and look at it in the dim moonlight. I hear Jayden fall to his knees, but it takes a few seconds to look at him again, and I can finally define the feeling that holds me captive, holds me to watching every bit of this.

*Fascination.*

Jayden whines. Writhes. Cries, even. But none of it evokes any kind of sympathy in me. Instead, I crouch down a few feet away, noting how similar he looks to a dying raccoon I'd once seen after it had been hit on the road.

The same frenetic movements possess Jayden as had that raccoon, until he's thrashing and moving in ways that won't get him anywhere. His eyes roam and rove, fixing on my mask and on Rory's, and even when his limbs have stopped and his breathing has gone shallow, his eyes still move.

To me.

To Rory.

And finally, to something neither of us can see as they go still, then glaze over in death.

*I should feel worse than this.* I should feel something, anyway. Anything at all, other than a dull satisfaction that Jayden is dead along with most of the others that bullied Daisy until she'd done something that ended up in her death.

But try as I might, I can't get excited or upset about this. Not like I thought I would, at least.

"Didn't I tell you to stay?" Rory asks, not sounding particularly upset about it.

"You did," I say, straightening as he steps away from the body. "Are you mad at me?"

"No." He shakes his head, then motions for both of us to head back into the woods before he says, with surprise, "I'd just love to know where you got a taste for dead and dying things, is all."

"Maybe I've always been this way?"

"Okay, well, that would mean you *are* just as fucked up as we are." He's quiet as we walk, until he asks, "Hey, this doesn't count as our date, right? Because I still want a real date in the next few hours, or I guess I could wait a day at *most*."

"Does it count as a date? Did you take Phoenix on a murder date?" I ask, more curious than anything at what this *would* be considered, in a relationship kind of way.

"I did not."

"Then this is definitely a date. Because I want to say that I was the one who got to go murder with you on our first date." My smile is wry as I take off the mask, and when Rory does too, I'm surprised to see the fondness in his grin, and the way his eyes dance.

"I'll allow it, then. I suppose. But just this once, and just so we can hold it over Phoenix's head. I told him to get us funnel cakes, by the way. Do you like funnel cakes?"

"Doesn't everyone?" I ask, eyes narrowed at the question. How could anyone *not* love them? Unless they just don't love fun.

"God, I knew you were perfect, Bailey."

P hoenix doesn't forget the funnel cakes. He doesn't forget anything, but after we've thrown our murder gear into the SUV as sneakily as possible and changed into the clothes we'd stashed in the back, Rory and I meet him in the fairgrounds. He's waiting for us at a table, a large funnel cake generously topped with powdered sugar, along with a cup of chocolate sauce.

"I love you," Rory proclaims, sinking down across from him as I do the same, sliding up next to my personal furnace as the chill takes hold in my less than warm clothes that don't hold a candle to Phoenix's jacket. Rory doesn't mind, obviously. Not when he hooks an arm around my shoulders and drags me against his chest with a kiss to my temple. "Seriously, though. Marry me?"

It's crazy how calm they are. How all of us are, even though we just *killed a man.*

Well, Rory had done all the work, obviously. I just stood there, in case something had gone wrong. But still, it should bother me that we came straight here without even...doing what? Honoring the dead? Calling for help?

Jayden was pretty far past help when we'd left him to bleed all over the parking lot.

*Shouldn't I be reacting more than this?* Or is this just the normal way to go about things? As if all we'd done is run an errand, instead of committed murder.

"I'd be a terrible house husband," Phoenix quips, pulling

me out of my thoughts. He tears off a piece of funnel cake as his foot hooks around my ankle and pulls my leg toward him under the table. "Did everything go okay?"

"Everything went *amazing*," Rory replies enthusiastically. "And we've discovered Bailey's new hobby."

"It's not that new," I protest, snagging one of the water bottles and taking a drink. "Or that interesting."

"What is it?" Phoenix asks, just as blasé about the murder as Rory is. As I am, I guess.

"Darling Bailey really likes playing with dead things."

# Chapter 29

I t's hard not to just stare at the phone in my hand listlessly. I'd rather not answer Nic's texts at all; and certainly not at eight am. But I know she's going to get more and more worried the longer this goes on, and since we're not actively fighting anymore, I probably need to get over the grudge I'm still holding onto for her visiting Evan and talking to Ava about me.

After all, Ava's dead, and Evan will be before Halloween is over.

And as today's the thirty-first, I doubt he has very long.

*Good morning,* I text, sending that before adding. *I hope you have a good Halloween. I'm not feeling the greatest.* It's absolutely a lie. There's nothing wrong with me, but I need a reason for her not to come over. And if there's a chance I can infect her so that she might miss out on the last days of the festival or worse, Halloween night, then she'll steer clear of me.

Even if the idea that I could get her that sick that fast is stupid, at best.

*Oh no!* She texts back, and the speech bubble appears again, showing me she isn't done. *Do you want me to come over?*

So much for my plan of keeping her away. I lean against the low wall outside of the library parking lot, my hip sore from sleeping on it wrong. Both boys are still asleep, as far as I know, but my brain had been so loud I knew the moment I woke up that I needed to walk.

And the cold air that makes it possible for me to see every breath that puffs out from between my lips has done wonders in quieting down my thoughts. I think of how to respond, but the distant whine of sirens pulls my attention upward, just in time for me to watch the cop car zoom on by.

I wonder if it's for Ernie. Though I haven't seen him in a while, I've heard from Rory and Phoenix he's still around. Maybe he's finally worn out his welcome.

*Nah. Don't worry about me. I'm going to go back to sleep for a while.* It's another lie. It's all fucking lies, but I push off of my low-wall seat and keep walking, my strides eating up the distance to the small hotel.

*If you're sure. Just let me know if you need anything?* I tell her I will, and slide my phone back into my pocket as I round the street corner that puts me back in sight of the hotel, and I see the door that'll take me straight back to the boys' bed.

My feet stop, steps coming to a dead halt on the edge of the sidewalk as I look at the scene in front of me. There are three cop cars scattered in the parking lot of the hotel, and as I watch, the boys' door bangs open, revealing Phoenix.

In handcuffs.

"*Fuck,*" I whisper, but before I can dart forward, I stop. There's nothing I can do for him, even though my heart pounds in my chest and I search for ways to do something that will get him away from the cop car and his current arrest.

But I'm not a cop.

And Angleson is with them, to make things worse. She's ignoring Rory, who walks out of the room behind her, his hair messy from sleep and face full of distress. Through some manner of luck, he looks up, meeting my eyes even from over fifty feet away.

And even from here, I can see the small shake of his head that tells me my instincts were right and that staying away is going to be better for me than going over there. I can't do anything for either of them right now. I'll just add to the suspicions.

But hell, I'm not sure what I can do from over *here* either. Hopefully Rory will know, and I can talk to him once Phoenix has, unfortunately, been taken away and the other officers go with him.

The only bright side I can see is that they won't find anything in the room. Rory and Phoenix are smart enough that they don't keep their murder clothes, masks, and weapons in the room. Instead, they're stored in a hidden compartment in Phoenix's SUV, where the spare tire sits. Sure, the cops will probably find them eventually, but it would take a while.

I wait, backing up into a neighboring yard that's thankfully overgrown with large, leafy trees and thick bushes that, even in fall, provide great visual cover. My only regret is that now I can't see or hear anything at all.

But what's there to hear? It's obvious why they're arresting Phoenix. Though I'm not sure *how* they've gotten the evidence to charge him.

My concentration is broken when cop cars zoom by, all three of them in a line, and when I stand up, I see Phoenix's SUV following with Rory behind the wheel. He slows just a little when he passes me, but doesn't stop.

He can't. They'd know.

But I meet his gaze through the glass, stomach flipping around in my body like a caught fish, and swear I see the worry in his eyes.

*Fuck.*

If Rory is worried, then I should be devastated. He's the one who's good at coming up with plans. He's the one who can make things better in a bad situation. That's the impression I've been going with, anyway.

I'm just Bailey.

My phone vibrates and I look down at it where I'm holding it clutched in white-knuckled fingers. I already know who it is, but Rory's name on my phone just solidifies my suspicions.

*They don't have any real proof. She basically admitted that when she arrested him. They're just trying to get him to fuck up.*

*Don't do anything stupid.*

*We just need to think of a way for them to completely disregard him as a suspect.*

*Seriously, don't do anything stupid.*

*I won't do anything stupid,* I promise in a quick text, and he reacts to it with a thumbs up, then goes silent.

But I get that, and I don't expect anything else. He has a Phoenix to get out of jail, after all.

*But so do I.*

My breath hitches, but I force myself to pull in a lungful of air as I stand up and move back to the sidewalk. The police are gone, all of them, so I prowl back to the hotel and use the keycard I'd swiped before my walk to get back in.

Unfortunately, I don't have Phoenix's murder clothes to wear, or Rory's, since they're well hidden in the SUV. But I can mimic it, to some extent, with the clothes I'd picked up from my house last night, post-festival and before I'd headed back to the hotel with the boys. I yank on black jeans, my sneakers that are pretty similar to the ones they wear, and a black hoodie on as well. The only differences are the fit of the jeans, and the lack of a zipper on the hoodie. After that I wind my hair back up into a braid, coiling it around my head and pinning it there with trembling hands as I think and work without paying attention to the movements my fingers make.

I have to find a way to convince the police Phoenix is innocent, and the only way I know how to do that, the one plan that comes to mind...is bad.

Worse than bad, it's fucking terrible. It probably won't even work, for one, and there's a good chance *I'll* be the one who lands in jail, right beside Phoenix, instead of actually getting him set free. But on that front, I'm trusting that what Rory had said is true.

If the police only have circumstantial evidence, if they don't have anything to really hold Phoenix on, then if I 'prove' that the murderer is still at large, then they would have more of a reason to let him go.

"This is stupid," I tell my reflection as I check it in the hotel mirror. This is *really stupid*. Yet here I am, closing the door hard behind me and taking off back the way I'd come, not quite knowing what I'm looking for, or where even to start looking.

It takes me two hours to find him.

Two *hours* of meandering through the parts of town where I've seen homeless people hanging out before. We don't exactly have much of a homeless population in Hollow Bridge. We're too small for that. But we've had people traveling through over the years who stay for a few days, or up to a week.

But it's at the rundown Methodist church where I find him, biting his nails as he sits on the porch steps and stares at the gas station parking lot next door. Ernie McMann has never looked worse, and definitely doesn't seem to have showered since the last time I'd seen him.

*Am I really doing this?* I can't help but ask myself, following the sidewalk around the church to where it connects to the parking lot in the back. I'll be on the other side of the building from the man, thankfully, and hopefully I'll be able to find what I'm looking for without him ever seeing me.

*But it's so wrong.* There's no way around that, especially not when my eyes land on a pile of junk next to the back loading dock of the large church that has served as the town's food bank since its inception long before I'd even been conceived.

My steps falter for a moment before I make my way to the pile, leaning over it to find something that would tell me this is, in fact, Ernie's junk. I don't want to touch anything, but I pull the end of my sleeve over my hand, looking through what lies on the smooth concrete.

If this is his stuff, then I'm in luck. There's a pair of knit gloves that I grab and stuff into the pocket of my hoodie, just as I hear the crunch of glass being stepped on from around the corner. *Fuck.* My heart leaps for my throat desperately, and I dart for the cover of a nearby dumpster with boxes piled in front of it.

Ernie rounds the corner just as I duck down, staggering toward the pile like his balance isn't what it should be. Or like he's drunk. As he comes close enough that I can see his eyes, I think that is probably the case.

My fingers flex against my sleeves, and I sink down further as my muscles tense to the point of soreness while he mumbles to himself and sorts through the pile.

*He's going to notice the gloves being gone.* My brain is so helpful to whisper that thought in my head over and over, as he paws through the rest of his shit once, then twice. *There's no way he doesn't notice.* Right?

Or...maybe not. With a grunt of recognition, he jerks something free that shines in the light, and my heart twists in my chest when I realize it's a fucking *knife.* God, I don't want to be anywhere near here. I don't want to be doing this, and the reality of my situation and the stupidity of my plan hits me while I'm hiding behind a dumpster from a man with a history of abuse and assault.

There's no way this is going to work. I cram my eyes shut against the burn of tears in my eyes. There's no way... But I refuse to give up my idea. I don't know what else there is for me to even *do* to help Phoenix.

And right now, helping Phoenix is the most important thing. That's the thought that steadies me. The one that makes it easier to draw breath into my trembling lungs as finally, Ernie walks back around the other side of the church, holding onto the wall for support and dropping the knife like he never cared about it in the first place.

But I wait, giving him ample time before I stand up and dart away, the gloves safely in my pocket and my feet creating more and more distance between me and the homeless man with every single second that passes.

*I need the knife.* The thought flickers through my brain and I pause, instead of completing my escape. It's perfect for this. For me.

Well, for Evan.

But my courage wavers when I sprint back to the building and peer around the edge of it. Ernie is at the far side, and if he sees me, this is all over. It's been incredibly lucky so far that he's so dense, and maybe not all there, and I keep my eyes glued to his back as I edge forward until I can bend down, grab it, and *run.*

I know this is a bad idea with every inhale, every soft sound of my sneakers against the sidewalk. It doesn't take much thought to route myself toward my destination, and it gives me time as I walk across town to think about how stupid of an idea this is.

I'm going to get caught, for one. I'll probably end up in jail. That's a given. My hands tremble at that, but I ball them into clammy fists at my sides as I focus on the walk instead of the consequences.

I wish I could think of anything else in the world to do to help Phoenix and Rory. If they only arrested him, then they think there's only one killer. But why wouldn't they? That's the illusion that Rory and Phoenix have worked to create, and as far as I know, everyone in town has fallen for it.

Surely if Angleson knew there were two killers, she'd have let it slip or asked if I knew who *both* of them were on any of the occasions we'd talked.

I check my phone as I make it to the hospital, going around it to the parking lot behind. Really, I should be thanking Nic for this, though she can never know what I've done. The knife is heavy in my pocket as I look around for Evan's signature red Mustang, which, according to Nic, his mom had driven here a few days ago so it would be here when Evan could leave the hospital on his own.

Normal people would've hitched a ride home with someone, instead of wanting to drive themselves. But Evan is a jock, and proud, and stupid.

And I am the luckiest person in the world, when I see the flash of red that's as far from the building as possible. Maybe his mom hates him, because mine certainly would've parked my car much closer, if not insisted on picking me up herself.

For the first time in my life, everything lines up perfectly. Like fate. Like a strange intersection of fate and luck and *want* that I've been straining for all morning. But there are still so many things that could go wrong, and I'm acting on instinct, instead of a real plan. After all, the only thing I have to go off of is how Rory killed Jayden last night, and how no one had seen us or even thought to look when we'd sat with his cooling body in the parking lot.

I don't get close to his car. But I'm also not as worried as I would be if Nic weren't the sheriff's daughter, and a twinge of guilt makes me twinge with discomfort. Nic hadn't told me about Evan for me to come here to kill him. And she hadn't vented to me about her mother's continued bad moods as she tried and failed over and over to get the town to set up better security systems.

Especially around important places, like the jail, city hall...

And the hospital.

Casually I walk past Evan's car, heading to the alley only a few feet behind it where boxes tower toward the high windows of businesses that are long gone. Only a few people live here, but there's no one in the alley and the windows of the inhabited floors have the blinds firmly drawn.

No one can see me here, if I'm careful. And I've never felt the urge to be more careful in my life as I sit down between two of the large containers. I slide to the ground between the boxes, my hood raised, and tilt my head back against the brick wall behind me to find the patience to wait.

For however long that takes.

Footsteps along the asphalt find my ears, but they aren't a surprise. Not when I've been watching Evan's slow journey from the hospital's back entrance and across the parking lot for the past five minutes.

He's exhausted, for one. Weak, for another, and I can tell he should've either stayed in the hospital another day or at the very least had someone come pick him up. My eyes stay fixed on him as he staggers, stumbles, and occasionally walks almost steadily toward his car that's parked on the edge of the lot, keys clutched in one hand.

I've thought a lot about this over the past six or so hours. And while the urge to pee is strong and unforgiving, I've refused to do more than softly whine to myself about it, while throwing myself the world's quietest pity party.

Instead, I focus myself by flexing my hands around the knife I clasp in my fingers. I look at Ernie's gloves that are thankfully big enough to fit *over* the pair I'd stolen from the hotel maid's cart before leaving this morning. There's no way this will get tracked back to me, Rory, or Phoenix.

Hopefully, I've thought of everything. Even if it means my

skin under both pairs of gloves is swelteringly warm even in the Halloween chill.

God, what a bad Halloween this has been. While I don't do much to celebrate it anymore, this is exceptionally bad by anyone's standards.

The first time I call out for Evan, voice soft and shaky, he doesn't notice. I wait, giving him another minute before I call again, making sure the knife isn't visible in the dim light from the street lamps at the edge of the alley.

I doubt he'll be stupid enough to walk into the alley. Especially after getting stabbed. But all I need is a chance to do this.

"Evan?" I call, voice soft. "Can you help me?" I push myself to my feet, eyes wide as I hide the knife behind my back.

He looks up at me and stills, keys in his hands as he sees me in my all black outfit. Though I've pushed the hood back to make myself look less menacing for this moment.

"Can you help me?" I ask again, and for a few moments, after I blink, we're not standing in the hospital parking lot.

We're in the woods.

On the lake.

*And I'm about to fall in.*

I'd looked at him that day, face numb with panic. He'd been the closest to me. To either of us, and I'd reached out, fingers stretching, hoping, and praying for help. Only for the ice to give out and Evan to leave with the others.

If he has any intuition or survival instinct, he'll do the same thing right now. But a part of me hesitates. When he takes that first step toward me and the illusion of the ice-covered lake shatters from my mind, my heart sinks and I realize I can't do this.

I can't lure him over here to his death. Not even to save Phoenix. If Evan is willing to help me right here and now, how in the world can I pull the knife from behind my back out and stab him with it, framing Ernie in the process?

*We used to be friends.*

Evan takes another step. Then one more, until the distance between us is maybe four feet at best. He looks me over, warring emotions flit over his face so rapidly I have no idea what he could be thinking. But I need to figure out a lie, for when he makes it over here to help and—

"No." Evan shakes his head, a look of derision crossing his features. "I don't know what this is, but I'm not helping you." He shakes his head again, relief coloring his features as he pushes off the responsibility of doing anything. "Tell Phoenix I said hi in jail." His voice is flat, derisive, and I tilt my head to the side as my heart hammers against my ribs.

"How do you know I've been talking to Phoenix?"

Evan's smirk is surprised, like he can't believe I'm asking. "Because you couldn't get enough of him before Daisy died." I flinch at the callousness of his words. "So I'm sure it's the same now that he's back here." I hate the cruelty, the coldness of his tone. But deep down, can I really blame him for it? He thinks Phoenix stabbed him.

"Okay." I sigh, my shoulders falling. "Thanks, I guess." He's already turned back towards his car, keys still clutched in his hand, when I move.

"For what—" he starts, turning just enough to look at me, and I see the surprise in his eyes when I bury Ernie's filthy, greasy blade deep in his chest.

Evan collapses. He slumps against me, his weight taking both of us to the ground, though I make no sound when his gasps fill the air. He fights, struggling against me, and I drag the blade free, surprised at how easy this is.

Like he'd just fallen onto the blade accidentally, and it had just slid right in between his ribs.

"You don't know anything about Phoenix," I whisper, extracting myself from under his crushing weight and rolling Evan over onto his back. I kick his keys away and move to stand over him, the knife blade dripping from where I clutch it in my fingers. "And you don't know anything about me."

There's very little hesitation.

*And I don't feel any remorse.* Not when my knees fold and gently, so carefully, I kneel over Evan and press the edge of the filthy, short blade against his throat.

"Please," Evan gurgles, eyes wide. "Please don't. Bailey—"

"I used to think that if I did something like this, it would be for Daisy," I interrupt in a cool whisper. I press the blade deeper, my hand trembling with the effort as it cuts into his throat. My heart pounds, and a sick feeling tries to creep over me, only for the coldness filling my veins to shove it back into oblivion.

"But now I realize that it's always been for me." Quickly, before that rogue part of me can tell me to stop, I drag the blade across Evan's throat and sit back on my heels, his blood spraying in arcs that splash across my black clothes and pale cheeks.

But I don't leave. Not for a few minutes, at least. Not until he's stopped writhing, and his body has grown cold between my knees. Only then do I stand and toss the blade down to the ground haphazardly, ripping the already torn side of one of the gloves until I've left a piece of it, too, tucked under Evan's body, as if in his struggles he'd somehow managed to rip it off of 'Ernie' and it had gotten trapped there, instead of me placing it.

*I hope they believe it.* My thoughts are a whisper as I look down at him, and the coldness in my veins has taken over, freezing my emotions solid. *I hope this sets Phoenix free.* I step back from him and away, hands clenching around nothing before I whirl around and leave, knowing I need to stop by the church on my way back to my house to place the bloody evidence there instead of keeping it on my person to bite me in the ass later.

## CHAPTER 30

Once things are all taken care of, I end up just going home, as lame as it feels.

It seems like the best option to me, at least so I can clean up. It takes longer than I had expected for me to scrub the blood off of my face. Though in reality, I'd probably overdone it; especially with how sore my skin is. Which is more obvious once the water is off and I'm staring in the mirror at the red, throbbing patch where there had once been the dark crimson of blood.

I'm too afraid to tell anyone what I've done. Rory and Phoenix will find out, eventually. I know that for a fact. So will everyone else, though I'm hoping they won't think it's me. But as the night gets colder, trick-or-treaters stream down our road, and I look at the kids dressed in fancy, garish costumes as they screech for candy, I start to wonder if I fucked up. If Evan's not dead, even though I *know* that's not the case.

Finally, when I can't take the stress of staring out the window and hoping his ghost isn't about to show up, I sink down onto my sofa, and bury myself in blankets. I go to sleep with the tv on, turned to a classic movies channel that's showing *westerns* of all things on Halloween.

If my parents try to wake me up, I never hear it. I only know that when my eyes do open, the ceiling fan spinning into view, I'm not alone. For seconds, I have no idea why my brain has come to that conclusion, until my ears finally join the party and I hear the television that's still on, though is decidedly *not* on an old movie channel anymore.

"—*found dead in the parking lot, just hours after he was released from the hospital. Police have no leads, as this happened when they were questioning their only suspect. Now, the police think the murders might be linked to a violent drifter who's made his way into Hollow Bridge...*" The voice trails off, and I realize that the volume has been turned down, instead of the reporter trailing off into obscurity.

Finally, it dawns on me that I'm not sleeping in the position I'd curled up in. My body is lying along the sofa, head pillowed on someone's thigh while, under my oversized comforter, a hand runs up my calf and back down, soothing rather than teasing.

"She's awake." Rory's voice is plain, as if he's answering a question, though his is the first voice I've heard. "With perfect timing, too. I think she got to hear the news."

The hand on my leg stills, fingers squeezing my calf muscle gently. "Are you awake?" Phoenix's low rumble comes from the other end of the sofa, and I realize he's the one stroking my leg.

"Yeah," I whisper into the comforter, burying my face in it. They don't sound particularly happy *or* mad. "I'm awake." Rory's hand buries under the blanket, and he curls his fingers against my scalp sweetly, nails scraping at my skin.

"Do you want to stop hiding? You look like you think we're about to kill you. If we were, I don't think Phoenix would be half asleep under your blanket, you know."

"Depends," I mutter, voice still obscured by the comforter.

"If you're upset with me, then I'd definitely rather stay under here. It's safer." I'm so exhausted. So raw...like my nerve endings were frayed by the knife I'd used to kill Evan.

God, the memory of killing him makes my stomach roll, and it's hard not to groan into the comforter as I try to chase the feelings out of my brain. More than anything, I don't need to spend the next day obsessing over the feeling of how easily the blade sank into Evan's chest, or how it was almost *satisfying* to drag it across his throat—

"*Mad?*" Phoenix's voice is muffled, and before I can stop him, he jerks the blanket off of me, letting most of it pool on the floor.

Now there's nothing hiding me from them. Dressed in my pajama shorts and a thin tee, I feel completely vulnerable between the two of them, fully dressed and still wearing their hoodies and shoes. My heart stutters, and I want to do something—move or hide or sit up—but Phoenix pounces too quickly, knees sliding to either side of my thighs on the couch and one hand splayed just below my throat.

"How dare you?" he breathes, so soft that I barely hear him. "Don't lessen what you did for me. For *us*." He slowly curls his fingers, the fabric of my shirt coiling with them as he pulls upward, towing me up into the air over the couch so there are a few inches of air between the cushions and my back. "I could never be mad at you, Bailey. Never in a million years."

Comfortingly, Rory cards his fingers through my hair, and pushes Phoenix away enough that he can swoop in instead, picking me up without much effort and getting to his feet with me in his arms. I yelp, trying to stay conscious about the fact my parents are probably downstairs asleep, and dig my fingers into the hair at the base of his skull, eyes wide. "What are you doing?" I hiss as he carries me across the large room to dump me on my bed.

"Anything you could ever ask," Rory replies seriously. "We

put you in a bad position. You shouldn't have had to do that. *Ever.* But you did. I'll do anything for you, Bailey. You saved him." He gestures to Phoenix, who moves to prowl closer, unzipping his hoodie and throwing it onto his shoes on the floor. He's already barefoot, his heated gaze is fixed on mine, and the sound of Rory's hoodie zipper as he shucks his off as well is what it takes to pull me back.

"Tell me what you did. Please," Rory requests, sitting down on the bed in front of me, the mattress dipping under his weight. "I trust you, Bailey. I just want to make sure that there's nothing we need to do to make sure this keeps going smoothly." His voice is kind and comforting, and he drags me forward until my knees are on either side of his waist and Phoenix can slide onto the bed behind me, burying his face against my throat as one arm snakes around my ribs.

"I remembered what Phoenix said," I admit, conscious of his mouth on my shoulder, though he doesn't do more than rest his face there. "About Ernie McMann being a convenient suspect for if things went the wrong way. And what you texted me, too, about there being only circumstantial evidence to implicate Phoenix." Absently, I reach out to find Phoenix's wrist, and I hold it tightly while Rory's hand strokes over my knee.

"I found Ernie. It took *hours*, but he was at this old church where the food bank is. I was just going to take his gloves to implicate him. But then I saw he had a knife—"

"A *knife?*" Phoenix interrupts. "You stole a *knife* from a violent—"

"She saved your ass," Rory points out patiently. "So you've lost your reprimanding privileges for the night, my love." His sweet smile when his gaze finds mine again warms me from the inside, and for the first time tonight, I don't feel cold.

"So yeah, I stole a knife from the lair of the violent drifter," I go on, lightly. "And I went to the hospital. Nic said..." My throat closes around the only piece of *real* guilt I've been able to locate so far. I've used Nic's friendship, her confessions to me about her mom's job and venting, to kill someone. She'd be heartbroken, and more than a little pissed off.

But I have no intention of ever telling her.

"She said Evan was getting out today. That he'd demanded his mom drop off his stupid red Mustang so he could drive himself home. Thanks to her, I also know that the county keeps denying the funds to better equip the hospital's security system, or fix any of the things that are broken. There are no cameras in that part of the parking lot, and Evan's car was in the worst place ever." I don't mean to spill the stupid things; like my hesitation, and the way I'd seen a flash from that day from the lake.

But I do. The details fall from my lips like rain, and once I start, I'm unable to stop. I tell them about nearly giving up. About how I'd thought I couldn't do it.

I tell them how it felt with Evan's blood on my skin and the knife dragging across his throat, opening up his jugular until he wasn't moving anymore, or breathing.

I even tell them how I'd stayed until his body was cold, unsure of what else to do, and how I'd left the evidence after. But for a few seconds after, when I'm trapped in my thoughts and the cycle of disbelief and acceptance, I don't realize they aren't talking, either.

"Oh, Bailey." Phoenix buries his face in my hair and sighs. "They arrested him a little while ago. It just wasn't in time to make the news. From what my mom said, the cops are more than sure he'd done it, thanks to what you left there. Thanks to *you*."

"I just wish I didn't feel like this." Tears sting at my eyes, but I blink them away with varying levels of success.

"Like what, sweetheart?"

"So..." I move my free hand, making an aborted motion somewhere around my chest. "A little bit guilty. I'm cold. I just feel empty and strange. Like maybe I'm not really me anymore, or that something broke in me when I killed him. It's dumb, right? Tell me it's stupid and to just get over it." I need something to push me past it. Something to make the empty ache less daunting.

"You're not dumb," Rory is quick to answer. "And you're not alone. Most people aren't born murderers, Bailey. Myself excluded, of course. But you can't be surprised that this has been a trauma for you. That it's *hard* to get past the first time."

"Evan is dead," I whisper. "I'm not the one who should be feeling traumatized, or upset." But more tears fall down my face, even though I can't place the emotions that have them there in the first place. "I'm—"

"Bailey, you're perfect," Rory interrupts, both of his hands coming to rest on my knees. "You can't hold yourself to the standards of anyone that's not us. You can't lower yourself like that."

"That's not narcissistic at all," I can't help but mutter, but he turns my words into a gasp when he jerks me forward on the bed, forcing my knees wider around him.

"I just have a healthy ego and good ideas about self love," the auburn killer chuckles softly, slanting a kiss against my jaw. "I also know how to make the bad feelings go away. If you'll let us help you."

"It's sex, isn't it? Your answer for every problem *can't* be—"

"It can be for this one." Phoenix follows my movement into Rory's lap, closing in behind me to keep me pressed between them without any chance of escape. But I don't want one. Especially when Phoenix's mouth closes on the junction of my neck and shoulder and his teeth scrape against me, so deliciously that I nearly sob.

"Let us take care of you," he adds, bunching both hands in my shirt. "Just this once. Maybe more than this once." Before I can reply, he has my shirt up and over my head with Rory's help, and my shorts don't last much longer.

"Can you..." I feel bad asking. But I want to see them. I *need* to.

"What, gorgeous?" Rory asks, lips pressed just under my ear. "What do you need?"

"I want you both naked. I want to touch you. Please." They always end up stripping at some point during or after we're fucking, since I've learned both of them prefer cuddling naked. But I don't want to wait this time. I want to run my hands across their skin, and reassure myself that they're real and here, and I didn't fuck this up like I thought I had.

"Anything you want," Rory is quick to agree, and within seconds, all of his clothes are gone, tossed onto the floor in a pile that Phoenix's clothes are joining as well.

This time, I don't wait for one of them to grab me. I reach over my shoulder, turning just enough that I can kiss Phoenix, though my hand that isn't curled in his hair reaches out for Rory, urging him forward instead of giving us space.

I don't *want* space, after all.

I want them.

He gets the memo quickly, his lips finding my throat, my shoulder, and even nipping along my collarbones as I taste every bit of Phoenix's mouth as I can before twisting to grab Rory's hair instead. I drag him up to me next, leaning forward on my knees to press myself against him like a cat.

My shock comes seconds later, when behind me, Phoenix decides he doesn't want to wait either. He pulls me back just a little, just my hips, until he can grind his body against mine, letting me feel his excitement as he rubs his cock between my thighs.

"Let me fuck you, Bailey," he purrs, leaning over to kiss Rory as well. Trapped between them like this makes it even better, because I feel every hitch of breath, hear every soft noise that both of them make. I've forgotten his question by the time he pulls away, lips shiny and slick from Rory's mouth.

"You can do anything you want to me," I assure them both, getting a snicker from Rory in response.

"Oh, don't promise us that," he purrs, lunging forward to nip at my lower lip. "Or I'll be begging you to try all of my kinks with me from here on out."

"And you think I'd mind?" Phoenix pushes me forward, then Rory wraps his arms around my waist and guides me almost into his lap. If I weren't braced on his chest, I would need my arms on the bed, but when Phoenix's fingers stroke along my slit, I realize it's intentional.

I kiss Rory again, letting him feel and hear my reactions as Phoenix sinks his fingers into me, stretching and fucking me on them sweetly.

But he's taking way too long.

"Just fuck me," I beg, pulling away from Rory's mouth. "Please, Phoenix, just—" Rory yanks me back to him, catching my mouth with a snarl. Like it's the signal he's been waiting for, Phoenix slides his fingers free, drags my hips back to him, and thrusts into me deeply, not stopping until I can feel his warmth pressed against my thighs, and the way he's leaning against my spine.

"Good girl," he purrs in my ear. "You're so perfect, Bailey." His hand comes up to tuck my hair behind my ear, and he presses his mouth against my shoulder as he fucks me. Slow, languid strokes aren't what I'd expected, and it doesn't instantly turn me into a writhing, panting mess. Instead, his movements build a slow burn in my body, every thrust sending tingles up my arms and back, until I'm scraping my teeth against Rory's lip, and I can't help the way my body moves, urging him deeper and harder.

But I can't go far. I can't go anywhere, really, since both of them are still pressed against me, trapping me between them in the absolute best way.

"You're so gorgeous," Rory murmurs, resting a hand on my face. His other slips between our bodies, and I jerk when he strokes my clit teasingly, his fingers wandering across my shaking thighs instead of teasing me further.

"And you're *ours*," Phoenix agrees fervently, one arm tight around my waist. "You'll always be ours, Bailey."

"Because we won't let you go," Rory agrees, hands still holding my hips as Phoenix *finally* starts moving faster, thrusts becoming uneven and erratic. At last he sinks into me, and I barely care that I haven't come when his body presses to mine, going limp as he trembles and comes inside of me.

Rory gives him a minute. It's kind of him, considering his whole personality, before he pulls me forward gently, my thighs sliding over his. He lifts me just enough that our eyes are on the same level, my hands are on his shoulders while he holds my hips, and then he drags me downward, sinking into me just as Phoenix had, though at a different angle.

"Oh fuck," I whisper, knees clamping around him. It feels just as good as Phoenix, just as *perfect*. Especially when the black-haired killer behind me grips my hips and uses his strength to move me along Rory's cock, making everything so much better.

This time, I come first. My lips part, and fear shoots through me when I realize there's no way I'm not about to scream. But Phoenix must have the same idea, because he jerks my head to the side and presses his mouth to mine, swallowing each and every sound that Rory drives out of me.

"You're so good, Bailey." I hear Rory's encouragement, and I can feel his fingers digging into my hips. "Seriously, you're wasted in Hollow Bridge."

"You're better than this place," Phoenix agrees, lips moving against mine before covering my sob at the next wave of my orgasm that rolls through me while Rory continues to fuck me. But he doesn't last much longer. His grip becomes sharper, tighter, and he pulls me down as far as I can go, until my eyes find his and his length is so deep in my body it makes me nearly see stars. Only then does he let out a soft *fuck* of his own and come, Phoenix leaning over my shoulder to taste the sounds he makes as he does.

I can't get enough of watching them. Of feeling them on either side of me, and the way they're so perfectly effortless. But as if they can sense my thoughts, both of them break away, Phoenix sinking his teeth into my neck as Rory catches my lips in another deep kiss.

"Thank you," Rory purrs, kissing me chastely. "*Thank you* for saving him. I know you didn't do it as just a favor. I know he means as much to you as he does to me. As much as *both* of you mean to me," he amends, eyes glinting. "But thank you."

"Thank you isn't enough," Phoenix echoes against my throat. "But I'm willing to spend the next eighty years or so figuring out what is."

Warmth blooms in my chest, causing my fingers to grip both of them more tightly. But I don't let them see, if I can help it. Instead, I hitch a crooked grin over my lips and say, "That's generous of you, to assume we're all going to make it to a hundred. Did you know there's a history of scurvy in my family?"

Phoenix can't help it. He laughs in spite of himself, the warm sound echoing in Rory's grin and the way his fingers dance over my skin approvingly.

Neither of them let me help them clean up. Not even our clothes. But by the time they're done, and they're in bed with me, Phoenix pressed to my chest and Rory against my back with one knee between mine, I can barely remember any of the bad feelings that I'd been struggling with before.

They've chased it all away. The indecision and the almost-guilt. The hollowness, and any ache that I couldn't get rid of before. Instead, I'm warm, with Phoenix murmuring to Rory over my shoulder and they hold me between them as real, pleasant sleep finally reaches up to drag me under.

# CHAPTER 31

It's been years since any cars drove over Hollow Bridge. Definitely more years than I've been alive, and every crack in the crumbling stone and gap wide enough for me to wiggle my fingers shows the reasons why.

But that doesn't mean the bridge isn't safe, as long as you aren't lugging a two ton vehicle over it.

My fingers scrape against the stone as I sit perched on one side, staring down at the river that streams around stone columns built into the river bed centuries ago. The stones are covered in green growth, from moss to ivy, down by the river, and if I were to jump or fall from here, I'd most certainly break something.

With my luck, I'd break my skull.

*I can't go back.* The thought is absolutely dramatic, but still one that won't leave my head since I'd woken up early this morning, before the sun had even properly risen.

By now it's a little past seven am, and while the sun peeks through the trees, it's cold enough that I shiver despite wearing one of Phoenix's hoodies that I'd swiped from their hotel this morning.

*Two days.* That's really all it's been since my life went from questionably abnormal to, well, whatever this is now. Before that, I knew what Phoenix and Rory were, sure. But I wasn't...

Well, things are just different now, since I killed Evan to save Phoenix.

It's hard to know what to feel when everything in me says that a nice person, a decent person, would be a wreck over killing Evan. Even if it was for a good cause. *Even if he did deserve it.* But for me, the only twinge of guilt was from planting the evidence with Ernie's glove and knife, though even that guilt is easily chased away everytime it bubbles to the surface.

Judging by the fact Phoenix is free and Ernie has been arrested, things are wrapping up neatly enough that none of us has to worry. For now, at least.

But here I am, staring down at the rushing river under Hollow Bridge, and worrying.

*What am I going to do?*

*Where am I going to go?*

*Seriously, what am I going to do?* My parents don't know. No one will know, and that's part of the problem. I can't tell Nic or Nolan, and the feeling of a divide suddenly cracking into existence has persisted. At this point, it feels like Nic and I are on two different continents with how dishonest I've been to her, and from all the things I haven't told her.

"Fuck," I sigh, the word barely more than a breath. I've really picked a shitty situation to throw myself into without any forethought as to how I'd handle the consequences that come along with killing someone.

Footsteps scrape on the stones behind me, and I glance over my shoulder in time to see Rory moments before he sits down beside me, arranging his legs over the edge of the bridge. Within seconds, Phoenix is on my other side, doing the same as he presses the length of his body to mine.

"We thought you ran away," Rory informs me, leaning his

shoulder against mine. "We almost went to your house to check on you. But then we heard someone talking about the crazy girl hiking to the bridge."

"Figured the crazy girl had to be you," Phoenix murmurs in explanation. "Are you okay?"

I scrape my nails against the stone under me, not sure how to answer just yet. "Two days ago, I killed someone for you." I sigh, tapping my heels on the rock making up the side of the column I'm perched over. "To be clear, I don't regret it. I don't even really feel bad." I look at both of them, catching their eyes while I say it so they know it's not just a bunch of words meant to make them feel better.

"But things feel different. How do I go back to being best friends with the sheriff's daughter after this? How do I look at them when they talk about how those five never deserved to die like that?" I scratch again over the stone, and wince when my nail protests. Thankfully, I stop before it splits, though I do examine my nails to make sure they're unscathed.

"You fake it," Rory replies. "You know, I'm sure we could come back here for a while. We could take a semester off, or—"

"Or you could do what you should've done years ago," Phoenix smoothly interrupts on my right. He doesn't continue until I tilt my head up to look at him, and even then his answer is just a raise of his brows, leaving me to work it out.

"You think I should leave Hollow Bridge." The words feel strange when I say them out loud. As if it's the natural conclusion of things. "You want me to run away."

"What's still here for you, Bailey?" he demands, voice persistent. "You can always come home to visit your parents. But I know you want to finish your degree, and you can't do that here. Not how you want to. You could leave, like you wanted to when you were younger."

"And it's not like we're totally running away," Rory adds helpfully from my other side. "It's not like we're going far. You could come back to visit whenever you want, like he said. Just, you know, maybe let all of this die down first. Your parents *love* us, too. They'd so support you coming to live with us."

"*Coming to live with you?*" I parrot; swiveling to look at him instead. "You barely know me. I could be a shitty roommate!"

"Probably not as shitty as me," Rory replies sweetly. "And I don't need to know you longer. That's the cool part about having a fucked up brain, you know? I'm decisive. I knew the first time I laid eyes on Phoenix he was going to be mine. No matter what I had to do to convince him. It wasn't that hard, in case you were wondering. He's a romantic." He flashes Phoenix a grin, the latter rolling his eyes. "But it was the same for you. I knew I wanted you when I saw you in the woods, standing over a dead bird like you wanted to play with it. How could I *not*? And how can't you see this town wasn't made for you? There's another big perk to coming with us, you know."

"Not going to jail? Not being alone?" I offer, letting him drag me closer with a hand in my hoodie.

"Well, yeah," Rory chuckles, but then leans forward so he can whisper loudly in my ear so Phoenix can hear as well. "Come with us, because we'll let you play with all the dead things you could ever want."

The shiver that trails up my spine should be one of fear, or at the very least I should be creeped out. But instead, I'm excited.

"What if you get caught? Or if I don't want to kill people anymore?" I ask, needing the answers to those questions. "What if you decide you don't want me around anymore?"

"What if the sky falls?" Phoenix breathes, pressing his face to my neck. "What if I tumble off this bridge? He's good at controlling himself, and he's right. There won't come a day when we don't want you around. Even if you're a shitty room-mate." His hand loops around my waist, and Rory does the same, his long fingers twining around my throat so they can hold me between them.

"Come with us," Phoenix urges once more.

"*Stay* with us," Rory adds. "Where you belong."

"And be more appreciated than you are here."

They fall silent after that, and I let my fingers wander over Rory's fingers, over Phoenix's hands, until I can reach out for the two of them and pull them closer, the same way they normally do for me. But this time it's my fingers at their throats, gripping them lightly, like they're *mine* and always have been.

"Yes," I whisper, looking at one, then the other. "If you really want me to. If you're really sure—"

"Until the sky falls, until we die, and then again when we reunite in hell," Rory chuckles, pushing his face to mine and also letting me more firmly grip his throat.

"That's morbid," I point out, feeling Phoenix's lips and teeth at my shoulder, even through my hoodie when he lightly bites down.

"It's not morbid," he laughs lightly, his smile sharp against me. "It's romantic as hell."

"Then if it's romantic as hell, he gets to tell my parents," I tell them both, marveling at the feeling of holding them here, against me, with my hands on their soft, warm skin. "Because they're going to have questions, and none of the answers can even *mention* the word murder." But the smile fighting for life curves my lips upward, and before either of them can reply I'm dragging them both in for a kiss. Any thoughts of guilt or what I'd be leaving behind flit away on the wind that blows my hood back and stings my face in a way that makes me feel so damned alive, that there's no doubt this, at least, is not a dream.

And if it is, it's not one I'll ever willingly wake from.

# ABOUT THE AUTHOR

AJ Merlin would rather write epic love stories than live them. I mean, who wants to limit themselves to only falling in love once? She is obsessed with dark fantasy, true crime, and also dogs. From serial killers to voyeurs all the way down to the devil himself, AJ's specialty is in writing irredeemable heroes who somehow still manage to captivate their heroines (and her readers).

Made in the USA
Monee, IL
09 November 2023

46048690R00175